LONGING

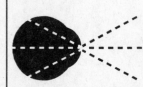

This Large Print Book carries the
Seal of Approval of N.A.V.H.

LONGING

MARY BALOGH

THORNDIKE PRESS

A part of Gale, Cengage Learning

GALE
CENGAGE Learning·

Farmington Hills, Mich • San Francisco • New York • Waterville, Maine
Meriden, Conn • Mason, Ohio • Chicago

GALE
CENGAGE Learning

LIBRARY OF CONGRESS CATALOGING-IN-PUBLICATION DATA

Balogh, Mary.
    Longing / Mary Balogh. — Large print edition.
        pages cm. — (Thorndike Press large print romance)
    ISBN 978-1-4104-7815-3 (hardcover) — ISBN 1-4104-7815-7 (hardcover)
    1. Triangles (Interpersonal relations)—Fiction. 2. Large type books. I. Title.
PR6052.A465L66 2015b
823'.914—dc23   2015005120

Published in 2015 by arrangement with NAL Signet, an imprint of Penguin Publishing Group, a division of Penguin Random House Company LLC

Printed in Mexico
1 2 3 4 5 6 7 19 18 17 16 15

Dear Reader,

Most of my books are set in England. But this one is set in my native Wales, and I immediately felt a change in myself, a heightened emotional involvement, as I wrote it. Wales is a land of hills and mountains, sea and cliffs, its own ancient language and culture, a deep spirituality, and music. Always music — the harp, church congregations singing in full harmony, choirs, particularly male voice choirs, often in the past made up of coal miners. Just the thought of it all can bring me to tears. Most of the Welsh coal mines are gone now, but there was a time when they dominated and blackened the countryside along the beautiful river valleys of South Wales.

Longing, my first all-Welsh book, originally published in 1995, has always been very precious to me. It is set in one of the coal-mining valleys in the first half of the nineteenth century, at a time when the owners were almost all wealthy Englishmen and life for the Welsh workers was hard, to say the least. Many of them became involved in the doomed Chartist movement to improve their living and working and political conditions.

The Marquess of Craille is a new owner,

having only recently inherited and come to Wales. Siân Jones is the illegitimate daughter of an owner but has deliberately identified with the workers. She is the widow of a miner and is now engaged to the leader of the local Chartist movement. She is soon caught in the middle of a conflict between two men who seem destined to be natural enemies.

A common theme through the book is music, in particular the Welsh song "Hiraeth," roughly translated "Longing," that soul-deep yearning we all feel for our homeland and what is beyond our reach and our full understanding. The story is a deeply felt piece of the history of my own people and a passionate love story between two people for whom a future together seems an impossibility.

I do hope you will love this book as much as I always have.

Mary Balogh

For my younger daughter
Siân
(pronounced Shahn)
whose name I have used as the heroine
of this, my Welsh book,
with love

PRONUNCIATION GUIDE

Glanrhyd Glan-HREED
Cwmbran Cum-BRAHN(*u* as in *put*)
Emrys EM-riss
Huw Hugh
Iestyn YES-tin
Siân Shahn
Gwyn Gwinn
Gwynneth GWINN-uth
Rhys Hrees
Hywel Howell
Penybont Pen-u-BONT
Angharad Ang-HA-rad
Ceridwen Care-ID-wen
Mari Marry
Marged MARR-ged
Dafydd DA-vith (*ith* as in *with*)
Blodwyn BLOD-win
Ifor EYE-vore
Ianto YAN-toe
Dilys DILL-iss
Gwilym GWILL-um

Cefn Kevn

Fach Vach (*ach* as in composer *Bach*)

Duw Dew

Eisteddfod Eye-STETH-fod

Hiraeth mawr HEE-ryth mour (*yth* as in *python, ou* as in *ouch*)

Bore da Bore-e DAH

Y deryn pur U DER-in PEER

Llwyn on Hloyn ON

Gymanfa ganu Gu-MAN-vu GA-nee

1

It was rather late in the day to go walking, especially in a strange place. But the night was warm and moonlit, and the hills beckoned invitingly. Besides, a day and a half of traveling had made him stiff and restless, and since his arrival soon after noon he had been busy with his housekeeper and his butler. His agent had called to pay his respects and make arrangements for the coming days. And there had been Verity to amuse. If the journey had made him irritable, it had made her positively petulant. It was harder for a six-year-old to sit still and idle for hours on end than it was for an adult.

Now she was in bed, coaxed there by an elderly and indulgent nurse, and put to sleep by the stories he had read to her.

He was unable to give in to his own tiredness. Everything was so strange. He had been the owner of this property for longer than two years — ever since the death of his uncle, his mother's brother — but he had never been here before. He did not even know much about it except that the quarterly reports sent by his agent showed it to be extremely prosperous. But then aristocrats, whose names and titles and wealth had grown out of large landed estates over several centuries, still frowned upon the idea of making money out of industry. It seemed very middle class and not quite the thing at all. Times were changing, but very often times changed faster than people.

Alexander Hyatt, Marquess of Craille, was the owner of a large area of land in one of the valleys of South Wales and the ironworks and coal mine on that land. The back of beyond, as his mother-in-law liked to describe it. It was not a compliment. She had been aghast when he had told her that he was going to take her granddaughter there for an indefinite period of time. It was in vain that he had reminded her that he also owned a castle there — Glanrhyd Castle — that had been built by his uncle's predecessor.

Alex, standing at his bedroom window, still fully clothed, decided that late or not, strange or not, he was going to go out for a walk after all. The little he had seen of the surrounding area during the day had fascinated him — the narrow valley with steep, heather-covered hills to either side, the river at the bottom with rows of terraced houses beside it and on the lower slopes, the ironworks below the castle, largely hidden by the trees of the park. Glanrhyd Castle itself was built above the valley floor, a little removed from both the works and the houses.

The hills fascinated him. Steep, and yet not sheer, they closed in the valley, making it like a little world cut off from the outside. He felt almost as if he were in a foreign country. In a way, he supposed, he was.

He took a cloak with him in case the night was chillier than it had felt through his open window. But it was still almost warm outside. He strolled the gravel walks bordering the sloping lawns of the park and stood still to breathe in the fresh air and to listen to the sounds of insects. But he was not satisfied with such a sedate walk. The hills called to him. If he walked a little way across and up the slope beyond the park gates he would be able to look down on the valley and have a more panoramic view of it than he had had from the house. It would probably look lovely in the moonlight.

He did not intend to walk far as he soon

realized that the hills did not ascend smoothly from the valley to the top. Rather they were rolling hills with peaks and hollows and even some sharp, unexpected drops. But there was no real danger as long as he was in no hurry. There was light enough to see by. And his guess had been correct. From above, and without the obstruction of the trees, he could see that the town was picturesque despite the smoking chimneys of the ironworks and despite the black coal tips he could see farther down the valley. Moonlight gleamed off the water of the river, which was broader than it had seemed from below. The houses, in long, snaking lines, looked sleepy and hugged the side of the hill as if for protection. There were very few lights. Obviously his workers went to bed early. Not that it was really early. He supposed it was close to midnight.

He should turn back. But there was a pleasant coolness in the air now, and he was reluctant to give up this only part of the day he had had to himself. If he strolled a little farther on, he thought, he would be able to look back up the valley from the other end of the town. Perhaps he would be able to see the castle above the works. It had been fancifully built, with numerous towers and turrets and long windows. He had been

14

rather amused when he first set eyes on it. And rather pleased too. Somehow it escaped vulgarity, ornate as it was. Somehow it seemed to suit its setting.

He was not sure when he first became aware of a sound that was neither water nor wind nor insects. At first it was a feeling that seemed not quite associated with the ears. But it became more marked as he strolled on. It was the sound of voices. The murmured sound of many voices.

Alex stood still and concentrated. Where was it coming from? From below? But almost all the lights were out in the houses and the works were too far away, although some men would be on shift there. From the mine, then? No, the sound was coming from the hills.

He walked on more warily, more alertly, until the sound was unmistakably that of voices — men's voices. And then there was one voice, speaking above the rest until they all fell silent, and speaking on. In a strange language, doubtless Welsh.

As he drew closer, Alex realized that he was approaching another of those unexpected peaks, behind which there was presumably another dip and a hollow. He could tell that he was close now. The voice was distinct. Whoever it was was in that hollow. He climbed carefully, ducking down as he approached the top so that his head would not be seen against the skyline. He inched up the last few feet so that he could look down.

His jaw almost dropped. Certainly his eyes widened. It was a large hollow, far larger than he had expected, and it was packed tight with men, now silent. Hundreds of them. Every single man from the valley below must be there.

The man who was addressing them was standing on a slight rise at one end of the hollow, so that all would be able to see him. He was a big man, not particularly tall, but broad and strong looking. He had a commanding presence, as he would have to have, Alex thought, to have called such a large gathering to order.

A meeting? On the mountain at midnight? He noticed suddenly that not one of the men held a lantern or any other light. It was true that the moonlight was bright enough, but it was surprising nonetheless that there were no lights. It was a clandestine meeting, then?

At first he thought he must be wrong. The broad, dark-haired speaker stepped down to give his place to a tall, thin man dressed all in black. He too spoke in Welsh, but it was

16

clear from the way he spread his arms and from the tone of his voice when he began to speak that he was a preacher. And that he was praying. The men all bowed their heads reverently and remained silent throughout the lengthy prayer, only the occasional "Amen" interrupting the preacher's voice.

A prayer meeting? Alex frowned and then felt amusement. He had been told that the Welsh were a devout people and that they were nonconformist almost to a man. But a mass prayer meeting at midnight when they should be at home asleep? He felt again the foreignness of this new home of his.

He probably would have retreated and left them to it if he had not spotted the woman. Like him, she was not part of the meeting. As far as he could see, its members were exclusively male. Like him, she was silently spying on it. She was hiding behind some large rocks a little lower than his hill and some distance away. She would not be able to see him. He edged over a little to his left to make sure.

He wondered what she was doing there and why she could not join the prayer meeting openly. Unless women were forbidden to do so. It looked as if that might be the case. It was impossible to tell if she was young or old. She wore a dark dress, which

17

blended well with the rocks, and a lighter shawl, which was drawn up over her head. But she looked slim. She looked young. He watched her, intrigued, and ignored the feeling that he was spying on something that was none of his business.

Actually it was his business. This was his land. These were his people.

And then the prayer was finally at an end and the preacher stepped down to be replaced by the first speaker. Alex wished he could understand what was being said but realized that he must become accustomed to hearing Welsh spoken all around him. He was the intruder, after all. It was their country, not his.

And then suddenly he did understand. The language had switched to English — heavily accented but nevertheless quite understandable. The Welshman was introducing a speaker who was English. His fame had spread throughout the land and they were honored and privileged to have him bring his oratory to Wales. Would they all welcome Robert Mitchell?

They did so as a small, bespectacled, insignificant-looking young man took his place on the rise and lifted his arms for silence. He did not get it for some time. The men were applauding and whistling.

18

Robert Mitchell? Hell!

Robert Mitchell was one of the more famous of the Chartist orators who were traveling endlessly and tirelessly throughout the industrial districts of England and Wales these days, trying to persuade the people to put their signatures to the great Charter that was to have been presented to Parliament a few months ago but which still had not appeared there. The most famous orator of all, Henry Vincent, was in jail in Monmouth.

This was a Chartist meeting? Alex flattened himself against the hill suddenly and grew cold. He had not realized that Chartism had taken a hold at Cwmbran. Barnes, his agent, had never made mention of it. But Alex might have guessed, he supposed.

Robert Mitchell was speaking in a voice whose volume and resonant power belied his appearance. He was explaining simply and clearly what the object of the Charter was, what six basic demands it was to make of the government — the vote for every British male, annual Parliaments, secret ballots, and so on. Alex was quite familiar with the Charter's demands. He was even sympathetic to them. But Chartism had somehow become the movement of the industrial working classes and it had become a move-

19

ment of protest. Many feared that it had become revolutionary in its aims and methods.

This secret midnight meeting made him feel suddenly uneasy about Chartism. Why the secrecy if the aims were open and honest ones? He had never had to think too much about it before. It had never touched him closely. Now suddenly it was very close indeed.

The woman was still there, he noticed as Robert Mitchell harangued the crowd with the necessity of adding their signatures to the Charter and of paying their pennies to join the Chartist Association.

"There is power in numbers, my friends," he shouted, stabbing the air with one fist and causing Alex to break out in a sweat. There was danger in the idea even if it might seem a reasonable one. Such was the power of the man's oratory that his audience was responding to it with raised fists of their own and with shouts of assent. There were even some fervent amens.

"Everyone will sign the Charter." The speech had ended and the stocky Welshman was back on the rise, though he still spoke in English out of deference to the guest speaker. "Unanimity is essential, men. Those who do not sign tonight or pay their pennies tonight will be asked why tomorrow."

There seemed to be a definite threat in the words. But there were no dissenting voices, only universal enthusiasm as far as Alex could see. He would have a few questions to ask of Barnes tomorrow. But first, he would dearly like to know who the leader was, the strong, fiery Welshman who seemed to hold the men in the palm of his hand as well as Mitchell had. And who the preacher was.

The woman was moving away, cautiously leaving the protection of the rocks behind which she had been hiding and circling behind the rise that stood between her and the gathered men. The meeting would be breaking up soon. She was making her escape in good time. She was making her way in his direction, Alex could see.

He waited until she had passed the slope on which he lay, without looking up and seeing him, and then he followed her as she quickened her pace, her shawl held close about her head and shoulders. She had a long, lithe stride. She was undoubtedly a young woman. And a shapely one. His eyes moved over her from behind. Long legs. Shapely hips.

He waited until she hurried down into

another hollow. Once out of it, he could see, she would be able to turn directly downward and would be in the town within a few minutes. He came up behind her, reaching a hand around to cover her mouth even as she sensed his presence and turned her head sharply. Large, frightened eyes looked into his while he hurried her behind some rocks so that they would be out of sight of anyone leaving the meeting early.

"You were not invited to the party?" he asked her, turning her so that her back was against the rocks. He removed his hand from her mouth but stood very close to her, his body almost against hers. Oh, yes, she was young. And beautiful. Her shawl had slipped from her head to reveal long hair worn loose. It looked almost black in the shadows. So did her eyes.

"Who are you?" She spoke to him in English, with a strongly lilting Welsh accent.

"It is a pity women are not invited to sign the Charter," he said. "Would you have signed it and given them one more signature?"

She leaned her head back against the rock. Some of the terror had gone from her eyes, but she was breathing raggedly. "I don't know who you are," she said. "You are

English. A spy? Did Mr. Barnes bring you in?"

"Who was the man leading the meeting?" he asked. "The dark, well-built Welshman?"

Her lips clamped together.

"He is from Cwmbran?" he asked. "He works there, perhaps?"

"I didn't know him," she said. "I don't know who he is. There are men from other valleys at the meeting. They are not all from Cwmbran."

He nodded. He did not believe her for a moment. "And the preacher?" he asked. "The one who opened the meeting with a long prayer? Who is he?"

Again the clamped lips. "I don't know him either," she said when he waited for an answer.

"And I suppose," he said, "you did not recognize any of the men at the meeting either. They were all from other valleys. They just happened to choose this site for their meeting."

"I suppose so," she said lamely after a while. But she lifted her chin. "Who are you? Have you come to make trouble? It was a peaceful meeting. There was no harm in it. It is merely a petition to be presented to Parliament."

" 'There is power in numbers, my

friends,' " he quoted softly. "The words can be made to sound almost seditious, can't they?"

"There is power," she said, "in a number of signatures. That was what he meant. Who are you?" The fright was back in her eyes and in her voice suddenly. "What do you want with me?"

It must have been sudden fright over her realization of the fact that she was alone on the mountain with a stranger, he thought. She tried to step forward and around him, but he stood his ground so that for a moment, before she flattened herself against the rock again, her body pressed against his. Firm, generous breasts, warm thighs. He set one hand against the rock beside her head.

"And who are you?" he asked. "Are you from another valley too and don't know yourself?"

Her chin came up but she said nothing for a while. "I shall scream," she said.

"Then I shall do this." He leaned forward and set his mouth over hers. But it was not a wise move. Her mouth was warm and soft. And he too was suddenly aware of how very alone they were, surrounded by shadows and cool night air and the droning of insects. Seduction had not been on his mind when he had pursued her and was definitely unwise under the circumstances. He drew his head back a few inches.

Her eyes were wide with terror and indignation. But she was a woman of some courage, he realized. Her chin stayed up and her eyes remained steady on his and she got herself silently under control.

"My guess is that you would not be over-eager, anyway, to make your presence on the mountain known to any of the men back there," he said. "I have the feeling that they would be a trifle annoyed. Who are you?"

"Let me go," she said. "Any one of them would pound you into the ground for touching me. But I'll not betray you if you will not betray me."

"Ah," he said, "an amicable bargain." He took one step back from her. "So all those men would punish me for frightening you and stealing a kiss from you, would they? All those men you do not know."

She ignored his last words. "I was not frightened," she said.

He grinned at her and wished that circumstances were such that he could attempt seduction. It would be very sweet. He thought ruefully of how long it had been since he had had a woman. Too long. But now was not the time.

He stepped to one side so that she could

make her escape. "If I were you," he said, "I would stay off the mountains this late at night. There are too many dangers for a woman alone."

"Thank you." Her voice was heavy with sarcasm. "I shall remember that."

"And I shall remember this night," he said, "and some of the faces of the men at the Chartist meeting. Perhaps I will see those faces again one day — in the other valleys. I believe I may see yours a little closer than that."

"Not if I can help it," she said.

He grinned and gestured to the downward slope just beyond the shadows in which they stood. "Go," he said, "before anyone else comes down and sees that you are out of your bed at this hour and in a place that no woman has any business being."

He watched her make the effort not to bolt like a frightened rabbit. She lifted her shawl over her head again, her eyes on his, and then walked past him and out into the open, her back straight.

"Good night, maiden of Cwmbran," he said softly.

She did not answer him. He noticed her pace quicken and her head come down as she hurried through the hollow and turned at its end to take the steep slope down to the town. She did not look back though he could almost see that her back was bristling with panic lest he was following her and was about to pounce on her again.

And so he was no farther forward than he had been before he caught up to her. She was a woman who could keep her mouth shut. He just hoped that she would keep it shut concerning him too. He was not sure that he wanted it known that he had unwittingly come upon a Chartist meeting. He did not wish to become embroiled in local politics when he had set foot in Cwmbran for the first time only hours before.

He should not have stopped the woman or spoken to her, he thought now that it was too late to do differently. Or kissed her. He should certainly not have done that. A fine first impression it would give. He was thankful that she had been where she was not supposed to be and would therefore be reluctant to tell anyone of the experience — even when she knew who he was, which would surely happen soon.

But he should not have kissed her. Brief and unplanned and one-sided as it had been, it had aroused needs in him that he normally kept well under control. Only two long-term mistresses in the almost six years since his wife's death, and none at all since his engagement to Lorraine a year ago — an engagement they had broken off only the month before.

Strange! He had kissed Lorraine several times, usually at greater length than he had kissed the unknown Welshwoman. But never once had he become as aroused physically as he had now.

It was just as well, he thought ruefully, striding with unwise speed across the hill in the direction of Glanrhyd Castle, that he had some distance to walk and that the air was now distinctly cool.

Robert Mitchell. Chartists. *There is power in numbers, my friends. Everyone will sign the Charter.* Hell! What had he walked into? He had come to Wales for some peace and quiet after a broken engagement. Had he walked unwittingly into a nest of hornets?

Siân Jones held the corners of her shawl tightly in each hand and tried not to run as she hurried down the slope to the town. It took every ounce of willpower not to do so and not to look over her shoulder. Her back crawled with panic. Every moment she expected to feel his hand again, clamping down on her shoulder or over her mouth.

Who was he? Whoever was he?

At first, foolishly, she had thought he was

the devil. There had been the large, strong hand over her mouth, the swirl of a dark cloak, the largeness of his body, which he had placed between her and freedom. But a strange devil who had looked like an angel when she had finally seen his face. Even in the shadows his hair had shone very blond. And his eyes were light — blue or gray. She guessed they were blue. And he spoke with a very refined English accent.

Who on earth was he? Some spy? The country was full of them. And full of soldiers too. He might be a soldier, though he had not been wearing a uniform. He had been sent to spy on the meeting. And he had seen it. He had seen them all there — Owen, Emrys, Huw, Iestyn, Grandad — oh, dear Lord, Grandad. And the Reverend Llewellyn. He did not know their names. She had told him nothing. But it would not take him long to find out. Owen most of all. Owen was the first one he had asked about. Oh, dear Lord, Owen had led the meeting. The spy would have had a good look at him even in the darkness.

She was almost running despite herself by the time she reached the valley and turned to hurry along one of the streets and to let herself quietly into one of the darkened houses. No one would catch her. Gran slept upstairs and would not come down even if she was awake. Grandad and Emrys would not be home for a while. Siân undressed hastily in the kitchen and drew on her nightdress before diving into the cupboard bed that had been hers when she first came to Grandad's at the age of seventeen and that had been hers again since Gwyn's death and the death of their son.

She lay shaking beneath the covers, waiting for her grandfather and her uncle to come safely home. Though there was nothing safe now about home. Tomorrow perhaps they would all be rounded up. What would happen to them? They could not all be taken off to jail, surely. And they could not all be dismissed from their jobs. There would be no one left to work except the women. All the men had gone up the mountain to the meeting, even those who disapproved of the Charter. They had all gone up to hear the famous Mr. Mitchell.

And she had gone up out of fear and curiosity — she always seemed to have more of the latter than any other women she knew. She had wanted to know what it was all about and if there was any basis to the hostility the owners and the government felt toward what was apparently a peaceful and lawful movement. But she remembered the blond Englishman repeating something Mr. Mitchell had said — *there is power in numbers, my friends.* Of course, when he repeated that to whoever had sent him, it would sound seditious enough, as he had said.

And Owen. Siân remembered what Owen had said and shivered. *Everyone will sign the Charter. Those who do not sign tonight or pay their pennies tonight will be asked why tomorrow.*

Oh, Owen, Owen. He surely would be thrown out of work tomorrow. He surely would be arrested and clapped in jail. He would be hauled off to Newport or to Monmouth for trial — trial by those who would interpret his words and Mr. Mitchell's as constituting treason.

The English spy had seen Owen's face clearly. Perhaps he would be unable to identify Grandad or the others who had been in the crowd, but Owen he had both seen and heard. And the Reverend Llewellyn, who did not even approve of the Charter.

The door latch lifted quietly and two dark figures tiptoed inside.

"Grandad?" Siân whispered. "You have come safely home?"

"Safe, *fach,* me and Emrys both," he

whispered back. "No danger at all. Just an old meeting it was."

"Go to sleep, Siân," her uncle Emrys said, not bothering to whisper. "Stayed awake worrying about us, did you? There is silly you are, girl. The morning shift comes early. To sleep with you now."

"Good night," she whispered.

She could not tell them about the very real danger there was. The danger that would surely break over their heads in the morning. Or over Owen's anyway. She listened to their footsteps on the stairs as they tiptoed up to bed so as not to disturb Gran, and felt physically sick.

And then she remembered that he had kissed her. She could remember the blind terror she had felt at the largeness of his body — he was very tall and had appeared dauntingly strong and well muscled. He might well be a soldier. And the terror and fright she had felt when his mouth had covered hers. His lips had been parted. She had thought — she had fully expected — that he was going to rape her.

He would be able to identify her too. He had said so.

Siân pulled the blanket over her head and burrowed underneath it, her knees drawn up, as if by doing so she could hide from the menacing Englishman, half devil, half angel, who had stolen a kiss from her and had it in his power to have Owen thrown into jail. Perhaps even hanged for treason.

Dear Lord. Oh, dear Lord, she prayed fervently.

2

Josiah Barnes was a short, balding man with a large stomach that proclaimed he drank too much beer. He was an unmarried Englishman who lived in the stone lodge cottage inside the gates of Glanrhyd Park. He kept very much to himself, associating with the owners of the other ironworks and mines at the heads of the valleys on terms of a type of junior partnership. They respected him as an excellent agent who in a dozen years had made Cwmbran as efficient and prosperous as any of their own works.

Alex was a little in awe of his knowledge. He felt his own terrible ignorance of both business and industry during his first full day at Cwmbran, when Barnes showed him around the ironworks. It all looked bewilderingly strange to the eyes of an English aristocrat, who had spent almost all of his twenty-nine years on a large country estate or in London. He was listening carefully to what Barnes said, trying to absorb at least some of what he was saying.

Alex was unable to converse with any of the workers, though he nodded affably to them. They spoke to each other in Welsh — though of course he knew for a fact that they understood English.

Alex found himself distracted somewhat from what his agent was telling him by his curiosity about the workers. He looked keenly at each of them, trying to recognize faces. It was hopeless, of course. He was almost convinced, though, that one of the puddlers — they were the most highly skilled and prized of the ironworkers, according to Barnes — was last night's chairman. The man was bared to the waist now, his upper body and arms glistening with sweat. He looked rather like a prize-fighter. But Alex was not sure he would be able to swear in a court of law that he had been the man.

Look as he would, he could not see his maiden of Cwmbran among the women workers. He would certainly have recognized her. He would have enjoyed seeing her too — and he would have enjoyed watching her reaction to seeing him.

"That was all extremely interesting," he said to his agent at the end of the afternoon.

It was a rather lame remark, he realized, and one that might well invite contempt from the man who had made his works so prosperous. "The coal mine tomorrow, then? I shall want to know too about the human factor — numbers employed, hours worked, wage levels, extra benefits, and anything else there is to know."

"I shall have the books in your office by tomorrow morning, my lord," Barnes said.

"And about workers' organizations," Alex said carefully. "Are there any?"

"Some Friendly Societies," his agent said. "Some workers pay into them and then have benefits in times of sickness or such. But no unions if that is what you mean, my lord. Any known members of unions are immediately dismissed. All the other works do likewise. Unions are disruptive. The running of the works is best left in the hands of men who understand all that is involved. We do not need to be told what to do by ignorant workers and held to ransom by united action."

It was as Alex had thought, then. "Is there any interest in Chartism in this part of the world?" he asked. "It is quite strong in the industrial cities of the Midlands and the North, I have heard."

"They are prowling around here," Barnes

said, "trying to work the men up into a fever against the government and against law and order. The men know that anyone who attends their meetings will be sacked instantly. We don't need that nonsense here, my lord."

Alex dismissed him for the day and hurried homeward so that he could take tea with his daughter. He hated to leave her alone all day in a strange place, with only an elderly nurse for company. Poor Verity. He should have forced himself to remarry long ago. He should have married Lorraine soon after their betrothal instead of hesitating and procrastinating until she suggested breaking it off.

So mass meetings were strictly forbidden — or any united action that might spell trouble to those in authority. The men of Cwmbran had risked a great deal in gathering on the mountain last night. And they had somehow kept it a secret from Barnes. There must be a great deal of trust and self-discipline among them — and no informers.

He did not know why he had not told Barnes about last night's Chartist meeting. He was rather amused by the thought that if Barnes's rule was to be enforced there would be almost no one to run the works or hew the coal from the mine today. And yet he ought not to be feeling amusement. Those men had definitely been doing what they knew was strictly forbidden at Cwmbran, or anywhere in the Welsh valleys. And the Welsh leader — one of his puddlers if he was not very much mistaken — had actually told the men that unanimity was essential, that those who did not sign or join the Chartist organization would be asked why today.

Alex wondered how exactly the men were to be asked. Politely and verbally? Or in some other way?

And yet he had said nothing to Barnes. Perhaps it was that he was new to Cwmbran, he thought, and had no desire to stir up trouble yet. Not until he had got his bearings and knew what was what, anyway. Or perhaps it was that he was sympathetic to the aims of Chartism. The six demands of the Charter seemed quite reasonable to him. They should at least be negotiable. And there was nothing seditious about presenting a petition to Parliament. There was nothing in it to make all law-abiding men fear a repetition in England of the revolution that had destroyed France just fifty years before.

Whatever the reason, he was keeping mute

about something that might well lead to trouble.

He took the stairs up to the nursery two at a time when he was inside the house, pushed open the door, and swept up his shrieking daughter into his arms to twirl her about.

"How is my favorite girl?" he asked her. "Have you missed Papa?"

Siân was drying dishes after the evening meal although her grandmother had protested. Siân had been working a long shift underground all day and was weary from the backbreaking task of dragging coal carts from the seams where the miners cut the coal to the shaft, up which it would be hauled. All day she wore a harness around her waist so that she could more easily drag the load. Sometimes, in the lower tunnels, she had to go down on all fours. The darkness and the heat and dust did not help.

But she was drying dishes anyway. Her grandmother had not exactly been idle all day long. The house was clean and tidy, as it always was, the dirty work clothes from the day before had all been washed and dried and folded and put away — washed with water that had had to be hauled a pail at a time from a distant pump and heated over the kitchen fire. And warm bathwater had been waiting for her when she came home — and had been waiting for Grandad and Emrys when they came home before her from the iron furnaces. And of course Gran had cooked the meal for them.

Perhaps, Siân thought, she would have been more tempted to sit down to rest her feet, as Gran urged, if she did not feel it necessary to occupy her hands. They were talking about the Marquess of Craille, absentee owner of Cwmbran, who had come on an unexpected visit of inspection. He had spent much of the day at the iron-works.

"A proper Englishman," Emrys said, seated at one side of the dying fire, his legs stretched out, almost touching those of his father, who was seated at the other side. "Wasn't he, Dada? You should have seen him, Mam. Strutting about the works like a prize turkey, nodding about at all of us just as if he was really interested in us instead of just in the money he makes off our sweat. I almost spit at his back, but Barnes was watching like a hawk."

Does he have blond hair? Siân wanted to ask. But she just rubbed hard at a plate that was already dry. She would bet a week's wages that he was blond. And tall. The man who had been up on the mountain. The man who had kissed her.

"Now, now, Emrys," Gwynneth Rhys said to her son. "We have not heard any bad of him have we, now? And the fact that he is English is not his fault, poor man. We will have a little respect for your employer in this house, if you please."

"We do not know any bad of him?" Emrys looked at his mother incredulously. "When he and his uncle before him have been bleeding us dry all our lives, Mam, and hiding behind the coattails of Barnes? When we work like dogs just to feed ourselves and keep a roof over our heads and are threatened with the sack if we try to get together to improve our lot? I'll give him bloody marquess and English airs."

"Emrys!" His father's frown was thunderous. "You will apologize to Mam and to Siân for using such language in this house. You may be thirty-five years old, but I am not too old and feeble to take you out the back and blacken both your eyes."

"Sorry, Mam, Siân," Emrys said sheepishly.

"Perhaps he is not a bad man," Hywel Rhys said. "Perhaps there will be some changes around here once he has seen for himself and assessed the situation."

41

Emrys snorted. "There is stupid you are sometimes, Dada," he said. "Nothing will ever change. We exist to make the rich richer, more is the pity. That is why the Charter is our only hope."

"I think," Gwynneth said, squeezing out the cloth over the bowl of water as if to wring every last drop out of it, "Dada had better blacken those eyes for you after all, Emrys. There is disrespectful you are, calling your own father stupid."

"It is what comes of stopping going to chapel," Hywel said. "Emrys has become godless."

Emrys had given up on God, Siân thought sadly, when his wife and infant son had died in a cholera outbreak ten years ago — and two years before Siân came to Cwmbran to live. Apparently he had taken exception to the Reverend Llewellyn's preaching at the funeral that such was the will of God and that the bereaved husband must give praise that the two of them were in heaven where they were needed more.

Emrys had stood up in chapel in front of most of the people of Cwmbran and sworn profanely before pushing his way out of the front pew and past the coffins of his wife and son out of the chapel, never to return.

There were those in Cwmbran who still

looked at him as if they expected to see horns sprouting from his head.

"I get tired of listening to fools," Emrys said now. "Though the Reverend Llewellyn did go up the mountain last night, to give him his due. And prayed long enough that I expected to see dawn in the sky before he had finished."

His mother clucked her tongue but said nothing.

They were going to talk about the meeting, Siân thought. And blank terror gripped her again. She could not understand why the whole day had gone by and nothing had happened. But something surely would happen. It was the Marquess of Craille himself who had witnessed the meeting and who had had a good look at least at Owen and at the Reverend Llewellyn. And he would recognize her. He would perhaps think himself able to squeeze more names out of her.

Perhaps he was waiting for some special constables to arrive, she thought. Or a company of soldiers. Perhaps the arrests would not be made until tomorrow. Or perhaps they would come tonight. She was sorry suddenly that she was on her feet. There was a buzzing in her head.

"Four hundred and fifty-seven signatures,"

Emrys was saying. "It was a good night. Of course there were at least five hundred there. Some men came up from the other valleys, Mam."

"I do not want to hear it," Gwynneth said, tight-lipped. "I do not want to have to visit my men in jail. And I won't do it, either. There is shameful it would be for chapel people, Hywel."

"Silly, Mam," Emrys said, getting to his feet to set an arm about her shoulders. She shrugged them but did not push him away. "How can they put us all in jail? There would be no one left to work. And no one to guard us." He grinned at Siân and winked.

"They will put who they can in jail," his mother said. "Beginning with those with the biggest mouths, Emrys Rhys."

He chuckled and kissed her cheek. "No one knew about the meeting except those who were meant to, Mam," he said. "You are very quiet, Siân."

She folded the towel deliberately and hung it up to dry. "I am afraid too," she said. But she could not say more. How could she warn them that the meeting had been watched last night — by someone who was not meant to. Doing so would be to reveal that she too had watched it. Besides, what was the use of a warning? It was too late. "I am afraid for Owen."

"Owen can look after himself, *fach,*" Emrys said. "You don't have to be afraid for him."

"I walked home from work with Iestyn," she said. "He signed the Charter but would not join the Association, he told me. He believes in the six points but is not willing to organize to enforce them. But he told me that those who will not join are going to have pressure put on them. Is that right?"

"Iestyn Jones should have been a girl," Emrys said scornfully. "How old is he, Siân? Seventeen? Eighteen?"

"Seventeen," she said. "He works as hard as everyone else, Emrys. The fact that he is sweet-natured and that he would love nothing more than to study and be a preacher does not make him into a — girl, as you put it."

"You are partial," he said, "because he is Gwyn's brother, Siân. Your brother-in-law. But he is too cowardly to pay his penny and stand up for what he believes in."

"That is not being a coward," she said indignantly. "Perhaps it is the opposite, Uncle Emrys. It would be a lot easier for him to do what almost everyone else is doing. Including Huw, his own brother. But

Iestyn believes in law and order."

"Well," he said, "it is only by acting together that we are going to get anywhere in this life. Perhaps he will be persuaded to see things differently, *fach.*"

"Persuaded?" She looked at him warily and remembered what Owen had said the night before.

"Enough," Gwynneth said firmly. "You may throw the dishwater out the back if you will, Hywel. Enough talk of Charters, is it? There are better things to talk about in one's own home when work is done and evening is here. We can be thankful for home and family and nice summer weather."

"Yes, Mam," Emrys said affectionately. "Sit down and take the weight off your feet, Siân. I do hate to think of you down in that mine every day, girl, doing the hardest job there is. I could still plant a fist in Barnes's nose for sending you there."

"He gave me a job at least," she said, sinking gratefully into the chair he had recently vacated. "That was more than I could get at Penybont."

"He gave you a job all right," Emrys said. "He did it to humiliate you, Siân."

"Well," she said quietly, "he will not succeed in doing that. Many other women do

46

the same job. There is no reason why I should not be one of them. I am not afraid of hard work."

"You should not be working at all," her grandfather said gruffly. "I take it as a shame that any woman of my family is forced to work outside the home. Especially in the mine. Emrys and I earn enough to keep your gran and you in the house."

"But, Grandad —" she began.

"But Siân has her pride," Emrys said, cutting her off. "When she came to live with us after my sister died, she was too proud to make it seem that she was asking for charity. And again after Gwyn died."

"Oh, there is wicked," Gwynneth said indignantly as she sat at the kitchen table, a pile of darning on the table before her. "As if our own granddaughter would be accepting charity by coming to live with her own gran and grandad. Don't talk nonsense, Emrys."

And yet it would have seemed like charity, Siân thought, looking into the last embers of the fire and setting her head back against the chair. Emrys understood that. She had grown up alone with her mother, who had been driven out first from the chapel and then from the community of Cwmbran when her womb had begun to swell. She had been housed close to Penybont farther up the valley by the man who had disgraced her — Sir John Fowler, owner of the Penybont works. Siân had never been invited to call him Dada or even Papa. She could not quite think of him as her father, though he had sent her to an expensive girls' school in England when she was old enough to go. And he had tried to provide for her at the age of seventeen when her mother died by offering her in marriage to Josiah Barnes. It would be an excellent match, he had told her. Barnes was an important and powerful man.

But Siân had refused to marry him. Lonely and caught between two worlds, she had wanted to join the one to which perhaps she could belong. She could never belong in Sir John Fowler's world. No one there, including Josiah Barnes, would ever let her forget her origins or her illegitimacy. And so she left her mother's cottage, where she had no wish to live any longer. But she had been refused a job in any capacity at her father's works.

She had come to her grandparents' house in Cwmbran. She had come begging. But not to live on their charity. Two days after they had taken her in Josiah Barnes gave her a job — grinning at her as he offered it

48

and undressing her with his eyes. It was the lowliest, hardest, and dirtiest job for women. She had accepted and worked in the mine for three years, until she married Gwyn Jones, a miner, and moved into the small miners' house he shared with his parents and brothers. Such had been her determination to fit in.

After Gwyn's death from a cave-in underground that had killed two other men too, Siân had gone back to work though she was pregnant. Gwyn's family was large and it had been a time of low wages. But after her son had been stillborn a month early, she had moved back to her grandparents' and returned to the mine though her grandfather had tried to use his influence to get her a better job in the ironworks.

Siân started suddenly as there was a knock on the door and the latch lifted after her grandfather's call.

"Good evening, Mrs. Rhys, Hywel, Emrys, Siân," Owen Parry said, cap in hand. "Lovely day it has been, hasn't it, now?"

The only time Owen ever looked uncomfortable or sheepish, Siân thought, was when he came calling on her, though he had been coming several evenings a week for months. He was courting her.

"Good evening, Owen," Gwynneth said.

"Yes, a lovely day indeed. All my washing dried in no time at all."

"Hello, Owen," Siân said.

"Well, Owen," Emrys said, "a good number of signatures there were on the Charter last night. And almost no one missing from the meeting."

"Yes," Owen said, "but a few did not sign. And more would not pay their pennies to join the Association. It was a disappointment."

"There will always be some who will not follow others," Hywel said. "And I myself am a little uneasy, Owen. I could not countenance any violence, mind."

"There will be no —" Owen said.

Gwynneth coughed significantly. "And to what do we owe the pleasure of your visit, Owen?" she asked, smiling sweetly at him.

Owen flushed and turned his cap in his hands. "Siân," he said, looking at her, "will you step out with me for some air, then? A lovely evening it is. I won't keep her out late, Mrs. Rhys."

Siân got to her feet and reached for her shawl behind the door. She was twenty-five years old and a widow, but Owen always gave the same assurance to Gran, who was now nodding her approval.

"Let me see now," Emrys said. "It is half

past eight, Owen. Have her home on the dot of nine, is it?"

"And not half a minute later, mind," Hywel added.

"And no going up the mountain," Emrys said as Owen opened the door and stood to one side to let Siân pass him.

"My watch stopped," he said. "I left it home in the dresser drawer. And what are you going to do about it, Emrys Rhys?"

Grandad and Emrys were laughing merrily when the closing door cut off the sound. Siân smiled at Owen.

"Imbeciles," he said, drawing her arm through his. "A couple of comedians. It is time they thought of something new to say, though."

Siân laughed outright.

"Did you have a hard day?" he asked her as they walked along the street and turned at the end of it to stroll up into the lower hills above the valley and the river and works and rows of terraced houses. "I didn't know if you would be too tired to come out."

"But the air is lovely," she said. She drew a deep breath of it. "It feels so good and smells so good after the dust of coal underground all day."

"Your hair is what always smells good to

me," he said, moving his head closer to hers for a moment. "You wash it every day. I like that about you."

Although she bound it every time she went underground, it was always gray with coal dust by the time her shift was at an end.

"Did you see the Marquess of Craille today?" she asked. "He was touring the ironworks with Mr. Barnes, Grandad and Uncle Emrys said. He looks really English, they said."

"As blond as they come and dressed up like a toff," he said. "And Barnes was all puffed up like a peacock, showing him around."

Any doubt that Siân might still have had about the identity of the man on the mountain the night before finally fled. The Marquess of Craille was blond.

"I wonder why he has come," she said. "He has never been here before."

Owen shrugged. "For a pleasant holiday," he said. "To watch all his slaves sweating for him."

They were up on the lower hills and turned to look down, hand-in-hand, at the valley below them. The river still looked clean from up here, Siân thought. And peaceful. The sun was setting over the hills on the other side. She tried to put out of her mind the marquess and her terrible dread of what must surely be about to happen. Perhaps this would be the last evening. The last time she would walk in the hills with Owen. Despite herself she felt a welling of panic. She breathed deeply again.

"I don't think there can be a lovelier place on earth, can there?" she said. The hills had never yet failed to bring her some measure of peace. She had missed them during her years at school with a terrible emptiness that had seemed to lodge in the pit of her stomach.

Owen laughed scornfully. "It is hell down there," he said, gesturing with his head first at the ironworks and then at the coal mine. "We work like slaves, Siân, and the likes of Craille rake in the profits. The English. Robbing the riches of our valley. Our country. Though we are much to blame. We stand for the poor treatment we get and console ourselves by saying it is all God's will — the Reverend Llewellyn's favorite phrase. He is as much our enemy as Barnes and Craille, if we but knew it."

"Don't," she said. "Soon you will be talking about unions and strikes and the Charter. Don't spoil the evening. I have been hearing too much about last night's meeting." And she knew too much. More than any of the unsuspecting men. She felt sick suddenly with worry for Owen.

"Such things have to be talked about," he said. "Especially the Charter, which is to be presented to Parliament any day now and will bring equality and freedom to the common man. To us, Siân. Once we can vote, we can have some say in the condition of our own lives. We will no longer be slaves. All the men of the valley have to be persuaded to sign it and to force its passage through Parliament. This is no time for fear of how our masters will punish us."

Siân felt coldness in her nostrils and the beginnings of dizziness in her head. This was worse than last night.

Owen stopped talking to wrap an arm about her waist and turn her against him. He kissed her hard and long. She set her arms about his neck. Life would be good with Owen. He had a skilled, secure job and the rarity of a house of his own since his mother's death the year before. He was respected by the other workers. He was handsome. She would be able to give him sturdy children and would be able to get out of the mine. Except that it all seemed a little calculated. She had been determined to be one of her people. Was she now trying to force her way to the top just so that she could be more comfortable than most of the others? If she was honest with herself, she would have to admit that she did not love Owen as she had always dreamed of loving a man. But then she had not loved Gwyn that way either. Perhaps there was no such thing.

And perhaps there was no such thing as a comfortably secure future with Owen. Perhaps they had no future together. How long would it be before the Marquess of Craille made his move? Should she warn Owen to run away? But he would not go. She knew he would not. She tightened her arms about his neck.

"Mmm." He nuzzled her neck. "We will go up the mountain, then, will we, Siân?"

It was a question he had asked twice before. All the town courtships were conducted on the hillside. It was tradition. There was nowhere else to find any privacy in the crowded houses and narrow streets of the valley. Advanced courtships proceeded on the mountainside, higher up, where there was more assurance of being quite alone. She had been up on the mountain once with Gwyn a week before their wedding. It was where she had lost her virginity, as she had known she would when she had said yes. That was what going up on the mountain meant. The ground had been hard and cold. She had been almost unable to breathe beneath Gwyn's weight.

"Not tonight, Owen," she said, wanting to go, wanting to settle her future once and for all, wanting to forget her sick fears. Owen was a chapelgoer despite his frequent criticisms of the minister. If he took her up the mountain, he would marry her afterward. Asking her to go was just one way of proposing to her. She wanted to go with him — part of her wanted to go. "Not yet."

"A tease are you, then?" he said. "Your kisses say yes, Siân. Very gentle I will be if you come with me. You think I cannot be gentle because I am big?"

She kissed his lips. "Give me time," she said. "I am sure you can be wonderfully gentle, Owen."

"Summer will be over soon, mind," he said. "It will be cold on the mountain when autumn comes."

"I don't mean to tease." She turned her head to rest her cheek against his shoulder. "I just don't want to go yet, Owen." But part of her did want it. She wanted the reassurance of a man's loving. She had liked that part of marriage with Gwyn — except for that one time on the mountain. There was comfort in being that close to another human being.

"Next week I'll be asking again, mind," he said. "You are the prettiest woman in Cwmbran, Siân Jones, married or single."

She smiled at him. "And you are the handsomest man, Owen Parry," she said.

He kissed her again, briefly. "Home now, then, is it?" he said. "And early rising for the morning shift?"

She nodded and smiled ruefully.

"Ah, Siân," he said, bending his head close to hers once more, "you were not made to be down the mine, girl."

"No man or woman was," she said, "but we all need to eat." She linked her arm through his and raised her face to the sunset. She breathed in fresh air once more before they descended the hill to the town. She hoped she would be able to sleep. She hoped that by some miracle her terrors were unfounded.

3

Alex took his daughter for a walk during the evening. She should have been going to bed, according to her nurse, but she was fretful and he felt guilty for having left her alone all day. She had had nothing to do beyond exploring as much of the house and the park as her nurse had allowed. Apparently her nurse was rather fearful of Wales and the Welsh and had not given her a great deal of freedom.

Alex took her to walk on the hills. They looked very different in the light of evening, he found, the heather brightened on their side of the valley by the rays of the evening sun. Last night seemed now rather like a dream.

It was definitely picturesque, he thought, stopping to gaze down into the valley and across the river to the hills opposite. Verity clung quietly to his hand. Picturesque and peaceful. A different world. It seemed that he must be separated by oceans and continents from his own world. But it felt strangely good to be here. Perhaps in time he would come to understand the industry on which the wealth of the property depended. Perhaps he would come to know the people who lived and worked here. Perhaps he would be content to stay for a while.

"What are they doing, Papa?" Verity was pointing downward.

He smiled. He had noticed them too, the couple below, though he had kept his eyes off them until now. They obviously thought themselves unobserved.

"They are kissing," he said. "Men and women do that when they are considering marrying each other. And when they are married. It is to show that they care for each other."

"Like you kiss me at bedtime," she said. "But you do not take so long about it, Papa."

"It is a little different with men and women," he said. "But we must not stare and intrude on their privacy, even if they cannot see us. What do you think?" With a sweep of one arm he indicated the slope about them, the valley below, and the hills and sunset opposite.

"I think it is very lovely, Papa," she said, "though I do not like all that smoke coming from those chimneys down there." She wrinkled her nose and pointed to the iron-works, where the furnaces were kept lit day and night. "I think Grandmama was wrong, though. She said we were coming to the back of beyond, and she made it sound like somewhere no one would wish to be."

He smiled. The setting sun was turning the sky orange behind the hills opposite and was making a gold ribbon of the river. He glanced down involuntarily at the lovers again. They were no longer embracing, but were still standing close together. A tall, slim woman with long dark hair, and a broad-chested, dark-haired man only a little taller than she. He had seen them both before, if the distance did not deceive his eyes. He was last night's leader and today's half-naked puddler. She was the maiden of Cwmbran. Though perhaps not a maiden after all.

Alex felt a sudden and quite unexpected stabbing of envy and loneliness. They seemed somehow a part of their surroundings. A part of this picturesque and remote Welsh valley whose steep hillsides closed it in away from the world.

Except that the world had come looking

for it last night.

The sun was dropping behind the hills opposite, deepening the orange to red. Already it was dusk in the valley. Soon it would be dark. He felt something — some longing, some yearning that he could not quite grasp or name. Some sense, perhaps, of being an outsider in something that was beautiful. Some sense of being in a place where he did not belong but wanted to belong. Some sense of — home. But no, that could not be it. He could not put words to the feeling. The valley was lovely despite the signs of industry, and he was seeing it at its loveliest, at sunset on a summer evening. Was it surprising that he was affected by its beauty and a little dissatisfied that there was no one with whom to share it except his young daughter?

The two lovers, he saw, looking downward again, were making their way down toward the terraced houses, arm in arm.

"Well," he said, looking at his daughter, who was unusually quiet, "shall we go home before it gets dark and we get lost?"

"But I am with you, Papa," she said, still holding tightly to his hand. "Are we going to live here forever?"

"Perhaps not forever," he said. "But for a while. Will you mind?"

"No," she said. And she added with the candor of a child, "It annoys me to be with Grandmama sometimes. She thinks that if I am enjoying myself I must be doing something wrong. That is silly, is it not, Papa?"

Yes, very. But one had to be loyal to one's mother-in-law. "Grandmama wants you to grow up to be a proper lady," he said.

"If a proper lady frowns all the time, I do not want to be one, Papa," she said firmly.

He wisely dropped the topic. But she was not quite finished.

"Nurse is just as bad," she said. "She would not let me go downstairs today to talk with the servants, as I do at home. And she would allow me to walk only just outside the house, with her close by. You know how fast and how far Nurse walks. She will never allow me out here on the hills. She thinks I might get lost or eaten by wolves. There are no wolves, are there, Papa? People have funny ideas about Wales, don't they? I think Nurse is just lazy."

And rather elderly. He had kept her as Verity's nurse because she was the one woman who had been with his daughter since birth — and because it was his mother-in-law who had originally selected her. But Verity needed more than a nurse. She needed companionship, but he could not spend a great deal of his own time with her.

"Perhaps it is time for a governess," he said. "You are six years old, after all. I shall have to see what I can do." He should have thought of it before they came. He should have seen about hiring someone and bringing her with them.

"Grandmama taught me how to read and do sums," she said, tripping along at his side. "I don't need a governess, Papa. Just someone to take me out. Someone who is willing to do things with me."

A governess. Yes. "I'll see what I can do," he said.

He wondered foolishly and uncharacteristically what *he* would do for companionship. And he thought again about the strongly muscled puddler and the dark-haired woman whom he himself had kissed the night before.

She had aroused an unwelcome yearning in him. He could still feel it.

Alex slept, as always, with his window wide open. He woke during the night with the feeling that something had woken him, though he did not know what. It must be the moonlight, he thought, opening his eyes to find it in a bright band across his bed. In a short while it would be right on his face.

If he turned over onto his side, could he ignore it? He felt too cozy and too lazy to get out to close the curtains. But he did so with a sigh. Moonlight on his head would definitely keep him awake.

He stood at the window for a few moments before pulling the curtains. He rested his hands on the sill and drew in a deep breath of fresh air as he looked out over treetops to the hills. It was as bright a night as last night. Though a little chillier, he thought, shivering slightly. He reached up a hand to one of the curtains.

But his hand froze there. There it was again. The sound that had woken him. He remembered it now that it was being repeated. A mournful and prolonged howling. Wolves? He frowned. Were there wolves? There was more than one of them. But more than one animal too. There were howls, but there were also bellows, as if there were cattle out there.

Alex shivered again. The sounds seemed somehow out of place in the peace of the valley. And almost human in their plaintiveness. He must remember to mention them to Miss Haines, his housekeeper, in the morning. And to Barnes. He did not want Verity wandering outside the park, governess or no governess, if there really were wild animals out there.

He pulled the curtains together and went back to the warmth of his bed. He heard the sounds three times more before falling back to sleep.

Siân came surging awake and up to a sitting position in her cupboard bed. Oh, no. Oh, Lord. Dear Lord. Pray no. Pray she had only been dreaming. She stared wide-eyed into the darkness, listening intently. But there was nothing. She had been just dreaming after all.

After a minute or two she lay down again, but she still stared upward, alert for the sounds she dreaded to hear. It was just that she had been worrying about Iestyn. Dear, sweet-tempered Iestyn, always her favorite brother-in-law. He had been only twelve when she had married Gwyn. She had tried to fill his thirst for knowledge by sharing her own remembered store of knowledge from schooldays, though he had learned to read and write at Sunday School. She had listened to his dreams and her heart had ached for the boy who was destined for the mines regardless of dreams. She had been worrying about him all day and when she had fallen asleep. That was what had made her dream the sounds.

And then she was sitting bolt upright again, in a cold sweat. Howls, wails, bellows. *Scotch Cattle.* Oh, Lord. Oh, dear Lord. She prayed frantically and incoherently.

Scotch Cattle!

She had not heard them many times in her life, but the sound of them had always had the power to turn her legs to jelly and her stomach to a churning mass. She had always burrowed far beneath the bedclothes and pressed her fingers into her ears. But this time she could not so dissociate herself from what was going on outside. This time Iestyn might be involved. It might be Iestyn they were after.

But he was just a boy. And he had signed the Charter. Surely they would not hold it against him that he had refused to pay his penny to join the Chartist Association? They must have bigger prey than Iestyn.

But even that thought was not consoling.

The Scotch Cattle were a secret organization of men who appointed themselves enforcers of group action in the valleys. They always worked at night and always wore disguise. No one knew who they were. It was said that Cattle worked in valleys other than their own so that they would not be recognized and so that sentiment would not soften their hearts. But who could know for sure?

If ever there was an attempt to form a union or to get unanimous action on a strike, the Scotch Cattle became active. For always there would be some dissenting voices, some men who for one reason or other refused to act with the majority. There was usually a warning first, a frightening nocturnal visit from the Cattle or perhaps merely the leaving of a note if the recipient was known to be able to read. Then punishment — the destruction of possessions, sometimes total. And very often a whipping up on the mountain.

Siân had always considered it a scandal and a disgrace. Life was so very hard. Surely the only way it could be made bearable was for the people to cling together in love and mutual support. And they did much of the time. Life was lived richly in Cwmbran despite the long hours of work and the hard and dirty conditions and the danger and low wages. But always times like this came along to spoil everything. And to terrify them all in their beds.

But there were men — and women too — who would say that the Cattle were necessary. She remembered Owen saying the night before that unanimity was essential. Perhaps it was. But did it have to be enforced by terror and violence? She would never believe so.

And then the howling came again, and Siân pressed a clenched fist against her mouth to stop herself from screaming and giving in to panic. Who were the recipients of their visits? Was it just the warnings tonight? Or were there men even at this moment being dragged up the mountain? She heard a creaking on the stairs and moaned.

"Siân?" It was Emrys's voice.

She pushed back the blankets and stepped out barefoot onto the kitchen floor. "Uncle Emrys?" Her voice shook. "Scotch Cattle?"

"Yes, *fach,*" he said. "Scared, are you?"

She crossed the room toward his darkened form and pushed her hand into his reassuringly warm one. "I hate it," she said. "It is not necessary, surely?"

"There were those who would not sign the Charter," he said, crossing to the window and holding the curtain back with his free hand so that he could peer out. "It is important that everyone sign. The government in London must be made to see that it is not just a few cranks who are demanding the changes."

"But if anyone's conscience is against it

—" she said.

Emrys clucked his tongue. "This is not the time for conscience, *fach,*" he said. He looked carefully up and down the street. "There is nothing to be seen. It looks as if no one on our street is for it."

Siân heard herself sobbing before she could stop herself. "Will it just be those who did not sign, then?" she said. "Not those who did not join the Association?"

"I don't know, *fach,*" he said. "But back to bed and back to sleep now, is it? And keep our noses out of places where they do not belong? We have to be up early." He squeezed her hand tightly before letting it go.

"Yes," she said, climbing back into bed and pulling up the blankets. She wished he would sit down beside the fireplace for a while so that she could feel a friendly human presence close by. But she heard his footsteps going back up the stairs and a low, murmured exchange with her grandfather.

Their noses did belong where the Scotch Cattle were. It was their own people who were being terrorized. People who were acting from conscience rather than cowardice, surely. It was not cowardly to hold out against the majority. Not when there were

Scotch Cattle ready to enforce the majority stand.

And then the howling and bellowing started again, and Siân dived beneath the blankets, shivering and pressing her hands to her ears.

Iestyn, she thought. Oh, Iestyn. *Dear Lord, protect him. Let them be after only those who did not sign. Lord, keep Iestyn safe.*

And then she remembered the Marquess of Craille and the fact that there was danger not only from Scotch Cattle. She burrowed deeper.

The next day was a busy one for Alex. He made the planned visit to the coal mine in the morning and received a visit from the closest neighbors of his own class during the afternoon.

But first, at breakfast, he tried to find out what animals he had heard the night before. Neither his housekeeper nor his butler had heard anything. And neither knew anything about either wolves or cattle in the valley or on the hills. He had the feeling that they were being deliberately evasive, though he could not imagine why. Did they believe that he would go scurrying back to England and dismiss them all from their jobs if they admitted to the existence of wild animals in the vicinity?

He had some surprising and disturbing answers from Josiah Barnes later, when he asked the same questions.

"Scotch Cattle, my lord," he said shortly. And he went on to explain just as Alex was forming a mental image of Scottish animals in the Welsh hills. "Workers out on the prowl and in disguise to punish some of their own for an offense against the masses."

Alex frowned and looked inquiringly at his agent.

Barnes was tight-lipped. "They are up to something," he said. "This happens when they are trying yet again to form a union or when they are trying to persuade everyone to go out on strike. I have not heard rumblings of either lately."

"Chartists, perhaps?" Alex suggested.

"Could be," Barnes said. "One never knows, my lord. I have some sources, but even they can button up their lips at times. These are a damnably closely bonded people. They can have a meeting of a thousand people up on the mountain and not a word of it leak out to any of the owners or their agents. I shall look into it, my lord."

Alex remembered both Robert Mitchell and the Welsh puddler calling for united action to bring the Charter successfully to the notice of Parliament. Scotch Cattle! He had never heard of them before. But he would never forget the sound of their night cries. The very memory of them made his spine crawl.

The coal mine was more unpleasant than the ironworks, he discovered during the course of the morning. Josiah Barnes seemed rather taken aback when he insisted on going actually underground. Alex suspected that Barnes did not go down often himself.

The air underground was heavy and very warm and laden with dust. Many of the men worked without shirts, their upper bodies glistening with sweat and coal dust. Children, some of them seeming very young, operated ventilation doors, opening them as people or carts went through, shutting them immediately again behind them. Women, harnessed at the waist to coal carts, hauled them along the tunnels, sometimes having to bend double and move on all fours in the lower sections. One of them almost butted him in the stomach with her head before seeing him and looking up, startled, to reveal a grubby face and large clear eyes. Her hair was bound with a dirty cloth.

"How old are those children?" he asked

Josiah Barnes when they were aboveground again. Alex felt grubby with soot and was glad he had thought to wear his very oldest clothes.

"How old, sir?" his agent repeated.

"At what minimum age are they employed?" Alex asked.

"They are not supposed to be down there before the age of twelve," Barnes said evasively.

"But they sometimes are?"

"Sometimes one turns a blind eye out of kindness to their families," Barnes said. "Some of them need the extra income, my lord."

Were wages that low? Alex wondered. And yet Barnes had assured him earlier that his workers were well paid. At the moment they were still sharing in a time of prosperity, though sales had fallen off along with profits and the workers were due for a wage reduction. It was all quite routine, his agent had assured him when he had expressed concern. Wages fluctuated with the market. Everyone knew it and accepted it. And yet as far as Alex was aware, his agent's salary was constant. He felt very ignorant — yet again. Wages had not yet been reduced, though they would be next week. The workers were to be informed of the change when they collected their pay this evening.

He had lived a very protected life, he supposed. About the hardest workers he had seen before coming here were the chimney sweeps who were called in to his houses occasionally. He had always refused to employ any who used climbing boys. And yet here everyone seemed to work long hours in hard, dirty jobs for a wage that sounded to him pitifully small — even before the reduction. And some of them even felt obliged to send their young children to work.

Yet there was not much he could say. What did he know about the working of industry in comparison with the confident, efficient Barnes? At the moment Alex's sole task was to learn. It was a frustrating task, when much of what he had seen disturbed him, but it was a necessary one.

He was grateful during the afternoon to receive a visit from Sir John Fowler, owner of the Penybont works farther up the valley. Sir John brought his wife and daughter with him. Although Alex and they would not perhaps have moved in quite the same social circles if they had been in London or some other fashionable center, they were at least from the same world. He greeted them graciously, listened to Fowler's rather pompous speech of welcome, and sent for

Verity to come down for tea. Lady Fowler and Miss Tess Fowler cooed over her and made much of her while Alex talked with Sir John.

The Penybont workers were to have their wages cut too. It was an economic reality, Sir John explained. The men and their families understood that and accepted it. They had learned from long habit to enjoy the good times and endure the not so good. And of course there was no real suffering. Even the reduced wages were sufficient to satisfy their needs. And the truck shops, the company shops, were always ready to give advances on wages to those families who were less skilled at managing their money than others. Child labor? It was a reality. Parents were not forced into it. If they chose to send their children to work, who were the masters to stop them?

"Do these children not go to school?" Alex asked.

It seemed there were not many schools. The few there were in any of the valleys were mostly dame schools, run by women not well qualified to teach, though two own-ers' wives in other valleys were attempting to sponsor schools themselves and had brought in schoolmasters. The Sunday Schools often taught the rudiments of read-

75

ing and writing.

"I am considering hiring a governess for Verity," Alex said. His words drew the ladies into the conversation.

"Oh, yes," Lady Fowler said. "She is quite old enough, my lord. And a dear child. We had a governess for Tess when she was but five years old. A very superior woman. English, of course, and a gentlewoman."

"I suppose I should have thought of it before coming here," Alex said. "I don't like the thought of someone else making the choice for me, and yet it seems there would be no likely candidates here, if any."

"Now Tess would be your perfect choice," Sir John said with a laugh, sounding as if he were only half serious. "She had the best of schooling in England and is always looking for something new with which to amuse herself, the puss."

Tess smiled dazzlingly at Alex. She was a pretty little blond, perhaps eighteen years of age. The sort of girl he instinctively avoided at any social function he attended. The sort of girl who was fresh from the schoolroom and in search of a husband and a dazzling match. As a marquess, and a wealthy one at that, he was definitely a dazzling match.

"It would be a quite delightful arrangement," Lady Fowler said with great enthusiasm, "and most convenient. She could come here two or three times a week, my lord, to teach dear little Lady Verity. I am sure they would become the best of friends in no time at all. Tess would be like a mother figure."

Tess tittered at the idea.

Alex's smile was polite and hid the real amusement — and the slight twinge of alarm — he was feeling. He had noticed from the start how very smartly the girl was dressed and how carefully her hair was styled. Almost as if she was about to take tea with the queen. It was quite obvious to him why she had been brought on this visit with her parents when it might have been more appropriate for Fowler to come alone the first time.

"Would you like that, Verity, dear?" Tess asked, all tender big blue eyes, taking his daughter's hand in hers. "I would like it of all things. It would be no trouble at all."

"I can read and do sums already," Verity said. "My grandmama taught me. I want someone to take me running and climbing in the hills."

"Oh, dear," Lady Fowler said, tittering, "what comical ideas little ones have, my lord. That would not be at all ladylike, Lady Verity."

"Then I do not want a governess, Papa,"

Verity said.

"I have the notion," he said entirely on the spur of the moment, "that she should learn something of the Welsh language and something of the country and the culture in which we have decided to live for a time." He hoped fervently that Miss Tess Fowler did not speak Welsh.

"This country is quite wild," Lady Fowler said, "and the culture much inferior to our own. It is not easy to be forced to live in exile here. Fortunately, of course, there are several other ironworks at the heads of the valleys and a superior circle of acquaintances of our own kind with whom to mingle. I believe you will not find our company inferior to what you have been accustomed to, my lord. And the language of these people is a barbarian's tongue. No civilized person would be able to get his tongue around it."

"I refuse to pay heed to anyone who does not speak English to me," Tess said. "It is nonsense that they all speak Welsh when they understand English perfectly well."

She did not speak Welsh, Alex understood with some relief.

They stayed for an hour and before they left renewed the offer for Tess to come to Glanrhyd Castle as often as he wished in order to give instruction to Verity. Alex smiled and bowed over the girl's hand when they took their leave.

"It is too kind of you," he murmured, shamelessly using all his charm on her. "I am quite sure you have far more pleasant things to do with your time than running in the heather on the hills with my daughter."

"Papa," Verity said when their carriage had disappeared down the driveway, "I would be lucky to coax that lady to stroll in the garden." Her voice was filled with disgust.

He chuckled. "I believe you are right," he said. "You would be no better off than with Nurse. Would you like to learn Welsh?"

"I think Cook and the maids were speaking it in the kitchen when I was sitting on the stairs this morning," she said. "I escaped from Nurse when she nodded off to sleep for a while. They could not see me. But it was no fun because I could not understand what they were saying."

"If you learned the language, imp," he said, chuckling again, "you would be able to eavesdrop to better effect. But I don't know where I am likely to find a governess who is qualified to teach it to you as well as a competent dose of other knowledge. And one who is willing to romp in the hills with you."

He asked Miss Haines about it a little later. The housekeeper was not at all encouraging at first. He would have to go down to Newport, the largest Welsh town that was anywhere close, and ask around or advertise there, she supposed. Or to Cardiff. But Cardiff was smaller. Certainly none of the teachers at the dame schools were in any way qualified to teach the daughter of the Marquess of Craille.

But she came back a short while later. She had thought of someone. There was Siân Jones, who lived right in Cwmbran. She had been educated at a private girls' school in England and she spoke Welsh.

"And would such a lady be prepared to be a companion to my daughter as well as a teacher?" he asked. "Would she have the energy to climb to the top of the hills above the valley, for example?"

Miss Haines looked doubtful. "Mrs. Jones is quite a young woman, sir," she said. "But I am not sure she would be willing to take on the task. It is merely a suggestion."

"Mrs.?" He raised his eyebrows.

"A widow, sir," she said.

He nodded. "Will you send for her?" he asked. "Ask her to call on me here at her earliest convenience?"

He liked the thought of it. Someone to

give Verity organized lessons. Someone to give her companionship and some outings and exercise. Someone to teach her something about the country in which he had property and in which they were to live for a while. Perhaps for a long while. For two days he had felt like a stranger in a foreign land. But he had also felt somewhat invigorated by the challenge of learning about something that was totally new to him. And then there was that feeling he had had up in the hills the evening before, that strange yearning for something he could not put a name to. It was a feeling he felt the need to explore.

He waited with some impatience to see what Mrs. Siân Jones was like. He would have to see if she was suitable — and willing — to be Verity's governess. He had not thought to ask Miss Haines what she did in Cwmbran. If she was not suitable, he would have to decide whether to send to his man of business in London to find him a governess or to go down to Newport and look for someone himself.

4

Angharad Lewis lived with her coal-miner father. She had lost her husband in the same cave-in as had killed Gwyn Jones. Unlike her friend Siân Jones, she had not gone back to work in the mine afterward. She wanted something better. She yearned for something better, for a grander home and for pretty clothes and money for some luxuries. She dreamed of a rich husband. She had found a job cleaning house for the Reverend Llewellyn and for Owen Parry. She had begun stepping out with Emrys Rhys two years after her husband's death, and there had been a growing fondness on both sides. But then she had got a job at Josiah Barnes's house to add to the other two, and finally her dreams had seemed within her grasp. She had stopped seeing Emrys.

Angharad was lifting a small tray of cakes from the oven when Josiah Barnes returned to his house from showing the marquess around the mine. She set it down and smiled at him.

"Good afternoon, Mr. Barnes," she said. "I have made you some little currant cakes for your tea. Your favorites."

He grunted. "I think you forgot to tell me something, Angharad," he said.

She tried to look blank, but her eyes slipped from his. She knew instantly what he was talking about. "Oh?" she said.

He took her by one wrist and squeezed hard so that her fingers splayed wide. "What were Scotch Cattle doing out last night?" he asked.

"It was to warn the Chartists, Mr. Barnes," she said. "Or rather, those who will not join them."

"Oh, aye," he said. "And when were they asked to join, pray?"

She looked flustered and tried in vain to flex her fingers. "There was a meeting on the mountain the night before last, Mr. Barnes," she said, not looking at him. "I didn't know anything about it. Honest, I didn't." The lie would make her afraid to go to chapel on Sunday.

"Angharad," he said sternly, "I don't like having things kept from me. I don't like being made a fool of. I thought you understood that."

"I didn't know about it until today," she said. "Honest."

He grunted and released her wrist. "Upstairs," he said, patting her on the bottom. "And out of those clothes."

She smiled at him. "Yes, Mr. Barnes," she said.

She pleased him, she knew — always keeping his house clean and tidy, cooking for him although it was not part of her original duties. And giving him his pleasure in bed. He was a single man and a lonely man, Angharad believed. And she had begun to believe in dreams. She would do anything to make her dream come true — including giving him information that she judged would not harm anyone in particular.

He did not undress when he followed her up a few minutes later. He merely loosened his trousers and lay heavily on top of her on the bed. She opened her legs for him, and he thrust himself inside her and rode her with vigor while his hands took hold of her naked breasts and squeezed them hard. He grunted and relaxed his full weight on her when he was finished before rolling to one side of her. He kept hold of one of her breasts.

"You are wonderful, Mr. Barnes," she

said, gazing worshipfully at him. "I do like a masterful man."

"You must just remember, Angharad," he said, "that a good woman does not keep secrets from her man. You must trust me. If I am your master, you must tell me everything you know. I have everyone's interests at heart, after all. You know that. I would be displeased with you if I thought you did not trust me and deliberately kept things from me."

"I trust you, Mr. Barnes," she said earnestly. "I think you are wonderful. It is just that I did not know this time. I'll tell you next time. I would do anything for you."

"I will expect better next time, then," he said. "Lie still now while I rest. I'll have you again before you go."

"Yes, Mr. Barnes," she said. She closed her eyes and dreamed of life in the stone lodge cottage. Her own spacious home to do with as she liked and money to buy ornaments for it and clothes for herself. The man who lived there with her in her dreams had Emrys Rhys's face.

The workers were paid in the Three Lions Inn, as they always were. It was owned by the company and many of the men never did make it out the doors before their pay pack was seriously depleted. Many a wife waited at home for her man to come, angry at his weakness, anxious about how much or how little money there would be left to stretch over the week's needs. Many thought with a sinking heart of the already impossibly high advance taken up at the truck shop and the resulting smallness of this week's pay, now being drunk up. Tomorrow or the next day they would be asking at the shop for an advance on next week's wages.

This evening many of the men drank deeper than usual — not with the once-a-week pleasure of having some money in their pockets, but with the impotent anger of their reaction to the news that wages were to drop ten percent during the coming week. Take it or leave it, the paymaster had said with a shrug when some of the more vocal men had protested. Profits were down. It was either a reduction in everyone's wages or layoffs. There were always more workers ready to move into the valley and work for even less if all they wanted to do was grumble. The Irish were always willing to work.

Siân waited at the end of a long line. The coal miners were always paid last, the women after the men. She thought of the long, hard hours spent underground each day and the almost inhuman conditions. And all for so little pay that it would scarcely buy sufficient food for the coming week. What would happen with a ten percent reduction? Yet she was one of the fortunate ones. Grandad and Uncle Emrys worked at the furnaces and were higher paid than most men. There were three wages going into their house and only four mouths to feed. There were no children. She tried not to listen to the complaints of some of the men with large families.

There were the usual murmurs about a union. Not loud murmurs with the paymaster still present, but quite unmistakable nevertheless. Owen was sitting with a large group of men at the far side of the room, Emrys among them. Her grandfather was sitting with a group of older men.

It was all they would need, she thought with an inward sigh of despair. As if they did not have enough troubles without that. There had been a curious silence at work during the day about the activities of the Scotch Cattle last night. And yet there had been a very definite awareness of the one topic that dominated all their minds. Siân had walked home from work with Iestyn, as she often did, and had asked him directly.

He had smiled at her. "Don't worry your

head about it, Siân," he had said. "You are tired after a day's work."

"And you are not?" she had said. "What am I not to worry my head about? Did they give you a warning? Did they, Iestyn?"

"It is not right to give in to threats," he had said. "It is only right to go with one's conscience, Siân. I am not afraid of them."

"You will not join the Association, then?" She had been whispering.

He had shaken his head. "You are not to worry about it." He had smiled again, but she had been able to see from the paleness of his face behind the coal dust that he was afraid. His face had reminded her for a moment of Gwyn's when he had been carried up from the pit, dead.

She was terrified for Iestyn. He was going to ignore a warning from the Scotch Cattle! As she waited in line for her wages, she thought for a moment that she was not going to be able to get her breathing under control but would collapse, gasping, on the floor.

Oh, Iestyn, she thought, as he passed her and smiled, his pay pack in his hand. *Foolish, brave boy.* She would have a word with Owen. Maybe Owen could do something about it. Maybe he knew someone who belonged to the Scotch Cattle, though she had never known anyone who was willing to admit as much. But if anyone knew, Owen would. She would have a word with him, plead with him. He knew that she was fond of Iestyn. She felt marginally better.

And yet now the men were reacting to the news of the wage cut with anger and the murmurings of a strike. Where would it all end? And what sort of a waiting game was the Marquess of Craille playing? But she dared not think of that. Oh, she dared not, she thought as her heart started to palpitate again.

"Well, Siân Jones," Ceridwen Hughes said, digging her in the ribs with one bony elbow and grinning to reveal crooked teeth. Unlike Siân, Ceridwen had not bathed before coming to the Three Lions for her pay. She had merely scrubbed her cheeks and the palms of her hands. "What did you think of him, then?"

Him today could mean only the Marquess of Craille, who had appeared underground during the morning to inspect the mine without any of the warnings they usually had if Josiah Barnes was expected. Siân had been trying not to think of that visit and the terror it had occasioned her. Life had been so full of terror in the past few days. She was mortally tired of it.

"I think he found it unpleasant," she said. "His nose was wrinkled." She remembered how she had stopped just in time before butting into him headfirst and how she had looked up and almost gaped at his immaculate splendor, so out of place in the mine. And at her realization that now it was beyond all doubt. The man on the mountain and the Marquess of Craille were one and the same man. And then she remembered the fear, almost amounting to nausea, as she had waited to be recognized.

"I saw him close-up," Ceridwen said. "He looked right at me." She lowered her voice. "I wouldn't mind stepping up the mountain with that one for a good go. What do you say?"

"I don't think he would go with either of us, Ceridwen," Siân said with a smile. She tried to feel real amusement at the thought. She was tired of feeling afraid. "Ah, at last. It is almost our turn." Her back ached with the long wait following upon a day of work.

She raised a hand in farewell to Owen as she turned to leave a few minutes later. He and the men with him were deep into their beer and animated talk. She shut her mind to what they were undoubtedly saying. She would not think of it anymore.

She sighed as she let herself into the house

a few minutes later and smelled the dinner her grandmother was cooking. It was good to be home and to close the door behind her. If only all her troubles and fears could be shut outside and left there. She smiled wearily at her grandmother and kissed her cheek.

"The line seemed to move even more slowly than usual," she said. "I am sorry to be late, Gran."

"There is no point in waiting for the men, at any rate," Gwynneth said, her voice curt as it usually was on payday. "Sit down, *fach*, and eat." She spooned generous ladlefuls of stew onto Siân's plate at the table. "They can eat it cold later. There is wicked it is of the owners to pay the men in the pub. And clever too. They get their money back almost before it leaves their pockets. And women and children go hungry."

"Wages are going down next week," Siân said quietly. "Ten percent, Gran."

Her grandmother sank onto the chair at the other side of the table. "Oh, *Duw, Duw,*" she said. "How can we live on less, then? Are we supposed to eat grass?"

Siân slid her pay package across the table. "We will manage, Gran, as we always do," she said. "I just worry about Gwyn's folk." Gwyn's father had the coughing sickness that so many miners ended up with after spending years working underground. He was not able to work any longer. Only Gwyn's older brother Huw and his youngest brother, Iestyn, were working in that house and yet there were eight mouths to feed, counting Huw's three young children. "Perhaps . . ."

Her grandmother spread the money before her on the table and divided it in half. She pushed the one half back toward Siân. "Yes, take it to them, *fach,*" she said. "For the little ones, is it?"

"But Huw is so proud," Siân said with a sigh. "I will have to slip it to Mari on the sly."

"Men!" Gwynneth Rhys said. "I suppose they are all drowning their sorrows down at the pub and whispering about a strike — Grandad and Emrys among them."

"And Owen," Siân said. "I can't really blame them, Gran. For some it is a matter of life and death. Really and truly. But we do not need that kind of trouble on top of what we already have with all this business over the Charter — and Scotch Cattle last night." She swallowed. "They called on Iestyn. He has been given three days to join the Chartist Association. But he says he will not."

"Oh, *Duw.*" Her grandmother was about to say more, but she was stopped by a knock on the door. Owen? Had he left the pub early, then? But the door was not opened as it usually was if it were Owen or one of their neighbors. Siân got up to open it.

"Mrs. Siân Jones?"

She did not recognize the man, though he was well dressed.

"Yes," she said.

"You are wanted at the castle," he said in English. "By his lordship. You had better be quick about it. He does not like to be kept waiting."

Siân felt suddenly as if she were looking at the man through a long tunnel. This was it, then. He had recognized her after all this morning and had found out who she was and where she lived. She concentrated on not showing the sick dread she felt. She would not show fear before one of his servants. Or before him either.

"Me?" she said with studied calm, speaking too in English. "The Marquess of Craille wishes to see me? What about?"

"Don't be daft, woman," he said, betraying his Welsh origins for a moment even though he kept to the other language. "Would he tell me? Wash your hands and face and get yourself up there if you know what is good for you."

Siân's lips tightened. And anger rescued her from perhaps cringing after all. She had bathed and washed her hair and changed into clean clothes not two hours ago. Her grandmother had hauled water from the pump and heated it so that she could clean herself after work. And yet this man — a mere servant when all was said and done — thought to treat her like a worm beneath his well-polished boot?

"It is very late," she said. "I have just come home from work."

The groom turned away in disdain. "I would be there in half an hour if I were you, missus," he said. "Or it may go badly with you."

Yes, badly. It would go badly whenever she went. She wondered if the Marquess of Craille would punish her merely for being there as a spy at the meeting, or if he hoped to coerce her into giving some of the men's names. Perhaps after all he found himself unable to identify any of them, including Owen. She felt a glimmering of hope. But he had summoned her to the castle. Absurdly she had a mental image of dungeons and racks. The castle had been built less than a hundred years before. It was not a real castle at all. Besides . . . She closed the

door and turned to stare at her grandmother.

"*Duw!*" was all her grandmother said from
her place at the table. She held one hand
over her heart.

"He must have found out who I was,"
Siân said. But she must not worry her
grandmother before she had to. Or anger
her. Gran would be very annoyed if she
knew that Siân had gone up the mountain
at midnight. "I almost ran him down this
morning, Gran, when he came down the
mine with Mr. Barnes. He must be going to
dismiss me. But he would not lower himself
to do that in person, would he? Whatever
can he want?"

"Don't go," Gwynneth said, her eyes
round with fear. "Stay here, *fach.* We will
send Grandad when he comes home."

"No," Siân said. "It is me he has summoned, Gran. I had better go and see what
he wants. Probably something we will laugh
about afterward." She tried to smile.

"Don't go," her grandmother repeated.
"My Marged —" She spread her hands over
her face. Marged had been Siân's mother.

"Oh, Gran," Siân said, realizing suddenly
what her grandmother's fears were. She
hurried across the room to put her arms
about her. "No. He has not even seen me

except this morning when I must have looked anything but inviting." *And once up on the mountain, when he kissed me.* "That is ridiculous. Besides, you cannot think that I would . . ."

"Mr. Barnes," Gwynneth said without removing her hands. "It is the sort of thing he would do, Siân. I have heard about wicked English gentlemen and their her — har—"

"Harems?" said Siân.

"It would be just like Mr. Barnes to have you brought up to the castle first," her grandmother said. "There is wicked he is, *fach.* And all because you would not marry him. Don't go. Wait for Grandad to come home, is it? Or run along and see if the Reverend Llewellyn is at home."

Siân kissed her grandmother's cheek. "No, I shall go," she said. "He cannot very well kidnap me, after all, can he?"

"Then I will come with you." Gwynneth got determinedly to her feet, undoing the strings of her apron as she did so.

"No, Gran," Siân said. "I shall go alone. It is silly to expect the man to be some sort of ogre just because he is an English marquess and lives in a castle. Besides, Grandad and Uncle Emrys will be angry if you are not here to give them their dinner when they come home."

"And serve them right too," her grandmother said, bristling, but she sat down again. "I shall send Grandad up there if you are not home at a decent time, Siân."

Siân, almost sick with fear, considered her appearance. Should she pin up her hair and put on her Sunday dress? She thought of all the dresses bought for her by Sir John Fowler and left behind in her mother's cottage. But she was not going to dress up for the Marquess of Craille. Not just to be dismissed from her job and interrogated about the men at the meeting. She took her shawl from the back of the door and wrapped it about her shoulders. She lifted the weight of her hair outside it as she left the house and closed the door, leaving a worried-looking grandmother behind her. She raised her chin, squared her shoulders, and strode purposefully along the street.

She had never been close to Glanrhyd Castle. Despite her resolutions she felt her knees tremble and her heart beat with uncomfortable thumps as she walked between the wrought iron gateposts and through the massive gates, which stood open, and past the two square stone houses just inside them. One of them belonged to Josiah Barnes, she knew. It might have been

97

her home.

A straight and wide stone driveway sloped upward to beautifully laid out formal gardens, with the house beyond, all turreted towers and arched windows and aristocratic magnificence. She headed toward the main doors beneath a high stone archway and at the top of a steep flight of steps. She had the uncomfortable feeling that she was doing quite the wrong thing, that she should be seeking out the servants' entrance. But she did not know where it was. She lifted the heavy wrought iron knocker and let it fall back against the door. She resisted the absurd and cowardly urge to turn and run.

She was in for it, she thought, as the door opened. But she felt curiously calm as she stepped inside the large hall. There was no going back now. And she would show no nervousness before the Marquess of Craille.

She would not.

It seemed rather late in the evening to be having a caller, Alex thought, looking up in surprise from his book when his butler opened the door to inform him that Mrs. Siân Jones was in the salon downstairs. It was almost dark outside. He had not expected her to come until morning. Did she know why she had been summoned and was she that eager? He closed his book and went down. It would have been better if she had come in the morning. Verity could have met her and had some input into his decision. But then if he found her quite unsuitable, as he somehow expected he would, it would perhaps be better for his daughter not to meet her at all. Verity had been in bed for an hour or more.

She was wearing a faded cotton dress and a shawl that had seen better days. Her very dark hair was in heavy, shining ripples down her back. She looked no different from the way she had looked up on the mountain that first evening — and the next. For one moment he wondered why she had come, and he stared at her, thinking that she was even more beautiful than she had appeared in the moonlight. And then he remembered what his butler had called her. Ah, not his maiden of Cwmbran at all. The large puddler must be Mr. Jones. But, no. Miss Haines had called her a widow.

"Mrs. Jones?" he said, stepping into the salon and hearing a servant close the door behind him.

"Yes," she said.

She stood straight and tall, her feet slightly apart, her chin up. She looked directly at him with eyes of a clear dark gray. And beautifully lashed. She gave him no title and offered no curtsy. She really was quite startlingly beautiful. He wondered if it was the stolen kiss that was making her look defiant. Had it been that good?

"Will you have a seat?" He gestured to a chair beside her.

"Why?" she asked. "What do you want of me?"

She was frightened, he realized suddenly, and doing an admirable job of masking it with pride and disdain. She was expecting him to renew the questions he had asked her on the mountain? She did not know why she had been summoned, then?

"I wish to discuss the possibility of employing you," he said, and wondered even as he spoke if he really wished to do so. Have a woman who sneaked alone up the mountain to an all-male clandestine meeting in the middle of the night teaching his daughter? And a woman who stood on the hills, embracing her lover for all to see? Would she be a suitable teacher and companion for Verity? But by God, she was lovely. He remembered how after kissing her very briefly, he had had to fight desire all the way home across the mountain.

"You already employ me," she said.

"Do I?" He wondered in what capacity.

"I almost collided with you this morning," she said.

He tried to picture any near accident he had had while on horseback that morning and could remember nothing. "I went down the coal mine this morning," he said.

"Yes." She looked at him calmly. She still had not seated herself.

The eyes. Good Lord. The woman had been dirty and sweating. She had looked more like a beast of burden than a human. Certainly she had not looked like a shapely, feminine, beautiful human. Her hair had been hidden beneath a filthy cloth. But the eyes. Was it possible? He stared at her.

"That was you?" he asked.

She said nothing.

"It must be backbreaking work," he said lamely.

"Yes."

There was hostility emanating from her though her face was expressionless. Why? Had he forced her into that job? Did she not feel that he paid her enough? Had she heard about next week's cut in wages? Despite the assurances of both Barnes and Fowler, he could not feel easy in his mind about that. Or was it just the memory of that stolen kiss? Should he apologize for it? But he was not sorry. In fact, it would give him the greatest pleasure to repeat it — not a thought to be pursued at this precise moment.

"You have been recommended to me as a possible governess for my daughter," he said. "Won't you have a seat?"

She stared back at him. "A governess?" she said.

"I am told you were educated at a private girls' school in England?" He looked inquiringly at her.

"Yes," she said. "For four years."

He wondered suddenly how a girl from this Welsh valley, who had ended up hauling one of those carts in a coal mine, had come to be at a school in England. She was clearly Welsh. She was speaking flawless English, but she was doing so with a lilting accent that clearly came naturally to her. And her name was Welsh — both names. She offered no explanation.

"I would imagine, then," he said, "that you are qualified to instruct a six-year-old child."

She said nothing. She was clearly not going to sit down. He did not offer her a seat again.

"I want something more than just that, though," he said. "I want someone to teach her Welsh."

She raised her eyebrows. "Welsh?" she said.

"This little part of Wales will be mine for the rest of my life," he said. "It is possible that I will live here for much of my time. My daughter will live here with me. If I do not remarry and produce sons, it will all be hers one day. It seems logical that she learn the language of the people who work for me."

She smiled. It was not a very pleasant expression. "It is a barbaric tongue," she said.

"Let me guess," he said, clasping his hands at his back. "You were told that at school."

She inclined her head.

"Nevertheless," he said, "I would have my daughter learn this barbaric tongue. And something of the history and customs and culture of Wales. This is a very beautiful valley."

"It *was* beautiful," she said quietly.

He raised his eyebrows at the impertinence. He was responsible for spoiling its beauty? That was what her tone had implied.

"My daughter also needs someone willing to play with her," he said, "and take her for walks. And runs. She is fascinated by the hills. Hills for children are irresistible. They

103

must be climbed."

"They have that effect on many people, regardless of age," she said. "Hills are meant to be seen over."

He half smiled and had that yearning feeling again very fleetingly. It was gone even before he could begin to grasp at it. Hills were meant to be seen over. He must remember that.

"Can you oblige me?" he asked. "Can you give my daughter what I need for her?"

She was silent for a long moment. "No," she said at last.

"Why not?" He frowned. He had expected to be the one making the decisions. It seemed as though Mrs. Siân Jones was turning the tables on him.

"I have work already," she said.

"And you enjoy it?" His frown deepened.

"Other women do it," she said. "I am no different from other women."

He suspected that she was. In beauty if in nothing else. He felt unaccustomedly dazzled by it. He was used to having his favors courted by all the most beautiful ladies of fashion. But then this woman was not a lady. Not in social status or in dress, anyway. But she had a dignity that he found appealing.

"You would live here," he said. "You

would have a room of your own close to my daughter's and a clothing allowance." He glanced at the clean shabby dress she wore. It did nothing to detract from her loveliness. "I would pay you . . ." He named a sum.

Her eyes widened.

"You are interested?" he asked.

Color flooded her cheeks. "No," she said.

"How much do I pay you to work in my mine?" he asked.

He was staggered when she told him, though he had already seen some of the books in which the wages of his men were recorded. How could anyone live on such a pitiful — pittance?

"Is that before or after the cutback?" he asked her.

She smiled again — the same way she had smiled before. "Before," she said.

Good Lord! "Would you not prefer to earn what I have offered you to be a governess?" he asked. "Would you not find the work more pleasant?"

He was surprised to see her lips tighten with what could only be anger. "Can you afford to pay me so much?" she asked. "I thought everyone was suffering with the reduction in iron sales. You included."

He felt anger too. Was she daring to use

sarcasm on him? "Will people suffer?" he asked. "I know that no one likes to have less money than they have been accustomed to. But will there be actual suffering?"

She looked at him and said nothing. He waited for her reply but she obviously had no intention of making any. Mrs. Siân Jones, he decided, was a prickly woman. Beautiful, but lacking in the sort of soft charm that he expected of women. Her lover doubtless derived enormous pleasure from that luscious body — his eyes strayed downward to her generous, well-formed breasts for a moment and he remembered again how they had felt against his coat — but he had better be a strong man himself, in character as well as body, if he was to hold her tamed. Yet again Alex was not sure that he wanted her teaching any of her qualities to his daughter.

"You are adamant in your answer?" he asked. "You would not like to meet my daughter, perhaps tomorrow, before you give your final answer? She is an eager child and has some charm, I believe."

"I will be working tomorrow," she said. "She will be in bed by the time I get home and bathe and have a meal."

"Is that why you came so late this evening?" he asked. "Do I keep you working for such long hours? You were working this morning."

"Today was longer than usual," she said. "I had to stand in line for over an hour, as I do once a week, to collect my wages. All your mine girls do."

Good Lord. She hated him. It was there in her voice and in her eyes. Had Barnes painted too rosy a picture of his workers and the conditions under which they lived and worked? Was this girl — this woman — typical of the way his other workers felt about him? Or was she the sort of person who felt bitter about life and took it out on anyone who got in her path? It would be interesting to know the story behind her four years at an English school. Any decent private girls' school would have cost many times more for one day than she now earned in a month.

"Thank you, Mrs. Jones," he said, making her a half bow and turning toward the door. "I will not take any more of your time. Thank you for coming so promptly." He opened the door and stood to one side.

She did not move for a while. "Will I now be dismissed?" she asked. Her face looked like marble. "I would ask you please not to have my grandfather and my uncle dismissed too. This has nothing to do with them, and they have been good to me."

He stared at her long and hard. He felt again that he had stepped into an alien world. Was it possible that life could be so cruel in her world? Or was she given to theatrics? He rather suspected the latter.

"Mrs. Jones," he said, "you are welcome to pull coal carts in my mine for as long as you wish. You appear to enjoy doing so. Your grandfather and your uncle and any other relatives you have may continue with whatever they do in my employ. I am not much given to spite."

She licked her lips and hesitated. She spoke in a rush. "Not even about the other night?" she asked. "Why have you done nothing? I thought that was what this summons was about."

"If I had wanted to discuss that matter," he said, looking closely at her, "I would have summoned your lover, Mrs. Jones."

Her eyes widened. "My lover?"

"The dark-haired puddler who looks as if he is also a prizefighter," he said. "I would speak to him, Mrs. Jones. But I choose not to. Not yet, anyway."

She seemed about to say something else. Thank you, perhaps. But instead she hurried across the room and past him without another word. He stepped into the doorway and nodded to a servant who was standing close to the outer doors. The man opened them for her and then closed them quietly behind her.

Alex stood staring broodingly at the closed doors before turning abruptly and climbing the stairs back to the haven of his library. Perhaps it was as well she had refused, he thought. He was not at all sure she was the sort of woman he would want as Verity's companion and teacher. And he was not at all sure it would be good for him to have her living in his house, close to him whenever he was at home.

In fact, he was quite sure it would not be good for him. The thought definitely had its attraction, of course — as temptation always did.

Alex smiled suddenly despite himself. Siân Jones might lack charm and wisdom, but she was abounding in courage. She had been afraid at the start and afraid at the end, but between times she had quite effectively spat in his eye — metaphorically speaking.

It was a shame he was to have no further dealings with her.

Tomorrow he would have to decide whether he was going to send to London or go to Newport himself. He did not particularly relish doing either. He sighed as he sat down in the library again and picked up his book.

5

The following evening Siân waited for Owen to come to take her to the weekly choir practice at the chapel. Her grandfather had gone already. Emrys, though he had a good voice, never went since the practices took place in the chapel and both the mixed choir and the male voice choir were conducted by the Reverend Llewellyn. Emrys had no use for the preacher though he had admitted years ago that the words spoken at his wife's funeral had been meant to comfort rather than chastise him.

"Llewellyn is a fool," he was fond of saying. "He preaches acceptance of our lot when we should be fighting to change it."

Even the fact that the Reverend Llewellyn had attended the Chartist meeting and led it in prayer and signed the Charter did not mollify Siân's uncle. The preacher had not joined the Association and had spoken out against it. It was right to ask for changes, he had said, but it was not right to insist.

"Bloody idiot," Emrys had said before being commanded by his father to apologize to the women for using such language in the house.

Siân always looked forward to choir evenings. Singing was the most relaxing thing in the world to do, she always thought, and one of the most joyous, especially when one sang in company with a hundred or more others who loved it as much. Actually to call the mixed group a choir was rather comical since it consisted of at least three quarters of the Sunday congregation. And they did not really need to practice since they all knew the hymns by heart — some of them had to do so if they could not read — and were well familiar with their own particular part. Hymns in chapel were always sung in four-part harmony.

The male voice choir always practiced after the mixed one. Siân thought it unfair that men singing in harmony together sounded so much lovelier than women or mixed voices. But she loved to stay and listen to the men. They did not practice in order to sing in chapel — the women would not have consented to be quiet themselves since it was mainly to sing that they went to chapel. The male voice choir practiced to sing competitively. They sang a few times each year at minor competitions and once a year at the big *eisteddfod,* or music and poetry festival, that was held in one of the valleys. This year it was to be in the neighboring valley. The Cwmbran male voice choir had been beaten only twice in the past ten years — both times by their bitterest rival.

The *eisteddfod* was the big social and cultural event of the year in the valleys. Cwmbran would virtually empty out on that day while all its people trekked over the mountain to whistle and cheer for friends and relatives and to hiss and heckle rivals. It was also the big annual hunting ground for young people. Many an intervalley courtship began at the *eisteddfod.*

There was a knock on the door and Siân jumped to her feet, smiling. Owen let himself in and greeted her grandmother, who was mending one of Emrys's shirts.

"Ready for choir, are you then, Siân?" he asked. "Sharpened your voice, have you?"

"I hope not too much," she said, wrapping her shawl about her shoulders. She took his arm as they stepped outside. She was feeling almost lighthearted again after several days of anxiety. Everyone at home had approved her refusal of the job she had been offered last night — though treacherously she sometimes found herself wishing that she had given herself a little longer to make up her mind. The Marquess of Craille, though he knew Owen's identity, was not going to do anything about the meeting he had observed — not yet anyway. She chose to ignore the suggestion of a threat in those last words. Mari had accepted with tearful gratitude the half of her wage pack that Gran had given back to Siân, though she had sworn that Huw would kill her if he found out. There had been no reaction at work today to the reduction of wages except for a few sullen murmurings. Perhaps there would be no serious talk of a strike after all. And during the day Siân had convinced herself that no harm would come to Iestyn. He was just a boy, and he had signed the Charter after all. The Scotch Cattle had just been flexing their muscles, letting everyone know that they were still around.

"I love choir evening," she said. "It will be lovely just to sing and sing."

Owen smiled at her. "Stay for male voice practice, will you, then?" he asked. "And I will walk you home afterward?"

"I'll stay for a while," she said. "Maybe not to the end, though, Owen. Sometimes it goes late if the Reverend Llewellyn is not satisfied."

"A perfectionist he is," Owen said.

"I know." The warmth of the summer air was acting like a tonic on her tired body. It had been unnaturally warm and dry for a few weeks. "Owen, I was called up to the castle last evening. The Marquess of Craille offered me a job teaching his young daughter."

He looked at her in some amazement. "Going up in the world again, Siân, are you?" he said. "I should bow to you and kiss your hand?"

"Silly." She laughed. "He had heard about my going to school in England. But he also wants his daughter to learn Welsh."

"Queer," he said. "What did you say?"

"No, of course," she said.

She expected him to react as her family had reacted. They had assured her that she had done the right thing. Uncle Emrys had echoed her grandmother's fears. The Marquess of Craille could have only one reason for wanting to lure her to his castle, he had said. She expected Owen to be even more protective of her.

"Perhaps you should have gone," he said. "It would have got you out of the mine, Siân. I hate the thought of you working down there. It is not right."

She was touched. "But other women have to," she said. "I am no different from them, Owen."

"But you are," he said. "You are brave and stubborn to a fault, Siân Jones, but you are ten times the lady any of them are."

"You know that I don't want to be," she said. "You know that I want more than anything to belong, Owen." Perhaps it was a hopeless dream. Although she did not think herself better than anyone else in Cwmbran, she did know that she was different. That somehow, in some ways, she did not quite fit in. Although most people were perfectly friendly toward her, she had no particular friend or friends, apart from Owen and Iestyn. No women friends except perhaps Angharad Lewis, with whom a bond had been created when their husbands had died together. But even that friendship had cooled since Angharad and Emrys had stopped seeing each other. Most of the other women treated Siân as if she was a little above their level. "You think I ought to have taken the job, then?"

Owen shrugged. "Well, it is too late now if you have already said no," he said. "But you could have kept your ears open there, Siân. It is always useful to know something about the movements of the owners and what they

116

are saying and thinking."

Siân frowned. "You mean that you would want me to act as a kind of spy?" she asked. "What a horrid idea."

"You think Barnes does not have his spies among us?" he asked. "Why should Craille be shut up in his castle like a god when we have to be looking over our shoulders all the time? It amazes me that Barnes did not get wind of the Chartist meeting the other night. He usually finds out somehow."

The subject had been switched slightly. Siân did not return it to the unpleasant suggestion that she take a post in the marquess's home in order to spy on him and report back to Owen.

"The Scotch Cattle gave Iestyn a warning the night before last," she said. "Did you know?"

"Him and two others," he said. "You have some influence with him, Siân. Advise him to pay his penny and be done with it."

"He will not," she said. "He listened to the Reverend Llewellyn and he agrees with him. Iestyn can be stubborn when he believes in something."

"Advise him," he said. "It is not worth taking a beating up on the mountain for the sake of a penny."

"It is not just the penny," she said. She

was growing frightened again suddenly. "They would not really hurt him, would they, Owen? He is just a boy. And he went to the meeting and signed. He is not against the Charter."

"It is not enough just not to be against something," Owen said. "Sometimes you have to be for something, *fach.* Especially when your whole way of life and your dignity as a man are at stake. And the freedom of your people."

"That sounds almost revolutionary," she said. "What is the purpose of the Association, anyway? If the Charter is rejected by Parliament, there is nothing else to be done, is there?" She was very much afraid that there was a great deal more to be done. She remembered learning all about the French Revolution at school. And that had happened not so very long ago.

"We will not let the matter drop," he said.

They were approaching the chapel. There were several other of their acquaintances making their way along the pavements toward it.

"Owen," she said quickly and quietly, "don't let them do anything to Iestyn. Do you know who they are? Do you know any of them?"

"No one knows who Scotch Cattle are,

fach," he said.

"Someone must," she said. "I thought you might. You are one of the leaders of the men. The main leader, in fact."

He smiled and returned the greeting of one of his friends.

"There must be something you can do," Siân said. "Someone you can contact. Please, Owen? He is just a boy acting out of conscience. He is a threat to no one. Please do something. Please see to it that he is not punished. Not beaten, anyway." The thought of anyone being dragged up the mountain and whipped horrified her. To picture Iestyn . . . "Owen, please try to do something. For my sake?"

He covered her hand with his and patted it. "I'll see what I can do," he said. "But I don't know Scotch Cattle, Siân, or have any influence with them at all. Just get him to pay his penny. It is the easiest solution."

Siân sighed as they stepped inside the chapel. It was not the easiest solution when one was up against a boy with strong convictions and religious faith. But she was not going to get herself all upset again. Deep down she was convinced that no harm would come to Iestyn. Just the warning and the fear it engendered were punishment enough to a young boy who had not totally defied his leaders.

She stepped past two women in one of the pews and took her usual seat between Mrs. Beynon and Ceris Pritchard in the soprano section. Owen made his way to join the baritones.

"I am in the mood for singing," Mrs. Beynon announced. "We will raise the roof off between us, will we, Siân Jones?"

"At least one foot straight up in the air," Siân agreed, laughing.

The Reverend Llewellyn, standing in the high pulpit, rapped on it with his baton to call for silence. Like chapel on Sundays, choir was never late starting. It was more likely to begin two minutes early.

Despite the overall warmth of the evening, there was a chilly breeze that would quite likely feel downright cold up on the hills. Or so Verity's nurse said when her charge begged Alex to take her there for an evening walk again. They would stroll through the town instead, he suggested, not to ruffle Nurse's feathers. Nevertheless his daughter was bundled inside a cloak and bonnet before she was allowed over the doorstep. Nurses were of a tyrannical breed, Alex thought, remembering his own.

A few children were playing on the streets

and stopped to stare at them as they passed. But both were used to such a reaction at home. Apart from the children, the town seemed almost deserted.

Alex did not make conversation with his daughter. He had something of a headache and was feeling irritable. It was the unaccustomed feeling of lack of power, he supposed. And the helpless frustration of not knowing or understanding what he should know and understand.

He did not know anything about the iron-making and coal-mining industries or even about business in general. He knew nothing about industrial workers. He knew nothing about Wales or the Welsh. He had almost made up his mind in the course of the afternoon to have his trunks packed and to return forthwith to his familiar estate in England, never to return. But he was too stubborn to give in so soon. He would be damned before he would run away.

He had studied the company books carefully during the morning. He had glanced at them before, but without real consideration. He was appalled at the wages his workers were receiving, especially when he remembered that this week they were to be lowered by ten percent. But then he was ashamed to admit that he did not know much about prices. Was it possible to live comfortably on such wages, as Barnes and Fowler claimed? Perhaps it was.

His curiosity had taken him to the company shop, called the truck shop. His arrival there had caused something of a sensation, he had felt. Certainly the three women who were shopping there when he went in went scurrying out with such haste that it seemed they must have thought he brought the plague with him.

Prices had seemed high to him. Not that he was in the habit of shopping for groceries. Really he knew nothing about such matters. Two other women came in while he was there. Both looked at him saucer-eyed and did not react to his affable nod, but neither retreated. One made her purchases, paid for them, and left. The other whispered to the shopkeeper in Welsh, flushing as she did so. The shopkeeper pursed his lips, drew a ledger from a shelf, and wrote in it. The woman made a few purchases, did not pay for them, and hurried away, her head down.

The woman had asked for and been given an advance on next week's wages, the shopkeeper had explained.

"The day after payday?" Alex had asked, frowning.

The shopkeeper had shrugged. "She had

a large advance last week," he had said. "There was very little in the wage pack last night. Her man drank it up as usual. There are four little ones at home."

On further inquiry Alex had discovered two disturbing facts. One was that a large number of women would be taking up advances on their husband's wages before the week was out. The other was that wages were paid at the Three Lions Inn, which apparently he owned, and that the men, naturally enough, often sat down for a drink or two before taking their pay home. A few had more than one or two drinks.

Alex had not been pleased and had explained his concerns to Barnes after luncheon. Perhaps, he had said, wages should not be lowered after all. It appeared to him that his workers were not living in any great comfort and could ill afford to be paid ten percent less than they had last week. His examination of the books had shown that the company profits were handsome enough to take the slight loss that the current lower demand for iron would entail. And he himself was a wealthy man even apart from the Cwmbran works.

Barnes had been aghast. The wages paid out were the main expense of operating the works and mine, he had explained. When profits fell, expenses had to be cut. It was good business sense. Otherwise the business collapsed. Wages were the only expense that could realistically be cut.

But there were people behind those wages, Alex had pointed out. It was not an impersonal expense about which they spoke. But Barnes had repeated what he had said before, that the workers were comfortably well off and fully expected to be paid less in tough times. He had added something that had silenced the arguments Alex was still prepared to make. What would happen to the workers, Barnes had asked, if the business collapsed and the works had to be closed? Sometimes what might seem to be cruelty was in fact kindness. Wages must be reduced for the workers' own good.

Company profits looked healthy enough to Alex. But what did he know? There was that frustration again of not knowing. That realization that he must trust the experience of his agent, even when it went quite against the grain to do so. Being at Cwmbran was a humbling experience, Alex was finding.

Besides — Barnes had not finished and again he had had a telling argument, one against which Alex had no defense at all — there were coal mines and ironworks all across the valleys, and people and news traveled. The owners had to work together so that what one did they all did. Only so could chaos be averted. If wages were lowered in all works except one, there would be mass discontent and strikes and untold suffering. The master who had thought to be unrealistically generous to his workers would make all the others suffer.

All the other owners and agents, Alex had learned, had been living and working in the valleys for years and knew how the industry was to be kept profitable — for the sake of both workers and owners. He had been there for only a few days and had had no previous experience whatsoever with industry. How could he come here now and change things and perhaps destroy what he did not understand? He could not do so. And so his workers must live on ten percent less this week than last. The same cut had been made right across the valleys.

The lowering of demand was likely to continue for some time, Barnes had told him. It was part of the cycle of business and not to be worried about. Things would swing upward again eventually. But in the meanwhile it was possible that in a few weeks' time wages would have to be reduced a further ten percent.

Alex had said nothing. But he had decided

there and then that he would fight against such madness. He would meet personally with all the other owners if he must and argue the point. But he would not jump the gun. Perhaps it would not happen. Or perhaps by the time it did he would know more, understand more. But he was feeling sick at heart and troubled at his own inability to act from personal conscience as he usually did.

"I can hear music, Papa."

Alex came back to the present and his surroundings with a start. He felt instantly guilty. He had been away from Verity all day again and now was ignoring her. He had spoken scarcely a dozen words to her since leaving home.

"Music?" He listened carefully, tightening his hold on Verity's hand and drawing her to a stop in the middle of the pavement. She was quite right.

"It is people singing, Papa," she said. "In that building at the end of the street." She pointed ahead. "Is it a church? It looks funny."

"A chapel," he said. "Not quite the same as the church we go to. Most Welsh people go to chapels. It's a choir singing. Let's walk a little closer, shall we?"

It was a male voice choir. A large one

judging by the volume and richness of sound. Mellow basses, sweet tenors — the balance was perfect. He had heard about Welsh song, Alex thought as they drew closer and could hear the music just as clearly as if they were inside the building. This must be a particularly fine example of it. By unspoken consent he and Verity stopped walking again to listen. The choir was singing in Welsh.

"Ah," Verity said regretfully when the song came to an end, "is it finished? Are they not going to sing any more, Papa?"

"I don't know," he said, watching a group of women leave the chapel, but no men. "But we had better walk on. Nurse was right. That breeze really is chilly when we stand still. I don't want you catching a cold."

But they had taken no more than two or three steps when the music began again and they stopped once more by mutual but unspoken consent. The choir sang without words and without accompaniment, producing a harmonious sound that made Alex think of wind on a lonely mountain or foamless waves on a full tide. It was achingly sweet. And then a single voice — a single tenor — sang a haunting melody above the choir's accompaniment. His voice was as clear as a bell, but he sang in Welsh, so that the words, though heard, had no meaning to the two listeners.

Alex closed his eyes. It was so sweet that it was almost unbearable. His chest ached with unshed tears. And that feeling washed over him again with almost overpowering force — that feeling he had had first up in the hills. He opened his eyes when he sensed that the song was nearing its end and felt himself an outsider again. The music and the choir were inside the chapel and he was outside on the pavement. It was not a conscious thought. Merely a feeling.

And then the song was over.

"Ahh!" Verity sighed with contentment. "I wonder who that was singing, Papa."

But before he could reply, the chapel door opened and another woman — this one alone — stepped out. She closed the door quietly behind her. She was dressed the same way as the evening before — and the same as on two other occasions when he had seen her. She was not a woman with a large wardrobe, it seemed. But she too must have felt the chill of the breeze. She lifted one fold of her shawl over her head before crossing the ends beneath her chin and tossing them over her shoulders. She turned and hurried toward Alex and Verity. But she suddenly became aware of them standing there and looked up. And stopped.

He touched the brim of his hat to her. "Good evening, Mrs. Jones," he said.

"Good evening," she said. Her eyes turned to Verity and then she moved again and would have hurried past them.

"What was that song?" he asked her.

" 'Hiraeth'?" she said. "You mean the last one they sang?"

He nodded. "Heer — ?"

" 'Hiraeth,' " she said. "It is an old Welsh song. It is one of my favorites. No, it *is* my favorite. It touches me here." She pressed a hand to her left breast and flushed and removed the hand when she noticed his eyes following the gesture.

"What is it about?" he asked.

" 'Hiraeth' means" — she sketched small circles with her hand for a moment — "it is difficult to translate. Longing. Yearning. It is the longing one feels for perfection, for the absolute. For God. That reaching beyond ourselves. The yearning that is never fully satisfied, except perhaps in heaven. I am not explaining it very well."

"Oh, yes, I think you are," he said. It was almost as if he had known. As if he had understood the Welsh words. Or perhaps some ideas conveyed themselves through music and emotion without the necessity of words.

She looked at him rather uncertainly. "It is part of the Welsh soul," she said. "*Hiraeth mawr* — the great longing. Maybe it comes from the wildness of nature. From the hills and the valleys. From the sea. Maybe — I am sorry. I am sounding foolish." She glanced at Verity again.

"My daughter Verity," he said. "She is six years old. This is Mrs. Jones, Verity. I asked her to be your governess, but she was unable to accept the position."

"My grandmama taught me how to read and do sums," Verity said. "But I want to learn to sing. And I want to speak Welsh. I think you must speak it. You sing when you talk. That means you are Welsh."

Siân Jones smiled at his daughter. God, but she was beautiful. Alex wondered if she would be as lovely dressed in all the finery of a fashionable lady at a London ball. He rather suspected that she would. But not lovelier. And she had been inside that chapel. She belonged. He felt a wave of loneliness again. This Welsh adventure was doing strange things to him. He did not normally think of himself as a lonely man.

"My mother spoke it to me almost all the time when I was growing up," she said in answer to Verity's comment. "Since she died, eight years ago, I have spoken almost nothing else."

"But your English is very good," Verity said politely.

"Thank you." She smiled again, but she looked uncomfortable. She looked once more as if she was about to move on past them.

He spoke on impulse. He had not yet sent to London, and he had made no decision about going down to Newport himself. But he certainly had not intended to pursue this option any further. Indeed, he had concluded that she would not after all have been a suitable choice.

"Perhaps," he said, "you have had a chance to think further about my offer during the course of the day. Perhaps you would like to change your answer?"

He was surprised to see that she hesitated before looking into his face. "No," she said.

"Or perhaps you would like a few days before giving a final answer," he said. "How does a week sound?"

"I don't need —" she began. But she did not complete the sentence. She bit her lip and looked at Verity.

"Do you go to that chapel instead of going to church?" Verity asked.

She nodded. "It is where my family and friends go," she said. "Most of the people of Cwmbran, in fact. Not many people go to the church. It is English and we are Welsh. The singing is dismal there." She laughed, a low musical sound that did strange things to Alex's insides. Her eyes danced and her face lit up with merriment when she laughed. Her teeth were white and perfect.

"If you were my governess," Verity said. "I could go to the chapel with you. I could sing those songs if you taught me Welsh. Or is it only men who can sing?"

Siân Jones laughed again. "Oh, no," she said. "We all sing. You cannot be Welsh and not sing. You would be exiled to somewhere horrid, far, far away."

"The back of beyond," Verity said.

"Well?" Alex asked, looking at Siân, compelling her through a knack he had learned in a lifetime of commanding servants to look back.

He saw her hesitate again. "A week," she said. "But I don't think it will be yes."

"Fair enough," he said. "I shall await your answer. You will come in person?"

She hesitated yet again and nodded. And then she smiled at Verity once more, tightened her shawl beneath her chin, and strode on past them. He turned his head to watch her walk down the street. She did not look back.

God, he thought, shaken, he wanted her. He wanted to bed her. To make love to her. To a Welsh laboring woman who harnessed herself to a coal cart in his coal mine by day. To a woman who could look him directly in the eye and address him without any bending of the knee or courtesy title. To a woman with the foolishness and courage to sneak from her home at night to spy on a men's political meeting. To a woman who yearned for the absolute. To a woman who was part of the soul of Wales.

He could remember the feel of her body against his. Tall, shapely, generously breasted, firmly muscled. He could remember the warmth and softness of her lips within his own. He could remember the surge of desire that one brief kiss had aroused in him.

He hoped she would refuse the offer he had renewed. It would not be a good thing at all to have her living and working under his own roof. He was not sure he would be able to keep his hands off her, and it had never been his way to defile his servants or those dependent upon him.

He wondered if she would come to tell him if her answer was no. He should have specified that she must come anyway. But he supposed he could send for her at any time. She was his employee, after all. And a very lowly one at that.

"Papa," Verity said, tripping along at his side, "I wish I could speak like Mrs. Jones. I could listen to her talking all day long."

Yes, so could I, her father thought. Siân Jones's soft Welsh accent was not by any means the least of her attractions.

And he was fooling himself if he thought he was hoping she would turn down his offer, he admitted ruefully to himself.

6

It was perhaps even more spine-chilling now that he knew what it was. Alex had woken at the first howling and bellowing and was standing now at his open bedroom window, as he had a few nights before. They were out again tonight, then, the Scotch Cattle. What was it this time? he wondered. Chartism again? Or was it something to do with the lowering of wages? Sometimes, Barnes had said, there were attempts to form a union and to get everyone out on strike. Was that happening now?

More and more as the days passed he felt ignorant and helpless. Frustrated. He beat a tattoo against the windowsill with the side of one fist.

Perhaps they were merely having a meeting and had decided to chill everyone in the valley with that prolonged howl, he thought when some time passed and there was no repetition of it. But it came again just as he was about to turn back to bed, loud and long. Bone-chilling.

He was angry suddenly. Angry at the knowledge that this was his property and his industry and that these people were his workers and his dependents, and yet everyone seemed to know and understand more than he. He felt almost like a child again, expected to behave himself, to be seen but not heard. Goddammit, he thought, turning from the window and striding across the room and into his dressing room, he was going out there to see for himself what was going on.

Doubtless it was dangerous, he thought fewer than ten minutes later as he ran down the stairs, fully clothed and wrapped about with a dark cloak. But to hell with danger. He was spoiling for a fight if someone would just take him on. Scotch Cattle keeping him awake at night and putting terror into his people, for God's sake! He would like nothing better than to get his hands on one or two of them.

There were long intervals of silence between the howls, and even when they came they were difficult to locate. Sound had a strange echoing quality in the hills. It took him almost half an hour to come upon the men making the noises, and then it was only to find that they were well below the height to which he had climbed. He flattened himself behind some projecting rocks and peered cautiously downward.

There were eleven of them by his count. Too many of them to be confronted, blast it, and they were all in a group together. They looked ominous too, with dark hoods covering their heads and shoulders, slits for their eyes. Some of them had horns attached to the hoods — cattle, of course. Only one of them was unhooded, but the reason was quickly obvious to Alex. He was their prisoner and had apparently just been brought up from the town below. Two of them had him by the arms. From what Alex could see by the imperfect moonlight he was slight in build. Apparently no more than a boy.

The devil, he thought, furious. Instinct would have had him on his feet and down the slope without a chance for thought. But he had had the weight of many responsibilities on his shoulders for too long to act purely from instinct. It would be madness. He had no weapon beyond his bare hands. His fists would be handy enough against one opponent or even two — perhaps even three. But against ten? There was nothing he could do at the moment to help their prisoner. He had to stay where he was and watch impotently — again.

The two men who held the boy tore off his shirt, his only upper garment, and then forced him down onto the ground, facedown and spread-eagled. Four of them worked to confine his hands and feet to stakes that Alex was unable to see from where he was. He clamped his teeth together, and felt the sweat cold on his back.

Were they going to kill the boy? Although going to his aid would be suicidal, Alex crouched into position, ready to hurl himself downward to try to create some sort of diversion. But they came out for punishment, Barnes had said. That was their function. Not execution.

One of the men was speaking — it was impossible to tell which one. His voice was muffled by the hood and gruff in tone. It was probably disguised. But Alex could hear clearly what he said. It was only later that he felt surprise at the fact that the man spoke in English.

"The last one," the unidentified man said, "and just a boy. You signed the Charter, Iestyn Jones, but refused to go the extra mile with your friends and fellow workers. You were too afraid of the consequences. You must be shown that cowardice too has its consequences. Ten strokes will be your punishment. Only ten. You are fortunate."

Alex closed his eyes and then opened them again to watch, sick to his stomach, while two men, one on each side of the boy, whipped him alternately, ten times in all. The boy did not make a sound.

The damned brutes! Alex thought, incensed. He would find them all, every last one of them, and grind their bones to powder.

Two of the others stooped down to cut the boy's hands and feet free after the whipping was over, but he scarcely moved. The Scotch Cattle howled once more, looking downward to the quiet, darkened town, and then ran off together across the hill to disappear into the night. Alex wondered if anyone was sleeping down there.

He straightened up, looked down at the inert form of the boy, and then went running and leaping down the steep slope toward him. He was neither dead nor unconscious, Alex saw in some relief. His legs were moving.

"It is all right," he said, kneeling beside the boy and touching one hand to the back of his head. "It is all over now."

The boy's breathing was labored. Even in the moonlight the marks across his back looked raw. He appeared to be no older than sixteen or seventeen.

Alex looked about him and picked up the boy's shirt. He set it gently over his back, though even so the boy flinched and an inward breath hissed into him.

"Come," Alex said, "I'll help you up. Do you think you can stand?"

"Give me a minute." They were the boy's first words.

Alex took off his cloak and draped it as lightly as he could on top of the shirt. It was a decidedly chilly night. "You took it bravely," he said. "What is your name?" He had not heard it clearly when it was mentioned.

For the first time he saw the boy's eyes turn upward to him. "It was nothing," he said. "Just a crowd of bullies. Nothing. I'll be all right in a minute." He grimaced and closed his eyes.

"It was Scotch Cattle," Alex said. "I have been here long enough to know about them, lad, and to know why they are on the prowl at this particular time. But I understand why you want to say nothing." He touched his hand reassuringly to the boy's head again. "When you are ready. Take your time."

But he was aware suddenly of two people

scrambling up the hill toward them. A man and a woman. They stopped when they saw him — perhaps they thought he was a lingering member of the Cattle. But then the man came striding on again and the woman came running up after him.

"I think your parents are coming for you," he said.

The man said something gruffly in Welsh when he was still some way off. Warning him away, Alex suspected. But he was too young a man to be the boy's father. Alex stood up.

"He will be all right," he said. "He just needs a few moments to catch his breath. They gave him ten lashes."

"Iestyn?" Siân Jones's voice was trembling as she hurried past the man she had come with and went down on her knees beside the boy. She smoothed the hair back from his face with one hand and leaned over him to kiss him on the cheek. She was murmuring to him in Welsh. She totally ignored Alex's presence.

"I'll be all right, Siân," the boy said, speaking in English. "Only ten lashes it was. Just give me a minute here and I'll be up and chasing you down the hill."

"Oh, Iestyn," she said, switching to English, "you silly brave boy. There is proud I

141

am of you. And I could beat you black and blue myself." She burst into tears.

"Black and blue?" the man said. "That would be just the color of your eyes if I had my way, Iestyn, before I started on the rest of you. You have Mam and Mari crying their eyes out down there and the children whimpering and Dada roaring and coughing and swearing to kill you if Scotch Cattle have left any of you alive. And all over an old penny."

The boy laughed weakly. "There is good it is to know that you love me so much, Huw," he said. "Are you going to leave me lying here all night, then?"

"To catch your death?" Huw said. "It would be no more than you deserve, you stubborn cub. Ten lashes was it? They should have given you at least twenty. Perhaps they would have whipped some sense into you."

Siân was still crying and smoothing her hand over the boy's head. "Frantic Huw was when I went over to see if you were one of the ones they had come for, Iestyn," she said. "He does not mean a word of what he is saying now. He is only angry with himself because he could not stop them from dragging you away. Oh, Iestyn, my pet, did they hurt you bad?"

142

They seemed to have forgotten Alex except that they had switched to his language, perhaps out of unconscious deference to his presence. But the man called Huw turned to him suddenly.

"What are you doing out here, sir?" he asked stiffly. "I thank you for coming to the aid of my brother. That is your cloak? It will get dirty on the ground, and bloody too, I wouldn't be surprised."

Siân whimpered.

"I came out to see what manner of animal Scotch Cattle are," Alex said. "We do not have that particular form of wildlife in England. I am sorry to say that there were too many of them for me to come to the boy's assistance until it was all over. There were ten of them. I wonder if your brother recognized any of them."

"No," Huw said quickly, "he did not. None of them. And I did not when they came to the house to take him away. They are not from this valley. Up with you, then, Iestyn. Are you going to rest there all night, cozy beneath that cloak, while Siân and I are shivering up here?"

He bent and wrapped one of the boy's arms about his shoulders. The boy groaned for the first time, but he pushed himself to his knees, rested there for a moment, and then got to his feet with his brother's help. Alex's cloak and his own shirt fell to the ground.

"Iestyn," Siân whispered, her eyes fixed on his back, one hand over her mouth. "Oh, Iestyn, my boy."

"Let's get his shirt on," Alex said, as the boy sagged against his brother. "Then I'll help get him home."

"Thank you," the brother said gruffly, "but we can manage, sir. I suppose we will be in trouble with you too now, but I'll not hide from you. I am Huw Jones. This is my brother Iestyn. Siân is our sister-in-law. She was married to our brother, who was killed in the mine three years ago. She has nothing to do with all this. She has no business even being out of her bed. If Gwyn was still alive, he could take her across his knee and give her what for. But you leave her out of it. I will answer for what has been going on here."

While he spoke, Siân was easing Iestyn into his shirt.

"I think it is the Scotch Cattle who should answer for it," Alex said quietly. "Good night, Mr. Jones. You are a brave boy, lad."

"I'll manage him," Huw said as he started down the mountain, and Siân made to take Iestyn's free arm about her own shoulders.

"You go back home to bed where you belong, Siân. I may warm your bottom with my own hand if I catch you doing anything so foolish again as coming out when Scotch Cattle are about. You had better be sure to creep in without Emrys finding out you have been gone."

His brother moaned again as they continued on their way down. Siân stayed where she was.

"He is right, you know," Alex said. "I had to take my courage in both hands to leave the safety of my home. But at least I have a man's fists with which to defend myself. Do you make a habit of doing this sort of thing?"

She whirled on him. He guessed that she had forgotten about him again for the moment. "He is just a boy," she said fiercely. "An intelligent and sweet-natured boy with a conscience and a strong sense of what is right and what is wrong. He would not do what was against his conscience even though they warned him the other night and everyone knows what happens to those who ignore their warnings. I thought perhaps they would spare him because he is a boy and his offense against them was not so very great. I begged Owen to intercede on his behalf. I begged."

"Owen?" he said.

Her face, distraught one moment, was blank the next. "Nothing," she said. "It does not matter."

She turned to leave, but he caught at her arm and held it. "Your lover?" he said. "He has influence with the Scotch Cattle?"

Her eyes widened and he glimpsed fear in them for a moment. "I have no lover," she said. "And I know no one who has influence with them. I know no one who knows any of them. No one knows who they are or where they come from." She shivered violently.

She was not wearing her shawl tonight, he noticed for the first time, but only the thin, shabby dress that she was always wearing when he saw her. He picked up his cloak from the ground and threw it about her before she realized his intent. He gathered her to his side with one arm about her shoulders and held her there.

"You will catch your death dressed like that on a night like this," he said. "Come along, I'll escort you most of the way home and see you safely there."

Her teeth were chattering. He was aware of her body pressed to his side, her breast against his chest. Her leg brushed his own as they walked. He felt warm suddenly despite the fact that he was not wearing his cloak. He had no idea what time it was. Well past midnight at a guess.

"You are fond of the boy?" he asked. "How old is he?"

"Seventeen," she said. "He was twelve when I married Gwyn. I loved him almost as if he was my own."

"Where does he work?" he asked.

"In the mine," she said, "just like his father and Huw and Gwyn. And me."

"How did your husband die?" he asked.

"A roof cave-in," she said. "He was careless. It is quite common, you know."

No, he did not. He knew nothing except for the fact that he had been glibly drawing income from Cwmbran for the two years since he had inherited it.

"You were fond of him?" he asked. A foolish question.

"He was my husband," she said, "and just my age. You would not believe how pale a man can look when he is dead, even when his face is blackened with coal dust." She shivered again.

"Pardon me," he said. "I know so little. I am learning, but with painful slowness. I am trying to learn."

She looked up into his face with — incredulity? Curiosity? He could not read her

147

expression. But he saw anew how very beautiful she was. And her face was only inches from his own.

"Which is your house?" he asked.

She pointed to a terrace of attached houses just below them. "The end one," she said. "I can go alone now. Thank you." She turned inward against him as if to shrug free of the cloak. But his arm anchored it too firmly to her shoulders. She looked up at him again, dismay and something else in her face.

He could feel the blood pulsing through his temples. His arm held her to him involuntarily. It did not occur to him to release her. He touched the fingertips of his free hand to her cheek.

"It was a severe beating," he said, "but he took it bravely and has nothing to be ashamed of. Scotch Cattle, I take it, are content with one punishment and do not press the point?"

"No." She swallowed.

"Stay off the mountain when this sort of thing is going on," he said. "It is not safe for a woman. When men's passions run high, they are not always answerable for their actions."

She stared mutely at him, and he realized that his words applied more to himself than to anyone else this night — and on the last night he had encountered her up here.

"Thank you for going to help Iestyn," she whispered. "You heard Huw say that he had signed the Charter. You will not punish him again?"

"I see no wrong in the Charter," he said. "Only perhaps in what its rejection might lead to. If it is rejected. I have no intention of punishing any man I know to have signed it — or any man who went to a meeting at which it was being discussed."

"Then you are very different from Mr. Barnes and all the other owners," she said. She was breathless suddenly and lifted her hands to his shoulders as if to push him away. "Good night."

"Good night, Siân," he said. "It is a pretty name. I have not heard it before."

"It is Welsh," she said foolishly.

He smiled. And could not after all resist. He should have released her as soon as she said good night. Or as soon as she tried to release herself from his cloak. He should have wrapped his cloak about her and allowed her to hold it herself. He should have kept three feet of space between them as they walked. Now he could no longer resist. He closed the distance between their mouths and kissed her.

They were standing, he thought immediately, in perhaps the same place as she had been standing with her lover when he and Verity had looked down on them. He had felt slightly envious then and lonely. Now he was in the lover's place. He found the thought arousing and drew her closer. Her arms, he noticed with some surprise and interest, had come about his neck.

He opened his mouth and licked at her lips, but she kept them closed and trembling. It seemed she was unaccustomed to such kisses. Or unwilling to allow the greater intimacy of them to him. He moved his hands hard down her sides, past warm, full breasts, in to a small, firm waist, over shapely, feminine hips, and around to equally shapely buttocks. His hands followed the curve of her spine as they came back up her body. It was arched. She had put herself against him from shoulders to knees — or he had put her there and she had stayed.

She could certainly be in no doubt about the extent of his desire for her — especially through her thin dress. She was one of his workers. The teacher he wanted for Verity. The Welsh puddler's woman. He ended the kiss with reluctance, withdrawing his mouth from hers, moving her away from him with his hands at her waist. Her eyes opened and gazed, bewildered, into his.

He inhaled slowly. It was the look a woman beneath him on a bed would have.

"Go now," he said. "I'll watch you safely home."

Safely! There was only one danger to Mrs. Siân Jones on the mountain — the one that was going to watch her home.

She continued to stare at him before biting her lower lip and turning abruptly away.

"Siân," he said, and she stopped without looking back. "I will still be expecting you to call at the castle with your decision."

She lowered her head and he was afraid for a moment that she was going to give him his answer there and then. But after a silent pause she continued on her way down the hill.

He drew cool breaths of air into his lungs. He wondered if he could have had her there on the ground if he had so chosen. He would be willing to bet half a fortune that he could have. Under different circumstances he would have put the matter to the test. But under these particular circumstances it had been impossible.

Governess and mistress, he thought. He wanted her as both. He wondered if she would take the one post and if he could then persuade her to accept the other. And if he wanted to so complicate his life and so compromise his principles. He had always chosen his mistresses from outside the ranks of those dependent on him.

But Siân Jones was uncommonly lovely and alluring. Something inside himself yearned for her. Not just to mate with her body, though that was definitely a part of it. He could not put the rest of it into coherent words in his mind. She somehow seemed to represent a world he had glimpsed so fleetingly that he could not even recall the image of it to his mind. A sweet and wonderful world that he wanted to inhabit.

"Hiraeth." Yes, in his mind he could hear the aching beauty of the song again. The song about the sort of longing he felt.

She had disappeared from sight. He turned his steps homeward. He had better hope, he supposed, that she put temptation beyond his grasp by refusing to be Verity's governess.

God, what a night. What a strange world it was that he had stepped into quite unwittingly by deciding to pay his Welsh property a visit.

Iestyn was at work the next day, pale but

smiling at Siân as usual when she deliberately made a detour to the seam at which he was working. He had not removed his shirt, she noticed, as he usually did and as all the other men had done.

He was one of the fortunate ones, if there had been any good fortune in his experience. Two other men had been visited by the Scotch Cattle the night before, men who had neither been to the meeting nor signed the Charter nor joined the Chartist Association. Unlike the others who had been given warnings, they had remained obdurate, for reasons of their own. Both had had all the furniture dragged out of their houses and chopped to pieces. And both had been given twenty lashes up on the mountain. The one who was a miner was not at work today.

Siân waited all day to see Owen in the evening. It was a strange, unreal day. Life just could not seem to get back to normal again. *She* just could not seem to get back to normal. She dared not think about the night before. And yet she could think of nothing else.

They went walking again, though they took a different route from the one they usually took, wandering through the town past the chapel and past the ironworks and the gates into the park of Glanrhyd Castle in order to stroll on the hills beyond, the hills that led within a few miles to Penybont.

They held hands and talked about trivialities while they were still in town. And as luck would have it, they ran almost directly into the Marquess of Craille and his daughter as they were coming through the gates from the park, obviously intent on their own evening walk. He seemed unavoidable. Siân nodded to them both, unsmiling, and continued walking. He touched the brim of his hat and inclined his head.

Siân was very aware suddenly of the fact that her fingers were laced with Owen's.

"Mrs. Jones," Verity called cheerfully. *"Bore da."* She laughed gaily, then clapped one hand over her mouth. "Oh, no, that means good morning."

"Nos da," Siân said. "Good night."

She felt thoroughly disturbed as they walked on. She followed Owen's lead without question as he turned up into the hills beyond Glanrhyd and led her higher. She felt horribly guilty. She felt as if she should be making a confession to him. But he was not her husband or even her fiancé. Besides, it had been only a kiss.

Only! It had been a lot more than a kiss. She had felt against her abdomen his readiness for more. And she had wanted more. She was still not sure that she would not have gone the whole distance with him if he had not pulled back for some reason. She grew hot and uncomfortable at the very thought. And she remembered Ceridwen's crude words about going up the mountain with the marquess — for a good go, as she had put it. Siân felt wanton, dirty. That was precisely what she had wanted and almost got. A good go. Her cheeks burned.

"He has asked me again to take that job," she said. "I saw him outside chapel the other evening after practice. He gave me a week to decide."

"You are wavering, then?" Owen asked. "Take it, Siân. You deserve better than you have. It would be a thumb of the nose to old Barnes, anyway, wouldn't it?" He laughed.

She could not believe she actually was wavering. It would be asking for trouble. For undoubtedly she found him almost ir-resistibly attractive — she had not really admitted that much to herself until last night. More attractive than she had ever found any man — Owen included, God help her. But she was a cart girl in a coal mine and her mother's bastard daughter. He was a marquess. It would be funny if it were not also frightening. Perhaps this was the way things had been with her mother.

She did not want to be like her mother. She did not want her mother's life. The prospect was horrifying — cut off from her family and her people and her chapel, totally reliant for support and emotional satisfaction on a cold lover who saw her only as a body to be used for his lust and his pleasure.

Oh, no!

"I don't know," she said. "I don't know if it is what I want or not, Owen." And yet her words showed that she was still wavering.

"I don't like you looking weary every night," he said. "And she seems a cheerful enough child."

"Lonely too," she said. "I expect she is lonely. She is an only child, and she can hardly mingle with the children of Cwmbran, can she?"

"Not when she is his nibs's brat," he said. "Do children who have everything feel lonely, Siân?"

"Yes," she said with conviction. She had had almost everything she could possibly have needed as far as material possessions went. Sir John Fowler had been generous in that way. But she had had no friends with whom to play. She had been an outsider as surely as Lady Verity Hyatt was. "They need the companionship of others as much as other children do, Owen. Things cannot take the place of people."

"Well, then," he said, bringing them to a stop and drawing her down to sit beside him on the heather, "take the job, *fach,* and make her a little happier. And yourself. And me too. I'll be happier thinking of you there than down the mine."

Would he, she wondered, if he knew why she really wanted to take the job? But that was not quite true, either. She wanted to be Verity's governess. Yes, she did. It was the girl's father who made her hesitate. He was the reason she did not want to accept the job.

He was the temptation.

"Perhaps I will, then," she said, drawing her knees up and wrapping her arms about them. "Yes, perhaps I will. I really would like to, Owen."

She noticed suddenly how high up on the mountain they were.

7

They sat in silence for a while, Siân gazing down into the valley, Owen, propped on one elbow, gazing at her.

"Oh, I don't know what to do," she said. "You tell me, Owen." But she laughed as she said so. In some ways it would be re-assuring to be a child again and be told what to do, but she knew she would never easily give up control of her life to any man. There had been a few battles with Gwyn . . .

"Tell you what to do? All right," he said, pushing himself into a full sitting position beside her. "Lie back in the heather and let me love you."

She felt a lurching of alarm. "Oh, no," she said. "No, Owen."

He set his mouth to hers and let it rest there for a few moments. "Gentle I will be," he said. "It is because I am big and Gwyn was smaller, Siân? But you are not a maid and it will not hurt. I will worship you with my body, *cariad.*"

Cariad — love. It was the first time he had used such an endearment. And she wanted it suddenly. She wanted something to block out last night's uncomfortable memories. Owen was her own kind and she was fond of him. He was attractive and had great strength of character — she knew that there were many girls and women in Cwmbran who envied her because Owen was stepping out with her. She would belong again as Owen's woman, as she had belonged all too briefly as Gwyn's.

But it was a step she could not take lightly. "Just kisses," she said, lifting her face. "Just kisses, Owen. Please?"

"A man needs more than kisses," he said. "Especially when it is the dusk of evening and he is up on the mountain alone with his woman. It is inside you I need to be, Siân." He took her hand and brought it against him, palm in, so that she could feel his need, his readiness.

She was no maid, as he had said. But even so she snatched her hand away in some alarm. Two nights, two different men. She wanted to get up and run suddenly. Run away. But from what? From herself? Was she a wanton that she had aroused need like this in two very different men in such a short interval?

"I don't want to do it, Owen," she said. "I would be sorry tomorrow. Let it be kisses. I like your kisses."

They were warm and firm. She always felt the strength and dependability of Owen when he kissed her. She wanted his kisses now to blot out the memory of those others. She did not like the Marquess of Craille's kisses. She did not want to remember them. He used the inside of his mouth as well as his lips. And his tongue. She could remember it licking against her lips. And she could remember the raw feelings of sexual desire it had aroused in her. She wanted Owen's kisses again. Warm kisses of affection. But if only Owen could kiss like that and make her feel like that . . .

"Just let it be kisses," she said softly.

"You are afraid I would take my pleasure and not pay the price?" he said. "Married we will be, Siân. We both know that."

"Do we?" she said. He had never mentioned marriage before.

"I have been courting you since last winter," he said.

"You started walking me home from chapel during the winter," she said. "Was that courting?"

"You are a beautiful woman, *fach,*" he

160

said. "Has any other man asked you to step out since last winter?"

"No," she said. "Only you."

"Last summer," he said, "they were about you like flies. Since winter they have known that they would face the fists of Owen Parry if they came near. They have known that we are courting."

It was a pleasing idea. The idea that he considered she belonged to him, that everyone else believed it too. And the idea that he would protect her, with his fists if necessary. And yet it somehow made her feel like a piece of property to be guarded by force. What if she did not want to be Owen's woman? What if she wanted the attention of one of those other men who apparently did not dare approach her now?

"You would not really fight for me, would you?" she asked him. "I mean, if any other man asked me to step out?"

"I would," he said, tightening his arm about her. "Everyone knows I am not a man to be crossed. And you are my woman, *cariad.* You will be my wife. Next summer, is it? In chapel with all the valley in the pews?"

It sounded almost as if she had no choice. What if she said no? But she had no wish to say no. She had had her eye on Owen Parry long before he had started walking home from chapel with her during the winter.

"Owen," she said, resting her head against his shoulder, "I want more than anything to be like other women. I thought I was when I married Gwyn. Don't marry me and then die as he did."

"It takes a lot to put Owen Parry down," he said, chuckling. "Siân." He set his mouth against hers again. "Let me in, *cariad*. A wedding it will be next summer, or sooner if your belly swells before then. Let me in. Under here, is it?" His hand slid up her leg beneath her skirt, from her ankle to her knee.

It was a decision that must be made in a moment. She returned his kiss, holding his hand still on her knee with her own on the outside of her skirt. If she took him into her now, she would be drawn into the protection of his strength and of his world for the rest of her life. It was what she wanted more than anything. Or she could hold back, defer the decision for a while longer.

"I don't want to," she whispered. "Owen, I don't want to." She was well aware that he might take no notice of her protest. If he did not, she would give in. She did not want the ugliness of rape between them. And part of her did want it — very badly. Part of her yearned to give herself over to his care.

He flung himself away from her and got to his feet. He stood staring down the valley toward Cwmbran.

"I'm sorry," she said, clasping her arms about her knees again. "I did not mean to lead you on by coming all the way up here with you, Owen. I did not realize how high we had climbed." Because she had been agitated by their brief meeting with the Marquess of Craille. "I just want kisses."

"Did you ever go up the mountain with Gwyn?" he asked, looking over his shoulder at her.

She hesitated. "Yes," she said. "But only once, a week before the wedding." She had agreed to go because she did not want to have it for the first time on their wedding night, in the small bedroom between his parents' and Huw and Mari's. She had wanted to be quite alone and private with him the first time.

Owen looked back down the valley. "It is because of your mother," he said. "You do not give yourself easy, Siân Jones. Maybe it is what I have always liked most about you, that aloofness, that holding yourself dear. Though the part of me that is throbbing and in pain at this very moment does not like you particularly well."

"I'm sorry," she said. *That holding yourself dear.* She wondered what he would say if he knew about last night. She rested her forehead on her knees and closed her eyes. She did not want to think about last night.

"So am I," he said quietly. "I can't kiss you yet, Siân. I can't touch you. Give me a few minutes."

They were quiet for a while. She was grateful to him for showing such restraint. She should not have come up so high with him. She had not meant to do so. It must have seemed that she was willing.

"Owen," she asked, "did you try to stop Iestyn from being punished last night?"

"I told you," he said, "I don't know any Scotch Cattle."

"Who does, then?" she asked. "If you do not, Owen, who does?"

"He got off lightly, didn't he?" he said. "Nothing in his house destroyed. Only ten lashes with the whips. He was even able to go to work today, I heard."

"Iestyn would have been too stubborn to stay at home," she said. "But his poor back, Owen. You should have seen it. Red and raw. They even drew some blood."

"Well," he said, "he got off lightly enough, Siân. He should not have held out against the rest of us."

A thought struck her suddenly. "Was it you?" she asked, looking up at his back. "Was it you who arranged for the lighter punishment, Owen? Was it? Would he have had twenty like the other men? Was it you?"

"I don't know any Scotch Cattle, *fach*," he said. "I have no influence."

But she leaped to her feet and crossed the short distance between them to wrap her arms about his waist from behind and to rest her cheek against his shoulder.

"It was you," she said. "You stopped them from destroying his mam and dada's house, and you talked them out of whipping him too badly to go to work today. You did, didn't you?"

She heard him blowing out his breath. "The less you know about such things the better, Siân," he said. "We will go back down, will we? It will be dark soon."

"Owen," she said, kissing the side of his neck, "I love you. I love you, I love you."

He turned and wrapped his arms tightly about her and kissed her hard. "Do you want to get it after all?" he said. "Don't tempt fate. Down to Cwmbran we will go and it will be to bed with you — alone, at your grandad's. Hold hands, is it?" He released her and held out a hand for hers.

She took it and held it tightly. She smiled

warmly at him. "Thank you, Owen," she said, falling into step beside him. "Thank you for doing that for me. I knew there was something you could do. You are wonderful."

"You know nothing about it, Siân," he said quietly. "And I thank the good Lord for that. But I like to see you happy, *cariad*. I do like that."

It felt good suddenly to be Owen's *cariad*.

Alex had had news from London that was both disappointing and disturbing. The Charter, despite many thousands of signatures from all parts of the British Isles, had been rejected by Parliament. It had been inevitable, of course, when Parliament was controlled by all the largest landowning families of the realm, who had a vested interest in keeping things the way they were.

But although Alex was among the largest of those landowners, he had hoped that things would be otherwise. It was high time the masses of the British people had more say in how the country was run. He had been able to see that especially since coming to Wales.

But it had been rejected.

His letters advised him to prepare for trouble. The industrial workers would not take the rejection lightly. Perhaps they would do no more than grumble. Perhaps they would do nothing more seditious than get together some other petition. Or perhaps they would strike and riot and cause all sorts of disruption in the quiet running of the country. Who knew with the ignorant masses? Alex was advised to swear in special constables or — better still — to bring in soldiers as a show of strength, just to discourage the majority from listening with any seriousness to the revolutionary minority.

Britain did not want to invite anything like what had happened in France just fifty years before.

Alex was a little worried. The Chartists he had encountered on the mountain had urged the men to join an association in addition to signing the Charter — for just such a situation as this. What was the point of an association if the Charter was passed? The organization was intended to prepare some action in the event of its being rejected. And it had appeared that almost every man of the valley had been at the meeting.

The Chartists were prepared to enforce membership and to punish severely those who held out against them. According to Barnes, there had been two other whippings up on the mountain the other night, apart from the one Alex had witnessed. Only three men had defied the order to join? It was a serious matter. And the men would not be happy at today's news, especially at a time when they had the other grievance over the drop in their wages.

And yet the last thing Alex wanted to do was give a show of force himself. Especially soldiers. He would bring soldiers in only as a very last resort. Damn it, he was in sympathy with the people!

He summoned Owen Parry to Glanrhyd Castle — the leader of the Chartist meeting. One of the puddlers at the ironworks. Siân Jones's lover. He was trying hard not to think of Siân Jones. He hoped she would not come back to the castle.

When Owen Parry was shown into the library, it was obvious he had come straight from work, although his face and hands were clean. He wore work clothes, and there was a suggestion of gray dust about them and about his dark curly hair. He was a big man — not very tall, but solid in build. The solidity looked to be all muscle and very little fat. He was not a man one would care to cross, Alex thought with an inward sigh as he looked up at Parry. The man held his cap in his hand, but made no attempt to bow his head or pull at his forelock or show any other customary sign of subservience. Alex was becoming used to the proud Welsh.

"Owen Parry?" he said. "Thank you for coming so promptly. Have a seat." He gestured to one at the other side of the desk at which he sat.

Owen Parry looked at it as if he suspected some trap and then lowered himself gingerly into it. He looked steadily into Alex's eyes. Alex found himself wondering quite irrelevantly if the man was gentle or rough with Siân.

"Parliament has rejected the Charter," he said bluntly. "I had word this morning."

Parry's jaw hardened for a moment and then his face went blank and slack. Stupid. "What is that to me?" he asked after a short silence, which Alex had decided not to break.

"A great deal, I would imagine," he said. "Since you campaigned for it and chaired a large meeting up on the mountain for it."

Still the blank, stupid look. The man shook his head slowly. "I don't know what you are talking about," he said.

Alex sighed. This was not going to be easy. "I am not setting a trap," he said. "I am as sorry as you that it was rejected. Or perhaps not quite as sorry — I believe it was very dear indeed to your heart. I watched your meeting. If I had been going to take any disciplinary measure concerning it, I would have acted before now. But I need to know what your future plans are likely to be."

Owen Parry had a gift for making himself appear totally without character or intelligence. If Alex had not seen him on a few previous occasions, he would surely have been convinced. He waited again for an answer.

"You have the wrong man," Parry said. "I don't know anything about any Charters. What are they anyway? And what does Parliament have to do with them? I don't know anything about any meeting on the mountain. I don't know what it was you saw. I should get back to work if you will excuse me."

"Not for a while," Alex said. "I pay your wages. You will not lose them for the hour or so you are away from your job this morning. Let me put it this way, then. The government is expecting trouble and in no mood to take it. Having said no, they have to flex their muscles and show that they mean no. It would be unwise to do anything further — for a while anyway. Let it rest for a year or two."

Owen Parry stared at him. He shrugged.

"Whatever you say," he said. "Whatever it is you are talking about. My English is not as good as it could be. I don't understand too well what you are saying."

"I would hate to be put in a position of having to enforce law and order when I am basically in sympathy with you," Alex said.

The man merely shrugged again.

"Don't put me in that position," Alex said quietly.

Parry laughed. Just as if he really did not know what was going on. Just as if he really was all at sea in a foreign language.

Alex sat back in his chair and surveyed his visitor for a few silent moments. Siân's lover. He assumed they were lovers. They had been walking hand in hand up into the hills last night. It was unlikely they were doing so merely for the exercise. Besides, he knew from experience how mere kisses and the light roaming of hands could turn her hot and ready. Had she been like that last night for Parry? It was none of his business. Absolutely none whatsoever. He pursed his lips.

"Perhaps we should work on a local scale rather than on a national one for a while," he said. "Perhaps we could talk, you with some other representatives of the people, and I. There are many things I do not

171

understand, many things that disturb me, many that I need explained. Perhaps we could talk. See what we could do together to improve conditions, to make life happier and more prosperous for all of us. Would you care to attend such a meeting if I arranged it?"

For a moment the mask of stupidity slipped and Alex glimpsed naked hatred and incredulity. He felt quite taken aback. Was he, then, so much the enemy that he was hated and his every word disbelieved? Then the mask was firmly in place again.

"I don't know anything about meetings," Parry said with a laugh. "Who would come with me? And what would I say? You have the wrong man. I just do my job by day and mind my own business by night. I don't need to be made happier. Or more prosperous. I have my wages."

"You are content that they have gone down ten percent?" Alex asked.

The man shrugged yet again. "I take what I am given," he said. "I am not a troublemaker."

Alex drummed his fingers on the desktop. "What do you know about Scotch Cattle?" he asked.

Owen Parry laughed. "This is Wales," he said. "Not Scotland."

For the first time Alex felt patience deserting him. "If you were as stupid as you are pretending to be," he said, "I doubt you would have a job as one of Cwmbran's most skilled workers, Parry. Do you know who any of them are? I would be willing to bet you do. It would be strange indeed if one of the leaders of a movement did not know the identities of any of the enforcers of that movement's decisions."

"Look" — Parry spread his hands before him, palms out — "we don't mess with Scotch Cattle. We don't talk about them. And we certainly don't know them."

"They are disembodied spirits," Alex said. "Totally unknown to anyone but themselves. I have a message for them, Parry. I trust it will reach them somehow. I will not have my people terrorized. Chartists want freedom and democracy for all British men. Well, then, let Chartists grant that freedom of choice to its followers and to those who choose not to follow. Perhaps I will let the property damage and the whippings of two nights ago pass this time. But if it happens again I will hunt down the Scotch Cattle, especially their leader, and I will see to it that they are treated as they treat their victims — with a strong dose of their own medicine. See that they are informed of that."

The blank look became blanker, if that were possible. "How am I supposed to do that?" Owen Parry asked.

Alex got to his feet. "I am sure you will find a way," he said curtly. "Good day, Parry. You may return to work."

Owen Parry got to his feet without a word and left the room. Alex felt the childish urge to pick up a book and hurl it after him. Instead he curled his hands into tight fists at his sides. The man looked as strong as an ox. Alex just wished — damn it, he just wished he had an excuse to fight him. He wanted nothing more at this precise moment than to punch that blank, stupid look off the face of the Chartist leader.

God, he wanted to fight someone.

Siân went up to Glanrhyd Castle in the evening. The summery weather seemed at last to have broken. It was a cloudy, chilly evening, with a suggestion of rain in the air. But she had promised to go and so she would do so. She still convinced herself as she walked through town and past the ironworks that she had not quite made up her mind. She had not even told Gran where she was going when she left the house. But deep down she knew that she had decided.

She wanted the job badly. She hated the one she already had, and no telling herself that other women did it and had no choice and that she wanted to be like other women could take away one iota of the hatred. There had been an accident during the day — a cave-in, as usual. It was not fatal this time or even very serious — one man had broken his arm. But Siân had been close when it had happened and her heart had chilled to his single scream and she had felt the paralyzing terror that all miners felt at such moments that the whole seam was going to come down on their heads and crush them or bury them alive.

She wanted to be Lady Verity Hyatt's governess. She liked teaching and was good at it — she taught at Sunday School. She liked children. And she liked cleanliness and fresh air and civilized living, though she felt almost guilty admitting as much.

Only one thing made her seriously hesitate. And it was a big something. She found him so very handsome and attractive — as what woman would not? And she knew that she had attracted him — on a purely base and physical level. A man like him would not think twice about seducing a woman like herself. Sir John Fowler was such a man. And yet, to be fair, she had to admit, the marquess had been the one to end their last embrace on the mountain. She had been witless with desire. It was a humiliating and rather frightening admission to make to herself. She would be playing with fire by taking a job in his home.

She was shown into the same room as before in Glanrhyd Castle. It was a large, high-ceilinged, square room, with an ornately painted ceiling and heavy-framed portraits hanging on the walls. There was a carpet underfoot. She had once heard that there were seventy-two rooms inside this building. To house one man and his daughter. It seemed almost obscene.

And then the door opened and he stepped inside. She felt rather as if she had been punched in the stomach. He was so very immaculately and elegantly dressed and so very blond and handsome. And he looked so formal and remote as if he could not possibly be the same man who had kissed her and touched her and desired her on the mountain.

"Mrs. Jones," he said briskly, advancing into the room as someone closed the door behind him, "you did come. Good. What have you decided?"

He had called her Siân on the mountain. He had obviously put the encounter behind him. This was a business meeting. His manner was totally impersonal.

Well, then, she would act the same way. She looked him calmly in the eye. "I would like to give it a try," she said. "But on one condition." She had known all along that she could do it only on that one condition.

"Oh?" He lifted one eyebrow and clasped his hands behind him. Those two gestures reminded her quite decisively of the fact that they were from two different worlds. He was utterly the autocrat, unaccustomed to having his will so much as questioned.

"I will not live here," she said. "I will continue to live with my grandparents."

He regarded her silently for a moment. From very blue eyes. Beautiful, compelling eyes. She wished she had not come. She hoped he would be unable to accept her one condition.

"I can see no serious objection to that," he said, "though I believe you would be more comfortable here."

"No," she said quickly. "No, I would not."

"Very well," he said. "You will start next week. At nine o'clock on Monday morning. You will consider your other employment terminated as of this moment. I shall see to it that you are paid for the full week."

She felt a rush of elation. And then a wave of panic. It all seemed so irrevocable suddenly. And she was still not sure she wanted to come.

"How did it come about," he asked her, "that you were educated at a private school in England?"

She had not prepared an answer to the question. She stared at him for a moment. "Someone paid for it," she said.

"Oh?" Again there was that autocratic lifting of his eyebrows.

She clamped her teeth together and stared back at him.

"My curiosity is not to be satisfied," he said. "But your case is unusual, Mrs. Jones. Are not most people here illiterate?"

The question angered her. It was the old English perception of the Welsh as barbarians.

"Most people can at least read and write," she said. "They learn at Sunday School as children. Most people would like to learn more, but there are no schools and no money to send their children to school elsewhere."

"Except for that spent by your benefactor," he said. "Why did my question anger you? Is it a sore point with you that there are no schools?"

"Perhaps some of the children would prefer an alternative to laboring in the works or the mine," she said. "Perhaps some of them would like to be clerks or lawyers or — or preachers."

"I am new here," he said quietly. "Give me time, Siân."

She flushed at his use of her name and was aware for the first time that they were quite alone in the room. And what did he mean? Give him time for what?

"How is the boy?" he asked.

It was another reminder of their last encounter. She felt her flush deepen.

"He has been at work," she said, "though he should not have been."

"I suspect," he said, "that his slender, boyish form hides a great deal of courage and stubbornness. Why else would he not have paid his penny? There have been no repercussions? No other threats?"

"No." She shook her head.

"If there are," he said, looking at her very directly, "or to anyone else of your acquaintance, I would be grateful if you would let me know."

No. Oh, no. She almost took a step back but stood her ground. He was not going to be using her as a spy any more than Owen was. She was coming here to teach his daughter.

He smiled suddenly. "You now look," he said, "exactly as your lover looked when I summoned him here this morning to question him about the Chartist movement and about the Scotch Cattle. I could have sworn through most of our interview that there was no one at home behind his eyes. I am not the enemy, Siân, though I suppose I cannot expect you to believe that yet."

He had summoned Owen? But he had told her that he intended to do nothing about the meeting he had witnessed on the mountain.

"The Charter has been rejected by Parliament," he said softly. "Had you heard?"

She closed her eyes and swallowed. Oh, dear Lord God. What now? She dreaded to think of what was likely to follow. She shook her head.

"Siân," he said, "give him some advice from me. Will you? Tell him not to do anything that will force a confrontation with the authorities. It is a confrontation these men cannot win. There are other slower, more patient ways to go about bringing change. He is a stubborn man. I believe it is a Welsh trait. But give him that advice. Perhaps he will listen to you."

It was a firm and implacable warning. Quietly and courteously expressed but quite unmistakable. She felt weak in the knees and dizzy for a moment.

"Damn you," he said more quietly still. "Damn you, Siân Jones. Do you want him in jail? Or dead? I'll not wait for your answer. You people are expert at giving the silent treatment. Go now — you are dismissed. You will return on Monday. Verity will be pleased by your decision. She said good night to me in Welsh last night. Is it really *noster*? As in *pater noster*?

"*Nos da,*" she said, clearly separating the words.

"Ah," he said. "Very much more musical than I made it sound. *Nos da,* then, Mrs. Jones." He opened the door and gestured to her to precede him through it. He signaled to a servant as she passed him to open the outer doors. He did not say any more but turned to climb the stairs.

It was raining outside — a dreary, chilly drizzle. Siân lifted one fold of her shawl over her head and hurried down the driveway toward the gates. She felt horribly upset. And wonderfully elated. The Charter had been rejected. Owen had been summoned into the marquess's presence. The marquess had wanted her to spy for him. *Damn you,*

he had said to her. Grandad would have
threatened to blacken his eyes for using
such language. She had done the wrong
thing. She should have said no. She should
have kept to the life she had embraced at
the age of seventeen.

But she would not have to go down the
mine again, she thought, lifting her face to
the drizzle. Not ever again. The good Lord
be praised, she was finished with the mine.

And the Lord forgive her for being so glad.

8

It had rained miserably for two days straight, but the clouds were finally breaking up by Sunday morning with the promise of sunshine later or by the next day at the latest.

Siân walked to chapel arm in arm with her grandmother. Mrs. Bevan, their neighbor, walked with them while Mr. Bevan walked behind with Siân's grandfather. Emrys, as usual, had stayed at home.

Sunday was Siân's favorite day of the week, with the mine closed down for the day and chapel and singing and the Reverend Llewellyn's sermon to look forward to in the morning and Sunday School in the afternoon. And then tea at home with the family and Owen. And relaxation — blessed relaxation.

This Sunday was a little different. Owen would not be coming to tea. There was a meeting at his house. A meeting to decide what was to be done now that the Charter had been rejected. There was a movement afoot, centered in Newport, to rally the men of all the valleys in some united action. Siân cringed from the thought and hoped that the very largeness of the idea would make it impossible to bring to reality. The Marquess of Craille's warnings rang constantly in her ears.

And today was a little different in another way too. Her absence from work in the mine had been noticed and people had begun to ask her about it. Word had begun to spread. She had told her own family, of course, and Gwyn's. Her grandfather had repeated what he often said, that she did not need to work anywhere outside the home. Her grandmother had cried a little, worried about what would happen to Siân at the castle with the marquess. Gran was the one who had been most hurt by what had happened with her daughter, Siân knew. Emrys had roared and offered to smash the marquess's nose flat if he so much as looked sideways at Siân. Gwyn's mother and father had said very little. Mari had been pleased for her and Iestyn delighted — "That is where you belong, Siân," he had said with his sweet smile. "You are a born teacher. Just a pity it is that he does not have ten daughters. Very happy I am for you." Huw had called her a fool and had told her that Gwyn would not have stood for it if he had still been alive.

Everyone else was beginning to look at her with marked curiosity, Siân thought self-consciously. She felt again as if she was something of an outsider and hated the feeling. But oh, dear, she admitted to herself, she had so enjoyed the last three days.

"So, Siân," Mrs. Bevan said now, "you have had some good fortune."

"With my new appointment?" Siân said. "Yes, I am very pleased about it."

"I am sure you will do very well at it," Mrs. Bevan said. "The Sunday School children all want to be in your class, including our Gwen and Willy. And you have had the schooling, thanks to your dada."

It somehow seemed ludicrous to hear Sir John Fowler referred to as her dada, Siân thought.

Her grandmother's lips tightened. "I would thank you not to mentioned him, Mrs. Bevan," she said. "Hywel is all the dada Siân needs. And schooling can sometimes be the devil's snare. I will be praying hard in chapel for Siân."

"Oh, Gran," Siân said with mingled amusement and exasperation.

Tardiness was not a vice with the people of Cwmbran. Although there were fifteen minutes still to go to service time when they entered the chapel, most of the pews were already full. It was not often there were empty places by the time the service began. Sometimes latecomers — those who came with only five minutes to spare — had to sit up in the loft with the organist or even on chairs squeezed into the aisles. People came for the singing and for the frequently fiery sermons of their preacher — and for the socializing.

Siân always sat two seats from the front with her grandparents, Owen one pew behind, the Joneses opposite. This morning, though, as she was walking down the aisle slightly behind her grandmother, someone in a pew close to the back plucked at her sleeve and whispered loudly to her.

"Mrs. Jones," Lady Verity Hyatt whispered, and smiled with bright mischief when Siân turned her head in surprise to look down at her. "You are going to be my teacher. We came to the chapel this morning."

Siân looked past her to see the marquess sitting next to her, looking blond and elegant and handsome and as out of place in chapel as a cat would look in a dog kennel. He also looked a little uncomfortable. He nodded to her.

"Sit by us," Verity whispered loudly. She still had hold of Siân's sleeve.

It was one of those moments when there was no time to think rationally. Had she done so, Siân realized later, she would have smiled at the child, told her that she always sat at the front with her grandparents, and reminded her that they would meet tomorrow. Then she would have continued on her way down the aisle, no more than a few seconds having delayed her. But there was no time for rational thought. She felt conspicuous. She felt as if everyone's eyes were on her — and knew she was not far wrong. She smiled and ducked down into the pew beside Lady Verity Hyatt.

Verity wormed her hand into Siân's and smiled up at her. "I am glad you are going to be my governess," she whispered. "I can't wait until tomorrow. There is only one sleep left."

"Hush, Verity." The marquess bent his head close to the child's and spoke very quietly. "You know we are always as quiet as can be in church."

"But this is chapel, Papa," she whispered. "There were only seven people in our church last Sunday, Mrs. Jones, counting Papa and me. It was boring." She wrinkled her nose.

"Sh."

This time Verity looked somewhat apprehensively up at her father and hushed, though she did turn her head to smile at Siân again and shrug her shoulders. Siân guessed that for the child this visit to a Welsh chapel was the treat of the week. It was a powerful and painful reminder of her own childhood, when as often as not she had watched from a window of their cottage as the people of Penybont went to their chapel. Sometimes her mother had taken her to the Anglican Church. Yes, she could remember the boredom and the envy she had felt of all the children who would be going to Sunday School in the afternoon. Unconsciously she squeezed Verity's hand, which was still in her own.

She looked up and ahead to confirm that Owen was indeed in his usual pew close to the front. She wondered if he knew she was there. And she wondered how he would feel about her sitting where she was. And how everyone else would feel. There was an unnatural hush in the chapel, a self-conscious hush. It seemed certain that everyone was aware of the presence of the Marquess of Craille. Usually the chapel hummed with the sounds of muted gossip until the Reverend Llewellyn climbed the steps to the pulpit.

Oh, dear, Siân thought, she should not have sat down here. She felt remarkably uncomfortable.

The singing was not self-conscious. The congregation sang the opening hymn with its usual harmony and enthusiasm while the Reverend Llewellyn conducted from the pulpit. Siân was very aware as she sang of the silent man standing at the other side of Verity. He held a hymnbook open in his hands but did not sing. Of course, he would be unable to, she realized. The words were in Welsh. And the service would be in Welsh. Verity would be even more bored than she had been last week. Throughout the opening hymn she stood staring up at Siân, still clinging to her hand.

The minister noticed the visitors during the hymn. After it he welcomed them in heavily accented English and all heads turned. Including Owen's. Siân met his eyes before he turned back again.

He had not given her any details of his interview at Glanrhyd Castle. "Bloody Marquess of bloody Craille," he had said when she asked — her grandfather had not been within earshot to reprimand him for his language. "A fox and a weasel he is,

Siân. Dangerous. He is worse than Barnes. You keep away from him, *fach*. Keep with the child."

He had refused to say what had given him such an unfavorable impression of their employer. Siân wondered what threats the marquess had made, and which of those threats he would carry out if he found out about this afternoon's meeting. But the very thought of the meeting set her stomach to churning. She concentrated on the part of the story of Job that the Reverend Llewellyn was reading from the Welsh Bible.

Job had been tested by the Lord, the minister said in his sermon. He had been tested to the limits of his endurance. And ultimately he had passed the test. He had come to see that suffering in this life cannot be avoided. But instead of being destroyed or embittered by his experiences, he had been strengthened and ennobled by them. They all had something to learn from Job.

It was very obvious to Siân as his sermon became more impassioned and some of the members of the congregation, swept along by his rhetoric and emotion, responded to it vocally, that he was talking directly to the Chartists, that he was making his position quite clear. They had done what was their legal and moral right. They had asked for freedom and democracy and the end of oppression. But having been rejected, it was now their task to endure, to be strengthened and ennobled by suffering.

She wondered if the Marquess of Craille had even an inkling of what the sermon was about. Owen, she could see, was sitting with shoulders and head thrown back. Iestyn had his head bowed.

Finally the service was over. Siân had prepared herself for the end. She would smile quickly at Verity, she had decided, and then hurry outside to wait for her grandmother and for Owen, who always walked her home. She certainly did not want to be trapped into leaving the chapel with the marquess and his daughter. Everyone would think she was putting on airs.

But it was not be that easy. Released from the necessity of being silent, Verity caught at her hand again and launched into speech.

"I enjoyed it much better than our church," she said, "even though I could not understand the words. It was fun with all these people. You have a lovely voice, Mrs. Jones. Everyone in here does. Papa was the only one singing last week. It sounded funny. Tell me who some of these people are. You are going to teach me Welsh, are you not? Maybe next week I will understand what is being said."

"Verity." The marquess's well-manicured hand came to rest on his daughter's shoulder, and Siân found her eyes focusing on it and then moving up his arm and shoulder and face until they met his eyes. "Mrs. Jones will be anxious to go home. You will have all the time in the world next week to talk with her — if she is foolish enough to let you get away with chattering."

"I don't mind," Siân said. "Children sometimes need to talk." *Especially when they are lonely,* she almost added, but the words would sound impertinent.

She turned to leave, but the Reverend Llewellyn was standing at the end of the pew, right hand extended.

"The Lord be praised that you saw fit to join us in our humble prayers of praise this morning, my lord," he said.

The marquess reached past his daughter and Siân to shake the offered hand. "We heard the singing from outside during both a choir practice and last Sunday's service," he said. "We decided to hear it from the inside this morning. You have a choir to be proud of, sir."

The Reverend Llewellyn's chest expanded. "The best male voice choir in Wales we have here, my lord," he said, "as we will prove at the *eisteddfod* in two weeks' time. And the best in Britain or in the whole world, I can say with confidence too. There are no singers like the Welsh. We are not afraid to open up our throats and praise the Lord with the vocal cords he gave us. Are we, Siân Jones?"

The marquess smiled politely while Siân murmured assent. Most of the congregation had already filed outside, she could see. She had not after all succeeded in avoiding being conspicuous.

"And lovely it is to see the little one," the minister said, beaming down at Verity and resting one hand lightly on her head. "Coming to Sunday School this afternoon, will you be, *fach*? We will put you in Mrs. Jones's class."

"Vark?" Verity wrinkled her nose and looked up at Siân.

"Fach," she said. "It means little one. It is an endearment."

"May I, Papa?" Verity swiveled her head to gaze pleadingly at him. "May I go to Sunday School? Please? Please, please, please?"

"It will be all in Welsh," Siân said. But she saw the agonized longing for one more treat in the child's eyes. "But I am willing to take you if it is all right with your dada — with your papa. Perhaps you would like to come home with me for dinner first." She was looking at Verity and seeing herself, she knew. She should have said nothing. She should not have interfered. The child after all was Lady Verity Hyatt, daughter of an English marquess.

"Lovely." The minister rubbed his hands together and then had his attention called elsewhere.

The marquess looked down at his daughter and then at Siân. "It will serve her right if she is horribly bored," he said, and then took Siân completely by surprise by grinning. He looked boyish and incredibly attractive when he did so. Something inside her did an uncomfortable somersault. "Will your grandmother mind?"

"Not at all," Siân said, wondering how her grandmother would react.

"Oh, please, please, please." Verity was bouncing on the spot.

"Very well," he said, looking down at her. "But behave yourself and watch your manners. And do as you are told. If you do not obey Mrs. Jones at all times, I will want to know the reason why afterward. Understood?"

Verity's smile was radiant. "Yes, Papa."

He bent down and kissed her upturned mouth. "Thank you," he said to Siân. "I hope she is no trouble. I will come to meet her after the school is over."

She nodded. There was something curiously intimate, she thought, about standing thus with him in the now-empty chapel, a child between them. She thought it might be possible to like the Marquess of Craille. She remembered suddenly seeing him kneeling beside Iestyn on the mountain, his hand resting reassuringly on her brother-in-law's head, his cloak spread over the boy to keep him warm. She remembered his offer to help Huw take Iestyn back home. And his telling Iestyn that he was a brave lad. A fox and a weasel, Owen had called him. Perhaps she had better not fall too easily into the trap of liking the marquess. He was, after all, all-powerful in Cwmbran. And some people were hungrier this week than last because the marquess of Craille's first act after his arrival had been to cut wages.

The street outside the chapel was far from empty. Almost the whole of the congregation gathered there every Sunday after service to talk and to gossip. And today, of course, they had the extra treat of watching Mrs. Siân Jones emerge a full two minutes after the last straggler, holding one hand of the Marquess of Craille's daughter while he held the other.

Siân tried not to feel embarrassed. After all, she had freely taken the job of Verity's governess and everyone must know about it by now. But she thought regretfully of all the efforts she had made during the past eight years to fit in, to be part of the community that had spurned her mother, to belong so that she would no longer be lonely. She wondered if her insistence on living at home with Gran and Grandad would save her from being cut off as she had been cut off throughout her childhood and girlhood. But it was too late for regrets now.

She led Verity first to where her grandmother stood with a group of neighbors and explained that the child would be coming home for dinner. And then she took her toward a group of men, all listening to something Owen was saying to them. He stopped talking and looked at her, unsmiling. She had a sudden, unreasoned fear that even Owen might turn against her. Unreasoned because he had urged her to take the job and had been pleased when she decided to do so. But of course it was since then that he had called Verity's father the bloody Marquess of bloody Craille.

Her world would fall apart if she lost Owen, she thought.

"Verity is coming for dinner at Gran's," she told him, "and then to Sunday School with me."

He turned from his friends. "I thought perhaps you had not even noticed I was at chapel," he said in Welsh before looking down at Verity and switching to English. "So you are going to go to school today as well as all next week are you, *fach*? Hold hands, then, is it?"

Verity set her free hand in his and tripped along the street between him and Siân. "Vark means little one," she said. "Mrs. Jones told me. Chapel was fun. I am going to meet other children at Sunday School. What is your name?"

He was offended, Siân thought, because she had sat with Verity and the marquess instead of in front of him, where he liked to look at her during the sermon, he had told her once to make her laugh and blush.

Again she felt that quiet, unfounded fear of losing him. Of being isolated between two worlds again, as she had been for the first seventeen years of her life.

She wished as she watched him talk with Verity — oh, she wished she had let him in when he had begged to be let in up on the mountain. She wished she belonged to him now, body and soul. She wanted him. She needed him. He was her rock and her anchor.

Alex had no idea how long Sunday School lasted. It was something of a real school, he had gathered, in which children actually learned to read and write. The chances were, then, that it would last quite a while. He did not go to meet Verity too early, but even so he paced up and down the pavement before the chapel for more than half an hour before the doors finally opened and children came rushing and whooping out.

It disturbed him that they had only this small chance for schooling. There should be a school in the town, accessible to all children daily, just as there was on his estates in England. Perhaps some of these children would like to be clerks or lawyers or preachers, Siân had said to him.

But he was given no time to brood on the matter. Siân Jones herself was coming out of the chapel, Verity holding her hand. His daughter whooped just like the other children when she saw him and came hurtling toward him, talking as she came.

". . . and they have a wooden settle that I sat on and all the dishes set up on a dresser, and Mrs. Jones sleeps in the dearest little cupboard bed right in the kitchen, and

Uncle Emrys — Mrs. Jones's Uncle Emrys — made me say good afternoon and thank you to him in Welsh and then laughed at me, and Mrs. Rhys — Mrs. Jones's grandmama — scolded him, and she held the loaf of bread right up against her stomach as she sliced it, and . . ."

He stooped down and swept her up into his arms, feeling a rush of almost painful love for her. She was still so young. So easily excited. So lonely. He should have married Lorraine or someone else before now and had more children. No child should be without brothers and sisters if it could be helped.

"I hope you were a good girl," he said, "and remembered to say thank you to Mrs. Rhys, either in English or in Welsh. Did you?"

Siân was standing quietly a few feet away. "I shall say good day, then," she said. "I shall be at Glanrhyd Castle at nine o'clock tomorrow morning."

He spoke from impulse and from a reluctance to turn away and lose sight of her until tomorrow morning. Tomorrow he would not even see much of her. He could hardly hang about in the nursery all day. And the sun had come out to make a rather pleasant day after all.

"Come walking with us for a little while?" he asked, setting his daughter's feet back on the ground. "I thought we would walk along the valley and look at the river."

"It is dirty," she said, "until you get past the houses and the mine."

"Then we will walk past the houses and the mine," he said. "Will you join us?"

He saw her hesitation and compelled her shamelessly with his eyes to say yes. She nodded and fell into step beside him, Verity and about six feet of space between them.

She was quite right. The river was very dirty and smelled unpleasant.

"There are no waterworks in the town?" he asked, and realized even as he did so how strange it would seem that he had to ask her such a question. This was his property. It was something he should know.

She laughed, a rather bitter and derisive sound. "No," she said.

"It seems unhealthy that there are not," he said, frowning. "This is quite a sizable town."

"There is no money for such an improvement," she said. "I heard somewhere that more children die in the valleys of South Wales than anywhere else in the country."

He was appalled and looked uneasily at the water, which was also quite obviously

the town sewer. It all looked so very picturesque from up in the hills.

But Verity wanted to tell him about the
Sunday School and he gratefully let go of
the topic of the river. It was something —
yet another thing — that he must look into
at a more appropriate time, and with
Barnes. Just as was the matter of a school.

"One of the worst things about mining,"
he said later, "is that the waste has to be
dumped somewhere. Coal tips are not attractive features of a landscape, are they?"
He looked with some distaste at the black
hills of slag to one side of the buildings and
great wheel that denoted the entry to the
coal mine.

"Industry is not attractive," Siân said.
"But it is a fact of modern life. We have to
make the best of it. I hate to see my valley
being gradually made black and ugly. It was
so very beautiful. It is where our music and
our dreams and our passion came from.
And now it is being —"

"Raped?" he suggested.

She looked even lovelier when she
blushed. "It does seem an appropriate
word," she said. "Will we just destroy the
beauty of our world? I wonder."

Verity had run on ahead. And finally the
town with its terraced houses and the mine

201

were past and it was as if they were walking in a different world. The river water seemed already cleaner and the grass all about them was green. Alex drew in a deep breath and the air seemed to be free of the smoke that belched eternally from the chimneys of the ironworks.

"Industry is so new," he said. "We have not yet learned to adjust to a way of life so totally different from that lived by our ancestors for hundreds and even thousands of years."

"The valley was all like this a mere hundred years ago," she said, gesturing ahead and to either side of them. "Sometimes I think I was born in the wrong age. But we cannot choose, can we?"

Verity had gathered some sticks and was throwing them as far out into the water as she could. She looked happy and absorbed in her game. She looked as if she had forgotten their presence.

"To me," he said, "all this is more of a shock than it is to you. I have lived all my life on a country estate, where everything is run much as it has been run for generations. I know it and understand it and feel competent to run it both well and wisely. Industry was little more than a word to me until I decided to pay a visit here. I feel rather as if

I have been transported to a different planet or even universe. Do be careful not to trip over that root."

She circled around the root and stepped closer to him as a result. He offered his arm without thought and she took it. It was only her touch that made him aware of what he had done. From the way she looked quickly up at him and the way her arm suddenly stiffened, he guessed that she had had the same realization at the same moment. It would be very easy, he thought, to develop a friendship with this woman. He should not have offered his arm. It was not at all the thing. She was, after all, only his servant. He had a vivid memory of her as she had looked when she had almost butted him in the stomach down in the mine.

They strolled on together arm in arm, neither one having the courage to arrange matters differently.

"I feel totally out of my depth," he said. "I know and understand only what I have been able to learn since my arrival. There is so very much that I still do not know and do not even realize I am ignorant of. Like the lack of waterworks, for example. I had not even thought to ask. In the meanwhile I have to defer to the superior knowledge and experience of my agent. He has, after all, run a prosperous business here for a dozen years."

Was he trying to justify himself to this woman? he wondered. Was he trying to convince her that if there were things wrong at Cwmbran — and there was obviously an appalling number of things wrong — it was not really his fault? Of course it was his fault. He had been the owner of this property for two years and had done nothing to shoulder the responsibility that ownership always brought along with it.

"Prosperous, yes," she said quietly. "We are all marvelously wealthy. One of us even owns a home with seventy-two rooms."

It was a remark that deserved a blistering setdown. Except that he could not deliver it. He had spoken to her as to an equal. He had never before bared a part of his soul to a servant. Could he blame her for responding in kind?

"Verity" — he called ahead to his daughter — "it is time to turn back. We are already late for tea." He used the excuse of turning around to disengage his arm from Siân's.

"Wealth brings with it responsibility, Siân," he said. "I am not convinced that abolishing wealth would solve anything. Would it bring equality and justice to the world? Ideally it would, I suppose, but I do not believe that human nature will ever allow for the ideal. I have always taken my responsibilities seriously." Except his responsibilities to Cwmbran.

Verity had turned obediently back toward the town. She was taking little runs up the hill and faster runs down again. She still seemed lost in her own child's world.

"If you feel bitter about anything," he said to Siân, "then complain to me. Give me details, like the detail you gave me about the children dying. Tell me all the things that are wrong here. I cannot even think of putting right what is wrong if I do not know about it. I asked your lover if he would be willing to attend a meeting with some other representatives of the people here to talk about improving life and conditions. But he was playing stupid at the time. Am I so much the enemy that I am not to be given a chance?"

She was gazing at the ground before her feet, he noticed, her face shuttered — and very beautiful. Ah, they were from different worlds. It was pointless to try to build bridges. He did not know why he was trying, except that he had kissed her twice, and thought about her almost constantly, and dreamed of kissing her again.

He thought she was about to answer, but

Verity came hurtling down the hill at just the wrong point and collided with Siân, who bumped sideways into him. He had to spread both arms and brace his feet to save all three of them from landing in a heap on the grass. Verity was shrieking with laughter and Siân was laughing too — as was he.

"That might have been quite spectacular," he said, "had we been a few feet closer to the river. No more, please, Verity. Mrs. Jones, will you come and take tea with us?"

"No," she said quickly, "thank you. My grandmother will already be wondering where I am."

"I will not press the point, then," he said. "I believe Verity and I will take the hill route back to Glanrhyd. You will continue this way?"

She nodded and smiled her farewell to Verity.

"You are going to teach me and play with me tomorrow," Verity said. "It is going to be fun. Only one more sleep." And she bounded off up the hill.

"I shall see you tomorrow," Alex said. Without thinking he did what he very rarely did with any woman. He took Siân Jones's hand in his and raised it to his lips. She looked startled and blushed deeply before turning sharply and continuing along the river path past the coal mine without saying another word.

Looking after her, he felt a welling of loneliness that was becoming almost familiar to him. They were worlds and universes apart. The only way they could ever come together was physically, and he was not even sure of that. Not by any means sure. But it would not be enough anyway, he realized uneasily. He wanted her liking, her friendship, her respect. He wanted them to be able to meet on terms of equality. He wanted them to inhabit the same world.

He sighed and set off upward in pursuit of his daughter.

9

Owen coaxed the fire in the grate back to life with a poker and set the kettle to boil. Siân took a seat by the table and watched him. It was not often Owen brought her to his own house, but the clouds had moved back over with evening and it was trying to rain.

"Just for a cup of tea, is it?" he had said, taking her arm and leading her toward the house.

It was one of the few houses in the valley that had only one occupant. It was kept clean and neat, Siân saw, though there was a pile of unwashed dishes on one end of the table. Angharad came in twice a week to clean and tidy. Sometimes, when Siân had still been working in the mine, she had almost envied her friend her job — except that she could never have brought herself to go into Josiah Barnes's house. It was after Angharad had gone to work for him that she had stopped seeing Emrys — and that she had seemed almost embarrassed with Siân.

This could be her home next summer, Siân thought. No, it would be her home. She had no doubts about marrying Owen. She wondered if she should get up and set out cups and saucers, but she left it to him to entertain her. She did not belong here yet.

"How did the meeting go?" she asked. She was insatiably curious about such things at the same time as she dreaded to find out that trouble was brewing.

"Well," he said, "everyone was angry, of course, that the Charter was rejected out of hand. What we were asking for was so reasonable. But no one was prepared to leave it at that. I was glad to find so much strong feeling and determination." He turned to the dresser and lifted down two clean cups. No saucers. Siân hid a smile.

"What is going to happen, then?" she asked. "Not another petition, surely. Isn't it a waste of time, Owen?"

"There will be something," he said. "Some big demonstration, probably. Some show of solidarity. Signatures on a page sometimes do not mean a great deal to men without imagination. Perhaps it will mean more to see the men behind the signatures."

Siân's heart sank. "Here?" she said. "Demonstrations in Cwmbran?"

He shook his head and sat on a chair at the table. "That would be meaningless," he said. "It would be on too small a scale. It has to be something bigger, Siân. Some big march by all the men of all the valleys on one place. Newport, probably. John Frost is from Newport."

"John Frost?"

"He is the leading Chartist here in Wales," he said. "He is the one trying to organize everyone. We will give him our support. We will inform him that he can count on us. We are going to invite him here to speak to us."

"Here?" she said. "Just to the men who were at the meeting this afternoon, Owen? You don't mean another mass meeting on the mountain, do you?"

"Everyone has the right to listen to what Frost has to say," he said. "If everyone is to be expected to march when the time comes, then everyone must have a chance to listen and decide. Everyone will have to be persuaded."

The kettle was boiling. He got up to make a pot of tea.

"Oh, Owen," Siân said, "is it wise? There could be trouble over it. The Marquess of

Craille knows about the last meeting. He has decided to do nothing about it, but he will not be so indulgent the next time. He has said that the government will be expecting trouble and will not stand for it."

Owen sat down at the table again, leaving the tea to steep in the pot. He looked at her steadily. "He has spoken to you about it?" he asked.

"By way of a warning, not a threat," she said. "I believe he is genuinely concerned, Owen. He wants to work on a more local level and find out what needs doing here to improve life and conditions. Perhaps it would be better that way. Perhaps something really would get done."

Owen laughed, though he did not sound amused. "And you believed him," he said. "I wondered why he suddenly decided to put in an appearance here, Siân, when we all know the opinion the bloody English have of the Welsh. Haven't you wondered? Haven't you worked it out for yourself by now? He is a part of the government. He is a member of the House of Lords, isn't he? Parliament never had the smallest intention of discussing the Charter and perhaps passing it into law. Craille came here to keep us in line, Siân. To show muscle. To confuse us and quieten us down if he can — we are only the ignorant, barbaric Welsh, after all. He came to squash us if we will not be quietened. He's a bloody snake. You had better not listen to a word he has to say."

Siân felt shaken. Was it true? It sounded so very reasonable. "He seemed genuinely concerned," she said, "about the fact that there are no waterworks in town. About the large number of children who die here."

"And when did he express this concern?" He was looking closely at her.

She flushed. "After Sunday School," she said. "He and his daughter asked me to take a stroll beside the river with them."

He was quiet for a while before getting up once more to pour the tea. It was almost black, Siân saw. He had used far too much tea. But perhaps he liked it that way. It was something she must remember. She found the silence uncomfortable. She felt guilty for agreeing to take that walk, though it had been quite innocent with Verity present.

"And they came to chapel this morning and you sat with them," Owen said at last. "There will be people who saw you walking with them."

"I was not trying to hide," she said. "Was there something wrong in doing so, Owen?"

"I had to fend off several remarks this afternoon," he said. "All of them jokes, Siân.

Certainly nothing to take offense over. No one would have dared. But all the jokes concerned a handsome Englishman and the loveliest Welshwoman in Cwmbran."

"Owen," she said, "it was with Lady Verity Hyatt I sat this morning and with her I walked this afternoon. I am going to be her governess. Of course I am going to be in company with her a great deal." She knew she was not speaking the strict truth. It was with the marquess she had walked this afternoon. Verity had amused herself.

"Just be careful," he said quietly. "Sometimes, Siân, it is possible to get a bad reputation even when you are innocent. And people will remember who you are."

She was on her feet in an instant, white with anger. "What is that supposed to mean?" she hissed at him, hands on hips. "How dare you, Owen. How dare you!"

He got up too, his chair scraping on the bare floor. He took her wrist in one large hand. "Calm down," he said. "Hush, *fach,* or Mrs. Davies next door will hear and think I am beating you."

"People will remember who I am," she said, her eyes flashing at him. "The daughter of a whore, Owen? Is that it? Like mother, like daughter? They will expect me to whore with him? The Marquess of Craille?"

213

Owen made a sound of frustration and pulled her into his arms. She found them about her like iron bands when she tried to pull free. "Spitfire," he said. "I am only warning you of what could happen if you are seen too often in his company as well as his daughter's. You know what people can be like with their nasty gossiping tongues. I trust you."

"Do you?" Anger was gone from her suddenly to be replaced by guilt as she remembered that the Marquess of Craille had kissed her twice, and that the second time she had participated fully in what had developed into something more than a kiss.

"Cariad." His arms had loosened and were cradling her. "I have had an idea. I have put it from me before because things are unsettled this year and I wanted them all to be behind us before we came together. But I think it would be wise for us to have the wedding this year after all. Next month, perhaps. And then no one will dare even joke about you and Craille."

For a few moments Siân felt weak with longing. This year? Next month? She could be living here next month as Mrs. Owen Parry? She would have her own home, as she never had before. She would be the wife of one of the most skilled and respected workers in Cwmbran. Perhaps within another month or two she would be expecting a child. She would belong fully and finally. She would be able to reverse the process she had begun when she had accepted her new job. Owen would not want her to work outside the home once she was his wife.

"Owen," she whispered.

He kissed her firmly, almost fiercely. "I don't want you there," he said. "I thought I did when it meant getting you out of the mine and when I thought it would mean someone in that house to keep an ear open for what might be going on. But seeing you with him in chapel this morning, *fach,* made me realize that I don't want my woman within a mile of him. We will marry, will we, and you will come here to keep house for me and to warm my bed. And to have my little ones."

She turned her head to rest her cheek against his shoulder, and closed her eyes. She wanted to be rescued. She wanted it more than anything. She had felt the pull of her attraction to the Marquess of Craille in chapel during the morning and on the walk beside the river during the afternoon. She could still feel a strange somersaulting of her insides when she remembered walking close beside him, her arm linked through his, Verity playing ahead of them, just as if . . . She had begun to like him. She had begun to believe that he really was concerned about the people of Cwmbran. She was so very gullible, if Owen's interpretation of events was correct.

She needed rescuing. She wanted to be rescued. She willed her body and her emotions to feel the solid safety of Owen's arms and body.

"I want little ones," she said. "You cannot know how it hurt, Owen, when my Dafydd was stillborn."

His arms tightened comfortingly. "We will have sturdy sons like their father and beautiful daughters like their mother," he said. "I will talk to the Reverend Llewellyn, then? Next month, is it, *cariad*?"

She quelled an unreasonable panic and nodded against his shoulder. She had felt no panic when agreeing to marry Gwyn. And yet she wanted Owen more than she had wanted Gwyn. She needed him more.

He nudged her head from his shoulder and kissed her again. He was smiling and looking happy. Siân felt panic once more and guilt once more. His kisses did not ignite her as the marquess's had done. She was agreeing to marry him as a type of escape, she thought. And yet that was not so, either. She loved Owen. She had had her eye on him and had begun stepping out with him and had hoped for marriage with him long before the Marquess of Craille had taken up residence at Glanrhyd Castle.

"Come upstairs with me," Owen said, and she realized with a jolt of surprise as she listened to his husky voice and looked into his heavy-lidded eyes, that he was aroused. "We will make love in bed, will we, *cariad*? Where you will lie every night as my wife. Where I will put our little ones in you. Where they will be born. We will make love there now to seal what we have agreed to this evening."

She gazed back into his eyes. *Yes,* an insistent voice in her head urged her, *do it. It will be good. With Owen it will be good.* It would make her safe. She would belong to him. And it was something she both wanted and needed. It had been almost three years. All that time without what Gwyn had given her almost nightly. She had liked it. It had made her enjoy her womanhood.

"Cariad," Owen said, "I am on fire for you."

"I could not face Gran and Grandad or the Reverend Llewellyn with our news, Owen," she said, "if I had already lain with you." They were foolish words and surprised even her. "They will be pleased, I think. They will expect us to remain pure."

He held her for a few moments longer and then surprisingly chuckled and let her go. He seated himself at the table again and picked up his cup. "There is a good chapel woman you are, Siân Jones," he said. "It is like trying to storm a fortress with you, isn't it? Drink your tea before it gets cold. I will take you home as soon as you are finished. Expect punishment on our wedding night, though, girl. I will keep you awake and hard at it all night. It is a promise." He grinned at her.

Siân blushed. "Thank you, Owen," she said, weak with relief, dismayed at her own inability to save herself from she knew not what. "You are a gentleman."

"I will ask you to repeat that," he said, "the morning after our wedding. If you are not too exhausted to speak, that is."

She gulped down her tea without sitting down again. She took her shawl from behind the door and wrapped it up over her head and about her shoulders, though she could see through the window that the rain had come to nothing.

"Owen," she said, her back to him, "I want to belong to you more than I have ever wanted anything in my life." Her words were passionate, almost desperate. As if she was trying to convince herself. She felt his knuckles brush the back of her neck through the shawl.

He opened the door and took her arm through his as they stepped outside. *"Fach,"* he said, covering her hand with his, "be careful. I am happy for you that tomorrow you will go to work that is not dirty and will not exhaust you. But stay away from him if you can and don't listen to anything he will say to you. He is the enemy. It is as simple as that. Remember that the man who pretends to want to help us has already lowered our wages."

"I am unlikely to see him at all," she said. "I am to teach his daughter, Owen. I will be just a lowly servant."

"And say nothing to him," he said. "Nothing at all, do you hear me? He will try to worm things out of you that he will turn back against us if he can. Not a whisper about this afternoon's meeting or about John Frost or the demonstration. Very angry I will be if you betray us."

She shot him a look of indignation. "Was that necessary?" she asked. "What do you think I am, Owen?"

He patted her hand. "I am sorry," he said. "But there was one man at the meeting this afternoon — and others who murmured agreement — who suggested that I tell you nothing since you will be going into the lions' den every day. You cannot tell what you do not know, he said. I have paid you the compliment of trusting you, Siân."

She did not know whether to be pleased that he had done so or offended that he had even had to make a decision to do so.

Alex had told himself a dozen times that he would not meet her personally when she arrived on Monday morning to begin teaching Verity. It was quite unnecessary. It would be far more appropriate if Miss Haines met her and took her up to the nursery. He could find out later what planned course of studies she had.

But of course when the time came he could not resist. He was finding her altogether too attractive for his own good. It was time, he thought, that he went visiting Fowler again and had another look at Miss Tess Fowler, though the idea was far from appealing. It was time, then, to arrange a meeting with the other owners he had heard about but not met. Perhaps they had some daughters, or at least some women of his own class with whom he could make social contact. Loneliness was doing alarming things to his common sense and self-control.

It was the first time he had seen her with her hair up. She looked very brisk and businesslike as he came down the stairs. And quite as lovely as always. She was wearing the same dress as she had worn yesterday. He guessed it was her best dress. He had only ever seen her in one of two dresses, if he did not count the work clothes she had been wearing in the mine. It struck him suddenly that perhaps she owned no more than the two dresses.

"Good morning, Mrs. Jones," he said when she looked up, suddenly aware of his descent of the stairs. He recalled that he had dreamed of her the night before. She had been lying on green grass beside a clean, fast-flowing river, smiling up at him as he leaned over her. The dream had disintegrated, or he had woken up, before he had had a chance to touch her. Dreams always seemed to deprive a person of fulfillment.

"Good morning," she said.

He wondered if she would ever call him by any name or title. If he were worth his salt he would establish certain ground rules with her from this moment. She should call him *sir* even if she could not get her tongue around *my lord*. It was a simple courtesy expected of a servant. She had called him Alex in his dream, he remembered suddenly. "Alex," she had murmured, reaching up her arms to him in warm invitation. Even her lilting accent had been there in his dream.

"I'll take you up to Verity," he said with stiff dignity, lest she see into his thoughts. "She found it difficult to settle to sleep last night. One would have thought today was Christmas Day."

"Oh, dear," she said as she fell into step beside him to climb the stairs.

"There are some books," he said, "a few that my mother-in-law bought for Verity, some that I had as a boy. Perhaps during the day you can assess your needs as far as more books and other supplies are concerned. Perhaps also you can make some plan for a course of studies. She is very eager to learn your language, but that, of course, must be considered secondary to all else. Perhaps it can be taught during walks and play rather than in a formal manner."

"Yes," she said. "It will be more easily learned that way."

He spoke on the spur of the moment. "You will take tea with me in the drawing room at four," he said. "At that time you can present me with a list of your needs and an outline of your plans. For today Verity will take tea in the nursery."

"Very well," Siân said, pausing outside the nursery door, to which he had guided her.

He reached across her to open the door, looking down at her as he did so. It was a mistake. She was looking back, her gray eyes quite calm and steady. But they were only inches from his own. She smelled quite unmistakably of soap. For a moment it seemed more enticing to him than any of the costly perfumes he had ever bought for his wife or a mistress.

He opened the door hastily and drew back. He had almost, he realized with an inward shudder, closed the gap between their mouths and kissed her. At nine o'clock in the morning outside his daughter's nursery. And though she had stood quite impassive, he had felt something flash between them. Just as he had on almost every other occasion when he had encountered her. He wished suddenly that he had not employed her to teach Verity. And that they were not living in such a small, closed community. His desire for Mrs. Siân Jones was becoming quite a persistent need.

Verity was standing just inside the door, obviously expecting their arrival. She looked flushed and excited. *"Bore da,* Mrs. Jones," she said, and giggled. "I have books, but I can read them already. My grandmama taught me. I am going to show you all my toys. I want you to take me walking in the hills today. I want to climb right to the top and see what is on the other side. I —"

"Verity," Alex said firmly, "Mrs. Jones is your new teacher. She will decide what you need and what you are to do. Any arguments and I shall be interested to hear about them and discuss them with you later. Is that understood?"

She smiled sunnily. "Yes, Papa," she said. "But I —"

Siân held out a hand and took one of Verity's. "I would love to see your books and toys first," she said. "Then together we will decide how to spend the rest of the day, shall we? The walk will be for this afternoon, I think. But it is a very stiff climb to the top."

Alex, apparently forgotten, stood in the doorway watching for a minute or two while his daughter lifted her favorite doll carefully from its crib and laid it in her teacher's arms. Siân rocked it and cooed to it so that for a moment it seemed almost like a real baby and she its mother.

Alex left the room, closing the door quietly behind him. He had a busy day planned with Josiah Barnes. It was high time he got started on it. Four o'clock seemed very far distant.

It was a busy day. They did not settle to any definite studies, but Siân used the time to discover what was available by way of books and supplies, to find out what her new pupil knew already and where her greatest needs as well as her greatest interests lay. In some ways Lady Verity was going to be an easy pupil. She was eager and energetic and she seemed to like her new governess. There was none of the sullenness one might expect to find in such a situation. In other ways she might not prove easy to teach. She was a stubborn child who would want to do only what she wanted to do. The trick, Siân realized before the day was over, would be to make her want to learn what she ought to learn.

They took the promised walk up the hill outside the castle park after luncheon. And of course Siân had underestimated Verity's energy. She bounded up the slope like a mountain goat and was not satisfied until she was at the top and could look down into the next valley.

"Oh, look," she said, pointing. "It is just like ours. A river and a town and houses along the sides of the river like a snake." She wrinkled her nose. "And smoke."

"Yes." Siân sighed. "The beauty of our valleys could be destroyed in another ten or twenty years."

"You sound sad." Verity slipped a hand into hers. "Are they your valleys?"

"Yes." Siân smiled. "They are the valleys and hills of Wales. Quiet and beautiful and useless to anyone except the Welsh for hundreds and hundreds of years. But now people all over the world need our coal and our iron ore and our finished iron and so we are famous. But perhaps we have lost something too."

Verity was quiet.

"But that is too sober a thought," Siân said. "That town down there will soon be the scene of an *eisteddfod* — a festival of music and poetry. Poets and choirs and soloists and harpists will come from Cwmbran and Penybont and all the other valleys to compete. It will be great fun."

"You will be going?" Verity asked.

"I would not miss it for the world," Siân said. "And I will be singing a solo. More important, the choir you heard from outside the chapel will be competing. My grandfather and my brothers-in-law sing in it and Mr. Parry, whom you met yesterday, and several friends. They very rarely get beaten. All the people from Cwmbran will walk over the mountain to hear them win again and to cheer them on."

"Walk?" Verity said. "You will not go in carriages?"

"There are too many of us," Siân said. "And the way over the mountain is far more direct than the road that goes around."

"I am going to come with you," Verity said.

Siân wished then that she had said nothing. "It would be lovely," she said, "but I don't think your father will be willing. It is a very Welsh event. The English usually stay away."

"I'll persuade him," Verity said confidently. "You did not teach me any Welsh on the way up. Teach me some now."

Siân pointed out various objects and gave them their Welsh names. Verity repeated the words until Siân was satisfied with her pronunciation. They both laughed a great deal over the "ll" sound peculiar to the Welsh language. But soon enough the eternal attraction to a child of a downward slope took Verity's attention and she released Siân's hand in order to rush down the hill, whooping with glee. Apart from the costly clothes, Siân thought, watching her, there was very little difference between this child of the aristocracy and the children of the town.

Except that this child was lonely. Siân knew all about a lonely childhood.

It was a busy day but not by any means an unpleasant one. And always in the back of her mind was the awareness, half dread, half excitement, that it would not be over when her workday finished at four o'clock. She was to take tea with the Marquess of Craille.

It was to be a purely business meeting. He wanted to see the list she had been compiling all day of books and supplies she would need for Verity's education. And the course outline and lesson plans she had made during the past few days and today. There would be nothing more to it than that.

But all day she could not keep her mind off what had happened outside the nursery that morning. Or perhaps even before that. Try as she had to concentrate her mind on last evening and the excitement of knowing that she was now officially engaged to Owen and their wedding being planned for next month — try as she had, she had been unable to prevent herself from feeling that strong physical awareness of the Marquess of Craille that was tormenting her dreams. And then outside the nursery, when he had bent across her to open the door and had turned his head while she was being incautious enough to be looking directly at him, something had passed between them. Something unmistakably sexual in nature. She would be willing to swear that she had not been alone in feeling it.

And so she found herself all day dreading the approach of four o'clock and longing for it. And cursing the weakness of her very human nature.

10

He was standing at the window, looking out, when his butler opened the drawing room doors and she stepped inside, looking as calm and as neat as she had in the morning, despite the fact that she had spent all day with Verity and had taken her to the top of the hill after luncheon. He knew because he had seen them up there and had resisted the urge to go to join them.

"You are very prompt," he said, "as you were this morning. Verity was willing to let you go?"

"I believe she enjoyed the day," Siân said. "She kissed me when I left just now." She flushed and bit her lip. "I was touched."

"She is an affectionate child," he said, "and has no mother to kiss. My wife died when Verity was six months old. I suppose she will look upon you as some sort of mother figure, provided you continue to make school seem like great fun to her. I gather that is what happened today. Do have a seat. Tea will be here directly."

She took the chair he indicated and sat on the edge of it, very straight-backed. The tea tray was brought in almost immediately, and he signaled the servant to place it before her. He wondered if she was accustomed to drawing room etiquette, but she poured their tea with a hand that looked only slightly unsteady. He crossed the room to take his cup and saucer from her.

"I shall arrange for you to spend a little time with Miss Haines tomorrow," he said, "to be measured for some suitable work clothes. I shall have her order them."

He was up against Welsh pride again, he realized immediately. Her lips tightened and her eyes flashed. "Thank you," she said, "but I will choose and buy my own clothes as I can afford them."

Some things had to be set straight. "I must make it clear to you, Mrs. Jones," he said, "that I have always considered it my responsibility to clothe the servants who work in any of my homes. I believe you fall into that category."

Perhaps, he thought, seating himself, he would feel better, more in command of himself, now that he had put her in her place. He had done it in the icy tone of voice he always used when his authority most needed to be exerted. She was staring down into her cup, her face pale and set. All injured dignity. He resisted the quite inappropriate urge to laugh.

"I saw that Verity had her walk up the hill," he said. "She dragged you to the top?"

"Of course," she said. "What is the point of climbing a hill unless one goes to the very top?"

Having established the master/servant relationship between them, he ought not to spoil matters, he knew. But he could not resist. She was looking so very prim and injured and — beautiful. "I believe," he said, watching her face closely, "you have shown me at least one answer to that question on more than one occasion."

Her cup rattled against her saucer and color rushed to her cheeks.

"It is a favorite spot for lovers?" he asked.

"It is the only place to find some privacy when two people are stepping out," she said.

"Stepping out." He smiled as she looked up at him at last. "A quaint expression. Do couples who are . . . stepping out not keep running into others doing the same thing?"

"If they keep to the lower hills," she said. "Sometimes it is pleasant to meet other couples."

He could tell by the way her eyes had become locked on his and by the look in those eyes that she knew where he was leading her. It was very unwise of him. Teasing Siân Jones was a rather dangerous business, he realized.

"Ah," he said softly. "And if they want to avoid that possibility?" He watched her swallow and lick her lips. He knew she was acutely embarrassed. "Have you ever walked higher into the hills while — stepping out, Mrs. Jones?"

He had gone too far, he knew. And he knew he would be sorry. The air was charged between them.

She looked down suddenly and managed to set her cup and saucer on the tray despite a shaking hand. She had not drunk any of the tea, he noticed. "You wanted to know my plans for Verity's schooling," she said. "I have written down some ideas and a list of what I will need. I have kept it as short as possible."

Even then, while he was feeling some relief at her changing the subject, he could not leave it alone. "Perhaps one day," he said, "you will do for me what you did for my daughter today. Perhaps you will take me high up into the hills — so that I may see over to the other side, of course."

Her lips compressed again. One thing at least was clear. Mrs. Siân Jones knew nothing about the game of dalliance. Not that he had any business trying to play it with her. It was not something he was accustomed to doing, anyway.

"Leave the papers with me," he said. "I will see to it that you have what you need. And I will summon you if I need to question any of your plans. How musical are you? That is an insulting question to ask a Welshwoman, I know. But are you capable of teaching Verity? Do you play the pianoforte?"

"There was a pianoforte at my mother's house while I was growing up," she said. "Her — My — Someone paid for lessons for me. I had lessons while I was at school. Since my mother died I have not had access to a pianoforte, only to the chapel organ. There is quite a difference."

"Let us see how rusty you are," he said, getting to his feet and reaching out a hand for hers. There was a grand pianoforte in the drawing room, which looked rather magnificent to him though he had never learned to play himself.

She looked at his hand as if reluctant to set her own in it. But she did so. It was slim and dainty — and he could feel the calluses on the palm. It was a powerful reminder of the fact that this woman was from a different world from his own, that she was his employee and had been for some time — as a coal cart puller in the mine. Who had paid for her music lessons? he wondered. Who had paid for her schooling?

"I am out of practice," she said, gazing at the pianoforte. But she looked almost wistful. "I have no music."

"There is some inside the stool," he said, "though I imagine it is all very old. Do you know nothing from memory?"

She bit her lip. He wondered who exactly she was and what had caused the crash downward to a life she had not been brought up to. He wondered how painful it was to her to be reminded like this.

"Only a few Welsh folk songs," she said. "Nothing that would interest you."

"You know my taste in music, then?" he asked her. "Let me hear one of these songs, Mrs. Jones."

She hesitated before seating herself on the stool and looking along the keyboard as if it was something quite strange to her experience. He hoped she was not so totally out of practice that she would humiliate herself. He had head her sing with the congregation in the chapel. He knew that music was dear to her.

"This song is called *'Y Deryn Pur,'* " she said, setting her fingers on the keys. "It is about a bird."

At first he thought that she really was going to bungle it. Her fingers stumbled over the opening bars. But then a simple melody emerged and she seemed to be calmed by it. He stood behind her and watched her bowed head and her hands. He wondered how long it would be before the calluses on her palms disappeared.

She loved music, he thought. It was there in her touch and in the posture of her body. But she had lost her pianoforte as a girl.

"You are rusty," he said when she had finished. "Very rusty. But you have a delicate touch and a feel for melody. I am going to shorten your workday by half an hour so that you may spend an hour a day in here. Starting tomorrow. I will give you one month before requiring that you teach Verity what you know. Agreed?"

She did not turn around. She bowed her head a little lower. "Alone?" she asked almost in a whisper.

"I don't believe I would derive a great deal of enjoyment from listening to you stumble your way through scales and finger exercises," he said, knowing very well that for an hour each afternoon the drawing room was going to act like a magnet on him. "Does that song have words?"

"Yes," she said. "Welsh ones."

"Let me hear them, then," he said. "I know that your voice is not as rusty as your fingers."

He thought for a while that she would refuse. But then she began to play again, making no more than one mistake in the introductory bars. He did not know if she made any after she began to sing. He had ears only for her voice.

It was a sweet soprano voice, which sang with such depths of feeling that he found himself with an unfamiliar aching in his chest and realized that he was on the verge of tears. Had she not said the song was about a bird? He was close to crying about a bird? But he closed his eyes tightly and was washed away on that flood of longing that he had experienced only ever in this particular part of the world. That longing to which she had put a Welsh name. Heer — ? *"Hiraeth."* Yes. *"Hiraeth."*

"Well," he said, aware at last of silence, "you have made my pianoforte seem almost redundant, Siân. It is a haunting melody. Do all Welsh tunes make one want to cry?"

"We make music straight from the heart," she said, getting to her feet. "We are an emotional people." She turned. He guessed that she had not realized he was standing so close.

"A romantic people," he said. "A passionate people. Do you share those traits, Siân?" One step forward — half a step — and they would be touching.

"I —"

"Yes, of course you do." He lifted one hand to touch his fingertips to her cheek. "It is there in your voice when you sing. And in your body when you kiss."

If she had said something or moved, perhaps he would have been saved, he thought afterward. But she did neither. Her large, calm gray eyes focused on his.

And so his arm slid about her shoulders and the other about her waist, and he lowered his head and opened his mouth over hers. And took instant heat. Manual labor had hardened the muscles of her shapely woman's body and had made her wonderfully different from any of the other women he had ever held close or bedded. She was magnificent and infinitely desirable.

He teased her lips with his tongue until they trembled apart, and eased his way past her teeth and deep into her mouth. Her body came arching against his. He could feel her fingers winding tightly into his hair. She moaned. And turned hot in his arms. He hardened into full desire.

But there was one part of his mind that stayed aware of the fact that they were standing in his drawing room with the door unlocked and that it was possible, though unlikely, that some servant or even Verity could come inside at any moment. Had it not been for that sensible part of himself, he thought later, it was altogether possible that he would have had her down on the carpet and would have completed what they had begun. He was almost sure she would not have stopped him. Just as perhaps she would not have stopped him on the mountain the night the Scotch Cattle had come.

He softened his kiss and loosened his hold after a long time and took his mouth away from hers with the deepest regret.

"This is getting to be a habit," he said.

"Yes."

He could tell that she had not yet pulled herself mentally free of their embrace.

"What are we going to do about it?" he asked.

He watched awareness begin to come back to her eyes.

"Are we going to keep fighting it?" he asked. "We are not doing a very good job of that, are we? Or are we going to give in to it?"

Full awareness was back. "Give in to it?" Her eyes widened. "I'll not be your mistress." Color flooded into her cheeks.

"Won't you?" he said, sorry and relieved at the same time. "I suppose we will have to keep fighting it, then. You are a very beautiful woman, Siân Jones. More than that, you are wondrously attractive and desirable. I would make it well worth your while." Those last words seemed to speak themselves.

But she was quite firmly back in command of herself and pushed away from him. Anger, he could see, had come to her rescue as nothing had come to his, except that little corner of common sense that had kept him from tumbling her a few minutes ago.

"I'll be no man's little bit of afternoon fun," she said. "I'll bear no man's bastard children. I'll be no kept woman even if you were to offer me all the comforts in the world and all the material advantages my children could need."

Like an expensive private school in England and pianoforte lessons and an instrument to practice on? He understood in a sudden flash. His uncle? Was she his uncle's by-blow? The thought turned him cold. Was she his cousin?

"No," he said. "Such affairs are unequal things, are they not? All pleasure and convenience for the man, all danger and humiliation for the woman. And ostracism from a deeply religious community like this, I do not doubt. We will fight it, then, Siân. You are my daughter's governess; I am your employer. I am the Marquess of Craille; you are — an ironworker's granddaughter. Yes, we will fight it."

"I should not come here again," she said. "I should not have come here in the first place. I knew the danger."

Ah, yes. She was an honest woman. She had known, just as he had. And yet neither of them had done the obvious thing to avoid the danger. And how could he let her go now? Verity wanted and needed her. And she needed this job. And he? He needed to see her occasionally. He needed to know that she was able to return somewhat to the kind of life he suspected she had lived while growing up. As some wealthy man's illegitimate daughter. He did not think he was wrong about that.

"But you will come?" he said. "Verity has been so very excited at the prospect of having a young woman here, whose time will be devoted just to her. She needs a woman's touch. And some schooling." *And I need to see you.*

"Yes, I will come," she said almost in a whisper. She sounded bitter. "But not for this again. I don't want any more of this."

"Shall we both promise to fight it?" he asked. "This attraction that apparently neither of us really welcomes?"

She looked at him speculatively. He wondered if she really believed him. "Yes," she said. "It must be fought. I am engaged to be married. I will be marrying next month. I care for him. I want to make him a good wife. I want to belong to him and to the life he represents."

"Parry?" His heart sank.

"Owen Parry, yes," she said. "He is a good man. He deserves better than this."

He nodded without answering and her eyes wavered from his and she turned away. He strode across the room to open the door for her.

"Verity will be expecting you at nine tomorrow," he said. "Go straight up to her when you arrive. I'll not meet you as I did this morning."

She nodded, did not quite meet his eyes, and hurried past him.

He closed the door quietly and drew a deep breath. So that was that. The beginning and the end. Perhaps it was just as well that it had come into the open and been talked out. Now it was over. Now he could put her out of his mind.

Did she react to Parry as she reacted to him? he wondered. And yet she did not seem promiscuous. Why was she marrying the man if she did not feel that way about him, then? *I want to belong to him and to the life he represents,* she had said. *The life he represents.* She had grown up as someone's bastard, if his guess was not way off the mark. There had been privilege and gifts and — loneliness? The sense of belonging nowhere? Not in her father's world and not in her mother's? If her mother had been Rhys's daughter, then she would not have been in high favor when she gave birth to a child outside matrimony. Siân had not grown up with her grandparents.

No, Alex thought, crossing to the window again so that he could watch her walk down the driveway toward the gates, an affair with him was the last thing Siân Jones would want.

And perhaps she was his first cousin. He had not liked to ask. Though surely she would not have allowed any embrace at all if that were so. No, that could not be it.

But who the devil was her father? he wondered. It was none of his business, of course. *She* was none of his business, except the job she did as Verity's teacher.

It was over, he thought, turning firmly from the window. There was no future in it whatsoever. It was over.

Siân was feeling upset as she hurried down the driveway. Upset and confused. Last night she had agreed to marry Owen within the month. And yet this afternoon . . . She wondered if it was just the marquess's wealth and position that were so fatally attractive to her. Or was it his blond, blue-eyed good looks?

He had asked her to be his mistress. He had said he would make it well worth her while.

The sooner she married Owen, she thought, the happier she would be.

And then her steps slowed. Josiah Barnes was outside his house, but whether he was going in or coming out she did not know. There was no avoiding him, though. He had seen her and was smiling at her.

"Good afternoon." She nodded curtly to him and would have walked past, but he stepped out to block the driveway. "Excuse me, please?"

"Hoity-toity," he said. "You cannot stop to talk a minute with an old friend, Siân Jones?"

She stopped a few feet away from him and looked inquiringly at him.

"You have done well for yourself," he said. "No less than a job at the castle. Will you have a cup of tea with me?"

"No, thank you," she said. "My grand-mother will be expecting me."

"The lodge is too humble for you?" he asked. "You would marry the likes of Gwyn Jones and step out with Owen Parry, but Josiah Barnes is not good enough for you?"

She did not need this, Siân thought, annoyed. Not today when her emotions were already in turmoil.

"Or perhaps, Siân Jones," he said, "you have your sights set very high indeed. Higher than your mother set hers. A hand-some piece of flesh, isn't he?"

Righteous indignation was denied her. But she looked at him with cold dignity. "Excuse me," she said.

He stepped to one side and made an exag-gerated sweeping gesture with his hand to indicate that she was free to pass. She did so and did not look back.

It was a slight incident, one not worth

dwelling upon. But it suggested to her yet again that perhaps she should have remained in the world she had so carefully made her own over eight years. In all those eight years she had only rarely come face-to-face with Josiah Barnes, and never when she was alone.

As she hurried home, she did not feel nearly as happy as she should have felt after a day at a job she wanted and enjoyed.

It was not going to be easy to continue.

Josiah Barnes stood looking after her.

"Bitch!" he muttered to himself. He had been willing to marry her years ago despite her illegitimacy because the alliance would have drawn him closer to the other owners — and because at the age of seventeen she had been a juicy-looking morsel.

Yet she had refused him. He had not believed at the time that there could have been any greater humiliation — until three years later she had married Gwyn Jones, a mere coal miner.

And now she had somehow brought herself to the attention of Craille and got herself a job at the castle. Damn him for coming and interfering in a business that Barnes had come to think of almost as his. And damn her for somehow worming her way out of the mine where Barnes had put her.

"Bitch!" he said again as she disappeared from sight.

For a week Siân did not see Alex except for a few brief, distant glimpses. It was an enormous relief to find that it was possible to keep her job and yet avoid the terrible danger that she had known about in advance but had fallen headlong into with no fight at all on the very first day.

She loved her job. She would have hated to have to give it up. And the very thought of having to return to her old job gave her the shivers. She loved Verity and she loved devising ways to both amuse and educate the child. It was not difficult, she found. Verity was an intelligent and energetic little girl, who responded with enthusiasm to a challenge.

And it was wonderful beyond imagining, Siân found, to feel clean all day and to see the light of day and breathe fresh air all day long. It was wonderful during the evenings to be able to relax without that dreadful feeling of physical exhaustion and aching muscles that had been a way of life to her for so long. Miss Haines had sent away for two dresses and two skirts and blouses for

Siân to wear at work. Once she had accepted the fact that it was not charity that was being offered but a requirement for the servants in the employ of the marquess, she delighted in the prospect of having so many clothes and of being able to keep her best dress for Sundays and special occasions.

As wonderful as anything else was the chance to play on the pianoforte in the drawing room for a whole hour each day. For a day or two she had approached the room apprehensively and had sat there tautly for her hour, waiting for the door to open. But he was never there and never came. She was glad, she told herself. More than glad. She seemed to have no self-control where the Marquess of Craille was concerned and despised herself heartily for having fallen into the trap of being flattered by the attentions of a wealthy and handsome nobleman. Her cheeks often burned at those remembered words, *I would make it well worth your while.*

In a month's time she would be married. It had all been arranged with the Reverend Llewellyn, who had had a long talk with them about their marital obligations, and with Siân's grandmother, who would be almost solely responsible for organizing the usual celebrations that accompanied a wedding. Owen had no mother or grandmother to help. But the neighbors would all pitch in with enthusiasm, as they always did, helping with the baking, and coming to help clean Gran's house the day before the wedding. That was where the party would be based, but it would inevitably spill out onto the street, as wedding parties always did, since the house would not hold one quarter of the people who would come to help celebrate.

Weddings were always exuberant community festivals.

It was a happy week. Siân almost forgot any causes of unhappiness. Almost. She found Mari crying as she pegged out clothes on the line one afternoon. Their father-in-law had coughed badly all night and Iestyn had got him some medicine in the morning, using the money that was to have bought him the material for a new shirt to replace the one the Scotch Cattle had torn almost beyond repair. And there was an advance at the truck shop that would take almost all of next week's wages. They would be living on borrowed money again next week.

"But I must not complain, Siân," she said, drying her eyes. "There is wicked I am when we are not starving and all the children are healthy. There is Blodwyn Williams back in the mine this week because her man was hurt bad and there is the little one to feed as well as themselves. And her five months gone with another child. What a terrible world it is we live in."

Yes. It was a terrible reminder of how a handsome exterior and charming manners could gull her into thinking him a good man, Siân thought. And she was doubly ashamed of the way she had twice given in to a physical attraction toward him. And she was ashamed of herself for believing during their Sunday afternoon walk that perhaps he really did care about the people who were dependent upon him. Owen was quite right. He had his feet far more firmly on the ground than she ever would. He was right about the Marquess of Craille. A man who cared would not have lowered wages that even as they were would hardly stretch over a week's necessities.

When she was paid at the end of the first week, Siân gave half to her grandmother and took some of the rest to Mari. Mari took it after tears and protests — "Only for the little ones, mind, Siân, because you insist. Not for me and Huw, or for Mam or Dada. Just for the little ones." But Huw came storming into her grandfather's house no more than an hour after Siân had returned there, furious, and slapped the money down on the kitchen table.

"You will not shame me by giving money to Mari," he said to Siân, ignoring her grandmother and Emrys. "I will support my wife and my babies and my mama and dada too with Iestyn's help, Siân. Try this again and I'll slap you a good one."

Siân felt as if she already had been slapped. "I am part of your family too, Huw," she said, "though I came back to live here because there was more room. I was married to your brother. Don't shut me out. Let me help when I can."

"Tainted money!" he said, bringing the side of his fist down on the table beside the money so that Emrys, sitting quietly by the fireplace, raised his eyebrows and pursed his lips.

Siân looked at the money. "Tainted?" she said. "Because it comes from the Marquess of Craille? Where do you think your money comes from, Huw?"

"Who knows," Huw said, "how your money has been earned, Siân?"

"For shame, Huw Jones!" Siân's grandmother said, speaking for the first time.

"Someone," Emrys said quietly, "is asking to be spitting teeth for the next week. I will hear an apology, Huw, before you leave this house."

The anger went out of Huw's face. "It made me that mad," he said, "to see the money in Mari's pocket and know that I cannot support her properly myself. I should not have said that, Siân. It is what I have heard from some this week, but I have offered to blacken a few eyes or smash a few teeth over it, just as Emrys did just now. You should not have taken that job. It will give rise to gossip, unjust as it will be."

"I suppose," Emrys said, "that is an apology. You can refer to me anyone who has anything to say about my niece, Huw. Better me than Owen. Owen would kill him. I will only maim."

His mother tutted but said nothing.

Siân picked up the money and held it out. "Take it, Huw, please," she begged. "For the children? They are my niece and nephews. They are Gwyn's niece and nephews."

He looked at the money for a long time before taking it. "You have a good heart, Siân," he said grudgingly. "Sorry to barge in, Mrs. Rhys. I was that mad."

Oh, yes, there were a few reminders during that week that life was not all happiness. But mostly it was. There was a new job to be enjoyed and the *eisteddfod* to look

252

forward to and a wedding and a new life as a married woman to look ahead to. Siân was not sure if Owen would be willing for her to continue as Verity's governess after they were married. She rather hoped so. But perhaps she would not be able to for very long, anyway. By this time next year perhaps she would have a child. It was a warming and an exciting thought.

She was in the nursery with Verity one afternoon about a week after her job had begun. They had been unable to go outside because it was raining. They were painting instead, a favorite activity of Verity's because Siân did not seem to mind the mess as her nurse had always done. It would be time to clear away soon, Siân thought, glancing at the clock. It was almost time to go downstairs for her hour of practicing on the pianoforte. It was an hour of the day she loved. It was an hour for her and no one else.

But a servant forced a change of plans by arriving in the schoolroom with the direction that Mrs. Jones was to bring Lady Verity down to the drawing room as soon as possible and stay there with her for tea with his lordship and his guests.

Siân sighed inwardly as she hurried to clear away brushes and paint pots with

Verity and then whisked the child to her room in order to help her change her dress and wash her hands and comb her hair. There would be no practice after all today. How very dreary. There was another whole day to live through before she could touch that most glorious of all pianofortes she had ever seen.

Perhaps she had misunderstood, she thought as she descended the stairs to the drawing room, Verity's hand in hers. Surely she would not be expected to stay to tea. She would merely accompany Verity into the room and then make her escape. It would be quite pleasant to be home an hour earlier than usual.

Despite herself she found her heart pounding as they approached the doors to the drawing room and a servant opened them from the outside. She would see him again. For a few moments she would be in the same room as he. It was a thought and a feeling she tried to quell by thinking hard about Owen.

And then they were inside the room and even the shock of seeing him again paled beside the necessity of standing calmly while being introduced to Sir John and Lady Fowler and Miss Tess Fowler.

11

It was the most acutely embarrassing moment of her life, she was sure. It was several years since she had set eyes on Sir John Fowler. Strangely enough, she had never come face-to-face with either his wife or his daughter. She had only ever seen them from a distance. Tess had been a child the last time Siân saw her. Siân could remember her mother crying the day news of Tess's birth was brought — seven years after the birth of her own daughter. Perhaps she had thought that that was one thing she had been able to do for him that his lawful wife could not.

"I would like you to meet Verity's new governess," the marquess was saying now after his daughter had made her curtsy to his visitors. "Mrs. Siân Jones. She is quite a gem, educated in England, able to give instruction in music as well as in everything else. And also in Welsh, which is important to me as I explained to you before."

Siân fixed her eyes on him. She was not even sure if the ladies knew her, though surely they knew of her existence. Sir John had visited her mother twice every week.

"May I present Sir John and Lady Fowler to you, Mrs. Jones?" the marquess said. "And Miss Tess Fowler? Sir John owns the Penybont works, but then I daresay you know that already."

"Yes." Her lips felt stiff and did not easily obey her will. She looked at Sir John and inclined her head to him. "How do you do?" She could not look at the ladies, though she could tell by their very stillness that they did indeed know.

"Mrs. Jones?" Sir John had got to his feet on their entry and bowed to her now. He looked rather pale, Siân thought. He seemed thinner than she remembered him. She marveled now, as she always had, that he was her father. She felt no kinship with him. She wondered why her mother had loved him — she undoubtedly had done so. He had always seemed cold and humorless to Siân.

"I am sure Mrs. Jones is grateful to be employed in your service," Lady Fowler said with a hauteur that would have done justice to a duchess. "We must thank her for bringing dear Verity down for tea."

It was an attempt at dismissal that Siân would gladly have accepted. But the door had closed behind her and the marquess was motioning her to a seat, and she understood that she really was expected to stay for tea.

It was a dreadful half hour. Siân sat in silence, pointedly ignored by both ladies, while she felt the eyes of both men on her a great deal more than was comfortable. The only saving grace was that Verity was as exuberant and as talkative as usual and smoothed over what might have been a very awkward occasion for all of them. Siân wondered if the marquess could feel the atmosphere of tension in the room, and did not know how he could not.

Her eyes strayed to Tess at one point. The girl was small, dainty, pretty, blond. Dear Lord, Siân thought, they were half sisters. It seemed impossible to believe. And then she glanced at Sir John and found his eyes on her. Their last bitter encounter came back to her mind. If she would not marry Josiah Barnes, he had told her — and it was a better match than she could ever have hoped for — then he would wash his hands of her. Not only would she not marry Barnes, she had answered, but she would not touch a penny of Sir John's money for the rest of her life. No, not if the alternative was to starve. Two headstrong people battering their wills against each other. Perhaps after all she had inherited something from him.

Verity's conversation centered embarrassingly about Siân and what they had been doing together during the past week.

". . . and I went to Sunday School with Mrs. Jones and met lots of boys and girls and they all spoke Welsh but I didn't mind because I am going to learn it too. I already know lots of words. Don't I, Mrs. Jones? And Mrs. Jones is going to sing in the eist— in the *eisteddfod.* There, I got it right. I think she is going to win this year though she only came second last year. But she has the best voice I have heard. And I am going to get Papa to let me go with her over the mountain because it is the most fun of anything the whole year, she says. Don't you, Mrs. Jones?"

"Dear me," Lady Fowler said, interrupting this excited monologue, "I am sure your papa will allow no such thing, Verity, dear. Such amusements are very well for your papa's Welsh workers, but they are hardly the thing for a young English lady."

"I have never mingled with Papa's laborers," Tess added. "It would be lowering, dear Verity. You have to remember that your papa is their master and that they all look up to you as the lady of the manor."

Siân was aware that her shoulders had straightened and her chin had lifted only when she caught the marquess's eye. He was looking steadily and unsmilingly back at her, though Tess was simpering at him for his approval.

"Mrs. Jones does indeed have a lovely voice," he said. He had said very little for half an hour. "But then, being Welsh, she has an unfair advantage over the rest of us poor mortals. Will you sing for us, ma'am? The one about the bird?"

Verity clapped her hands.

If the floor would only open up, Siân thought, she would gladly drop through it. Had he not sensed her extreme discomfort? Or the intense, spiteful dislike of his lady guests? She looked up at him as he got to his feet and held out a hand for hers. She had not even had a chance to feel the embarrassment and discomfort of being in company with him. Only a little more than a week ago in this very room . . .

"We should be leaving soon, John," Lady Fowler said.

"In a little while," he said. "Let Mrs. Jones sing to us first."

Siân set her hand in the marquess's and allowed him to escort her to the pianoforte. At least this week, she thought, she could play with greater confidence. But she would rather be anywhere else on earth than where she actually was. She set her fingers on the keys and began to play the opening bars of *"Y Deryn Pur."* The marquess stood quietly behind her for a while after she began to sing and then went back across the room to join his guests.

She thought he had come back again, but when she looked up from the keyboard, it was to find Sir John Fowler standing close to the pianoforte.

"Well done," he said when she was finished. "Will you sing another?"

"Yes, please, Mrs. Jones," the marquess said.

Siân looked at her hands and realized she had no choice. Saying no would cause more of a stir than complying with the request. " *'Llwyn On,'* " she said, naming the other competition piece that she was to sing at the *eisteddfod*. " 'The Ash Grove.' It sounds lovelier with a harp accompaniment, but the pianoforte will do."

Lady Fowler began to talk rather loudly when she was only partway through the song, Siân heard. She continued anyway.

Sir John was still standing to one side of the instrument when she finished. His wife was talking to the marquess, pointedly pretending that she had not even noticed the ending of the song. Tess was talking to Verity and laughing.

"Your voice has matured," Sir John said quietly. "It is lovelier than ever."

"Thank you." She did not look up at him.

"I have heard," he said, "that you are going to be married again."

"Yes," she said.

"To a puddler?" he said. "Not a miner this time?"

"Yes," she said, "to a puddler."

"Your first marriage, of course," he said, "was a thumb of the nose to me. You went as low as you could go."

The old antagonism she had always felt toward him was back. "Gwyn was a worthy and hard-working human being," she said. "I married him for myself. I was fond of him. I was grieved by his death and by the death of our son."

"I would not have allowed you to go back underground if you had let me know you were with child," he said. "I did not know until it was too late."

"You would have had no say in the matter," she said angrily. "You are not a part of

261

my life."

"Siân —" he said.

"John." Lady Fowler's voice, sounding brittle, hailed him from across the drawing room. "Do come along. We have already stayed far too long for good manners. The marquess will think we have grown rustic indeed. Do come out to the carriage with us, Verity, dear, and wave us on our way."

She acted as if Siân was not even in the room. Sir John bowed silently to her before turning away and joining his wife and daughter at the other side of the room.

"Wait here, please, Mrs. Jones," the marquess said as he left with his guests and Verity.

She sat on the pianoforte stool, staring downward at the keyboard, feeling numb and very close to tears. He was her father. Her father! He had not even known that he was to be a grandfather. Because she had not wanted him to know. Because he was the last person she would have thought of informing. Because it should have been his business to find out what was going on in her life. But he had not cared. Not a word when she had married Gwyn. Not a word when he had been killed. Not a word when her baby — his grandson — had been born dead.

Siân reached out a finger and dusted off an already spotless key. She did not look up when the drawing room door opened and then closed quietly again.

He had invited her down to tea purely to convince Lady Fowler and Tess that he really had hired a competent governess for Verity and that his daughter was happy with his choice. They had been hinting since their arrival that Tess was still willing to come two or three times a week to instruct Verity — not for remuneration, of course. They had both been hasty to insist that it would be a labor of love and not by any means in the nature of employment.

Perhaps too, he admitted to himself, he had sent up the invitation because it gave him an excuse to see her again after more than a week of keeping himself very strictly away from her. He had even refused to take Verity back to the chapel on Sunday. He felt almost starved for a sight of her and for the distinctive sound of her voice with its musical lilt. He should not have given in to temptation at all, of course, but then he had the other reason for sending for her.

He certainly had not intended to arouse any sort of situation to cause anyone discomfort. It was quite unexceptionable to have his daughter's governess accompany her to tea. No one could be expected to take umbrage over having to take tea with a social inferior under such circumstances.

Perhaps things were different in Wales, he thought at first. So much was different in Wales. Perhaps there the social lines were observed more strictly. Certainly the atmosphere in his drawing room seemed thick enough to be cut with a knife, and Lady Fowler lost no opportunity of making Siân feel three inches high.

Alex blessed his daughter for being her usual garrulous self and for seeming totally unaware that anything was amiss. And something definitely was. It was not just that he was in a different country and did not understand its ways.

He thought he understood after he had tried to cover up for a particularly cutting rudeness of Lady Fowler's by suggesting that Siân sing to them. He noticed how Fowler got up and crossed the room to listen to her. He noticed how he talked quietly to her after she had finished singing. Even from across the room he could see the tightness and anger in her face, though he could not hear anything that was said — Lady Fowler and Tess were too loudly busy ignoring her very existence.

She was a beautiful woman. An unusually attractive woman. He knew that to his own cost. She was attractive to Fowler too. Perhaps there had once been something between them. Perhaps there still was. The thought made Alex clamp his teeth together with unreasoned fury. And perhaps now he was molesting her, though he was speaking quietly to her. Perhaps he was making suggestions . . .

And then another thought struck Alex.

Of course. But of course! It would explain everything. The whole ghastly atmosphere that had pervaded tea so that he was not certain if he had eaten food or cardboard. But it seemed an unbelievable idea. Looking at the two of them over at the pianoforte, it seemed unbelievable. Looking at Tess, it seemed impossible.

When the Fowlers were taking their leave, he took Verity by the hand to lead her outside to see them on their way. He asked Siân to stay where she was. It was perhaps not a wise thing to have done, he thought as he took his daughter back upstairs to the nursery and left her in the charge of her nurse. Siân had been looking upset, but he was hardly the one to comfort her. And the rest was none of his business.

It was going to be dangerous to be alone

with her.

He stepped into the drawing room and closed the door quietly behind himself. She was still seated at the pianoforte. She did not look up.

"The second song was lovely," he said. "It was familiar. 'The Ash Grove,' did you say? What did you call it? It began with that most unpronounceable of Welsh sounds."

" '*Llwyn On,*' " she said. "It sounds lovelier with a harp accompaniment."

"That is what you will be singing at the festival?" he asked.

"Yes," she said.

"Siân" — he stopped beside the pianoforte and rested his elbow on it — "I am sorry that you had to put up with such bad manners and such well-bred insults."

"It does not matter," she said.

"It does." He searched her impassive face. She was still looking down at the keyboard. "He was saying something to upset you. Was he insulting you?"

"No," she said.

He could not leave it alone. He could not mind his own business. He could not stay out of her life. "What is he to you?" he asked quietly.

She rubbed one finger over a key without depressing it and then looked up at him, her eyes huge and blank. "He fathered me," she said.

The way she expressed the relationship said volumes. "Ah." He nodded. "Then I was not mistaken. He turned you off when your mother died?"

"He turned me off," she said. "I turned myself off. We never could like each other. He resented me — perhaps for being conceived in the first place, certainly for always being in the way when he visited my mother. I resented him — perhaps for begetting me and stranding me in a world shared by no one except my mother and me. When Mam died, there was nothing left between us except mutual dislike."

And yet she did not look indifferent. There had been more than that, even if she did not know it herself.

"He made no attempt," he asked, "to look after you? After spending a great deal of money on your education?"

"He had a marriage planned for me," she said. "I would have been caught forever between two worlds. I don't think he ever understood that. Provided one is safe and well cared for, one must be happy. He has no imagination."

Alex had an uncomfortable memory of offering to make it worth her while to become his mistress. Of offering to strand her forever between two worlds.

"Whom did he want you to marry?" he asked.

She smiled fleetingly, though there was no amusement in the expression. "Josiah Barnes," she said.

He felt a little as if someone had punched him in the stomach. No imagination? she had said. Fowler must be a complete block-head. And another question flashed into his head.

"How did you end up working in the mine?" he asked. "Your grandfather and your uncle, I understand, are both at the ironworks. I have also learned since coming here that working in the mine gives a person a lower status than working at the ironworks. You had the worst job of all for a woman."

"I preferred it," she said, "to the alternative."

"Did Barnes give you the job?" he asked.

"He said there was nothing else available," she said. "It was take it or leave it. I took it."

"Your grandfather was unable to support you?" he asked.

She looked at him steadily. "I had lived a life of privilege," she said. "To anyone who had not lived it, it would have seemed that I had a far better life than most of my peers. I had something to prove — to my family, to the people of Cwmbran, and to myself."

He gazed at her, trying to imagine what it must have been like. What if he suddenly had to leave the life he had always lived in order to work in that coal mine, harnessed to a heavy coal cart in dust and darkness all day? He thought it altogether possible that his spirit would be broken in no time at all. Yet Siân Jones had done more than survive. She looked back at him with pride and dignity.

"It was not as bad as it may sound," she said. "You cannot imagine, perhaps, how I had yearned all my life to belong to my mother's people. She used to tell me stories about them and about her life as a girl. I longed for it. Here." She spread a hand over her left breast. "You would not be able to understand. Most people would not. The longing to be a part of something, no matter what the cost."

"Hiraeth," he said softly.

She laughed unexpectedly and then sobered again. "Not quite," she said. "But something like that."

"The cost was a few years of your life in the mine," he said.

"Yes." Her eyes grew luminous. "And my

269

Dafydd."

"Your husband?" he asked.

"My son," she said. "He never breathed. He was so perfect. So very perfect. But too small. He came too early. He never breathed."

Alex felt robbed of breath. He could feel her pain like a tangible thing. And he was not sure what sort of Pandora's box he had opened with his curiosity. She was being transformed before his eyes from a lovely and desirable woman into a very real person. Something in him wanted to stop her. He did not really want to know her. He did not want the burden of the knowledge. He could not have explained to himself why that was.

Perhaps because knowledge might transform his feelings from simple desire to — something else? And feeling something else for her would only complicate his life impossibly.

But it was too late to stop her or his own need to know.

"He told me," she said, "that he would not have allowed me to go back down the mine if he had known I was going to have a baby. But he had never made any inquiries at all. He had never shown any interest."

He had missed something essential. She

was looking down at the keyboard again and was scrubbing at one of the keys.

"You worked," he asked, "when you were pregnant?"

"Gwyn died," she said. When she looked up at him suddenly, her eyes were brimming with tears. "We needed the money. His dada was already home with the coughing sickness and Iestyn was still too young to be earning much. Gran and Grandad stormed at me and Uncle Emrys too, but I went. I had to prove that I was one of them. But I think it was the working that brought on my time too soon. He was dead. He never even had a chance to live. He was dead."

God! He watched a tear spill over from each eye and roll down her cheeks. He felt frozen to the spot. He could not even reach for her and hold her. The loneliness of her memories and her grief was too intense.

"Why were you allowed to work if you were pregnant?" he asked after a while. He was whispering, he realized.

"There is no rule against it," she said. "Sometimes it is necessary."

Lord God. "Is it still happening?" he asked. "Do you know of any woman right now who is with child and pulling one of those carts?"

"Yes." She scrubbed at one tear with the

back of her hand. "Blodwyn Williams. Her husband is injured and they have a little one to feed."

Alex felt as if all his insides had turned to ice. He stared down at her bowed head.

"*Who* would not have allowed you back down the mine if he had known?" he asked.

"Him," she said. "Sir John Fowler. He said it just a little while ago, standing where you are now. As if he cared. Just as if he cared."

"Perhaps he did," he said.

"There was not a word," she said, "after I had gone to live with Grandad and when I went to work in the mine. Not a word when I married Gwyn. Or when he was killed. Or when Dafydd was born dead. His own grandson, he was, my little one. Not a word. Or in the years since. Nothing until today. Yet he said he would have stopped me going back down the mine if he had known. Does he expect me to believe that he cares?"

"Perhaps, Siân," Alex said, "he really wanted to provide for you the best he could. He could not take you into his own home. He had a wife and daughter there. He planned a marriage for you. To a man with little imagination, it would have seemed a good marriage. Barnes has a steady job and a good income. He has considerable power. Perhaps your — father was hurt when you rejected his plans and returned to your mother's people."

"Hurt." She laughed a little. "Hurt."

"I am sorry," he said, "that I unwittingly brought you into this situation today. I had no idea."

"Well" — she got to her feet at last — "you had no way of knowing. I will be going home. It is late."

"And I am sorry about the child," he said. "I believe it must be about the most devastating thing that can happen to a woman. I am sorry, Siân."

"It was a long time ago," she said. "Perhaps I will have — I am going to be married next month."

Perhaps she would have Parry's child nine months after next month.

"Yes," he said softly, reminded again of what he had tried not to think of.

"It is what I want," she said. "It is what will make me happy." She sounded defensive, as if she thought he was going to argue with her or question her motives.

"I am glad for you," he said, feeling anything but glad. Feeling somehow bereft. Feeling lonely. "If he can make you happy, Siân, I am glad for you."

"He will make me happy," she said. "I am happy. I love him."

He nodded and straightened up from his position against the pianoforte. He realized that she was finding it difficult to walk from the room, not sure if she had been dismissed or not.

"Come," he said, "I'll see you out."

But he stopped her with a hand on her elbow before opening the drawing room door. "Siân," he said, "the singing really was beautiful. I had to call on all my powers of self-restraint not to throttle Lady Fowler when she so rudely talked above your singing."

She turned her head to smile at him, amusement in her face this time. She looked not only beautiful, but pretty too when she smiled like that.

"I believe," he said, "you cannot fail to take first place at your festival this year."

"But you have not heard the opposition," she said.

"I don't need to," he said. "I am highly partial. There could not be another contestant with a lovelier voice or one who sings with such feeling that I find myself fighting tears."

She actually laughed. "Perhaps," she said, "I should try to have you appointed adjudicator. Sole adjudicator."

He chuckled and opened the door. He had

felt the need to do something to rid her of the stricken look she had worn since walking into the drawing room and seeing Fowler there.

"I will try what bribery and corruption will do instead," he said. "Not that they will be needed. I want to come and hear you sing and see you win, Siân." The words were unintentional, but he realized that he meant them.

The laughter died from her face, though there was still a glow of warmth in her eyes. "Everything will be in Welsh," she said. "You would be horribly bored."

"Then you must be my interpreter," he said. "Besides, the language of music is universal. And besides again, Verity has her heart set on going, and who am I, a mere father, to fight the will of a six-year-old child?"

"You would have to take your carriage the long way around the heads of the valleys," she said. "You would never be able to walk over the mountain with the rest of us. You are used to soft living."

He stopped at the outer door, which a servant was holding open. "If ever I heard a challenge," he said, "that is it. If I do find the climb beyond my strength, perhaps you and Verity will take a hand each and drag

275

me to the top. You can roll me down the other side."

Laughter was back in her eyes and spilled over into sound. She turned away to leave the house.

"Good afternoon, Mrs. Jones," he said. He stood in the doorway for a while, watching her walk down the driveway to the gates. His smile faded. There, he had fallen into temptation again. He had committed himself to going with his people — and with her people — to their festival. He must learn its Welsh name. He would ask Verity.

He had shared laughter with her, Alex thought. And pain. She was becoming precious to him. He recoiled in some alarm from the word his mind had chosen.

12

The street outside the chapel was so crammed with people that it made a body wonder there was enough air to go around — or so Mrs. Beynon was proclaiming loudly to anyone who would listen. Most people seemed more intent on talking than listening. And on laughing. Children were darting about among legs and skirts, playing hide-and-seek. Mothers were calling shrilly for them to come back and behave themselves. Occasionally the more authoritative voices of fathers would bring them slinking to heel for a minute or two until they were forgotten and could start the game again.

The scene had all the chaos and all the cheerfulness of a normal *eisteddfod* day. It always amazed Siân that everyone could be up and full of energy so very early in the morning — although it was light, the sun had not yet risen and the air was brisk with the morning chill. But there was scarcely a man, woman, or child of Cwmbran who was not there in the street waiting for the trek over the mountain to begin. Inside the open chapel door stood Glenys Richards's harp, which would be loaded onto a little cart made especially for it as soon as the street had begun to clear, and hauled over the mountain by Ifor Richards and his two sons. Glenys always insisted on taking her own harp to the *eisteddfod*. It was a very good thing that the organist was not so particular, many people joked.

"Where is the Reverend Llewellyn?" Ianto Pritchard asked loudly enough for many people around him to hear. "Still sleeping, is he? Who will come with me to his house to give him the old heave-ho, then?"

There was cheering and laughter. The idea of entering the preacher's house in order to turn him out of bed was one that tickled all but the most deeply devout among them. But they were not to discover if anyone would have been bold enough to do it. The Reverend Llewellyn, clad in his best clerical black and newly polished black boots despite the long walk and climb he faced once in the morning and once again in the evening, appeared in the chapel doorway and raised both arms for silence. He got it almost instantly.

"Let us pray," he said, his practiced orator's voice carrying clearly to the most distant member of his flock.

Every head was instantly bowed. Even Emrys's, Siân noticed as she dipped her own and as Owen's hand took hers and he laced their fingers.

They had not come after all, Siân thought as the minister prayed. She had not seen the marquess since that disastrous afternoon when she had been invited to tea. But Verity had assured her that they were to come. She had been beside herself with excitement all week. He must have decided after all that it would not be appropriate. Siân tried to tell herself that the feeling she had was not disappointment. Or if it was, she thought, it was disappointment for Verity's sake. She had so wanted the treat.

"Well, well," Owen said when the long prayer was finally at an end and the massed "Amen" had given place to jokes and laughter and more shrill yelling at children impatient to be on their way. "To what do we owe the honor, I wonder?"

When Siân looked in the direction of his nodded head, it was to see the Marquess of Craille at the far edge of the crowd, Verity up on one of his shoulders. The child spot-

279

ted her at the same moment and waved with sunny enthusiasm. Siân had not mentioned to Owen that they were planning to come.

"I know they have heard the male voice choir practicing," she said. "I think they must be coming to cheer you on, Owen."

"Well," he said, tightening the pressure of his fingers about hers, "this is a holiday for you, *fach*. He can look after the child today. You will stay by me, is it?"

"Of course." She smiled at him. A dazzling smile, which she knew was not quite natural.

"And perhaps," he said, "they are coming to hear you sing. Have you sung for them at the castle?"

"Yes," she said. "I told you that I am to teach Verity music. I am given an hour each day to practice on the pianoforte. I have taken her downstairs a few times for a singing lesson."

"And him?" he asked. "You have sung for him, Siân?"

She wished she could control her blush. But she could feel her cheeks grow hot.

"He had me bring her down for tea one afternoon," she said, "when there were — visitors. He asked me to sing."

The crowd was moving off up the street in the direction of the hills. It would take them a good three hours to reach the next town, less than five miles away over the mountain as the crow flies. But they would be there in time for the opening of the *eisteddfod*. A town would be shamed indeed if its people walked late into the pavilion.

"I am nervous," Siân said. "Are you, Owen?"

"I have a whole choir to hide myself among," he said. "But you don't need to be nervous, *cariad*. A lovelier voice there is not in these valleys. You would have won last year if there had been any justice in Wales."

Siân laughed and remembered doing the same with the Marquess of Craille the last time she saw him when he had threatened to use bribery and corruption on the judges of the soprano solo competition. And when he had offered to let her and Verity roll him down the hill. Despite herself, she searched for him in the crowd, and found that he was quite close by.

"Wretched boys," Ifor Richards was proclaiming fiercely from the chapel doorway while Glenys stood beside him, wringing her hands. "Run away to hide, they have, because there is work to do. A good hiding I will give them both when I get my hands on them."

"I will not use that harp they have over by

281

there," Glenys wailed. "It will not fit my fingers and I will shame myself and all of Cwmbran by making errors."

"Hush, woman," Ifor said, his look thunderous.

Owen laughed, but even as he released Siân's hand to lend his help, he was forestalled.

"What seems to be the problem?" the marquess asked.

"It is this bloody harp that is the problem," Ifor said, too exasperated to be cowed by the identity of the man who questioned him but switching to English nonetheless. "Don't ask me why they can't manufacture something that makes the same sound but can be tucked nice and tidy under the arm. And Glenys will play only this one — as if every harp that was ever made was not exactly the same. So over the mountain it has to be carried, all five tons of it. A little cart I have put together to make the task easier, and two boys I have begotten to help their dada humor their mam. And where are they? Romping with the other boys, they are, with never a care in the world. There is sore their bums will be when my hand has finished with them. And trews down for it too."

Owen's shoulders were shaking, and Siân was biting hard on her upper lip. Poor Ifor would not appreciate laughter at this precise moment. Glenys looked as if she was about to have hysterics.

The marquess was grinning broadly. "Perhaps I can help," he said. "It looks to me as if two men will be enough for the job — one to pull the cart and one to hold the harp steady. Shall I do the latter?"

"Oh, *Duw, Duw!*" Glenys, hands to cheeks, whispered loudly in Welsh. "No, Ifor. It is the Marquess of Craille."

"If Cwmbran is not to be shamed over the mountain by turning up with a harpist and no harp," Ifor said, "I would accept the help of the King of England, if there was one. Right-o, man. We lift it as gentle as we can onto the cart and then bounce it all over the mountain, is it? There is a stupid thing it is to be married to a harpist, I tell you."

"Verity." The marquess looked around him and then directly at Siân, so that she realized that he had known she was there. Perhaps it was her he had been approaching. "Take Mrs. Jones's hand, will you, and promise me that you will not get lost."

And so when they started up the mountain, she and Owen, Verity was between them, holding a hand of each, and prattling excitedly. Owen looked ruefully at Siân and raised his eyebrows.

■ ■ ■ ■

Before they reached the top of the mountain, Alex was in his shirtsleeves, his coat hanging over the harp. And he was enjoying himself immensely. He had spent a few weeks wandering about the works by day and even visiting a few of the people of Cwmbran, in an attempt to get to know them and their concerns. It had all been without apparent success. And yet now, toiling up the mountain with the unwieldy harp and the useless cart — it would have been a great deal easier if the two of them had just slung the harp over their shoulders, he thought — and the exasperated Ifor Richards, he suddenly felt a part of it all. An outer part, perhaps, and one that could never fully belong, but a part, nevertheless. And accepted by the people among whom he moved.

He was the butt of merciless teasing and laughter by both men and women. Even one group of children danced about the cart, hands linked, and chanted at him to play them a tune on the harp before Glenys Richards shooed them away, looking as if she was about to have a heart attack. Alex was not sure if her concern was for him or her precious harp.

It made him feel good to be teased. He could not be quite hated if they teased him.

"Oh, ho," one wag said, "off comes the coat now. Next it will be the shirt and you will be expected to take it to your scrubbing board, Glenys Richards."

"But a lovely set of muscles, mind," a woman said. "Showing them off, he is, taking his coat off."

"Pretty soon," another man said, "it will be the marquess you will have on that cart, Ifor, and the harp left on the mountain to pick up on the way back. Pretty red in the face he is looking, muscles notwithstanding."

"One thing if his heart stops," someone else added. "He will be let straight into heaven because he will have a harp to play."

They all took the trouble to speak English so that he would know how he was being insulted.

"Perhaps," he said, "I will be posted beside St. Peter at the pearly gate so that I can help him keep out the rabble Welsh when they try to get in."

"There is a wit he has," the first man said. "You had better save your breath for holding the harp, man. Glenys will beat you about the head with it if you let it fall."

"Oh, *Duw, Duw,*" Glenys said.

The Richards boys appeared at the top of the mountain when the worst part of the exertion was over. They claimed to have lost their parents in the crowd.

"And lost the bloody harp too, did you?" their father asked them. "Two blind boys I have been raising and did not know it. Never mind, boys. I will lead you by the hand out the back when we get home tonight, one at a time. Sleeping on your bellies you will be all night, the both of you. Too sore you will be to lie on your backs."

"Oh, Dada," they protested in chorus.

Alex chuckled inwardly and wandered away. Almost everyone was taking a rest at the top, he noticed, and dipping into the contents of the picnic baskets most of them had brought with them. He strolled a little apart and for the first time was aware of his surroundings. He had not been to the top of the mountain before. The land fell away to either side of him over grass- and heather-covered hills to two valley floors, each with its river winding away into the southern distance, each with its little town snaking out along the narrow valley and its smokestacks and coal tips and giant colliery wheels. Farther north, on the Cwmbran side of the valley, he could see Penybont.

The scenery was wild and quite breathtakingly beautiful. One thing was certain at least, he thought. Man could not compete with God in the creation of beauty.

And then he looked down to smile at Verity, who had come running up to his side and had taken his hand. Siân was with her, he saw. He smiled at her too.

"We saw that you were free," she said. "I thought I had better bring Verity back to you."

"Thank you for watching her," he said. "I had more important things to take my attention. Mrs. Richards's harp." He laughed.

"Oh, yes," she said. "It is her most prized possession, and that includes Ifor Richards and her two boys." She laughed too.

"Is that the harp that will accompany you?" he asked.

She nodded.

"Then I am very glad that I risked life and limb to get it up here," he said. "I believe the boys will help their father down the other side with it in an effort to avert this evening's promised spanking."

"I am going to play with those children from the Sunday School again," Verity said, pointing, and ran off.

"Are you nervous?" Alex asked Siân.

"Yes." She smiled. "Every year I swear I

will never do it again. I feel sick with fear."

"You will be wonderful," he said. "You will win." He wondered if she realized how very beautiful she looked with her hair blowing free behind her in the wind at the top of the mountain, and her best dress flattened against her curves and blowing out behind.

"Winning is not really the point," she said. "Taking part is. I must get back to Owen." She turned and hurried back to where Owen Parry was standing with a group of men.

It had been a mistake to summon the man to the castle, Alex realized now. Parry, he felt, was his implacable enemy. It was a shame. Undoubtedly he was looked up to by the other men. He was a leader.

Alex wished matters could move faster. In the weeks since his coming to Cwmbran he had uncovered a whole host of facts that disturbed him. If he had his way, a great deal would have been changed by now. The lives of his workers and their families would have improved beyond recognition. But it was no easy matter to accomplish. Barnes balked on every issue, and on each he had a reasonable argument for delay or even abandonment. The most powerful argument was that things were done the same at all the works. Nothing could be changed unilaterally or chaos would result.

Then there must be a meeting for all the owners, Alex had said at last in exasperation. He would put his ideas to everyone. Surely everyone would want to bring about changes when they knew the facts. Sometimes being in one place for years was a disadvantage. It could make one unaware of what was going on under one's very nose. He would be able to contribute his fresh insight to the group.

Barnes was organizing a meeting to take place at Glanrhyd Castle next week. Then things would change, Alex thought. Then men like Owen Parry would realize that he was not after all the enemy. Then the people of Cwmbran would lose interest in the Chartist movement, which was apparently moving into a new and potentially threatening phase. His sources had informed Alex that leaders all over the country were now trying to organize mass riots. And one rumor had it that it was South Wales that had been chosen to lead the way.

But this was not the day to worry about such matters. This was a day to be enjoyed. And he was enjoying it, he thought, strolling back along the top as everyone began the descent, their rest period over. Despite everything, he was growing fond of this isolated and lovely part of the world.

He was enjoying himself despite the fact that Siân Jones's hand was in Owen Parry's and Parry bent his head to kiss her briefly. Alex pursed his lips. He would swear that the kiss was for his benefit. Parry was putting the stamp of his possession on Verity's governess.

Although Emrys Rhys was thirty-five years old, he was still a handsome man. His straight dark hair was still untainted with gray and was still as thick as it had ever been. He was still lean and hard-muscled. He still drew admiring glances from the women of the other valleys and soon had one of them clinging to his arm and laughing and chatting with him.

Angharad felt a pang of regret that she could not somehow combine his best qualities with those of Josiah Barnes — Emrys's good looks and virile strength and Mr. Barnes's power and money and house.

Angharad wanted to scratch the eyes out of the other woman, who was not even pretty in her estimation. She could not understand what Emrys saw in her.

And yet she did not care either, she told herself. Pretty soon now Mr. Barnes was going to realize just how comfortable she made his home. And he was going to realize that it would be far more pleasant to have her in his bed all night every night than for just brief snatches of time in the afternoons.

Let Emrys have his woman, whoever she was. Angharad did not care.

And yet in the pavilion, when all the Cwmbran people were seating themselves in a block together, the better to cheer their own, Angharad took the empty chair beside Emrys quite by accident — she was looking the other way as she did so, waving enthusiastically to some imaginary friend.

"Oh," she said, turning her head when she was seated, "it is you, is it?"

"Hello, Angharad," he said. "You are looking very pretty today."

His eyes had a way of looking her over from head to toe so that she felt warmed and caressed. She had forgotten it.

"Oh," she said tartly, "I am surprised you have noticed, Emrys Rhys. You seemed to have eyes only for the woman who was hanging on your arm outside."

He smiled at her. "Jealous, are you, Angharad?" he asked.

"Jealous?" She tossed her head. "You can have two women on each arm and it will not matter to me. I have my own interests."

"Yes." The teasing smile faded from his

face and he looked toward the stage, where the first competition was about to begin. "Yes, and so you do, Angharad. We had better be quiet or we will be frowned on by Cwmbran and hissed at by everyone else."

"I have nothing to say to you anyway, I am sure," Angharad said.

She sat silently at his side, stealing glances at his hands — strong, capable hands, their backs dotted with dark hairs, the square, short fingernails kept clean despite his job. And she remembered that whenever he had made love to her up on the mountain, he had always kissed her and whispered love nonsense to her while doing it and had always taken his time over it so that she could enjoy what everyone knew was really meant only for a man's pleasure. The only other two men she had known — her husband and Josiah Barnes — had always gone at it hard and fast.

Sometimes she longed for some of Emrys's tenderness again.

But she wanted more out of life than Emrys could offer. Mr. Barnes was her ticket to a better life.

After the first competition, when everyone got up to stretch and move about, Emrys found a different place to sit.

Angharad wiped away a tear with one

knuckle. She did not care.

The soprano section of the solo competitions came last. Siân could have wished it was first so that she might have enjoyed the other three sections. And by the time her turn came the weight of responsibility was heavy on her shoulders. Cwmbran had taken second in both the tenor and baritone solos and an ignominious fourth in the contralto solo because Dilys Jenkins folded under the pressure of competition and breathed in all the wrong places.

Siân, cold and clammy and sick with dread, lost her fear as she usually did once she was standing on the stage looking down at the audience and once she heard the familiar opening bars of *"Llwyn On"* on Glenys's harp. She forgot everything except responding with her voice to the beauty of the music and the poignancy of the words.

Always the most wonderful moment came at the end when the large audience applauded politely and the Cwmbran segment of the pavilion erupted in cheers and whistles and stampings. Siân always knew that it was for themselves and their own pride that they cheered more than for her individual performance, but that was the very fact that was precious about it. She never felt more a part of the community than she did at such a moment.

And this year that sense of belonging was to be multiplied ten-fold. For the first time the judges placed her first and the Cwmbran part of the pavilion went wild. Before they had all spilled outside while the stage was being set up for the next competition, Siân marveled that she had an unbroken bone left in her body. She had been hugged and kissed by almost everyone she knew and even by a few that she hardly knew at all. She had, it seemed, done Cwmbran proud.

Owen swept her up outside the pavilion and twirled her about before kissing her hard. And then Emrys and Huw and Iestyn and several other men she knew from the mine converged on her and lifted her up bodily until she was riding, laughing and clinging, on the shoulders of two of them.

"There is proud I am of you, *fach*," Emrys said when her feet were finally on the ground again. He held her in a bear hug for a few moments and kissed her loudly on one cheek. "I am going all around now, bragging that my niece is the winner of the soprano solo."

"Siân" — Iestyn smiled at her and hugged her — "you sang like an angel."

Huw kissed her heartily on the lips. "Gwyn

would be proud of you today, Siân," he said. "I am proud of you, girl."

And then it was Mari's turn and Siân's grandparents'. Her grandmother had tears in her eyes.

"Siân," she said, hugging her granddaughter, "you came by it honestly, *fach*. Marged had a lovely voice. It did my heart good to hear you in there."

It would be hard to remember a happier moment, Siân thought.

"Mrs. Jones. Mrs. Jones." Someone was tugging at her skirt. "I knew you would win. I just knew it. I told you, didn't I? The other ladies didn't sing nearly as well as you. I am going to tell everyone that you are my teacher."

Siân bent down to hug Verity. "Thank you," she said. "I am so very happy."

"Mrs. Jones. Many congratulations. It was a well-deserved win."

She smiled radiantly at the Marquess of Craille as he took both her hands in his, squeezed them tightly, and raised them one at a time to his lips.

"Thank you." She swayed toward him and lifted her face to his as she had done to a few dozen people before him — both men and women.

He kissed her. Briefly and fully on the lips.

It felt rather like being doused with water. Or more appropriately, perhaps, with fire. She realized what she had done, what she had invited, what she had forced him into, only when it was a few seconds too late to do differently. And having realized it, it was too late also to proceed in the only way that might have given the incident its least significance. She gripped his hands convulsively, felt herself blush from her toenails to the roots of her hair, and let her smile fall away to oblivion.

And then he released his hands from her hold and turned away.

Fortunately, there were a few other people crowding up to hug her and congratulate her.

The male voice choir competition as usual was both the climax and the highlight of the day. And as usual Cwmbran defeated their closest and bitterest rival by a few points — won by their tenor soloist in *"Hiraeth,"* the adjudicator explained. And so it was the tenor who was hoisted to shoulders and borne in triumph out of town and to the foot of the mountain on the way home in the late twilight. Three firsts for Cwmbran — Siân Jones, little Lloyd Pritchard in the children's recitation, and the male voice choir. It had been a happy day, a day to make one proud.

Darkness fell as they toiled up the mountain, the children far more subdued than they had been that morning — a few of them rode their fathers' shoulders. But it was not a deep darkness, the sky being clear and star-studded. The moon would be up before they reached the top, someone predicted.

"Well, *fach*." Owen's arm was about Siân's waist. "I get to escort the heroine of the day, do I?"

She laughed. "Your choir won too, Owen," she said. "I felt goose bumps when you sang."

"I am glad you won," he said. "You should have won last year too."

"It did feel good, I must admit," she said. "Everyone was very kind afterward."

He was silent for a while. "Craille is lucky I did not ram his teeth down his throat," he said. "Could you not have avoided that grand display he made, Siân?"

She had hoped that by some miracle Owen had not been watching. "His congratulations?" she said. "But everyone was congratulating me, Owen, and hugging and kissing me."

"On both hands and the lips?" he said.

"People will be talking, Siân. I don't like it. You are my woman and pretty soon I am going to have to start using my fists to stop the gossiping. But you are not doing much to help."

"Don't spoil the day," she said. But it was already spoiled. "No one is talking. There is nothing to talk about. He was happy for me. Everyone was happy for me. I think there can be scarcely a man in Cwmbran who did not kiss me after the winner was announced. And what do you mean by saying I am not doing much to help?"

"I am beginning to look like a fool," he said, "who cannot control my own woman."

"Don't," she said again, distress turning to annoyance. "I don't like it when you talk tough, Owen. I don't like being talked about as if I am a possession to be controlled, as you put it, by my owner."

"I think perhaps," he said, "Gwyn was too soft with you, Siân. Perhaps because you are Fowler's daughter and were educated in an English school and everybody thinks you are something a little bit special. You won't find me so easy to rule. You had better learn that now."

"What exactly am I meant to learn?" She could hear her voice shaking.

"That you are mine," he said. "That you

will not shame me by giving anyone even the whisper of a chance to link your name with any other man's. That you will learn to toe the line if you know what is good for you."

"I think you had better complete that thought," she said, "so that you can be quite sure that I understand you, Owen. If I know what is good for me. What would not be good for me? What if I do not — toe the line?"

"I don't want to quarrel," he said. "Let's leave it at that, Siân. We should be enjoying our triumph now, not going at each other's throats. We haven't quarreled before, have we? I didn't mean to spoil the day for you, *fach.*"

"What would happen," she asked, "if I did not toe what you perceived to be the line, Owen?"

He tutted. "A stubborn woman you are, Siân Jones," he said. "I am going to have my hands full with you, aren't I, *fach*? I will not put my hand to you unless you force me to it. There. Are you satisfied now? I am not a drinking man, Siân, or one given to sudden rages. And you are right. Everyone was kissing you and I did not think to object until he did it. He makes my blood boil if the truth were known. At least we know where we stand with Barnes. This man is pretending to be our friend just so that he can keep us beneath his broad thumb without our even realizing we are there. I hate that kind of hypocrisy."

I think he does care. Siân was about to say the words aloud, but she kept her mouth closed. She did not want to discuss the Marquess of Craille with Owen. He would not agree with her opinion anyway and perhaps he would twist the facts to distort her own image. He would accuse the marquess of slyness or oppression, for example, in stopping Blodwyn Williams from going to work while she was pregnant and in paying Blodwyn's husband compensation for the injury he had got at work — something no other owner had ever done.

Besides, she did not want to talk at all for a while. All the joy had gone out of her day. *I will not put my hand to you unless you force me to it.* She could not think of anything she would find more degrading than to be beaten by Owen, or any man. And yet if she forced him into it — or if he perceived that she had forced him — he would do it. She would have no recourse. He would be her husband in less than a month's time. He would have the right to discipline her in any way he saw fit.

Everyone was stopping on top of the mountain, as they had done in the morning, though not for a picnic this time. They were stopping for the traditional *gymanfa ganu*, the community singing that was always the windup to *eisteddfod* day. Glenys's harp would be set up, and everyone would sing in the moonlight until tiredness and good sense sent them trickling down the mountain in twos and threes and family groups toward their beds and sleep.

It was the part of the day Siân had looked forward to since her win. Now it was all spoiled. Now she wished she could just continue on down the hill. She disengaged herself from Owen's arm and went to sit with some of the women.

13

Alex was sitting apart from everyone else and out of sight of them too, behind an outcropping of rock. He sat with his knees drawn up, his arms draped over them, looking down to the moonlit valley that had somehow come to feel like home. He had stolen some moments for himself, Verity having attached herself to a group of Sunday School children who were now sitting in a ring among the adults, singing with them.

He was not feeling lonely. Not really. Certainly not in any unpleasant way. In fact he was feeling remarkably happy. And at peace with himself and the world and quite ready to tackle the hard task facing him in the coming week. He had been privileged today, he felt, and more thankful than he could express that Verity had pressed him to come and that he had given in all too readily.

What was happening there on the mountaintop should be hilariously funny. Almost a whole town was camped out there in the moonlight when they could be tucked up cozily in their beds, singing in glorious harmony. Glenys Richards was seated in full state at her harp, its little cart standing close by under the guardianship of her husband. And the Reverend Llewellyn, still immaculate in clerical black, was conducting with his baton.

It should have been funny, but it was not. It was expressive of the whole warm and wonderful culture into which he had stepped quite unsuspectingly just a few weeks ago. The sounds of harp music and singing somehow blended with the wild landscape and the moonlight. Man in tune with nature — despite the industry that was raping their valley down below.

The lives of these people were hard, he knew, and he was responsible for having made them harder than they need be. But even so they seemed to have the capacity to live and to love and to reach beyond themselves for what was permanent and beautiful. They were a people who had added a spiritual dimension to lives that might have been unutterably dreary. He was glad suddenly that he had it within his power to improve their daily lives. Soon. Starting next week, as soon as he had met with the other owners.

He looked up suddenly as someone came around the rock that shielded him from view. He expected to see Verity, but it was Siân. She stopped when she saw him but did not retreat. She appeared to be alone.

"Come and sit down," he said, and was surprised when she did so, without saying a word. She sat down quite close to him and clasped her knees with her arms.

"You are not singing with everyone else?" he asked.

She shook her head.

"It has been a wonderful day," he said. "There is a warm and strong sense of community in this part of the world."

"Yes," she said. "It means a great deal to be a part of it."

"And yet there is a mingling of communities too," he said with a smile. "I noticed that your brother-in-law was a great favorite with the girls from the other towns today. He was hand-in-hand with one of them before the day was out."

"Iestyn?" she said. "Yes. There will doubtless be many treks over the mountain for him in the coming weeks. The girl will be fortunate who wins Iestyn's heart."

"You are fond of him," he said.

"He was just twelve years old when I married his brother," she said. "He wanted so badly to go to school and to college. He wanted to be a minister. He used to try to learn what I remembered from school and taught him. But he never complains. He smiles his way through life."

They were quiet for a while. Companionably quiet while music surrounded them.

"This is all so beautiful," he said, indicating the valley with one arm. "Peaceful. It is well worth the climb."

She nodded and lifted her face to the moonlight. Her eyes were closed, he saw.

"Has something happened?" he asked. "To send you away from everyone else, I mean?" He did not believe she had come seeking him.

She opened her eyes and looked at him. "No," she said. "Nothing has happened. Just reaction to the excitement of the day, I think. I wanted to be alone."

"And I had stolen your spot," he said. "Do you want me to go away?"

She shook her head.

"It was a wonderful day for you," he said. "I was very happy that you won."

"Thank you," she said, and grasped her knees more tightly so that she could rest her cheek on them.

She wanted quietness, he saw, and gave it to her. He leaned back against the rock so that he could watch her. It was hard to tell if she was tired or peaceful or unhappy. She had her eyes closed again. But she was not uncomfortable in his company, as he might have expected her to be. And her presence only added to his contentment. It was the icing on the cake of a happy day.

It was a dangerous realization. If he had felt desire for her or the temptation to touch her and make love to her, he would have understood the feelings and fought them off. They were what he would expect to feel. But he felt neither, only a quiet pleasure to be sitting close to her in companionable silence.

Yes, it was dangerous, suggesting as it did that she was becoming to him more than a beautiful woman whom he desired to bed.

"Would you ever beat a woman who was your wife?" she asked suddenly without opening her eyes.

"Good Lord, no," he said, jolted by the sheer unexpectedness of the question. "I have never even laid a hand on my daughter."

"You don't believe there is the need for discipline?" she asked.

"Yes, of course," he said. "But there are

other ways of disciplining apart from violence."

"How would you discipline a wife, then?" she asked. Her eyes were open and she was looking at him, though she had not lifted her cheek from her knee.

"A wife?" He frowned. "I was talking about children. Unfortunately we need to discipline children because we have a responsibility to train them and they are never angels. I was not talking about a wife. A wife is a man's equal."

"But what if she does not toe the line?" she asked.

"What line?" he said. "Whose line? What if he does not toe it? Marriage is not an easy business. We have both experienced it. We both know that. It is something that has to be worked hard at every single day. If one partner refuses to make the effort, then they have a problem and an unhappy marriage. But violence would not solve anything."

"Is the husband not always right?" she asked. She spoke so quietly that he could not tell if there was bitterness in her voice. "Is he not the one who must enforce the toeing of his line?"

"Just because he is probably the physically stronger of the two?" he said. "It would seem a little unfair, would it not?"

"Life is not always fair," she said. "Especially to women."

"Do you know someone who is beating his wife?" he asked. "Is that what this is all about? If so, perhaps you had better tell me who he is. Perhaps I can bring pressure to bear on him."

"By threatening his job?" she said. "No, it was just a question. I was curious." She sat up suddenly, setting her hands flat on the grass on either side of her. "It has been a happy day. You were right. A wonderful day. And especially happy for me. I have always dreamed of winning a first at the *eisteddfod,* though I always persuaded myself that participating was the important thing. It was wonderful to win — for myself and for Cwmbran."

He acted purely from instinct. He set his own hand flat on top of hers. "But you are not quite happy," he said.

She turned her head to look at him "Yes, I am," she said quickly. "A little tired. Suffering from some reaction. But happy. I will be very happy when I wake up tomorrow and remember."

He wondered where Owen Parry was. The two of them were to be married soon. And there was a mountaintop to lose themselves on and moonlight in which to kiss, and a triumph to be celebrated. Why was she alone — and not altogether happy?

"I am happy," she said very softly. "Just being here, quiet like this, after all the excitement. This is the happiest time of the day."

He guessed that she acted with as little thought as he had when he had set his hand on top of hers. She turned her hand beneath his, leaving it spread, so that their palms and their fingers touched.

She seemed to remain unconscious of what she had done. They stayed silent for a long while until she sighed — a sound of contentment.

"I wish it could go on forever," she said. "Don't you sometimes wish certain moments could be frozen in time?"

"Yes," he said.

"But they can't." She sighed again. "I had better go and find Owen. He will be wondering where I am. It is time to go home, I think."

"Yes." He did not move. She looked down at their hands as if she was seeing them for the first time. He lifted his away from hers. "Good night, Siân."

"Good night —" Her voice stumbled over the absence of a name.

"Alexander," he said. "It is my name. Alex."

She looked into his face for a while before getting to her feet and brushing at her skirt. "Good night," she said softly as she turned away.

He stayed where he was for a while, though he knew that soon he was going to have to go looking for Verity. He would doubtless have to carry her down the mountain. She had never been up so late.

Yes, very dangerous, he thought. He too had wanted the moment to be frozen in time. Just sitting together like that, in near silence, their hands touching. Nothing more. He had not desired her tonight. This night and these surroundings were too magical for passion. It was a night for companionship and tenderness. He had wanted it to go on forever.

He could not put a name to his feelings for her, he thought. Or perhaps it was just that he would not put a name to them.

Angharad had not really enjoyed the day. She was not with anyone in particular, and though no one shunned her, she felt lonely nonetheless. She had let her friendships lapse lately, she realized. A miner from Penybont had tried to flirt with her, and one or two other men would have done so with a little encouragement, but she had not been interested.

Emrys had had another woman on his arm all afternoon and had done a great deal of laughing with her.

The climb up the mountain in the evening was tedious. She was tired, Angharad thought. She wanted her bed. She wondered what it would be like to have a carriage to take her home and a grand house all of her own to be taken to. And a man who loved her waiting for her there. Not that love really mattered, of course. Love never got a person anywhere in this life.

Angharad stumbled awkwardly on a large boulder in the darkness and turned over on her ankle. Mrs. Bevan and Mrs. Davies clucked over her in some concern as she stopped to rub it, but it was a strong masculine hand that took her elbow in a firm clasp to steady her.

"Oh," she said, looking up at Emrys Rhys, "it's all right. It's not hurt bad."

The other ladies moved tactfully onward.

"But it's not easy to see where you are stepping in the darkness," he said. "Hold to my arm, Angharad."

"Are you missing the woman who was holding it this afternoon?" she asked him tartly. "She was very pretty, I am sure."

"Very," he said. "You *are* jealous."

"Hm." Angharad injected a world of scorn into the single syllable.

Her ankle was not very sore and it was not very dark. But they climbed slowly upward and fell far behind everyone else. They could hear Glenys's harp, and the singing was starting when they drew level with a small, sheltered hollow, almost a cave, well below the summit.

Angharad did not resist when Emrys drew her into it and backed her against the rock face. They had not spoken a word in ten minutes. They did not speak now. She lifted her face to him as her arms came about his neck and he wrapped his about her waist.

He kissed her long and deep.

"Are you willing, then, Angharad Lewis?" he asked against her mouth.

Sometimes nothing mattered except the needs of one's heart. "I am willing, Emrys Rhys," she whispered.

She lay down on the sparse grass, his coat beneath her head and shoulders, and lifted her skirt while he unbuttoned his trousers. She spread her legs for him when he came down to her. But being Emrys, he did not immediately come inside for his pleasure. He kissed her and caressed her and murmured to her, and then came in when she too was ready for pleasure. He took his own and gave her hers without hurry.

She had forgotten, Angharad thought when it was over. She had forgotten what she had given up. And now at this precise moment she could scarcely remember why.

They were singing in full harmony on top of the mountain.

Emrys spoke finally, after they had lain quietly side by side for several minutes. "We will make this honest, then, Angharad?" he said. "I will talk with the Reverend Llewellyn and I will step inside the chapel again at last — for a wedding."

Angharad closed her eyes and stayed silent. She tried to remember why she had finished stepping out with Emrys. She tried to picture the lodge cottage inside Glanrhyd Park and the happiness she felt there, making it comfortable and dreaming that it was hers. She tried to remember Josiah Barnes starting to look at her and touch her. And then telling her one day, when she had not flinched from having her breasts fondled, to go upstairs and undress and lie down on the bed. And the sudden hope of a dream come true. But sometimes dreams did not seem so attractive when they started to come true.

"You are sleeping with him, then?" Emrys's voice, flat in tone, cut through her indecision.

Angharad wanted to deny it. She wished she could. But she could not lie to Emrys. That was why she had had to stop seeing him even before she was sure of netting Josiah Barnes.

"Well." He got to his feet and stood with his back to her, buttoning up his trousers. He reached into a pocket and she heard the jingling of coins. And then a small shower of them landed with a plop on her stomach. "Thanks for the treat, Angharad. It's quite a while since I had a woman up on the mountain. I hope it's enough. I can't afford to pay as much as Barnes does."

Angharad bit down hard on both lips while he strode away, leaving his coat behind. She would not let out a sound while he was within earshot. Then she felt about until she had three pennies in her hand and pressed them hard, with both hands, against her mouth. Hot tears ran diagonally across her cheeks.

Siân met Verity before she found Owen. The child was heavy-eyed and yawning and clutched at her skirt.

"Where is Dada?" she asked, and Siân

took her by the hand and led her back to the rock behind which he was sitting.

Siân heard his voice as Verity went around to him and did not go herself. She turned back to find Owen and saw him almost immediately. He took her hand and smiled, and they started down the mountain among a group of Owen's friends.

Siân wondered how the marquess would react to being called the Welsh Dada instead of the English Papa. Verity had even said it with a Welsh lilt.

She was in love with him. The realization came to her full-fledged and left her feeling quite calm. She held to Owen's hand, less than a month before their wedding, and half listened to the conversation he was having with his friends, and knew that she was in love with the Marquess of Craille.

Alexander. Alex. She had not known his name before tonight.

She did not feel panic-stricken at the realization. Perhaps because it had come without passion. There had been no passion between them even though they had sat with their hands palm to palm. She had not even noticed that consciously until it was time to leave. There had been no real physical awareness at all. Just — oh, just an emotional one.

It had been wonderful. Truly the happiest part of the day. Comforting and soothing. She really had wished that it could last forever.

She should be feeling upset and alarmed, she knew. How could she be planning marriage with one man and yet be in love with another? But it was unreal, that other. He was an English marquess, a man of rank and fortune. He was the owner of Cwmbran. There was no possibility of a future with him. That very impossibility kept her calm.

She would be alarmed tomorrow, she thought. But tonight was magical. Tonight was for unreality.

A man and his wife are equals, he had said. A marriage had to be worked on day by day. It would be unfair for a husband to enforce his will on his wife merely because he was the stronger of the two. How wonderful it would be to be his wife, she thought. But thought had to stop there. She could not allow it to stray farther.

One thing was for sure. She did not believe any of the things Owen accused him of. He was a good and a gentle man and given time he would lift the oppression of years from the workers of Cwmbran. He had already stopped Blodwyn Williams from going underground and doing heavy work while she was with child. He had done it out of kindness, not guile.

She loved him.

Owen's arm came about her waist. "We will go across the hill here and down to the houses," he said, "instead of going down into the town."

"Oh-ho," one of his friends said. "Watch him, Siân. A devil on the mountain is Owen."

She laughed as a chorus of teasing calls followed them across the hill. They were almost down. This was the route of their usual evening walk.

"You went away by yourself up on top?" Owen said. "You were upset, Siân? We quarreled, didn't we?"

"It was nothing," she said.

"It was," he said, "and it was all my fault. Jealous I was. But I know I have no cause. I was the one to urge you to go there to teach his daughter and as soon as you did I grew jealous. I am eating humble pie, you see. Forgive me?"

Now at last she felt guilt. "Oh, of course, Owen," she said. "Let's forget it."

"And I spoiled the day of your triumph," he said. "I was proud, *cariad*. Proud to know that it was my future wife standing up there on the stage singing to put everyone else to shame."

"Owen." She dipped her head sideways to his shoulder. "You did not spoil the day."

They walked on in silence.

"Tired?" he asked at last.

"Mm," she said. But she could not accept the comfort of the truce. "Owen, you would not really ever beat me, would you?"

"Don't be daft," he said. "Of course I wouldn't. You would never give me cause. You are a good woman."

Leave it, she told herself. He felt comfortable and safe. He was of the real world. He was her reality. A reality she wanted and one that would be fully hers very soon. Leave it. "But if I did give you cause?" she said.

He stopped walking to turn her into his arms. He was chuckling. "Then over my knee it would be with you," he said, "and a good hiding to make sure you never gave me cause again. Silly talk, this. Kiss me, woman." He lowered his head to nuzzle her neck below one ear.

She put her arms about his neck and clung to him. He had been laughing, joking. Not serious. She should not even have asked. He was Owen. She had known him for years. She had never seen him being even discourteous to a woman. He had been courting her for many months. He had always been gentle with her. Even when she had unwittingly led him on and he had expected that she would let him make love to her, he had stopped when she had said no.

Yes, it was silly talk. Silly thoughts.

"Owen." She kissed him back when his mouth came to hers. "Owen, time is moving so slowly. I wish our wedding day would come already. I wish we were going home together now."

"One word from you," he said, "and we will go higher up now, *fach,* and soothe ourselves for the wait. But it is not what you mean, is it?"

"No," she said sadly.

"Well, home to your gran's, then," he said. "The days will pass, *cariad,* and then we will make up for lost time, is it?"

"Yes."

She let him kiss her again and kissed him back before he took her home. This was reality and she wanted to cling to it. The unreality had been left behind, and also the calm acceptance she had given it. It must be left there — in the past, on top of the mountain. Something that never really was and never could be.

She would never give Owen cause, she thought, and so he would never be put to the test. She would never give him cause.

Six owners came to Glanrhyd Castle during an afternoon of the following week, and met there with Alex and Josiah Barnes.

Alex had called the meeting with the purpose of persuading his peers to raise wages back to their former level and of explaining to them the changes he wished them to join him in making so that the lives of their workers would improve. Everything had seemed so obvious and straightforward to him before the meeting began that he had not expected opposition beyond the natural reluctance most people feel to changing what has been common practice for years.

But opposition was stiff. Indeed, the other owners had misunderstood the invitation and had taken for granted that the Marquess of Craille wished them to come to a common agreement on what they were all separately beginning to realize — that wages must be cut another ten percent in the coming week. The market for iron had still not begun to recover and a loss of profit was soon going to put them all in serious danger of bankruptcy.

They were all agreed, even Josiah Barnes. Alex listened, aghast.

"These people cannot live on ten percent less," he said. "Most of them are having a hard enough time making ends meet now. My purpose in inviting you all here was to suggest very strongly that we put wages up ten percent."

They all stared at him rather as if he had two heads, Alex thought.

"Do you know anything at all about the running of a business, Craille?" Mr. Humphrey asked.

It was, of course, the best question with which to silence Alex. No, he did not know much at all. Almost nothing. Only what he had learned in his weeks at Cwmbran.

"Business," he said, "is not an impersonal, inanimate thing. Business is run by people. I have spent the last several weeks finding out as much as I can about the people who work for me and the lives they lead. I have watched them at work, and I have visited them at home. I have called at the truck shop. They cannot live on less than they have now."

"Most of them do not have the intelligence to manage their money properly," Sir Henry Packenham said. "Is that our fault, Craille? It is not a charity we run. It is a business."

"There are always other people willing to work for less," Sir John Fowler said. "The Irish would be only too glad to take these jobs."

"If the companies collapse because too much has been paid out in wages," Barnes added, "then there will be no work for anyone."

Mr. Humphrey provided the winning argument. "Perhaps you can afford to operate at a loss, Craille," he said. "We all know that you draw enormous incomes from your estates in England. The rest of us are not so fortunate. This is our livelihood."

It was a losing battle he fought, Alex knew even as he argued and tried to devise other ways of protecting profits besides reducing wages. But it seemed that there was only one other way — laying off some of the workers. That was even less acceptable to him as a solution. He had to admit to himself finally that there was nothing he could do to prevent the further drop in wages. And he could not act unilaterally. He reluctantly agreed with the idea that solidarity among the owners was necessary.

But it was a nightmare situation, one in which his head and his heart were at war and could come to no agreement with each other. He was going to have to study the books with great care over the coming days, he thought, instead of concentrating on the human aspect of the business as he had done so far. He needed fully to understand the concepts of profit and loss as they applied to this industry. He needed to know quite clearly exactly how profitable or unprofitable the Cwmbran works were.

If he then disagreed with the other owners, he would call them back and throw at them a whole new arsenal of arguments. And if that failed, then he might consider breaking the solidarity after all in order to deal justly with his own people. But it was not a decision he felt informed enough to make now. Perhaps after all they were right and as much the victim of circumstances as their workers were.

"I will have to authorize you to reduce wages next week, then, Barnes," he said. "But I do so with a heavy heart."

The other owners appeared to breathe a collective sigh of relief. They seemed unconcerned with the state of his heart, Alex thought. They probably wished him in Hades. Doubtless everything had run far more smoothly when Barnes had had the sole responsibility for running the Cwmbran works.

"And now the other matters I wished to discuss," he said, and saw wariness and some irritability return to the faces of most of his guests.

No one else seemed to feel any concern about child labor or the employment of pregnant women for heavy labor or the lack of compensation for workers injured on the job or the fact that workers were regularly paid their wages in a public house — that complaint even won for itself a hearty laugh — or the absence of waterworks or sewers in the towns. The list went on and on.

The only answer he received from the other owners was the one that had been made before — they were not running a charity, but a business. But this time he was even more reluctant to give in to the need for joint action — or joint inaction.

"I cannot see," he said to Sir Henry's angry objection, "that my putting in waterworks at Cwmbran will cause the collapse of the works at Penybont or elsewhere. But I do know that it will make life here cleaner and healthier and will perhaps save a few babies from dying."

"You have no imagination, Craille," Mr. Humphrey said irritably. "Dangle a piece of cake before one hungry person, and a hundred others will want it too."

"Perhaps if they are hungry," Alex said, "they have a right to want cake — or at least bread."

But his answer, he saw, only angered them further. He had no friends, no allies in this group. In the end he compromised. He promised to do nothing in haste but to see how the markets progressed over the next month or so. Perhaps the demand for iron would return to its former level and wages could be raised again and there would be profits left over to make some of the improvements he suggested.

He would give himself that month, he thought as he saw his visitors to their carriages, to educate himself thoroughly, to see to it that he knew as much about Cwmbran as Barnes knew. Then he could make some informed decisions without having to feel that he was trotting along in the wake of men he could not quite bring himself to like.

He dreaded the thought of having to meet anyone's eyes next week after wages had been reduced again. How would he be able to do it without squirming with shame?

He thought back to the day of the *eisteddfod,* less than a week ago, when he had felt accepted by most of the people of Cwmbran. They had tolerated and teased him and even talked and laughed with him. They had allowed Verity to mingle with their children.

How would he be able to face these people now?

How would he be able to face Siân? Although he had been careful not to be in company with her since the night of the *eisteddfod,* he had come to feel that they were in some way friends. He had felt on that night that they had grown comfortable with each other, that perhaps they had come to like each other.

Would she like him next week?

He was going to work night and day, he thought, to understand this coal and iron industry from the inside out. He was going to prove that there was a way people — his workers and he both — could control industry instead of being controlled by it.

14

Josiah Barnes was breathless and exhausted. He crushed Angharad's unprotesting body beneath his weight for a few minutes before rolling off to one side of her.

"There is wonderful it is with you, Mr. Barnes," she said, turning her head to look at him and smile. "Are you pleased with the news I brought you, then?"

He grunted and lay quiet for a while. "But you don't know exactly when," he said. "The information is not much use to me unless I know the exact night of the meeting."

"The men I overheard at the *eisteddfod* said it would be soon," she said. "It will not be hard for me to find out exactly when. I will let you know as soon as I hear."

"Yes, you will," he said, reaching for one of her breasts, "if you want me to continue to be pleased with you, Angharad. John Frost, you say? Coming here to persuade the men to riot?"

"I don't think they will, Mr. Barnes," she said, "especially if you let it be known you have found out about the meeting and put a stop to it. That would be best for everyone."

"Why would I do that?" he asked.

She looked at him appealingly. "I don't want to get anyone in trouble," she said. "Promise no one will be in trouble, Mr. Barnes."

He squeezed her nipple between thumb and forefinger until she squealed and then set his mouth over hers, thrusting his tongue deep inside.

"Just find out the exact night for me," he said. "And I will find a way of thanking you, Angharad."

"But you are pleased with me anyway?" she asked, putting her arms about his neck. "I try to please you, Mr. Barnes. I would do anything for you. I wish I could be here for you every night for the rest of my life."

He grunted and lifted himself over her and between her thighs again.

Siân was enjoying a quiet evening at home with her grandmother. Emrys and her grandfather were always late home on pay night. Siân was preparing lessons for Verity while also participating in a sporadic conversation about her wedding.

"I am happier for you this time, *fach,*" her grandmother said. "Not that I would wish to say any ill of the dead and I was very fond of poor Gwyn. But such a little house he took you to and so crowded it was. This time you will have a house all of your own with Owen. There is grand you will be — the queen of Cwmbran."

Siân laughed. "I don't want to be the queen, Gran," she said, "just a very ordinary person. And that is what I will be."

"I don't know that you will ever be that, Siân," her grandmother said fondly. "And Owen is no ordinary person, either, is he? I just hope he does not get into any trouble with all this nonsense of meetings. Mr. Frost is to come up from Newport next week, is it?"

"Yes, Gran." Siân's spirits dropped at the thought. It was to be a secret night meeting on the mountain again. Owen and Emrys were all fired up about it. Mr. Frost apparently had ideas of uniting all the men of all the valleys for one great demonstration against the government rejection of their Charter. But Siân did not trust the word *demonstration*. What exactly did it mean?

"There will be divisions among the men

329

again," her grandmother said. "There is foolish men are, Siân. It is women who should rule the world. Then we would see some good sense. The *eisteddfod* brought all of us together in a lovely spirit of togetherness, and now this old meeting will split us up again."

And there will be Scotch Cattle again, Siân thought, but she did not speak aloud. She looked down at her book and pretended to be concentrating on it so that they lapsed into silence again. Would Iestyn be willing to participate in a demonstration? Would those who organized it be willing for some men to stay at home? But her thoughts sickened her. She tried to bring her mind to the words on the page.

And then there was a knock on the door and it opened to admit Owen. Siân closed her book with a snap and jumped to her feet, smiling. She had not been expecting him.

"Owen," she said, "how lovely." But even as she spoke she looked into his face and saw his expression. "What is it?"

"Wages down another ten percent next week," he said curtly. "That is what."

Siân sank back into her chair and closed her eyes.

"Oh, *Duw, Duw!*" her grandmother said.

"One thing about it," Owen said, "it will open up the eyes of those who have been wavering about coming up to the meeting next week. It is not needed, some have been saying. Our owner has come, they say, and he seems a decent sort. He has talked to us and visited us. He has rescued Blodwyn Williams from the mines and paid her man for his injuries. He came to the *eisteddfod* with us and took off his coat to help Ifor Richards with Glenys's harp. He will put our wages back up again and all will be well with the world. This will open up their eyes wide."

The door opened again and Emrys and Siân's grandfather came inside.

"You have heard the news, then," Emrys said, slapping his pay pack down on the table. "Here, Mam. There will not be so much next week."

Hywel Rhys sat down heavily in his chair by the fire. "It is the Lord testing us," he said, "as he did with Job."

"I would like to give the Lord two black eyes," Emrys said, "and kick his backside up the mountain and down the other side."

Hywel was on his feet again. "Right-o, Emrys," he roared, "out the back, is it? It is not enough that you show disrespect to your mam, but you must blaspheme against the

Lord too. I will show you what for now without further ado."

"I bloody well will not take all this lying down, Dada," Emrys said, eyes blazing. "If John Frost will not organize a protest against the government, then I will. And I am sorry, Mam and Siân. I do mean no disrespect, but my blood is on the boil. Glad I am that I have no wife and little ones. But plenty of men do."

"John Frost will have a plan," Owen said quietly. "Sit down, Hywel. This is no time to be turning against one another when we should be uniting against the true enemy. A mass protest it will be, and a strike too, like as not. I will speak out for a strike."

"A strike? Oh, no, Owen Parry," Gwynneth Rhys said, her palms to her cheeks. "The little ones will starve and there will be no winning anything."

"The little ones will starve on eighty percent wages, Mrs. Rhys," Owen said. "And who knows that there will not be another cut in a few weeks' time? Are we to stand by and let the owners treat us as if we are just cogs in their machines, not flesh-and-blood human beings?"

Siân had not said a word. She had sat with her eyes tightly closed, trying to will it all to be a bad dream. He had betrayed her. Utterly betrayed her. She had begun to believe in him despite all Owen had said to the contrary. She had begun to believe that he was a kind man, that he cared for the people of Cwmbran, that he was going to change everything for the better. She had grown to like him. She had fallen in love with him.

He had betrayed her.

"Siân," Owen said, "you will leave your employment at the castle without even giving any notice. You will not go to work tomorrow."

She opened her eyes at last and looked at him. "Why?" she asked.

"I will not have you working directly for that bast— for Craille any longer," he said. "You will stay home here. If your grandfather cannot support you for the next few weeks, then I will contribute to your keep. My wages will be enough to support you after we are married even with the reduction. Tomorrow you will stay home here."

"Yes, you must, Siân," Emrys said. "And we do not need your money, Owen. We will look after our own women, and Siân is ours until she weds you."

"It will be for the best, *fach,*" Gwynneth said. "I have never liked the thought of your going up there to that house."

Had no one said anything, Siân thought

later, perhaps she would have decided for herself that she could not possibly go back to Glanrhyd Castle. Certainly the thought of ever seeing him again sickened her. But there was the fact that she hated to be told what to do. She always had. It was one of the weaknesses of her character. Her mother had always said she got it from Sir John Fowler.

"I am working with Verity," she said. "I am teaching her. She is a six-year-old child and in no way involved in any of this. I cannot just abandon her."

"But the point is," Owen said, "that you are working for him, Siân, that you are going up to the castle each day, and that you wear the clothes he provided for you."

"We are all working for him," she said.

"There is a difference." He pulled out a kitchen chair from beneath the table and straddled it back to front. "It does not look good, you going there to work. There will be those who will say now that you are turning against your own people and making sure you do not have to suffer with them."

It was something she feared more than anything. "They would be wrong," she said. "I will give my pay to Gran, and if she gives any back to me, I will give it to Mari to feed the children or to any other woman who has hungry little ones."

"Huw would see his babies dead first," Emrys said, "and you too, Siân."

"There will be talk if you do not give up your job," Owen said.

"About what?" Siân jumped to her feet. "About what, Owen? It always returns to this, doesn't it, and yet you were the one who wanted me to take the job in the first place."

The chair scraped across the floor as Owen got up too. "I will not have my woman in the same house with Craille day in and day out," he said, "and people wondering what goes on between the two of you there."

"Oh, *Duw*," Gwynneth said. "There is wicked people are if they are wondering any such thing, Owen."

Emrys was rolling up his shirtsleeves. "I think it is time you came out the back with me, Owen," he said. "Siân is not your wife yet and even if she were, I would not have you talk to her like that in this house."

"Tempers are short," Hywel said. "It is part of the test. We all turn on one another and prove that we do not have what it takes to be ennobled by suffering. Emrys, it is bedtime. Owen, we will say good night to you. Siân, you must make up your own mind about what you will do and then live with your conscience. But just remember that no woman in this family is compelled to work outside the home."

Emrys stamped his way upstairs without another word.

Owen and Siân stared at each other while anger waned.

"Come out to the gate with me," he said, "and say good night. Good night, Mrs. Rhys, Hywel."

Siân preceded him silently to the back gate and hugged her arms with her hands. It was chilly and damp and she had not brought her shawl.

"Cariad," Owen said, framing her face with his hands, "I love you. But you have a stubborn streak that is going to give me the devil of a bit of trouble. When we marry, you will be promising before the Reverend Llewellyn and as many of the people of Cwmbran as can squeeze inside the chapel that you will obey me. It is a promise that I will make sure you keep. Even though I love you."

She had made the same promise to Gwyn. But it had never been an issue between them. It would between her and Owen. It would always be an issue. They were two strong-minded individuals who did not always see eye to eye.

"I will obey you, Owen, once we are married," she said, not at all sure that she would be able to keep either this promise or the far more solemn vow she would make at their wedding.

"But not before?" His voice was soft.

"I realize now," she said, "that you will not allow me to continue to teach Verity once we are married. Let me have these last few weeks with her, then, while her father finds someone else. She is a dear child and is a joy to teach. And she is very lonely."

"You are making a mistake, Siân," he said. "The mood of the men is about to turn ugly. There will be us on the one side and the Marquess of Craille and Barnes on the other. And you in the middle. You will not be looked upon kindly. I will not look kindly upon you myself."

She swallowed painfully. "Perhaps," she whispered, "you want to change your mind about marrying me."

He searched her eyes. "Do you?" he asked.

There was panic in the thought. She shook her head.

"I love you," he said. "But don't expect a complacent husband, like Gwyn was. If you must be stubborn, get it out of your system within the next few weeks, Siân, or it will go hard with you."

There it was again, the threat. If she did not obey, there would be punishment. But perhaps the very marriage vow presupposed that. She would have to learn to be obedient during those times when they were opposed. Perhaps the occasions would not be numerous.

She nodded and moved her head forward for his kiss.

Alex was crossing the hall when Siân arrived for work the next morning. For a long time he had been careful not to run into her. He had seen her only in brief visits to the nursery or from the windows when she had Verity out in the park or when they were taking longer walks out on the hills. The day of the *eisteddfod* had been the exception to all that. But then that was not something he had planned. She had come and sat with him while everyone was singing on the mountaintop, and he had neither turned her away nor gone away himself.

The fact that he met her now, quite by accident, in the hall told him that perhaps it was not really so accidental after all. He had not slept all night — and had slept only fitfully for nights before that — wondering what the reaction would be to the announcement of next week's drop in wages.

338

He had wondered what her reaction would be.

He got his answer, loud and clear.

"Good morning," he said, stopping in the middle of the hall and clasping his hands behind him.

She looked up at him, startled, flushed deeply, jerked her head away again, and hurried past him and up the stairs. Her back, he saw, staring after her, was straighter than ever.

He felt an unreasonable flash of anger. How dare she ignore him. How dare she cut him so pointedly. She was his servant! But she had provided him with the answer he had lain awake worrying about. He had trouble on his hands. And so far, though he had spent long days toiling over books, striving not only to make sense of them but also to feel that he was thoroughly in command of their contents, he had found no evidence to support the idea that the business would collapse if wages were not reduced. His profits would be down — considerably. But not far enough to put him in danger of financial ruin, even if they were his sole source of income.

And yet he dared not act on his findings yet. There was so much more to learn, so much more to know. He could not risk so many livelihoods on the strength of half-digested facts. Especially when so many other men of experience, including his own highly competent agent, were strongly united in disagreement with him.

He summoned his housekeeper after half an hour in his study had convinced him that he could not concentrate on the books this morning.

"Go up to the nursery, please," he told her, "and ask Mrs. Jones if she will take luncheon with me today. Give instructions in the kitchen accordingly." But he stopped her when she turned away with a nod. "No, better yet, Miss Haines, tell Mrs. Jones that she is to take luncheon with me to report on my daughter's progress."

He did not want her, he thought, his jaw tightening, refusing his invitation and making him the laughingstock with his other servants. He did not even know quite why he had decided to have luncheon with her, anyway. Or perhaps he did. He felt the need to justify himself to her. Though how he could do that when he could not even justify himself to himself, he did not know.

He was not to be allowed to settle to his morning of study. A short while later Josiah Barnes was announced and ushered into his study. There was to be a midnight meeting up on the mountain in four nights' time, he told Alex. Chartists again. Apparently John Frost, the ringleader and big troublemaker from Newport, was coming to address the men.

"With your permission," Barnes said, "I will have it squashed. I know who the leaders are — there are three or four of them, though Owen Parry is the main one. I will have them dismissed from their jobs and threatened with arrest if the meeting goes on, and the others will all take fright and fall into line."

"No," Alex said. "There will be no dismissals. And no arrests. The men will be allowed to have their meeting. It is supposed to be a free country we are living in."

"Begging your pardon, sir," Barnes said, frowning, "but this is most irregular. There will be trouble. The men are not in the best of moods. They will use the meeting to air all their grievances. I would not be surprised to find that there is talk of a strike."

"I will take responsibility for what comes of the meeting," Alex said. "It will be allowed to proceed. How do you know about it?"

"I have my occasional informers," Barnes said evasively. "One of the men who was whipped a few weeks ago has no love for the likes of Owen Parry. Let me beg you to reconsider, sir."

"The meeting will proceed as planned," Alex said. "And you will not need to endanger yourself by spying on it, Barnes. I shall doubtless do that myself."

"Ah," Barnes said, brightening somewhat, "then you will be able to see with your own eyes exactly who is to be dismissed, sir. And you will know exactly what the plans are so that they can be squashed. I did not understand."

"And still do not, perhaps," Alex said. "I cannot help but sympathize with my men, Barnes. I believe if I had to live on what they now earn and support my daughter too, I might be willing to throw caution to the winds and demonstrate against the government and strike against my employer. That will be all, thank you."

Barnes stared at him, stupefied, and then turned and strode from the room.

Another enemy, Alex thought ruefully. He had enemies on both sides and felt very much alone and lonely in the middle. He wished fervently that his mother's brother had had some closer kin to whom to leave the lucrative ironworks and coal mine of Cwmbran. He wished he had never set eyes on this accursed valley.

And yet — he closed his eyes and pictured it as he had seen it that first night from up on the hills, just before he had come upon that other meeting. And as it had appeared from the top of the mountain on the night of the *eisteddfod*. And he heard again in memory the male voice choir as they had sounded when practicing inside the chapel, and the whole community singing during their *gymanfa ganu* — Verity had taught him the Welsh name for their communal singing. And Siân singing her Welsh folk songs to the accompaniment of the harp.

He felt on the verge of tears suddenly. And that mysterious, unnameable yearning rushed at him, taking him quite unaware and acting on him almost like the infliction of pain. No, he could not wish that he had never owned Cwmbran and never come here. He could not wish it at all. He was a part of it whether he liked it or not, and it was a part of him.

He loved it. And he loved its people.

He loved Siân.

He had never verbalized that realization in his mind until this moment.

Josiah Barnes, striding along the driveway toward his own house, was white with fury. For twelve years he had run the works and made them profitable. He had worked on an equal footing with Fowler and Packenham and the other owners. He had won their respect — and that of the workers of Cwmbran — through sheer hard work.

And now this fool had come along to ruin everything with his bleeding heart and his damned conscience. And his dangerous respect for what he saw as the rights of his men. Did he not realize he was headed for ruin — and that he would drag Josiah Barnes down with him?

Barnes had had control of the situation — he had the likes of Owen Parry exactly where he wanted him. The man would be dismissed and unable to find work anywhere else in the valleys, and the masses would take fright at the fate of their leader. All would be quiet again.

Parry of all people. Barnes had been elated with the sweetness of his knowledge and power. Parry was to marry Siân Jones within a few weeks. The marriage plans would come to nothing if the man was dismissed. Or if she did marry him regardless, then she would starve with him.

Yet that fool had put a stop to it all.

Somehow Barnes's fury focused more on Siân as the day wore on than on either the marquess or Owen Parry. There is no fury like that of a woman scorned, the old adage says. Perhaps it applied equally to men scorned.

If it had been an invitation, she would have refused it, Siân thought. But it was a command. She was to dine with him and report on Verity's progress. It was a reasonable command — he was the child's father. But she could have wished he had summoned her to his study, where she could have made her report formally and briefly. And she could have wished that it was not today of all days. She had begun the day by cutting him in the hall, refusing even to say good morning to him. Her back had bristled as she had climbed the stairs. She had expected to be called back and dismissed.

He was standing at a window looking out when she was shown into the dining room. He hurried across the room toward her and drew back a chair so that she could seat herself. Neither of them spoke a word. She did not look directly at him. He took his place beside her, at the head of the table, and signaled to the servants to bring on the soup.

"I understand that the lessons are going very well," he said. "Verity shows off new knowledge to me every evening and seems very enthusiastic about it."

Siân breathed a silent sigh of relief. She had not been invited under false pretenses, then. He really did intend to discuss Verity's progress.

"The secret is," she said, "to make it all seem like the playing of games, so that she does not realize that she is learning."

"The secret is," he said, "to give her attention and approval and affection. She is thriving under your regime."

Siân fought against the glow of warmth his approval brought. "She is particularly interested in music," she said. "I believe she has some talent at the pianoforte. I hope you will nurture it."

"I hope you will," he said.

It was the opening she needed. "I will be here for only two weeks longer," she said. "After I am married, I will have a husband and home to keep me busy."

She was aware of his eyes on her for a few silent moments as she sipped her soup.

"Is that your decision?" he asked. "Or is it Owen Parry's?"

"Both," she said, aware of the lie. "We make decisions together."

"I am sorry about it," he said. "Verity has become attached to you. She needs a woman with whom to identify and one to give her a sense of security. You will not reconsider — at least until such time as you are with child?"

Siân could feel her cheeks grow hot and wondered how he could seem so oblivious to the silent servants who were waiting to clear away their dishes and serve the next course. "No," she said. "I must leave."

He was silent while the servants were busy and then signaled them to leave.

"Is it entirely because of the demands of your marriage?" he asked. "Why did you ignore me this morning, Siân?"

Well. It was not to be avoided after all, then.

"I did not want to bid you a good morning," she said. "It was not what I wished for you. I came here to teach your daughter."

"You had your wish," he said. "It was not a good morning. Neither was last night a good night. Or the last week a good week. I cannot blame you for your hatred."

She could no longer even pretend to eat. She set her napkin on the table beside her plate. "If you had always been as I expected you to be," she said, "I would not have felt betrayed. In a way I can respect Josiah Barnes. He has never pretended to be anything that he is not. You have. You have pretended to care."

He was bound to dismiss her. She hoped he would. Then she could please Owen and her family without having to make the decision herself.

"Betrayed," he said softly. "Is that what I have done to you, Siân?"

"Yes," she said. "I had begun to think you were a kind man. I had begun to l-like you."

"Had you?" His voice was soft and devoid of expression. "That was a mistake. Men like me cannot afford to be governed by kindness, Siân. There is too much responsibility on our shoulders. But I cannot expect you to understand and I will not plead for your sympathy."

"And I will not plead for yours." She looked him directly in the eye and almost flinched away from his pale, drawn face. "I will let the facts speak for themselves — if you will allow them to speak and do not shut yourself up in your castle and shut them out."

"What facts?" he asked.

"It is always the children who start dying first," she said.

He recoiled rather as if she had slapped his face. "Is that not rather melodramatic?" he asked.

"No." She got to her feet, pushing her chair back with the backs of her knees. "If you will excuse me, I cannot eat any more and even if I could, I would not want to eat with you."

She waited for the inevitable words of dismissal.

"Siân." He got to his feet too, flinging his napkin down on the table. He drew breath to say more but merely released it instead. "No, there is nothing to say, is there? Go back to Verity, then. I'll have food sent up to you. Thank you for being so kind to her despite my perfidy."

"She is an innocent child," she said, "and in no way responsible for her father's sins. Just as I was not for mine."

She hurried from the room, wondering if the day would come when Verity hated her father as much as she, Siân, hated hers. And would yearn as much for his love. Would yearn as much to forgive him.

But then their situations were not really comparable, hers and Verity's. Verity was not an illegitimate child. And he clearly loved his daughter as her own father had not loved her.

Was that what she wanted? Did she yearn for Sir John's love? Did she yearn to forgive him? The idea was unfamiliar to her.

She made a conscious effort to smooth

out her frown before opening the door into
the nursery.

15

Siân never knew what made her more curious than other women. Or more courageous. Or more foolhardy. Or whatever it was that needled at her and nudged at her until she went to see something for herself. It was not that she was without fear. That first time, when she had gone up the mountain to hear Mr. Mitchell, she had been afraid every moment of the embarrassment of being found out, and in the event had suffered the fright of being caught by a stranger. And on the night when the Scotch Cattle had been out and anxiety for Iestyn had driven her from her bed and from the house, she had known stark terror.

But she went again on the night John Frost was to address the men up on the mountain. She tried not to go. She lay in bed for a long time after Emrys and her grandfather had left, trying to will herself to sleep. But she wanted to know what Mr.

Frost had to say, exactly what plan of protest he had. She wanted to know how the men of Cwmbran would react, how eagerly they would fall in with the plan. She wanted to know if the black mood of the men, so apparent all week, would turn ugly under such conditions and if they would discuss action other than the demonstration. Would there be talk of a strike?

She wanted to know what Owen's part in the proceedings was to be. She wanted to know how united all the men would be and how kindly they would look upon those who would inevitably disagree with their decisions.

She wanted to see if they were spied upon, as they had been the last time. That last time the Marquess of Craille had decided to do nothing with his knowledge. But he was not after all a kind man. He was a selfish and cruel and crafty man. This time if he had got wind of the meeting or if he stumbled upon it by chance, there would be trouble. Trouble for everyone. Trouble especially for Owen.

And so she went, hurrying up the mountain from shadow to shadow, her teeth chattering from mingled cold and excitement and dread, almost as if by her very presence she could hold at bay all the dangers she feared. Almost as if she thought that by listening to the plans she could prevent them from being seditious.

The men were gathered in the same place as before, though there were surely more of them. Siân flattened herself behind the same rock as had hidden her the last time and felt the same pounding fear as she had felt then. If she were caught . . .

If she were caught, it might go hard with her. Any woman caught there could expect to arouse the anger of the men and the particular fury of her own men, who would possibly feel obliged to assert their male dominance by chastising her — perhaps publicly. But she was not just any woman. She was the woman who worked directly for the Marquess of Craille and had refused to leave her job after the second reduction in wages even though it seemed to be general opinion that she ought to have done so. If she were caught, she might be taken for some sort of spy.

If she were caught, there would be Owen to contend with.

She was a fool, Siân thought, pressing herself closer to the rock. She had everything to lose and nothing to gain by coming up here. It was a darker night than before with clouds obliterating all but the occasional glimpses of the moon. Even so, there were no lanterns, no lights at all. Only hundreds of men packed shoulder to shoulder in darkness, waiting quietly for the meeting to begin.

He had watched the last meeting, Siân thought. He had caught up to her farther down the mountain, but it was obvious that he had listened to what had been said. He had seen Owen. She wondered where he had hidden and gazed fearfully all around. In the darkness it was impossible to see any lurkers. Did he know of this meeting? Was he here? Fear clawed at her back and fingered its way between her shoulder blades to her neck.

Finally the meeting began, led by Owen, like last time. John Frost, though he was a Welshman from Newport, chose to address the men in English. His speech was as long and as impassioned as Robert Mitchell's had been. The time for petitions was over, he explained to rumbles of approval from the men. The time to stand up and be counted had come. Any man who wished to assert his dignity and his right to freedom and a portion of the bounty of the land was now called upon by his very conscience to participate in a mass march on Newport. All the men from the valleys, in three great columns — from the east, from the west, and from the central valleys, were to converge on the town at the same time one night so that in the morning light the authorities would see what solidarity looked like.

It was to be a peaceful demonstration. No revolution, this. The men of Wales were to show to the country and to the world how they could assert their rights without trying to wrest them at sword's point from their rulers. And the eyes of the world would be on Wales. The eyes of the workers of England would be on them. Matters would be so organized that the Welsh would lead the way and the English would follow. Massive demonstrations all over the country would follow closely upon the Newport march. They would be the leaders, but they would not be alone.

Despite herself Siân found her attention riveted more and more on the speaker. More and more she found her emotions being swept along by his oratory. Her heart echoed the shouts of the men. Yes, oh, yes, it might work too. And they had the right, the moral obligation to stand up for themselves.

No exact date had been set, Mr. Frost explained, as there was still a great deal to be organized and secrecy was essential. But they were to be ready to march at a moment's notice in a month or so's time. In the meanwhile everyone was to join the Association and keep in constant touch with the leader who would be appointed in each community. And in the meanwhile too everyone was to gather what weapons he could to take along with him and more weapons were to be made — on the sly at the works, or in caves up in the hills. Weapons would be necessary, not to make the men the aggressors, but to give them defense if anyone should try to bar their way into Newport or break up the march.

Again there was a shout of approval.

But Siân was clinging to her rock, feeling dizzy and nauseated. Everyone was to join the Association. It was not to be left to the individual man and his conscience to decide. Everyone would be forced to join. Coercion and violence again. And weapons! They were to make and carry weapons. They would be an army. A rabble. The potential for violence would be there, merely awaiting the spark to ignite it.

John Frost's speech over, the meeting was addressed by many men, some from their own valley, some from the next, some speaking Welsh, others English. The vast majority

356

of those present seemed to approve of the plan for the demonstration. But the topic shifted inevitably to the present and immediate concerns of the men gathered there — to the fall in wages and the impossibility of feeding a family on what they could earn.

The mood of the men was clearly for a strike. The impassioned speeches of Owen and others were not necessary in order to persuade. But they did whip up feelings already at the boiling point and succeeded in turning the general mood ugly. They would strike tomorrow, ironworkers and coal miners alike, and they would stay out until Craille and the other owners capitulated and gave in to all their demands.

Fists waved in the air as the men roared their assent. It seemed that at any moment they would erupt from the hollow where they were gathered and stream back down the mountain. She had left it too late, Siân thought, her knees weak with fright. She should have made her escape five minutes ago. She would be lucky indeed not to be caught. She flattened herself once more against the rock.

And then she had that unreal feeling of déjà vu as a heavy, warm weight came against her from behind, pinning her to the rock, and at the same moment a hand slid between her face and the rock and clamped hard over her mouth.

"Hush," the Marquess of Craille murmured, his mouth against her ear. "To our right quickly. Don't resist me or you will be caught."

She already had been caught. So had they all. But when a heavy fold of his dark cloak came about her and his hand left her mouth, she ran with him without shouting out one word of warning to the men of her own kind.

For a while he thought that this time she had not come. It was a relief to know that she at least was safe, especially when it became obvious that peace and calm reason were not foremost in the minds of the men. The march on Newport, apparently so impressive and well conceived, was after all likely to be violent. He did not know if Frost was foolish enough to believe that weapons would be used only in self-defense when hundreds, perhaps thousands, of men would be defying law and government by marching in a demonstration of strength and solidarity. He did not know if men like Owen Parry were that foolish. But it was perfectly obvious to Alex.

His men must be stopped from participating. They must be protected from the consequences of their own foolishness.

But then the focus of the meeting shifted, and as Alex had feared and half expected, the talk turned to the necessity of a strike. It was while they talked that there was a rare break in the clouds and the moon shone down on the men and Owen Parry haranguing them — and on Siân Jones pressed against the rock behind which she had hidden the last time.

The men were in an ugly mood. They would not treat kindly anyone they found spying on their meeting, even if that spy was just a woman from Cwmbran. And this was not just any woman. Siân was Fowler's daughter.

Damn the woman, Alex thought, afraid for her suddenly. *Damn her.* It took him more than five minutes to edge his way from one side of the hollow to the other — blessedly the moon had disappeared behind clouds again. But finally he was close to her — the woman had not even had the sense to make her escape while the men were still all gathered in the same place — and able to press himself against her and get his hand over her mouth before she had a chance to cry out in alarm.

There would be no time to get her back

down the mountain and safely home. He could sense that the meeting was about to break up.

"Hush," he said against her ear. "To our right quickly. Don't resist me or you will be caught."

He wrapped his cloak about her and held her to his side as they ran across the hill away from the town. He did not stop until there was another rock face behind which to hide. He set her back against it and held her there with his own body.

"Are you mad?" he said. "Coming up here with a light-colored shawl, like a red flag to a bull?" He found her mouth with his own and kissed her hard.

She was sobbing when he lifted his head away. "I hate you. I hate you," she said, pounding the sides of her fists against his shoulders. "Creeping about in your dark cloak to catch everyone red-handed. If you knew about the meeting, why did you not simply stop it? Must you trick everyone into placing his head in a noose and then spring the trapdoor?"

"Hush." He kissed her again and waited for some of the tension to go out of her body before removing his mouth from hers once more.

"I hate you," she said, the passion gone

from her voice. "I suppose you will allow the demonstration to proceed too and will have an army awaiting them when they arrive at Newport. You will not get away with it. I shall tell Owen that you know — unless you plan to murder me up here on the mountain."

"Siân." He kissed her once more. "I do not hate. These are my men, my workers, my people. I have a responsibility to them. I care for them."

"You have a wonderful way of showing it," she said. "I suppose they will be shot at and thrown in prison and hanged and transported because you care for them."

"Trust me." He leaned more heavily against her and found the pulse at the base of her throat with his mouth.

"As I would an adder," she said. "Let me go."

"Siân." He lifted his head and looked into her eyes. Even in the darkness he could see the misery there. "Trust your heart. Your heart trusts me. Trust your heart."

He watched her bite her upper lip. "My heart is not to be believed," she said. "I have seen what you are like. I have seen my people suffer."

There were the unmistakable sounds beyond the rock of a meeting breaking up and of men scattering. Alex turned so that his back was to the rock. He wrapped his cloak right about Siân and held her tightly to him. They were well away from the path the men of Cwmbran would take back to the town, but he was not sure about the men from the other valley. No one came their way.

"Your grandfather and uncle were at the meeting?" he asked after a while. "Will you be missed when they get home?"

"Not unless they deliberately look in my bed," she said, her voice muffled against his coat. "They are not likely to do so. They will tiptoe past."

"Come." He took her by the hand and drew her away farther to their right and upward. "We are too close for comfort."

She did not struggle. He was not even sure why he had left the refuge of the rock since they had appeared to be quite safe there. But they would have had to stay there quite a while since there were always stragglers at such gatherings, men who stayed to talk long after everyone else had dispersed. It would be dangerous to try to take Siân home until everyone had left. Or so he told himself.

"Here," he said finally, drawing her down to sit on a level piece of grass and heather quite high up. "We will see the last of them going down and then I will take you home." He drew his cloak right about her, his arm clasped about her shoulders beneath it.

"What are you going to do?" she asked.

"Here and now? I am not sure," he said quite truthfully.

"About the demonstration," she said. "About the strike. About the men you must have seen even in the darkness and can identify. What are you going to do?"

"I am going to do what I should have done at the start," he said, "and what I have been trained all my life to do. I am going to take all the responsibility for those dependent upon me on my own shoulders and on my own conscience."

"What does that mean?" she asked.

"Precisely what I said." He looked down at the valley as the moon made another brief appearance from behind the clouds. "It means that I will be doing what I think necessary. It means I care."

He heard her drawing a deep breath as her head tipped sideways to rest on his shoulder. "Why do I always believe you when I listen to you?" she said. "It is against all reason. Why do I believe that you care?"

"Perhaps," he said, "because you recognize truth when you hear it, Siân. Perhaps because your heart knows that I am to be trusted."

But he was not at all sure that he was to be trusted in the present situation. He swallowed and rubbed his cheek against the top of her head.

"Or perhaps," she said, "because I am foolish and gullible."

"Siân." He closed his eyes and knew that he certainly was not to be trusted. "You have come up the mountain with me after all."

He waited through the silence that followed for her to turn the moment, for her to rescue them both.

"Yes," she said.

His hand fitted itself beneath her chin and held there for a few moments, stroking, before he tipped it up and set his mouth to hers. Her lips trembled beneath his but did not pull away. And then she turned in his arms and one of her own came about his neck. Her mouth opened.

"Siân." He feathered kisses along her jaw, up her cheek to her temple, trying to impose rationality on his mind.

"Alexander," she whispered.

It was the sound of his name that snapped his control. His full name, which almost no one else ever used, spoken with her lilting accent.

And then she was on her back and he was over her, his mouth finding hers, both of them wide and hot and seeking. He searched out inner heat with his tongue, plunging it deep into her mouth, stroking surfaces, circling her tongue.

Her hands were on him, strong and demanding, pulling him down to her, one going behind his back, the other tangling in his hair. She arched her back to press her breasts against his chest.

He was lost, the last vestiges of his control gone. She wanted it. She wanted him. And he loved her. By God, he loved her. In his physical need he could not remember any reasons why he should not have her.

He began to make love to her, his mouth on hers again, his hands roaming over her body, worshiping her curves, pausing at her breasts to stroke and arouse. He touched her nipples with his thumbs through the fabric of her dress and found them already hard with desire. His own need was throbbing in him like a heavy pulse.

"Siân." He had an arm beneath her and rolled her onto her side against him so that he could open the buttons down the back of her dress. Despite the chill of the night, her skin was warm beneath his cloak and her shawl. He moved his hands over her back. "My love."

She helped him remove her bodice and reached for the buttons of his waistcoat and shirt. And finally after frenzied moments he was able to draw her against him and feel the naked magnificence of her breasts against his bare chest.

"Ah," she said. It was almost a cry of agony.

"Beautiful." He kissed her softly on the mouth and trailed hot kisses down over her chin and her throat to one full breast. He spread his mouth over her nipple and breathed warm breath on it while he licked it.

She moaned again, arching up against him and clutching his hair with both hands.

"So beautiful," he said, moving his mouth into the valley between her breasts and up to suckle the other.

"Cariad," she murmured when his mouth returned to hers. "Ah, *cariad.*"

It sounded like a caress.

And then his hand was beneath her skirt, moving up slim and strongly muscled legs. For a moment rationality returned. If she did not stop him now or sooner than now, or if he did not stop, he would be unstoppable. It would happen. But it was too late for rationality, too late for control. She wanted him, and he wanted her. He loved her.

She lifted her hips as he withdrew her undergarments, and lay quietly gazing up at him as he adjusted his own clothing. She reached up her arms for him as he lowered his head to kiss her. Her legs and her arms and breasts gleamed pale in the faint light provided by a silver-edged cloud.

She was very ready for him. His hand found heat and wetness when it touched her between her legs and parted folds and stroked her. He would not have to use any expertise to prepare her body for penetration.

Siân. He did not say her name aloud again as he brought his body over hers and down onto it and felt all her soft, warm, womanly curves against the hardness of his own body. He could not see her. The moon had receded farther behind its cloud again, and he had his eyes closed. But she was Siân. Every inch of his body and every particle of his mind was aware that she was Siân. His beautiful Siân. His woman. His love.

He pushed his hands beneath her as her legs parted about the pressure of his, and kept them firmly there, a cushion between the hard ground and the press of his body. He found the entrance to her, pushed against it, and stopped there. He held still for a few moments, unconsciously giving her one last chance to avoid what was to happen. Her arms came about his waist.

She was slick with wetness. And soft and warm and wonderful. He drew a slow breath as her muscles clenched about him while he pushed inward, drawing him deep, contracting against him so that his control almost went. He held deep in her, regaining control, reveling in the feel of woman intimately sheathing him.

Siân.

He found her mouth with his without opening his eyes. It was relaxed and warm and open and inviting. He put his tongue inside.

She moved with him almost as soon as he began to stroke her, pivoting her hips up and down, contracting and relaxing her inner muscles, setting up a rhythm with him instead of lying still and letting him set its pace and depth. There was no sense of mastery with her, as there had been with every other woman he had ever possessed. Instead there was a sense of togetherness, a sense of give and take, a sense of making love with her instead of to her.

He found it infinitely exciting and satisfying. He prolonged it well past the time he normally spent inside a woman before spilling his seed. He wanted it to go on and on, this loving, this deep sharing of bodies, this intimate knowing and being known.

Knowing Siân. Known by her. My love. My love, my love.

"My love."

He could feel the growing tension of her body. She was no longer riding to his rhythm, but had twined her legs about his and was pressing up against him. God, he thought, she was going to climax. It was something beyond his experience in a woman. But Siân was beyond his experience. This was all new, this loving of a woman he loved, this giving as well as taking. This yearning to give her love, to give her himself, to give her everything there was to give.

He acted from instinct and from love. He had nothing else to guide him. He slowed and deepened his rhythm, concentrated on sensing the needs of her body, holding deep and still in her finally while he felt her tension reach a breaking point.

"Yes, my love," he whispered into her mouth. "Yes, come. Don't be afraid. Come."

And she came with shattering force, all

the tension in her muscles exploding into uncontrolled shudderings. She cried out. She called his name. He held her tightly until all the inner tremors and outer shaking had stopped and she lay relaxed beneath him. And then his body was aware again of its own hardness, of its own need for release. He moved in her once more, aroused by her very stillness, thrusting and withdrawing until the blessed moment when he spilled into her. Into woman.

Into Siân.

Heedless at last of the hardness of the ground beneath her, he relaxed all his weight onto her and lost himself for timeless moments.

She was quiet and relaxed and awake when he came back to himself and disengaged from her body to move to her side. He kept his arms about her and brought her over onto her side against him. He smoothed her dress down over her legs and drew it up over her breasts before drawing her shawl about her and his cloak over them both. Her eyes were open. She was looking at him.

"What does it mean," he asked, *"cariad?"*

"Love," she said. "It is used as an endearment."

"My love?" he said.

"Yes." Her eyes fluttered closed.

He kissed her softly.

"Say my name again, Siân," he said.

"Alexander." She did not open her eyes. A few moments later he knew that she was sleeping.

He closed his eyes and held her close. His woman. She was his now. He would look after her for the rest of his life. She would not wed Parry now. And he would never marry again. He would not treat her to the indignity of knowing herself his mistress while he had a wife at home.

She was his. He was going to love and cherish her forever. He was going to shower gifts on her. He was going to give her everything that wealth — and love — could give.

He loved her.

Siân.

My love.

Cariad.

16

When she woke up, she was not at all disoriented. She knew immediately where she was and with whom and what had happened. Just as she had known at every moment while it was happening what it was she did. She had not at all been carried away by passion. There had been passion, yes — more of it than she had ever experienced before. But she had not been made mindless by it. She did not have that excuse.

She had given up everything, she thought, her eyes still closed, her body still relaxed against his warmth, in exchange for an impossibility. She had given up Owen — she could not now marry him — and she had given up the effort of years to belong fully to the community of her grandparents and to their religion and values. It was all gone in exchange for one night of passion with a man not of her world.

Perhaps with a cunning and cruel man.

Only her heart trusted him. Her head was not sure.

She had known what was going to happen as soon as they had sat down and she had seen how far up the mountain they were and how very much alone together. Even before he had commented on it she had known. And yet she had done nothing to prevent it. He had given her the chance. He had not rushed her at all. At every stage until her body had been finally penetrated he had given her a chance. But she had wanted him. Not just physically — oh, not just that way. She would have fought if it had been only that. Her soul had yearned for him.

And so she had given up everything.

"Alexander." She tipped back her head and looked up at him. His name made him a real man to her, a real person. She could no longer think of him as the Marquess of Craille, as that impersonal figure of authority. He was part of her. They had made love. He had been inside her body. She could see his blond hair and sharply chiseled features in the darkness. He was looking back at her.

He dipped his head and kissed her warmly, open-mouthed. She marveled that she had never known a kiss could be like this. Even when it was without passion, as it was now, it could suggest intimacy and tenderness.

"Owen is not my lover," she felt compelled to say. "There has only ever been Gwyn. Until tonight."

He smiled slowly at her. She could see the expression in the darkness. She found herself smiling back.

"You called me *cariad,*" he said. "Did you mean it?"

"You called me my love," she said. "Did you mean it?"

He continued to smile. "Yes, I did, Siân Jones," he said. "My love."

"And I did, Alexander Hyatt," she said. *"Cariad."*

They had spoken the truth — she believed that he spoke it, and she knew that she did. Yet they faced an impossibility, a future that just did not exist. But there was this night. She had given up everything for this night and it was still not over. The present was possible even if the future was not.

He kissed her again, softly, almost lazily, while his arms drew her closer against him. He was splendidly tall and well muscled. She moved her body slowly against him, feeling him with her shoulders and breasts and stomach and thighs. She felt him harden with returning desire and enjoyed the quickening of sensation in her own body.

But this time, she knew, she could relax and enjoy every moment and try not to coax her body to react faster. He made love slowly, giving her time to participate and to gather together the excitement of their coupling to fling recklessly to the stars when she could bear no more. And to discover what was the other side of passion.

With Gwyn, although she had always enjoyed their intimacies, she had had to snatch what pleasure she could from his hasty, lusty lovemaking.

Alexander had made her feel that he was doing something with her rather than to her.

She let his hands arouse her after her bodice had been lowered again and her skirt raised. She let him touch her in places she would have thought embarrassingly unpleasant to be touched but found wonderfully and surprisingly erotic. And she touched him and learned from his sharpened breathing that it was possible to arouse a man further even after he was physically ready for the act of love.

She knew instinctively when the moment had come for their bodies to join. She turned over onto her back and reached for him.

"Let me take the hardness of the ground this time," he whispered to her, and strong arms were beneath her and lifting her to lie flat on top of him. He lifted her chin and set his mouth to hers.

"How?" she asked. She knew that there were different sexual positions, but she had experienced no other than the one Gwyn had always used and Alexander too a little earlier.

"Kneel astride me," he said.

When she did so, he drew her knees and thighs snugly against his sides and positioned himself before setting firm hands on her hips and drawing her sharply downward. She gasped as she knelt upright, and threw back her head, her mouth open. It seemed impossible that there could be room. And yet there was. She drew in on him when he was deeply embedded in her. He was magnificent. Ah, dear God, he was magnificent.

His hands lifted her slightly away from him and he began to move in her with deep, bold strokes that had her gasping and arching backward against his updrawn knees. Her head was still thrown back. She did not move with him. She hovered on the edge of pain, on the edge of ecstasy.

"Siân." He was moving more gently. His hands reached for her arms and drew her down toward him. She set her hands on either side of his head and leaned over him, gazing down into his face. Her hair fell like a curtain on either side of them. "My love. Ride me." He stilled in her.

And so she rode him, slowly and tentatively at first, with growing boldness as she found a rhythm that brought back the pain and the promise of ecstasy and that had him closing his eyes and moaning and finally moving his hands from the grass on either side of him to grasp her hips and drive into her rhythm.

They reached glory together and cried out together. And relaxed together into the panting aftermath of passion. And slept together after he had pulled his cloak over them.

One step closer to impossibility, Siân thought as she came back to herself. But she did not care. What had happened had been beautiful beyond imagining. And it was beyond putting into words. For it had not been a purely physical thing, though that was how it had manifested itself.

She had known love, she thought, for a brief moment in time. She was privileged. Surely the vast majority of people went through life without ever having known it. She was fortunate.

One of his hands was massaging the back of her head.

"You will not be marrying Owen Parry," he said.

"No." There was a pang of regret but no more. Perhaps tomorrow she would feel more. Perhaps then she would feel the great weight of her loss. But not yet.

"I will be good to you, Siân," he said. "I will love you and cherish you. I will care for our children. I will never marry again. I will not put you through that distress. You will not be sorry for tonight."

Ah. He did not understand the impossibility. She nestled her head more comfortably on his shoulder.

"I am not going to be your mistress, Alexander," she said.

His hands stilled. "Is that not what tonight has been all about?" he asked. "You have become my mistress tonight. My body is still joined with yours."

"We have made love tonight," she said. "Because we both wanted to do so and because there is something between us that had to be expressed this way. But that gives you no ownership of me. It does not make you my master."

"Ownership?" he said. "It gives me a responsibility. I have possessed your body. I have put my seed inside you. Perhaps even now you have taken my child into your womb. I will look after you, Siân. Care for you. Support you. For the rest of my life and as a clause in my will. It is not a question of ownership. I will not be harsh with you or demanding. I will never use violence on you — or on our children."

He made it sound so enticingly sweet to be his mistress. If it had not been for one fact, she might have succumbed. But it was that fact that constituted the impossibility.

"Alexander," she whispered, "I will not be like my mother. I will not live in luxury and loneliness. I will not be visited by you for the sole purpose of going up to our bedroom to make love. I will not have my children brought up in isolation from other children. I will not be your mistress or any man's."

"I thought you loved me." She could not tell if his tone was harsh or bleak.

"Tonight I gave up the future I had planned," she said. "I gave it up because I could not deny the present. I gave it up because I wanted you. Not only this coupling on the mountain. I wanted — oh, I wanted to give myself to you. I wanted to know that I had done that in my life. Given all for love. But I cannot base a future on that, Alexander. I will not be your mistress."

He drew a deep breath and let it out slowly. "This was the beginning and the end, then?" he said. "There will never be another time, Siân?"

She could not bear the thought of that, the finality of it. "Perhaps there will," she said. "If you want it and I want it at some other time. But I will not belong to you. I will not, Alexander. I will never again be any man's chattel. From now on I belong to myself. I will give where love leads me to give. But I will not be a kept woman."

She felt him swallow. There was a lengthy silence. She was very much aware of the fact that their bodies were still united. He was a warm and comfortable bed. She ached with love for him. Her chest and her throat were sore with unshed tears.

"It is time I took you home," he said at last.

"Yes."

And yet they lay for several more minutes before his hands came to her hips and lifted her off him and turned her to lie on the grass. She pulled on her undergarments and straightened her dress while he adjusted his own clothing. He was on his feet before her and reached down a hand to help her up.

"The next time curiosity brings you up the mountain to spy," he said, drawing her shawl about her shoulders and then flinging his cloak about her and drawing her against his side, "wear something dark over your dress, will you, Siân? I was terrified that someone else would notice you before I could get to you."

"All right," she said, setting her head on his shoulder and wrapping one arm about his waist beneath the cloak they shared. She was going to ask him again what he intended to do about the demonstration and the strike. She was going to ask if he intended arresting the leaders. She wanted to beg him not to. But she said nothing. She decided to trust him instead. To go with her heart and trust him.

They walked across and down the hills in silence, their arms about each other, until they came to the place just above the terrace where she lived at which they had stopped on a previous occasion.

"You will be safe alone from here?" he asked, turning her against him.

She nodded and lifted her face for his kiss. It was a long and lingering one.

"I am just beginning to realize," he said, "the enormity of the gift you gave me tonight, Siân. Everything in exchange for nothing. Thank you. But I will give something in return. All the way down you have been worrying about your people again, haven't you? I am going to prove to you that

I can be trusted. That is a gift you will value, is it not?"

She nodded again.

"Good night." He kissed her briefly. "Be careful."

She turned and ran lightly down the remaining part of the slope and along behind the terrace to slip through the back gate and into her grandfather's house. No one was stirring. Her absence had not been noted. She slipped quickly out of her clothes and into bed.

The night must be almost over, she thought, curling onto her side and pulling up the blankets warmly about her. But not quite. There was still a little of it left. Tomorrow everything would look different to her, she knew. Tomorrow reality would intrude. But there was still a little of the night left.

She closed her eyes and was again in his arms.

The men came out at the start of the early morning shift. All of them, in both the ironworks and the mine. Apparently on the issue of a strike at least there were no dissenting voices.

Josiah Barnes brought the news to Glanrhyd Castle early, while Alex was still at breakfast. He abandoned his meal in order to join his agent in the study, knowing what the news would be but rather sorry that he could not have acted himself before the strike began.

"Barnes," he said, closing the study door behind him, "I am glad you are here. I was about to send for you."

"The news is not good," Barnes said. "Everyone has come out on strike. Everything is shut down. If you went up to that meeting last night, you probably know about it, unless everyone spoke Welsh. You see the danger of allowing it to happen, sir? If you had stopped it and dismissed the leaders, we would not have this crisis on our hands."

"I will not forget," Alex said, "that you gave me that advice, Barnes. I will confirm the fact to the other owners that none of this is your fault."

"It is not that I am blaming you," Barnes said. "But if you will forgive me for saying so, sir, you do not have experience with this sort of situation. You are used to gentler living."

"Quite so," Alex said. "You are to put wages back up, Barnes, effective immediately. And you will send Owen Parry up here, if you please."

Josiah Barnes gaped at him. "Put them

up?" he said. "All the way up to last week's level? Oh, no, sir. That is not the way to do it. You don't crumble at the first hint of trouble. The men will hold you to ransom for the rest of your days if you do that."

Alex raised his eyebrows. "To last week's level?" he said. "No, Barnes. To the level they were at when I first came here. And that is the way I will do it."

"You will be the laughingstock," Barnes said, aghast. "You will never have control of your workers again, sir. Not to mention the trouble there will be in the other valleys if we put up wages here. We have to act together."

"On the contrary," Alex said. "We do not. Not when acting together is done for purposes of greed. I have discovered, Barnes, that my profits will be down if I raise wages, but that I would still be a wealthy man even if I had no other source of income. I have discovered that I am getting very wealthy indeed at the expense of hundreds of powerless men and women who can barely survive on what I allow them, and sometimes do not do so. Too many children die in this valley. Wages will be raised. Effective immediately."

"It will not —" Barnes began.

"Mr. Barnes." Alex's voice cut into his

agent's sentence like a whip. "You are an excellent agent. When I need information or advice, I know I can consult you and listen to an expert. On this issue I need neither. You will do as I have directed. And send Parry to me."

Josiah Barnes stood staring at him truculently for a few moments before turning on his heel and hurrying out.

Alex crossed the room and stood looking out of the window, waiting for Owen Parry. Perhaps he would refuse to come. Perhaps being on strike would give him the courage to defy the summons to Glanrhyd Castle. But he needed to talk to the man, Alex thought, even if it meant going into the town himself to seek him out.

Barnes might be right. Quite possibly he was. It was perhaps the worst of all times to correct a long-standing injustice on the very first morning of a mass strike. Perhaps he would give the indelible impression of weakness and break down all discipline forever after. But he could not justify holding out against the strikers for the mere sake of proving his will to be stronger than theirs. He could not justify starving innocent children just in order that he not be despised as a weakling.

Wages had to go up. He had realized it a

week ago but had meticulously plodded through every last detail of the business before making his decision, determined not to make the mistake of acting too soon and bringing disaster on all those to whom these works meant the difference between life and death. He had waited perhaps a little too long.

But perhaps not. Perhaps if he showed himself willing to take two steps toward his workers when they asked for only one, he could convince them that he was acting in good faith. Perhaps he could win their trust. Doing so had become even more important since the arrival of the early morning post. It seemed that the government was preparing for just such a demonstration as the men of the valleys were planning. Soldiers were being sent out to major towns to back up the authority of local constables and militia. Troublemakers were to be dealt with harshly.

He must persuade the men of Cwmbran not to march. And not to make weapons.

Siân was walking up the driveway. Was it only nine o'clock? he thought. It seemed as if the day must be half over already. She looked neat and businesslike as she always did and strode along with an almost manly stride that nevertheless succeeded in looking unmistakably feminine. She did not look like a woman who had spent most of the night up on the mountain making uninhibited and passionate love.

It did seem rather like a dream, he thought. Except that in his body he recognized the signs — satiety that could easily flame into renewed desire — that he had had a woman again after a long dearth. A beautiful, desirable woman who gave unstintingly.

Strangely, he was glad now this morning that she had refused to let him set her up as his mistress. Siân would not fit well in the pampered luxury of a love nest. She would not fit the image of a kept woman. She was free and independent and strong willed. She would not be happy as his mistress. And he would not be happy if he could not make her so.

But he could not afford to think of Siân this morning. He resisted the urge to go out into the hall to bid her good morning. Later. He would see her later.

Owen Parry came a little less than an hour later. He stood silently inside the study door as he had done on a previous occasion, looking steadily at his employer. There was perhaps a gleam of something like triumph in his eyes, Alex thought.

The thought flashed unwillingly into Alex's mind that he had taken Parry's woman the night before and destroyed the man's marriage plans. But he pushed the thought ruthlessly aside. Now was not the time for personal concerns.

"Have a seat," he said, and Parry sat in the chair he had occupied once before without taking his eyes off Alex.

Alex sat down behind the desk. "What is the purpose of the strike?" he asked. "What are your demands?"

The expected stupid look descended on Owen's face like a mask. He shrugged. "How am I supposed to know?" he asked.

Alex leaned forward, his elbows on the desk. "Let us not play foolish games," he said. "Even apart from the fact that you are the leader of the workers of Cwmbran and I know it and you know I know it, I cannot imagine that there is a man or woman out on strike today who does not know the reason. What are you striking for?"

"For survival." Owen's eyes narrowed.

Alex nodded. "And what constitutes survival?" he asked. "We both know that there are families who will not survive long during a strike. What will it take to get you back to work?"

Hatred was barely masked in the man's face. "A return of our ten percent," he said. "There are many families who cannot live on less."

"I have already given orders for the return of the twenty percent you have lost since my arrival here," Alex said. "To be effective immediately. No pay will be deducted for today's strike."

Owen Parry stared at him, surprise giving place quickly to blankness.

"That will end the the matter?" Alex asked.

"What is the catch?" Eyes narrowed again, Owen was making no further pretense of stupidity. "What is the bloody catch?"

"Nothing, actually," Alex said. "Wages will be raised regardless, and would have been even if there had been no strike this morning. I would have liked another day or two, perhaps, before you had your meeting. But I could hardly expect you to arrange that to suit my purpose."

Owen's face went blank again.

"I made you an offer once before," Alex said. "I asked you to arrange for me to meet with you and some other representatives of the people to discuss what can be done to improve the quality of life in Cwmbran. I renew that offer. Perhaps my action this morning will convince you that I am acting in good faith. I believe you will find that your colleagues who work for other companies will not have had their wages restored today."

Owen Parry sneered but said nothing.

"The march on Newport sounds like a good idea," Alex said. "But there are many things that can go wrong with such a plan. It is difficult to coordinate such a large undertaking so that everything goes exactly according to plan. With so many men involved, there is almost bound to be some shortness of temper, some recklessness, some one individual or two who can destroy the whole thing. The carrying of weapons is a dangerous thing. Anyone set to meet the marchers and ensure that they do not break up the peace or endanger the town might act hastily or unwisely and provoke a violent incident. And even if all goes well and peacefully to plan, the chances are that nothing at all will be accomplished. Would you not agree?"

"What march on Newport?" Owen asked.

"I believe that what was demanded in the Charter will come about eventually," Alex said, ignoring the question. "Unfortunately such changes take a long time. Years or decades. Sometimes even centuries. In the meantime, something can be accomplished locally if everyone acts together. There is a great deal to do in Cwmbran. But rather than imposing change from above, I would prefer to work with the people. Perhaps here in Cwmbran we can have a form of democracy. Will you speak to your men? You will know far better than I to whom to speak and what to say."

Owen Parry was silent for a long time. "I do not trust you, Craille," he said. "Not for a single moment. But perhaps others will. I will pass on what you have said."

"Thank you." Alex got to his feet and held out his right hand.

Owen looked at it and stood up too. He made no move to accept the handshake. "You were there?" he asked. "Or did you have spies reporting to you?"

"I was there," Alex said.

"Who told you about it?" Owen looked him directly in the eye. "Someone did. If there is to be good faith between us, we had better have such things out in the open. Who was the bloody informer?"

Alex shook his head. "There can be no useful purpose in disclosing that," he said. "Besides, I do not know the man's name. If we can learn to work together, Parry, there will be no further need of secrecy and spies.

391

There will be no your side and my side but only our side. I shall look forward to that meeting."

Owen Parry set two powerful hands on the desk and leaned across it toward Alex. "I will find out," he said. "The bastard will be sorry."

The man was not going to be easy to work with, Alex thought when he was alone again. But then he could not expect any of this to be easy, he supposed. He wondered if he should send upstairs to invite Siân to luncheon, but rejected the idea.

Josiah Barnes sent for one of the men who had been whipped by the Scotch Cattle and had his furniture destroyed. He waited impatiently in his office at the ironworks for the man to arrive.

He could not use Angharad. Part of his success over a dozen years was attributable to his knowledge of human nature. Angharad would give him information in the abstract — information that it would seem to her would harm no one in particular. She would do it in exchange for his approval and the hope he gave her between the sheets that one day she would be his wife. But she would balk at harming any one individual.

Gwilym Jenkins had no such scruples. He

seethed with resentment.

"It will hurt Parry," Barnes explained. "It will make him look like a fool who cannot control his own woman. It will make him look a cuckold. It will very likely topple him from power."

It was obvious that Jenkins found that prospect even sweeter than the money Barnes gave him to help replace his lost furniture. "I will do it," he said, nodding curtly. "It will quite possibly be guessed at anyway."

"But carefully," Barnes said. "It must not seem too obvious."

"Trust me." Jenkins turned his head and spat on the floor before leaving the office.

It would work too, Barnes thought, looking after him. Parry would be brought down or at least be made to look a fool and have his personal happiness ruined. Craille would be further discredited and would appear even more of a weakling than today's actions would suggest.

And best of all, Siân Jones would suffer. Perhaps only her reputation. Perhaps more than that if he was lucky, Barnes thought.

Nothing could make him happier.

17

"I really do not see the sense of it," Emrys said while they were sitting around the table at the evening meal. "If he took fright, which is what many of the men believe, why give more than we were striking for? Twice as much. Perhaps no one had told him what we were asking."

"Happy we should be and not question the reason why," his father said. "I do not remember the strike that was over in half a day. Or the strike in which we got what we were asking for and more."

"The dear Lord be praised," Gwynneth Rhys said, "that the children will no longer go hungry. And I do not believe the Marquess of Craille took fright. I believe he is a man who cares for justice and mercy. He has a little one of his own."

"But if he is like that, Mam," Emrys asked, "why did he put down the wages in the first place?"

"Pressure," Hywel Rhys said, "from the other owners. Word has it that none of the other valleys are back at work. Only ours."

"There will be trouble over that," Emrys said.

"Well, I think our marquess is a good man." Gwynneth nodded her head. "Clean off your plate, Siân. It is good food. You look tired, girl. Worrying, have you been?"

Siân resumed eating. Yes, she was very tired, both physically and emotionally. She was feeling a confusing mixture of happiness and unhappiness. He was going to prove that he could be trusted, he had told her last night — or this morning. It was to be his gift to her. And he had delivered early and in greater abundance than she had dreamed. He had heard at the meeting that the workers would demand a return of their ten percent. He had given back the twenty.

He had done it because he cared. Because he cared about the people of Cwmbran. Because he cared for her. It was his gift to her. A precious, precious gift.

But she had not seen him all day. She had told herself that she did not want to. She had told herself that she hoped he would not try to seek her out. But she knew now that she had deceived herself, that she had really hoped he would. Just to see him. No longer the Marquess of Craille, but Alexander. Her love. Her body, sensitive from last night's lovings, yearned for him.

"A penny for them, Siân, *fach.*" Emrys was laughing. "Seeing Owen tonight, is it? And the wedding less than two weeks off. Dreaming of wedding nights, is it?"

"Emrys!" His father's voice was stern. "There will be no coarse talk in this house, and your mother and Siân present."

And that was another unhappiness, Siân thought, one she had been trying to hold at bay. But it had to be faced, and soon. She was going to have to break off with Owen. Her stomach churned at the very thought of all that would mean to her future. And of how she would hurt him and perhaps humiliate him too.

"I'm sorry, Gran." She pushed her plate away from her. "I can't finish. Forgive me?"

Her grandfather frowned. "There are people starving in this world," he said. "And it is an insult to your grandmother's cooking, Siân."

"I'm sorry." Siân drew the plate back toward her, speared a piece of potato, and put it in her mouth. She chewed determinedly.

Her grandmother patted her on the arm. "I will tell Owen to bring you home early tonight, *fach*," she said. "You need a good night's sleep."

The next piece of potato felt rather like a pebble in her mouth. Siân swallowed it.

Owen came while she was helping with the washing up half an hour later. Siân found it difficult to meet his eyes. He was not looking as happy as she had expected.

"Well, Owen," Hywel said, "pleased are you at the outcome of today's action? It was far better than any of us could have expected."

"It do seem that way, Hywel," Owen said. "The strike over almost before it had begun, no deduction of pay for the morning we were off, a return to the wages we had a few months ago. Yes, it do seem that everything has worked out well."

Emrys chuckled. "You sound almost disappointed, Owen, man," he said. "I think you were looking forward to a good fight and a good battle of wills."

"That would be a wicked thing to look forward to," Gwynneth said, drying her hands on a towel, "with people going hungry. You may empty the dishwater out the back, Hywel, if you please."

"That it would, Mrs. Rhys," Owen said. "But I do not trust a man who gives so much so easily."

"You think he was scared?" Emrys asked.

"I think he is sly," Owen said. "You are ready to come walking, Siân?"

This was it, then. Siân folded her apron and put it away and reached for her shawl. She wrapped it about her shoulders while her grandmother was instructing Owen to have her home early.

"Not too far up the mountain, mind," Emrys said, "or the Reverend Llewellyn will be up after you with a big stick."

"Which I would break over my knee and give him back as two sticks to go and use on someone else," Owen said over his shoulder as he ushered Siân outside.

He took her hand in a firm clasp and walked along the street with her and up the slope to the lower hills, the walk they most frequently took in the evening. It was chilly and damp. Autumn was in the air. He did not speak or look particularly happy.

"You must be glad," she said, "that the strike was over so soon."

"Of course I am glad," he said. "It would be strange indeed if I were not. But our friends in the other valleys are not so fortunate. And they may well accuse us of strikebreaking here when we could have stayed out to help their cause."

"But we have no reason to be out," she said.

"Which is exactly what most of the men would say," he said. "It is not even worth calling them all together and taking a vote. But I don't like it. It is only by acting together that we will ever accomplish anything of lasting value. Craille took that away from us — that solidarity."

"That is what is bothering you?" she said. "I had not thought of that. But it is not his fault. Surely he acted from a concern for his own people and a recognition of the justice of their claim."

"That is not what is bothering me," he said. "That is a minor point."

"What is it, then?" she asked. "The rest of last night's meeting? What did Mr. Frost have to say? What is to happen?"

"You don't know?" he asked. "He did not tell you?"

"He?" She frowned. "Mr. Frost?"

"Craille," he said. "He spied on the meeting. Did he not tell you what happened there?"

She felt herself turn cold. "How do you know he was there?" she asked. "What makes you think that he was?"

"He told me." Owen looked at her. "He had me up to the castle this morning as the leader of the workers and he told me. Did he not report to you?"

"I have not seen him all day." She felt rather as if all the blood was draining from her head. "I was there to teach Verity."

He turned his head away and gazed ahead of them across the hill.

"Why do you think he would have told me about the meeting?" she asked. Did he know that she had been there too? Did he?

"Siân," he said, his voice very quiet, "someone told him about it. He admitted as much though he would not give me the name of the informer. But there is an informer. Someone told him about last night's meeting."

She grew even colder as she understood what he was saying. What he was asking.

"You think I told him?" she said, her eyes wide. "Owen, I did not. It was the last thing I wanted him to know. I did not tell him."

"Someone did," he said. "I had a meeting with some of the men before we went back to work this morning. Your name was brought up as one likely informer. Indeed someone has been putting it about as a certainty."

She felt sick. She stopped walking and turned to face him. "Who would say such a thing?" she asked. "And what do you think?

400

Do you think I would do that, Owen, when it was likely that he would have you dismissed from your job and perhaps arrested and that he would cause no end of trouble for the rest of the men? Do you believe it was me?"

He took her face in his hands and set his thumbs beneath her chin, none too gently forcing her face higher.

"No," he said after a lengthy silence, during which he searched her eyes. "No, *fach,* I don't believe you would do that to me. Or to the rest of the people here."

His trust paradoxically distressed her. She felt tears spring to her eyes and bit her upper lip. And she knew at the same moment that she must deceive him for a little longer. Now was certainly not the time to break off with him. She would appear guilty when she was not. She was guilty of other things. She was engaged to marry him and had been unfaithful to him. But she had not betrayed him. Or the people of Cwmbran.

"Thank you," she said.

"But you must not go back to Glanrhyd Castle ever again," he said. "You must see that now, Siân. Other men are not as trusting as I am. You are already suspected of being the informer. And there are those who have your motive all explained, too. He is a

401

handsome man, it is being said, and wealthy, and closer to the world in which you grew up than I am."

Siân felt herself blanching.

"You must put yourself quite beyond suspicion for the future," Owen said.

"You want me to leave my job just like that?" she said. "Although you believe me, Owen? Would it not appear almost like an admission of guilt? Or as if you had found me guilty and chastised me and forced me to leave my job?"

"All the better if it does appear that way," he said. "If the men think I have handled the situation by giving you a good beating and forcing you to do as you are told, they will be satisfied and will consider the whole matter at an end. I will even put it about that that is how it is — except that I will not beat you because I believe you. You will be protected if it is believed that I have dealt with you."

Siân closed her eyes. His thumbs beneath her chin prevented her from lowering her head. "No," she said. "No and no. I will not agree to such a thing, Owen. How can you even suggest it?"

"You are too proud for your own good, *fach*," he said. "You would be ashamed to have it thought that I had given you a good spanking, would you? It will be forgotten soon enough. No one will think the worse of you."

"I will not pretend to anything," she said, "just to clear myself of something I did not do. And I will not play the coward by leaving my job. I don't want to leave it. I like it. I like Verity."

And yet she felt sick. She was already pretending to something. But she could not tell him now. It would make her seem guilty of the other charge. And she was not guilty. Oh, he must believe that she would never have done that.

"Enough of this nonsense, Siân." His tone was harsher. He released his hold on her chin finally. "You must see that it is for your own good, and I am getting very tired of your stubbornness. In less than two weeks' time you are going to have to finish working, anyway, because you will be my wife. What difference do a few weeks make? Especially when being stubborn will increase the gossip and perhaps make a few people turn nasty."

"I will not do it," she said. "I will give up my job when I am ready to do so or when my services are no longer required. I will not give it up out of fear because a few people believe I might have told the Marquess of Craille about the meeting last night."

"Or because I ask it of you, *cariad*?" He was looking very steadily at her.

She dropped her eyes and swallowed. "It is not something you should ask, Owen," she said. "If I asked you to give up your job or if I asked you to give up your leadership of the workers because it might be dangerous to you to continue, you would not do so, would you?"

"Of course not," he said. "I am a man."

"And I am a woman," she said. "No inferior creature to whom a job and pride mean nothing, Owen. I am a woman."

Unexpectedly he smiled. He set his hands on her shoulders and drew her against him. "I had noticed," he said. "But damn you, Siân, you are a woman who is going to need a heavy hand."

He kissed her hard. She felt panic for a moment and terrible guilt. But she could not tell him now. God forgive her, she could not.

"It is going to be a toss-up on our wedding night," he said, "whether you will go over my knee or into my bed first. If you would prefer the second, you had better keep your mouth shut all day, girl, after you have said what the Reverend Llewellyn will have you say. Why are you crying?"

She shook her head and hid her face against his shoulder. Owen! She had come so close to loving him. So very close. She could not understand what that small something was that had held her back. He was everything she could want or need. Almost any other unmarried woman of Cwmbran or the neighboring valleys would jump at the chance to be in her shoes. She wished she loved him. Even now she wished it.

If only it had been Owen up on the mountain last night — loving her as she had been loved, making her feel as she had been made to feel. If only. With a wedding to look forward to and a whole future of married life and motherhood. If only she could love him, she would even be willing to subject her will to his and take the consequences when he was displeased with her. Or at least, she would try to be willing. If only she loved him.

"Owen," she said, "I care for you so very much. Please always believe that."

"You can show me on our wedding night, *fach*," he said, kissing her temple until she turned her head and he could kiss her lips. "You can show me all night and in the morning I will tell you if I believe you or not. If I don't, you will have to show me all over again. It might take a week before I am convinced."

She drew away from him. Owen affectionate and playful was so much more difficult to be with at the moment than Owen grim and masterful.

"Take me home?" she said. "Gran said I was not to be late."

He threw back his head and laughed. "And Gran is to be obeyed," he said. "You sounded just like a meek child then, Siân. I will have to ask Mrs. Rhys what her secret is. Back home it is, then, *cariad.* Pretty soon it will be back home to our own house. Then I will not drag my feet."

He took her hand again and laced his fingers with hers.

He stopped outside the drawing room door and set his hand on the knob, as he often did. Sometimes he turned it and went in for a few minutes — to listen to Verity's progress in her music lessons, he always said, not entirely untruthfully. She was excited when he did so and had to demonstrate for him all the scales she had mastered and play him one or two of the simple tunes she had learned. Sometimes he remained outside the door listening for a few minutes and then moved away.

Today it was Siân playing, not Verity. Verity was singing.

Siân. He had had difficulty sleeping last night despite his tiredness. He had had a great deal on his mind. But it was one fact alone that kept him awake. He had kept wishing that it was the night before. He had relived their lovemaking moment by moment and longed to have it again.

He longed to see her again. To hear her voice. To touch her. Alexander, she had called him. Not Alex, but Alexander. It was the first time she had called him anything at all. And then she had called him *cariad* — my love. She had told him later that she had meant it, that it had not been simply passion speaking.

Siân. He set his forehead against the door and then withdrew it again and opened the door.

"Good afternoon," he said. "Am I interrupting anything?"

"Papa" — Verity's face lit up as she came bounding across the room to take his hand in hers — "I am learning to sing a real Welsh song. In Welsh. I am ever so clever, aren't I? Mrs. Jones is teaching me. She says that when I am grown up perhaps I will be able to sing in the *eisteddfod*."

"I shall come and cheer you on when that happens," he said, "and carry you about on my shoulder when you win."

She laughed. "Come and listen to me."

He looked across the room at Siân, who was sitting at the piano-forte, looking back. Her cheeks were flushed, her eyes bright — devouring him as his were devouring her. God, he thought, it had been real. It had been no vivid, erotic dream. It had been real.

"May I?" he asked. "Is she ready for an audience yet?"

"Yes, indeed," Siân said, "since the audience will be partial. We have to work more on the pronunciation and the expression, but she has a sweet voice."

"Coming from a Welshwoman," he said, "that is quite a compliment."

Verity sang for him and then played him all her scales and a new tune she had not mastered at all. And then she had to tell him that King Henry VIII had had six wives and that Vienna was the capital of Austria and that Mrs. Jones had said her penmanship was improving.

"Not one blot this morning, Papa," she said.

"Goodness," he said, "soon I am going to have such a scholar on my hands that I will be put to shame."

She laughed with delight. "Don't be silly, Papa," she said. "Two of King Henry VIII's wives had their heads chopped off."

"Painful," he said. "I believe school is over for the day. Why don't you run up to the nursery and ask Nurse to order up tea? I need to speak with Mrs. Jones for a few minutes."

"All right, Papa," she said. "But come up later. I want to show you my penmanship sheet and the painting I started this afternoon. Good-bye, Mrs. Jones. May I sing again tomorrow?"

"Of course," Siân said. "What would a day be without song in it?"

Verity whisked herself from the room and shut the door behind her.

There was silence for a few moments as Siân stood beside the pianoforte and Alex stood several feet away. They looked at each other with some wariness but no embarrassment. Then he opened his arms and she walked into them, pressing herself against him while he closed them about her.

"You got home safely and undetected?" he asked.

"Yes." Her face was against his cravat. "Thank you for my gift."

"Gift?" he said.

"The proof that I can trust you," she said. "For giving more than you were asked for yesterday morning. It was a more precious gift than jewels would have been."

"Was it?" He kissed the top of her head. "I would like to give you all the jewels money can buy, Siân. But you would not accept them, would you?"

She lifted her head away from his chest to look up at him. "No," she said. "I do not need jewels. I need to believe in you, and now I do."

He feathered the backs of his fingers over one of her cheeks.

"You have told him?" he asked.

She shook her head and bit her lip. "Not yet."

"But you will not marry him, Siân?" He should be wishing that she would. He should be wishing for a secure and contented future for her. She would not be his mistress. He should wish that she would be Parry's wife, then. But he could not bear the thought of her being with another man. Least of all Owen Parry.

She shook her head again.

"What have they decided?" he asked. "Have they agreed to the meeting?"

She looked inquiringly at him.

"He has not told you?" he asked. "I want

to meet with Parry and other representatives of the people to discuss what else may be done to make life better here. He is to arrange it."

"I know nothing about it," she said.

He smiled at her. "I found it hard to sleep last night," he said. "I wanted you."

He watched a flush brighten her cheeks and knew that she had wanted him too. He lowered his head and opened his mouth over hers. But it was neither the time nor the place for passion.

"Come and sit down," he said, leading her to a sofa, and seating her close beside him, his arm about her shoulders. "Tell me something, Siân. If you had unlimited resources of money and manpower, what changes would you make in Cwmbran? What improvements?"

"Oh," she said. She set her head on his shoulder and was silent for a long time. "I would find a way to produce iron without all the smoke and dust and to mine coal without the danger of explosions and the coal tips and the coughing sickness that most miners seem to end up with. But you mean within the bounds of reality?"

"Yes." He rested his cheek on the top of her head. "Within the bounds of reality, though perhaps in time we can tackle those problems too."

"I would have waterworks and sewers put in," she said, "and the river cleaned up. I would make sure that no children worked. I would have schools for them all. And the chance for them to do something else in life than laboring in the works or mine if they wished and if they had the ability. I would have more doctors. And a level of wages below which it was not permitted to go. I would have pensions for the elderly and sick. And a library and speakers and readers coming in to keep us informed about the rest of the world. We already have music. I would have — is that enough?"

He chuckled. "I think quite enough to be going on with," he said. "And more houses, perhaps, so that families would not be so crowded together?"

"Oh, yes," she said. "Definitely that."

"I shall have to make you my program manager," he said.

"Are you really planning to do any of those things?" she asked.

"As many of them as I can," he said. And he realized even as he said it that he meant it. And that therefore he was making a huge commitment of time and energy and money to Cwmbran. No longer could he tell himself that he was here for just a short time. If he really did intend to make these changes — and he did — then he was committing himself to making Cwmbran his home for many years to come.

What had happened to the feeling that he was a stranger in a strange land? Ah, but there was that other feeling he had had right from the start, right from that walk he had taken out onto the hills with Verity — that feeling of longing, that feeling that somehow he had come home, though he had not quite understood it at the time. But that was what the feeling was.

He had come home.

And he had found his love there.

"Alexander," she said, "why?"

"Because I want to," he said, "and because I am able to."

"Is it because of me?" Her voice was so quiet that he could scarcely hear the words.

"Partly," he said. "Not entirely. But partly, Siân, it is because of you. I love this valley and this town and these people — but I cannot separate any of them in my mind from you."

"I must go," she said, lifting her head from his shoulder and getting to her feet.

He got up too and took her hands in his. He lifted them one at a time to his lips.

"I did sleep last night," she said breathlessly. "The few times I woke up I willed myself back to sleep quickly. I dreamed of you all night long."

He smiled at her. "Call me what you called me up on the mountain," he said.

"Cariad?" She raised her eyebrows and flushed. And then looked at his mouth. *"Cariad."*

He kissed her mouth softly.

"I must go." She drew her hands free.

He crossed the room to open the door for her and watched her as she descended the stairs quickly and lightly to the hall.

God, he loved her. Her body, her mind, her soul. Her. He loved her. Yet they had somehow got themselves into an impossible relationship. She was not his mistress and yet had not ruled out the possibility that they would be occasional lovers. They were not established lovers, yet she was willing to let him kiss her and hold her. She was willing to call him her love.

Siân Jones was an incredibly generous woman, he realized. The night before last she had given herself without any thought of getting anything in return. And now she was giving her love — yes, it was love — without demanding any type of security. Only the knowledge that she could trust him. She did not need jewels, she had said.

She needed only to believe in him.

If he possessed the universe, he thought, he would spread it beneath her feet. Well, he did not own as much, but he owned enough. He would spread what he had as a carpet for her, so that she would be able to look about her in Cwmbran and like what she saw.

And know that she had not trusted him in vain.

18

Alex woke in a cold sweat and found himself gazing up at the canopy above his bed and listening intently. The sound had died away by the time consciousness had fully returned, but he knew very well what he had heard.

Scotch Cattle.

Damnation! He clamped his teeth together and clenched his hands into fists at his sides. He had hoped to avoid this.

He was foolish, he supposed, to have believed that matters would move fast, that everyone would see things his way, that they would forget about the larger issue and throw themselves with enthusiasm into making Cwmbran a livable place and a model to all surrounding towns.

He had not not heard anything from Owen Parry in three days. He had heard plenty from his fellow owners, who were still holding out against their striking workers. None of what they had to say was complimentary.

The Chartists were still pressing forward with their plan. That was obvious. Yet again they were trying to force every man and boy to join their organization and prepare for the march on Newport. It was not going to be so easy to deflect them from that purpose, obviously.

Damn it all to hell! Some poor men were going to be punished again. For nothing. He wondered if Siân's young brother-in-law would be among them once more. Did Scotch Cattle punish the same man twice? He was going to have to call Owen Parry back tomorrow and see if something could be settled and to find out what progress had been made in organizing a meeting with representatives of the town's workers.

And then that chilling wailing and howling started up again and Alex got out of bed to cross to the window. Not that he could see anything from there, of course. Should he get dressed and go outside? Doubtless they would be gone before he could come up with them. If they were following their usual pattern, this must be a night of warning since they did not usually punish without a warning first. Besides, even if he went out and found them, what could he do —

one man against ten?

While he hesitated, he was chilled by another sound — screaming from within the house. Verity! She must have awoken and been frightened by the sounds. He grabbed a dressing gown, thrust his arms into the sleeves, and belted it about his waist as he ran.

Verity's nurse was just arriving at the child's bedside, but Alex waved her away and scooped up his screaming daughter in his arms.

"It's all right, sweetheart," he said to her. "It's all right."

"Dada, I'm frightened," she wailed. "There are wolves. They are coming to get me."

He had noticed ever since the day of the *eisteddfod* that she tended to give him a Welsh title when she was in any sort of emotional state.

"Papa has you," he said, tightening his hold on her for a moment so that she would feel the strength of his arms. "And we are inside a strong castle. No one and nothing is going to get you. Papa will not allow it."

"Wolves," she moaned against his neck. "Nurse said there would be wolves and I thought it was funny."

It was probably better for her to believe in

wolves than in wild men, he thought, having to make a quick decision.

"Just wild animals of some sort," he said. "They don't come close to Cwmbran or to Glanrhyd Castle because they are afraid of people. But in the night the sound of their howling travels a long, long way and makes them seem close."

"I'm frightened, Dada." She burrowed closer.

"I know." He pulled the top cover from her bed, sat down with her on an armchair, and covered her up warmly. "It is a frightening sound, isn't it? But there is nothing really to be scared about. Papa has you safe. Nobody is going to get my little girl."

She wriggled into a more comfortable position and sighed. "Stay with me, Papa," she said.

"Of course." He kissed her tousled curls. "Ah, there it is again. Listen to it with Papa's arms about you. You see? It is not so very frightening after all, is it? Not when you are here and it is there."

She sighed again and closed her eyes.

And yet it chilled him to the bone. Some poor stubborn men were being terrorized tonight and knew what they had to look forward to in a few nights' time if they continued stubborn.

There were no more howlings. Just the three. Alex sat for longer than an hour in his daughter's room, holding her fast asleep on his lap, before getting up and setting her gently back on her bed without unwrapping her from the bedcover. She did not stir. He gazed down at her with a love so intense that it almost hurt.

Siân woke instantly and sat up in bed to hug her legs and press her forehead against her knees. She was cold with terror. She doubted that it was a sound one could ever become accustomed to. It was intended to wake all sleepers and put terror into them. It succeeded.

Iestyn, she thought immediately. They would be after Iestyn again. She had spoken to him and he had assured her that he would not join the Chartist Association. Not when the men were to march with weapons and in such large numbers that the chances of a peaceful demonstration turning into a bloody riot were high. But surely they would not go after him again. Not twice.

She hated Scotch Cattle. She hated shows of violence and coercion. Could people not be allowed to decide for themselves what to do about major issues? Could not the majority rule without having to squash the minority? What use would unwilling men be in such a march, anyway?

"Siân?" It was Emrys's voice. He was coming down the stairs. "Are you all right, *fach*? Frightened?"

"I wonder if anyone in this town is not frightened," she said. "I hate this. I thought the ending of the strike would satisfy everyone for a while."

"That has nothing to do with the demonstration," he said, setting a reassuring arm about her shoulders when she got out of bed. "It is important that everyone join the march. It would not be very effective if twenty men went marching into Newport, now, would it? Anyone who blinked would not notice them passing at all."

"All right, Siân?" Her grandfather had come downstairs too. "You stay put tonight, girl. No running off down to the Joneses' to make sure young Iestyn is safe."

"They won't single him out again, will they?" she asked, begging for reassurance she knew they could not give.

But before they could give any answer at all, the howling began again, so close that they all jumped, and Emrys's hand tightened painfully about Siân's shoulder.

And then the door crashed inward, the latch shattering as it did so, and three large men wielding sticks and wearing sacks over their heads, with only slits for their eyes to look through, leaped into the kitchen while more stayed outside in the back garden.

"Bloody hell!" Emrys roared. "What do you want? You have the wrong place."

"In the name of the good Lord," Hywel Rhys said, drawing himself up to his full height, "state your business, Scotch Cattle."

One of them spoke in a hoarse whisper, his voice muffled by the sack. He raised one of his arms to its full length and pointed.

"Siân Jones," he said, "be warned. Informers are the scum of the earth. You will leave your employment at the castle and stay away from the Marquess of Craille if you do not want us to call on you again in three nights' time. Be sensible. Acknowledge your guilt and atone for it by doing as you are told."

"Get out of my house! *Duw, Duw,* what is the world coming to, then?" Gwynneth Rhys came storming down the stairs in a long white nightgown, her hair in two plaits over her shoulders, and picked up a broom. "Get out of my house, or I will sweep you out like dirt from under my feet."

The Scotch Cattle turned unhurriedly and left the house. Gwynneth slammed the door behind them though there was no latch to hold it shut.

Terror sometimes had the effect of almost totally incapacitating a person physically, Siân found, while leaving the mind lucidly clear. She lost her legs, and her hands shook beyond her control. Her stomach wanted to heave itself empty and her lips and tongue were paralyzed. Her lungs were drawing in too much air and expelling too little.

They were going to come back for her in three nights' time and drag her up onto the mountain and whip her, as Iestyn had been whipped. No, Grandad and Uncle Emrys would not allow it. Owen would not allow it. He would not. Oh, God, oh, God. Alexander!

"No, I have her, Dada," Emrys was saying. "Do you stand aside and I'll sit on the settle with her."

He had lifted her up into his arms, Siân realized, and soon he was sitting on the settle with her cradled on his lap. Her grandfather was chafing her hands hard enough to hurt. Her grandmother was coaxing the dying embers of last evening's fire into life and filling the kettle.

"She is just in shock," Emrys was saying. "Breathe in and out slowly, *fach.* Let the breath come out. Count slowly — one, two three, in and one, two, three out. That's it."

"I'll kill the bloody cowardly bastards for

this," Hywel said. "Picking on a woman, indeed to goodness. It is unheard of. It is against the teachings of the Good Book."

Siân's lucid mind registered a quite inappropriate amusement. Her grandfather would have reprimanded the Reverend Llewellyn himself if he had dared to swear in his house or in the hearing of women.

"That's right, *fach,*" Emrys said. "You have it under control now. Just shock it was, and fright."

Siân burrowed her head against his shoulder for a moment and then sat up. He lifted her to sit beside him on the settle, but still kept a protective arm about her.

"Well," she said, spreading her hands on her lap and noting that they were shaking as badly as ever, "at least now I know what it is like." She tried to laugh.

"My granddaughter, my own flesh and blood accused of being an informer." Hywel had abandoned his efforts to chafe her hands and was standing, feet apart, shaking one fist at the back door. "I'll bloody Scotch Cattle them if they dare to come back here. Let them dare face me man to man one at a time. I'll bloody well Scotch Cattle them."

"Hywel," his wife said softly.

He looked at her blankly and then with awareness. "May the Lord forgive me," he

424

said, "and you too, Gwynneth. And Siân."

"Well, if you don't, Dada," Emrys said, "I bloody well will. And don't ask me to apologize."

"Anyway," Hywel said, more himself again, "they will not be coming back. Staying home here you will be tomorrow and every day after that until your wedding, Siân, *fach,* and letting your grandad and your uncle look after you. You can help Gran about the house. She needs help."

"There will be the wedding to start cooking for any day now," Gwynneth said. "You will be safe when you are married to Owen, Siân, *fach.* He will not stand for Scotch Cattle visiting in the middle of the night."

"Neither will I, Mam," Emrys said. "But they don't exactly wait for an invitation, do they? They will have three days, Siân, to see that you have done what you are told. They will not come back. You will be safe. But until the wedding, anyway, I will sleep in this old cupboard down here and you will have my bed upstairs."

"No," Siân said, and felt suddenly as if she were two quite distinct persons, one standing back and observing in some amazement, and the other right inside her body, speaking and acting.

"It will be no sacrifice," Emrys said with a

chuckle. "Now that the nights are getting chillier, I will welcome the chance to sleep in a room where there has been a fire all day. My motives are selfish, you see, Siân. There, Mam has a cup of strong tea made for each of us. We will drink it down and then it will be upstairs with you while I mend the latch."

They all fell silent as the Scotch Cattle wailed again. A farewell salute from the hills. Only three howlings altogether — two from the hills and one from the town. They had come out solely for their visit to her, Siân thought.

"No," she said when all was silent again outside. "I was not talking about the beds, Uncle Emrys. I meant no, I am not going to stay at home. I am not going to give up my job. I am not going to stop going to the castle."

"Duw, Duw," her grandmother said.

"As stubborn as a mule," her grandfather said, anger in his voice. "As stubborn as our Marged."

"It is a pity you are not married already," Emrys said. "I know for a fact that Owen would take a hand to your backside, Siân, and a good thing it would be too, for all that I do not hold with beating women. Better Owen's hand than Scotch Cattle's whips, I say."

"Oh, Siân, be sensible," her grandmother said, and her face crumpled as she reached for her apron, which she was not wearing. She turned her head sharply to one side.

"That is exactly what they said." Siân was beginning to feel terror turn to anger. Every word they had said was engraved on her mind as if it had been chiseled there. " 'Be sensible.' Being sensible involves doing that which will save me from punishment. No. I will not be sensible. I am sorry, Gran. But I cannot be."

"Fach," Emrys said, "those whips hurt. You saw Iestyn's back. Raw it was for days, and all he got was ten strokes. They usually give twenty. They spread you on the ground and tie your hands and feet to stakes. They bare your back."

Gwynneth moaned.

The terror was back on Siân, cold in her nostrils, attacking her breathing. She counted again — one, two, three in, one, two, three out.

"Did you hear what they said?" she asked. " 'Acknowledge your guilt,' they said, 'and atone for it by doing as you are told.' If I stop teaching and stay home here, I will be admitting that I told the Marquess of Craille about the meeting on the mountain. I did

427

not tell him. I am not an informer. If I do as they demand, it will be only out of fear. I will not be controlled by fear."

"It is to avoid the whips, Siân," her grandmother said between sobs. "You will do it to avoid them, *fach*. And soon you will be married and leaving that old job anyway."

"No," Siân said. "If I once let fear dictate how I live my life, Gran, soon I will not be living it for myself at all. And I will not be able to live with myself either."

"There is brave you are, little niece," Emrys said, grudging admiration in his voice. "And there is foolish. Maybe Owen will use that hand even before you are married and save you from yourself."

Hywel got up without a word, leaving behind a cup of tea he had hardly touched, and went upstairs.

Gwynneth cried quietly.

Siân doggedly drank her tea to the dregs, even though she had trouble swallowing each mouthful. She dared not let her mind dwell on three nights hence. She would talk to Owen. He knew she was innocent. He trusted her. He would save her.

"Right," Emrys said when she was finished. "Upstairs with you, then, and to bed in my room."

"There is no need," she said.

"Siân." He got to his feet and looked sternly down at her. "There is little enough either Dada or I will be able to do for you, girl, if you continue stubborn, no matter how tough we talk. If they come for you, they will take you even if we put up a fight. At least let me do this for you. Let me at least make them have to fight their way past me."

She stood up and kissed him on the cheek. "All right," she said. "Thank you, Uncle Emrys."

"Foolish, brave girl," he said. "I could shake the living daylights out of you. But it would do no good, would it?"

She shook her head.

"Up you go, then," he said. "And you, Mam. Dry the eyes and blow the nose, is it? And console yourself with knowing that you have a granddaughter with more courage than sense. One of those warrior women she should have been, the ones I read about once in Sunday School when I was a lad, though why it was not the Bible I was reading I cannot remember. Amazons. That was them. Our Siân should have been an Amazon."

Siân went upstairs and climbed into her uncle's rumpled bed. She burrowed beneath the blankets and lay still, wrestling with her demons for an hour or more before falling asleep.

Josiah Barnes did not know why the Scotch Cattle had been out, he assured Alex when summoned the next morning. Someone had not wanted to go on strike, perhaps, though everyone had for the few hours it had lasted. Or perhaps someone did not want to join the Chartists in their next planned action. Barnes's informer had told him about the demonstration — but not the reason the Cattle had been out last night. Everyone was too terrified of the Cattle to inform against them, he explained to Alex.

Owen Parry did not know, either. He had not even heard the Cattle. He was apparently a deep sleeper. Had they really been out last night? He had heard nothing about it. Alex, who had summoned him, asked him only once. He knew by now that there was no getting anything out of Parry that the man did not choose to disclose.

"I don't want anyone hurt," Alex said. "Especially in such a useless cause. A demonstration like the one planned by John Frost is doomed to failure. Perhaps to worse than failure. In the meantime, we have important matters to deal with here in Cwmbran. When may I meet with you and the other representatives of the workers?"

"We are not interested," Owen said.

Alex stared at him in exasperation. "What is that supposed to mean?" he asked. "How can you not be interested in the well-being of your own people? You are their leader and work to assert their rights, don't you?"

"We are not interested in charity or in walking into the traps you set," Owen said. "We will win equality and our rights in our own way. We will not be beholden to you."

It was an answer so unexpected that Alex was quite unprepared to deal with it. "Do you speak for yourself?" he asked. "Or for everyone?"

"For everyone." Owen looked at him steadily. "I am the leader, remember? I speak for my people."

"Damn you," Alex said. "What have you said to turn them against me? Have I not demonstrated goodwill enough? Is it not worth at least talking?"

Owen said nothing.

Alex nodded curtly. "It will have to be done another way, then," he said. "Thank you, Parry. That will be all. Except for one thing. I believe I once told you that if the Scotch Cattle harmed my people again, I would hunt them down and deal out a like treatment. I meant what I said. I trust you

431

will pass on the message."

"I don't know any Scotch Cattle," Owen said. "No one does."

Alex dismissed him with a nod.

What he should do, he thought, was have his bags packed and Verity's and leave for the familiar world of his estates in England without delay. How could he keep trying to convince himself that he loved this valley and these people when hell could not be worse than living here? The lives of the people were almost intolerable, and yet they would do nothing to try to improve conditions. They hated him without reason — merely because he was English and the owner of Cwmbran, and it was ingrained in them to hate the owners.

But he knew he would not leave. There was a stubborn streak in him that he had not been fully aware of before coming here. Besides, he could not leave.

He sent up to the nursery to invite Siân to luncheon.

She knew, he thought, as soon as she joined him in the dining room later and he seated her at the table. Her face was pale and set and there were shadows beneath her eyes. She sat stiff and straight-backed on her chair. She had not once looked fully at him. She knew, all right.

He waited for the soup to be served and then dismissed the servants, telling them that he and Mrs. Jones would help themselves to the other courses from the sideboard.

He took her hand in his as soon as they were alone. It was as cold as a block of ice. He raised it to his lips. "Three days has been too long a time," he said. "Did you resent the invitation?"

She looked at him for the first time and shook her head.

He talked about Verity and their home in England. He talked about London and Brighton. He talked about his boyhood and university days. He spoke monologues. She looked as if she needed a good meal. He would not talk about anything that might take away her appetite. Not until the meal was done. Even so she ate precious little, he noticed.

"Siân," he asked at last, "on whom did they call last night?"

Her eyes looked back into his, and it was almost as if a curtain dropped behind them. "Pardon me?" she said.

"The Scotch Cattle," he said. "On whom did they call?"

She shook her head. A hint of fear in her eyes was immediately masked. "I don't know," she said. "Were they out last night?"

He sat back in his chair and regarded her steadily. "Your brother-in-law again?" he asked. "Is that it? Poor Siân." He reached out to cover her hand with his.

"No." She shook her head. "If they had called on Iestyn, I would have heard. It was not him. It was someone else."

"But you don't know who?"

She shook her head quickly, her eyes on her plate.

"Siân." He curled his fingers beneath hers. "I thought you trusted me."

"I do." Her voice was very low.

"Tell me, then," he said. "I want to help. I want to put an end to it — to the terror. I want to catch them at it."

"You don't understand," she said. "Scotch Cattle are enforcers. They enforce what the vast majority believes in. People may be terrified of them, but most people approve of what they do. They would not take kindly to your interfering."

"Wouldn't they?" He had not thought of that, either. Interference. Not help, but interference.

"No," she said.

"And you?" He watched her closely. "Wouldn't you like me to stop them, Siân?"

She hesitated for a long time. She licked

her lips. "No," she said. "You would only make it worse."

"How?" he frowned.

"If you came to the rescue of a man being punished," she said, "it might be thought that he had appealed to you, that he was your friend. Perhaps your informer. It would go the worse with him."

"Informer?" His voice was angry, though it was not against her his anger was directed. "Am I so much the enemy, Siân, that anyone who speaks to me or tells me anything is an informer?"

"Please." She drew a deep breath and closed her eyes for a few moments. "If they were out last night, it must have been to give a warning. If they come back again in a few nights' time to punish, don't interfere. Don't go out there. Please? Promise me?"

"Siân," he said, "it is my duty to protect my people. How can I —"

"Please." She was on her feet and was gazing down at him. "You must promise me. You must. Please."

My God, he thought, throwing down his napkin and getting to his feet to draw her firmly into his arms, what was this all about? What did she know? What were the Scotch Cattle up to that had made her so frightened? It was someone she knew. But who?

The brother-in-law again? He could believe that she would be frantic with worry if she thought the boy was going to have to endure another of those whippings. And doubtless this time he would have to take the full number of strokes.

But how could he promise her what she asked? It went entirely against the grain. But there was so little he could give her. And he loved her.

"Please?" She raised her face to his. Her eyes were large and luminous.

"I promise," he said, and watched in some dismay as she bit at her upper lip, lost control of her facial muscles, and began to cry.

"What is it?" He drew her face against his cravat and rocked her. "What is it, my love? Tell me." She was as cold as ice.

"No," she wailed. "It is nothing."

He lifted her face after a while and dried her eyes with his handkerchief before handing it to her so that she could blow her nose.

"I'm sorry," she said. "I don't often do that. I must be getting back to the nursery."

"Not until the redness has gone from your eyes," he said, setting the handkerchief on the table and drawing her back into his arms. "I see that it is something you cannot tell me. We will leave it at that, then. But

436

never feel that you cannot come to me, Siân. I am always here. Kiss me?"

She nodded.

He kissed her until he felt warmth flow back into her body. And then he kissed her some more. And realized something that had been nagging at his consciousness for days. This would not do. This having her but not having her simply would not do at all.

He could not live without her, he thought.

It was not just that he was in love with her. He loved her. She was the air he breathed.

He would not live without her. But she would not be his mistress. That left only . . .

But that was an impossibility. He was the Marquess of Craille. She was the illegitimate child of a baronet and an ironworker's daughter.

It was an impossibility.

But so was living without her.

"I must go back to the nursery," she said.

"I'll send word that you will be another hour," he said. "Come to bed with me, Siân. Come and make love with me."

She shook her head. "It would be sordid," she said.

Yes, it would. Dammit, it would.

He kissed her once more and released her.

"Forgive me," he said. "I did not mean disrespect."

"Thank you," she said, "for luncheon." And she was gone.

No, he thought, walking to the window and glazing sightlessly out, he could not live without her. But neither could he live with her like this. She was right. The snatched and very occasional lovemakings that they could doubtless enjoy over the coming months or years would be sordid. Up on the mountain or in his own house — with Verity beneath the same roof. It had not been sordid that first time because it had been spontaneous. It had been beautiful. But that could not be repeated.

What did she know? His thoughts returned to the mystery that had been gnawing at him all morning. Why was she so frightened? He cursed himself for promising to stay away if and when the Scotch Cattle returned to mete out punishment in a few nights' time.

Angharad was sniveling as she dusted. She cuffed ineffectually at her eyes when Josiah Barnes entered the house, and turned her face away.

"What is the matter with you?" He frowned, her misery breaking in on his more than good mood.

"Siân Jones is going to be whipped by Scotch Cattle," she said, sobbing and gulping in the middle of the sentence, "and it is all my fault."

"How so?" he asked, pulling off his boots. "Don't talk nonsense, woman."

"Someone has been putting about the rumor that she told the marquess about the meeting," she said. "But it was you, Mr. Barnes, and I am the one who told you. If I had not told you, he would not have known and no one would have thought it was Siân who told."

"If people believe stupid rumors," Barnes said, "it is not your fault, Angharad. And there is no stopping Scotch Cattle once they get something into their heads. It is unfortunate for Siân Jones, but that is the way things go. She could avoid the punishment. I hear she was warned not to continue her job."

Angharad wailed afresh. "But she went to work this morning," she said. "I saw her pass the house."

Yes. Barnes had to school his features not to smile openly. Yes, he had seen her walk past the ironworks.

"She is my friend," Angharad said. "I think I should say something, Mr. Barnes. I think I should tell Owen Parry. Perhaps he can stop them."

Josiah Barnes looked at her, thunderstruck. "Tell Parry?" he said. "Tell him what, Angharad? Tell him that it was not Siân Jones who was the informer, but you? Do you want to be the next one to receive midnight callers? Do you want to have your back bared up on the mountain and strips torn off it with Scotch Cattle whips? Have some sense, woman."

Angharad whimpered.

"Listen," he said, striding across the room to her, swallowing his distaste at her wet, reddened face and drawing her into his arms, "Siân Jones is asking for trouble by coming to work. She is being foolishly stubborn. Nothing is your fault, Angharad. Dry your eyes now and get upstairs and no more of this silly talk about going to Parry. I would not like you with a scarred back. I'll talk to Craille and see if he can persuade Siân Jones to stay home for a few days."

"Will you, Mr. Barnes?" she said, scrubbing at her eyes with the duster and gazing worshipfully up at him. "There is kind you are."

Coupling with a woman was too strenuous and too mindless a business to allow for much thought. But elation helped Josiah

Barnes enjoy the exercise with more than his usual vigor. Sometimes imagining that it was Siân Jones's body beneath him helped increase his enjoyment, but today he did not need to do that.

His little scheme was succeeding very well indeed. He had never for one moment expected that Scotch Cattle would be brought in to discipline her. Or that the stubborn wench was also so stupid.

She had gone to work this morning. If only Craille did not get word of why Scotch Cattle had made their visit last night, she would continue coming.

She would get the whips. Perhaps worse. Who knew what Scotch Cattle would do with a woman once they had her on the mountain and their blood was up?

Then he would see if she would hold her chin up and look at him as if he was a worm beneath her feet, Barnes thought as he lay spent and breathless on Angharad's body.

Then he would see.

"Oh, Mr. Barnes." Angharad's voice was weak with tears again. "There is wonderful you are. And you will talk to the marquess?"

"Yes, I'll talk to him," he said, rolling off her. It would take weeks for the cuts and welts to heal on Siân Jones's back. She would carry the scars to the grave. There

would be no wedding next week. He smiled.
"You are a good woman, Angharad. Rest a
while and I'll give it to you again."

19

It had been a mistake to come to choir practice, Siân thought wearily as she stood in the church porch after it was over, staring out at mist and rain. Though several other people were hesitating to step outside, as she was, and the porch was not large, there was space all about her. As if she was in some way untouchable — and invisible. No one's eyes quite touched on her and had not all evening. Her neighbors in the pew had both been intent on talking with the people on their other sides when they were not singing.

It all felt sickeningly familiar. The pariah.

Though it was not quite hostility she sensed, but more a deep embarrassment. How did one speak to someone who had been warned by Scotch Cattle the night before, after all? Did one pretend one did not know when everyone always knew — as they were expected to know — whom they had visited? She supposed that most people felt a strange sort of fascination with the knowledge that she had gone to work as usual today — and an inability to look into her eyes with the knowledge that she was facing Scotch Cattle whips in two nights' time if she continued to go to work.

There was blank terror in the thought that threatened to bring a return of last night's discomfort when she had been able to breathe in but not out.

She had been almost unable to sing. Or to concentrate on the Reverend Llewellyn's instructions. Or on his lengthy prayer for peace and good sense and an acceptance of the will of God that had preceded the practice.

She ought not to have come.

A hand clamped onto her shoulder suddenly and squeezed hard. She had not realized how much she needed to be touched until she felt it there.

"Home is it for us, then, Siân?" her grandfather said, his voice too loud and hearty. "Up with your hood, *fach.* A wicked, rainy night it is. Gran will have a pot of hot tea waiting for us."

She smiled at him and did as she was told. Owen had not come for her before the practice as he usually did. She had walked to chapel alone, her grandfather having gone on ahead. Owen had not come to practice either.

"Grandad," she said as they left the chapel and she took his offered arm, "this is all rubbing off on you, isn't it? That is the worst of it. If I were the only one involved, it would be just. I don't want you hated too."

"You are not hated, *fach,*" he said, "except perhaps by those few who believe that you informed against your own people. Most people admire your courage and think you the most foolish woman on God's earth."

"As you do," she said.

"As I do." He patted her hand.

"Perhaps" — she drew a deep breath — "perhaps you would prefer it if I moved away, Grandad."

"Moved away?" His voice, surprisingly, was thunderous.

"I have brought trouble on you," she said, "and on Gran. And I can't do the one thing that would smooth everything over again. I can't, Grandad. I cannot give in to threats. But perhaps they will destroy the house or the furniture. They sometimes do. I would never forgive myself if that happened."

"Siân" — his voice was harsh — "you must do what you must do. It will break your grandmother's heart, but she will respect you for it. And so will I. But you will not leave us. That would break Gran's spirit. If we have learned one thing in this life, Gran and I, it is that we cannot live the lives of those dearest to us. We can only love them no matter what they do. We learned the hard way. We learned too late in the case of your mother. We will not let you go. Even if it were true, what some are saying, we would not stop loving you."

"Grandad," she whispered, "oh, Grandad." She drew a deep breath, fighting tears. *I am so frightened,* she wanted to say. *So terrified.* But that was her burden alone. There was one thing she could do to avert what was ahead of her, to put the terror behind her. But she chose not to do it. Her terror was her own personal burden, then. She did not know if she most feared being dragged away by those large masked men — there was something bone-weakeningly horrifying about a masked face — or being spread out on the ground and confined and whipped.

Terror caught at her breathing again. She might have appealed to Alexander. Oh, dear God, she might have told him and he might have been able to intervene to save her. Instead, she had made him promise not to leave Glanrhyd Castle to investigate the next night visit of the Scotch Cattle.

He had promised.

They were just turning in at the gate of their house when they were hailed and turned to find Owen hurrying toward them.

"Hywel, Siân," he said in greeting. "I had a meeting. It went on longer than expected. Siân? How are you?"

She had not seen him since the night before. He would know, of course, just as everyone knew. She had expected to see him earlier. She had thought he would come to see her as soon as he had finished the day shift. But he had had a meeting. A meeting, it seemed, was more important than she was. In one way it was consoling. She was burdened by guilt over Owen.

She nodded her head and said nothing.

"Come inside, man," Hywel said. "It is madness to stand out here in the rain."

"I want to talk privately with Siân," Owen said. "Come and have a cup of tea with me, Siân. I will treat her with the proper respect, Hywel."

"See that you do," her grandfather said sternly. "These fists of mine can still do damage, Owen Parry, even if yours can do more."

Owen wrapped an arm about her waist as they walked away. He said nothing while they hurried, head down against the rain and the wind, toward his house. He took her cloak from her when they were inside, shook it out, had hung it behind the door. He did the same with his coat before turning to face her.

"Madwoman!" he said, reaching for her and taking her upper arms with hands that would leave bruises behind. His face was tight with anger. "What is this I hear, Siân? You went to work today?"

"Yes." She came against his chest and forgot that the burden was all her own. He was so very reassuringly large.

"Then all I can say," he said, "is that you deserve what you will surely get. You know, of course, that they tie you down. You know that they take the clothes from your back. You know that the whips are of leather and often draw blood. You went up after Iestyn and saw it all. Do you think they will strike more lightly because you are a woman? They will not. They believe your crime to be worse than merely refusing to sign a document or join an organization. You will doubtless be given the full twenty strokes, if not more."

Despite herself, she whimpered and pressed herself closer to him.

But he still had her by the arms and

moved her away from the sanctuary of his body to shake her violently until her head flopped on her neck and she was dizzy and disoriented.

"What will it take?" He was shouting at her. "What will it take to tame you, you bloody foolish, stubborn woman? You want to go over my knee, is that it? Right now? I have a heavy hand, Siân Jones, and will not spare it. You will be lying on your stomach on your bed tonight. Let's get on with it, then."

He kept his bruising grip on one arm and dragged her toward a chair.

"Owen" — she spoke coldly — "if you lay one hand in violence on me, I swear I will have you before a magistrate. I am not answerable to you. And why must men — some men — assume that women are to be controlled by pain? I will not be controlled by it or coerced by the fear of it. I will not give in to threats. And you will not save me from the whips even if you take me over your lap now and beat me until I have to lie on my stomach all night."

His hold on her did not relax as he stood quite still and stared down at her, his face white and set with anger. Then he drew her against him and pressed her head hard against his shoulder.

"Siân," he whispered. "*Cariad, cariad.* Why will you be so foolish? Why will you not let me hold you and protect you and guide you as a man should be allowed to do for his woman?"

"Perhaps because I am a thinking person as well as a woman," she said sadly.

He rocked her against him wordlessly.

"Owen," she said after a while, "you know some of the Scotch Cattle, don't you?"

"No one knows who they are, *cariad,*" he said.

"But you do." She lifted her head to look earnestly into his face. "You are the leader. You must know. Besides, I cannot forget how kind you were when it was Iestyn's turn. I know he was given ten lashes, but I know too that you had put in a good word for him and had reduced the sentence. I know you did that. You cannot convince me that you don't know any of them."

He shook his head.

"Owen," she said, "you know I am innocent. You know I said nothing to the Marquess of Craille. You know I would not so betray my own people. You know I am no informer."

"*Cariad,*" he said, "I know it. Other people do not."

"Then tell them," she said. "You have

450

influence. People listen to you. Tell them. I don't want to be whipped. Oh, please, I don't want to be whipped."

His face turned paler. "Bloody stubborn woman," he said, the anger back in his voice. "You can save yourself, Siân. Even though you went to work today. If you do not go tomorrow, they will not come back. Even if you do not go the next day."

She shook her head slowly.

"Fach." He was whispering. "I cannot save you."

"Please?" She spread her hands on his chest. "Tell them I was not the informer, Owen. It hurts to know that people believe that. That is what hurts more than anything."

"No," he said harshly, "there is something that will hurt more than that, Siân. The whips will hurt more."

"Tell them," she said. "Please?"

He gazed at her in silence for a long while. "I will see what I can do, *cariad,*" he said. "But I cannot promise anything. Fair warning has been given. You have been provided with a way out. Punishment will follow if you do not take it."

She smiled at him. "Not if you speak up for me," she said. "Thank you, Owen."

His face blurred before her eyes suddenly

451

as all her deep affection for him welled up in her and reminded her that she did not love him, that she was deceiving him by not breaking off their engagement, that she had lain with another man up on the mountain and loved that other man.

Owen!

If only she loved him. If only.

His kiss was gentle and rather brief.

"I'll walk you home," he said. "Unless you want that cup of tea."

She shook her head.

He kissed her rather more fiercely in the wind and the rain outside her grandfather's house a few minutes later.

"Siân," he said against her lips, "save yourself. Stay away from bloody Craille and his brat tomorrow. I want to protect you but can't. I feel like an impotent man. Only you can save yourself."

She pressed her lips to his. "I must do what I must do," she said. "But you are going to help me, Owen. I know you are. You are very wonderful."

Too wonderful to be deceived, she thought as she lay awake upstairs in her uncle's bed later. She should have been more open with him. She should have told him that she could not marry him. She should have removed from his shoulders the burden of feeling responsible for protecting her. But she had given in to cowardice. How could she tell him now? It was altogether the wrong time. She would wait until after . . .

But her stomach lurched and she felt physically sick as her mind pulled to a halt. She would not even think of before and after. Or of the event that separated the two. She burrowed farther beneath the bedclothes.

He had not slept at all, though he was lying in his bed. Three nights had passed. It was probably the night they would return if the poor men they had warned had not done what they had been instructed to do. He waited, all his muscles taut, for the first sign that at least one of their potential victims had proved stubborn.

Siân's young brother-in-law, as like as not.

And yet wakefulness and tautness of muscles did not after all prepare him for an expected horror, he found when the first unearthly howling and bellowing began. It was worse for being expected. He felt his blood run cold. He felt his breath catch in his throat.

Poor bloody fool, whoever he was that had defied them. Or whoever they were. He would not like to hear that sound and know they were coming for him, Alex thought. He closed his eyes and tried to lie still. He listened intently for a sound from Verity's room and prayed that tonight she would sleep through it.

There was a long wait for the second bout of wailing and bellowing. A silence filled with tension and horror. The whole of Cwmbran waited as he did, he guessed. The Scotch Cattle, whoever they were, were marvelously clever not to work in silence and secrecy. They were clever to prey upon the imagination of a whole townful of people. The first howl had heralded their arrival. The second was an indication that they had their first victim and were dragging him up the mountain. The third would mean that they had finished with him — poor beggar — and were setting out for their next victim. And so on.

How many victims?

But before he heard them for the third time, Alex was on his feet and pacing his darkened bedroom, his fists tight at his sides, his teeth clamped together. He regretted his promise to Siân more than he regretted any promise he had ever made. He felt utterly helpless and impotent, confined to the castle, while an unknown number of his people were being chastised out there on

454

the hills.

Why had he promised?

Why had she made him promise?

He wondered if she had stayed in her bed this time or if she had gone up the mountain again with her brother-in-law, as she had done the last time. Perhaps she was out there now, he thought, staring out the window into damp and gloomy darkness, while he was safe in here.

Damn you, Siân. He pounded the edge of his fists against the windowsill. *Damn you.*

He wondered if anyone ever became accustomed to the sound and could sleep through it or at least lie through it feeling nothing but indifference. His stomach churned sickeningly when finally the Scotch Cattle howled for a third time. Some poor fool's punishment was over. Iestyn Jones's, perhaps? Had he been first tonight? And how many more were there? Why were they being punished? For refusing to join the march on Newport?

Alex sighed with frustration. Tomorrow he would make it clear to Siân that his promise applied to this night only. He was not going to allow this to happen again. Even if it meant bringing in special constables or soldiers, he was going to put an end to such terrorism.

He stood at the window for longer than an hour, hardly aware of the fact that the air was cold, even with the window closed. But there was no further sound.

Only one victim?

The thought was somehow chilling. Only one? What was the crime that only one man out of the whole town was guilty of it?

He would find out tomorrow, he vowed. By God, he would find out.

She was not sleeping, of course, though she was lying on her uncle's bed upstairs. Neither was she undressed. She was wearing her oldest dress and shift. She was staring up into darkness. Her grandparents and Emrys were doing likewise, she guessed, though they had all gone to bed at the usual time and in the usual manner.

It was almost a relief, Siân thought, setting an uncontrollably shaking hand over her mouth, when the howling began. Almost a relief. It was beginning. Her hand, though icy cold, gradually stilled and she felt strangely calm. She sat up and swung her legs over the side of the bed. She sat very still, her hands in her lap, and waited. She listened to her grandfather going downstairs and saw light around the edge of her door. They had lit the lamp.

She wished, in her strange state of calm as she waited, that they did not howl up in the hills to warn of their approach. It took time for them to come down. Perhaps not very long. Perhaps ten minutes, perhaps fifteen. It seemed more like ten or fifteen hours. She wished they had just come to the house and howled and thrown open the door and come for her.

The waiting was the cruel part. Her heart was beginning to feel as if it were lodged in both her throat and her ears.

One, two, three, she counted slowly, closing her eyes. One, two, three in, one, two, three out. She counted more slowly for the outward breaths and opened her mouth. In through her nose, out through her mouth. She gripped the edge of the bed tightly.

Would they go away if she promised never again to go back to Glanrhyd Castle? If she begged and wept and groveled? Would they? Was it too late?

One, two, three in through the nose. One, two, three out through the mouth.

And then she gripped harder and doubled up until her forehead touched her knees as the howling began again and the door downstairs crashed inward. She lost control of her breathing.

She would beg. She would beg and beg.

457

She would promise anything. Anything they asked. She would do anything. Anything they wanted.

One, two, three; one, two, three.

Somehow she got to her feet.

Grandad and Emrys both had their shirtsleeves rolled to the elbows, she saw as she came quietly down the stairs. Gran had the broom. There were four Scotch Cattle in the kitchen, all hooded. There were more beyond the open doorway. Grandad was swearing the air blue.

"I believe," Siân said, her voice distinct and amazingly steady, "that you have come for me."

"That we have, Siân Jones," someone said in a gruff, hoarse whisper.

"I am ready," she said, lifting her chin.

But her family had other ideas. Siân stood quietly and watched, feeling curiously detached, as first her grandfather and then Emrys were overwhelmed and tied to chairs with lengths of rope that must have been brought for the purpose. Gran's broom was snapped over someone's knee.

"You do not need to drag me," Siân said, when hands finally clamped on her arms and two of the Scotch Cattle hurried her toward the door. "I will come with you." They should have gagged Grandad, that curious detached part of her mind thought. No one hearing him now would have guessed that he was a God-fearing man. It would take Gran a while to free him and Emrys from their knots.

But they dragged her anyway, their strides longer than her own so that she had to run to keep up to them and even so stumbled frequently on the darkened slopes. There were no moon and stars tonight. It was not actually raining but the air was cold and damp and the grass and heather underfoot were soaked and slippery. They rushed her upward in silence. She did not count them. Her mind was not lucid enough. But they all seemed like giants to her and there were many of them.

Please, dear God, she prayed. *Please, dear God.* A thought had struck her — strangely, for the first time. She did not know of any other woman who had been the victim of Scotch Cattle. What if part of her punishment was to be raped? It had never struck her before — before being alone on the mountain with perhaps ten large, strong men, all with their identities quite firmly concealed.

Oh, please, dear God, she prayed. *Please, dear God.*

She did not know where they were. Her

mind was incapable of registering direction or the normally familiar landmarks. She only knew that they moved steadily upward before stopping finally. Her arms were released and she found herself standing alone, staring down at the four stakes already driven into the ground and very visible even in the darkness.

She raised her chin though she did not lift her eyes.

"Siân Jones," the same hoarse voice as had spoken in her grandfather's kitchen said, "you have been accused of informing against your own people to the owner of Cwmbran and putting them all in danger. You have failed to comply with the demand that you end your employment. You have therefore been sentenced to twenty lashes with the whip."

Twenty. Oh, dear God. Her knees almost buckled. But now that the moment had come, she had found some inner strength, some inner stubbornness. She stood very still, looking down at one of the stakes.

Someone stepped up behind her — she did not turn her head. He did not open the buttons of her dress. He tore it open so that she felt it going from neck to hips. Then with a loud rending sound her shift was torn in two. She felt cold, damp air and the clawing of panic against bare skin.

And then she was facedown on the cold, wet, hard ground, her arms and legs being forced in four different directions and tied to the stakes. Four men worked simultaneously — and silently — and then she felt the hands of one of them pull the torn edges of her dress and shift back and down over her shoulders so that she was fully exposed from shoulders to hips.

Her back prickled. She pressed the side of her face against the ground and gripped the stakes with her hands. Whoever had tied her left wrist had tied too tightly, she thought irrelevantly. The blood could not flow freely. She would have pins and needles in her hand when she was released. There was something almost hysterically funny in the thought.

"She is a woman," another voice whispered. "She cannot take twenty. Ten will be enough."

"She is a woman who has betrayed us all," the first voice said. "She is lucky not to have twenty-five."

"Ten," the other voice whispered.

"Twenty," the first man said. "And let me see neither of you spare the whip."

"Fifteen," a third voice said aloud. "Split the difference and give her fifteen. Full force. The whips are damp. Fifteen with damp whips will feel as bad as twenty-five."

"Fifteen, then," the first man whispered grudgingly. "Be thankful that you have a champion here, Siân Jones."

But Siân was beyond thought. Let them just begin, she thought. Let them give her thirty strokes if they would just begin.

And then she was aware of a whistling sound and a thud and almost belatedly, it seemed, felt a needle-sharp pain that was too intense to be absorbed for a moment. Only the shock of it told her that one of her lashes had been delivered. A shock that felt as if it had stopped her heart and had certainly stopped her breathing. A knowledge that she had been hurt before her brain could fully register pain.

And then the second. The pain screeching loudly at her.

"Stop a moment."

She did not hear the voice. Her brain and her body grappled with a pain more intense than she had ever experienced or ever imagined — even during the past three days. And part of her waited for the third lash. For the unbearable one that would surely kill her.

"Open your mouth," someone was whispering, someone who was kneeling on the grass beside her head.

Mindlessly she did as she was told and a thick wedge of some rag was shoved between her teeth.

"Bite down on this," the voice said, slipping for a moment from its unidentifiable whispering.

But she neither saw him nor heard him. She only cursed inwardly at the delay.

Thirteen more lashes. She did not count. She did not think. She became raw pain. If she thought at all it was with amazement that one could endure such pain without passing out or without dying. And with surprise that it did not become dulled after the first few strokes but became more intense with each successive lash, as the whips whistled against welts already raw and bleeding.

She did not know it was over. She did not feel her wrists and ankles being cut free.

She did not hear the final howls and bellows and wails of the men who surrounded her spread-eagled body.

She was unaware that they had gone away.

She did not hear her grandfather's voice, Or Emrys's. Or Huw's or Iestyn's. She did not hear Iestyn crying or feel him stroking back her hair or kissing her cheek or telling her how proud he was of her.

And yet she did not lose consciousness.
Alexander, she thought.
Alexander, Alexander. Where are you?
Why have you not come?

20

Alex had not summoned Josiah Barnes. Doubtless Barnes would know. Everyone must know by now who the sole victim of the Scotch Cattle had been last night — except the Marquess of Craille. But he would not ask Barnes. He would find out from Siân.

She had known in advance and on the strength of her knowledge had extracted that promise from him not to leave the castle last night. He wondered if her fears had been realized. Perhaps not. Perhaps the victim had been someone else — perhaps her young brother-in-law had decided after all to toe the line.

He would invite her to luncheon, he thought. Or rather, he would command her to come to report on Verity's progress. She would hardly refuse a command. He was going to send Miss Haines up to the nursery with the invitation, but he decided to go himself. He would be able to see from her face if it had been her brother-in-law.

The nursery was very quiet. As he opened the door, he half expected to see the room empty. Perhaps they had gone for a morning walk since the weather was decent for the first time in several days. It would be wet underfoot in the hills, though.

But they were seated together at the table close to the windows, Verity bent over a sheet of paper, concentrating on some task she had been set, Siân sitting beside her, very straight-backed.

"Good morning," he said. "Don't let me interrupt you. Carry on."

Verity smiled sunnily at him. "I am doing penmanship, Papa," she said. "Look. All my letters are the same size."

"A miraculous improvement," he said, coming up behind her and looking over her shoulder. "And very neat and nicely shaped letters, too. I hope Mrs. Jones is pleased with you."

"Yes," Siân said. "She is trying hard."

He looked fully at her for the first time. There was not a vestige of color in her face, unless one counted the dark shadows beneath her eyes. Even her lips were bloodless. There were some cuts on her lower lip, as if she had bitten it. Her face was totally without expression. Although she looked at him when she spoke, he noticed that only her eyes moved. She held her head high and stiff.

She looked more like a marble statue than a woman.

God, had they killed the boy? Or hurt him badly? He wished more than ever that he had refused to promise what she had asked. He might have been able to stop it. He might have saved her this suffering.

"Carry on," he said again, patting his daughter's shoulder.

She bent over her paper once more. He was rather surprised that Siân did not reprimand her on her posture. She usually did in that gentle, positive way she had that always made censure sound like praise and that always had the desired result. Today Verity was allowed to hunch over her work. He said nothing himself.

He strolled to the other side of the table so that he could watch Siân without being observed himself. He would tell her soon that she was to take luncheon with him. He would get the truth out of her then. And he would kiss color back into her face and relaxation back into her body. She was sitting perfectly still and silent. He had the impression that she was paying no attention at all to what Verity was doing, even though her eyes were directed at the paper.

At first he thought it was a thread poking up from the neckline of her dress. He even caught himself about to step forward to tuck it back under. But such an intimate gesture would not be at all the thing. He wondered idly why anyone would use red thread in order to sew a blue dress.

And then he frowned and did take a step forward so that he was standing just a few feet behind her chair. Yes, he had not been mistaken. It was a scratch, a bloodline. Though more than the type of scratch one might give oneself carelessly with a pin. It was more like a — welt.

All his insides seemed to perform a complete and painful somersault suddenly. His knees almost buckled under him. He could feel the blood draining from his head and leaving it cold and clammy. The air in his nostrils felt icy. He clasped his hands very tightly at his back.

Several seconds passed before he felt sufficiently master of himself to move. He crossed the room to the bellpull and jerked on it. He waited beside it until Verity's elderly nurse came puffing into the room.

"Stay with Verity," he told her. "Perhaps you could take her for a stroll in the garden.

I have some important business to discuss with Mrs. Jones."

"Yes, my lord," the nurse said as Verity looked up in surprise and began to protest.

"You may take your doll with you," he said, smiling at his daughter, "and bring her downstairs with you for luncheon with me later."

Verity's protests stopped in the middle of a sentence. It was a rare treat to be able to take luncheon downstairs with her father. She bounded up from the table.

"Mrs. Jones too?" she asked.

"No," he said. "Mrs. Jones will not be joining us." He looked at her. "Come with me, please, Mrs. Jones."

She got slowly and stiffly to her feet while his stomach somersaulted again. He could not go to help her. He would not know where to touch her. Her face registered no expression at all.

"Along here," he said, following her from the nursery and directing her toward some guest bedrooms farther along the corridor.

She made no protest, even when he opened the door into one of them and motioned her inside. She made no protest when he followed her inside and closed the door behind him. She stood still and straight-backed in the middle of the room, facing away from him.

"The Scotch Cattle were out again last night," he said, leaning back against the door, wondering if it was possible for a man to faint, half expecting that he was about to find out.

"Yes," she said.

"They howled three times," he said. "I believe that means that there was only one victim."

"Yes."

"Who?" he asked. "Who was it, Siân?"

There was a lengthy pause. "I don't know," she said at last. "I have not heard."

He came up behind her. She did not move though she must have felt him there. She did not turn her head to look back at him.

Perhaps he had been mistaken after all, he thought. Surely he must be mistaken. Surely to God. He contemplated the top button of her dress, wondering how he could undo it without touching her flesh. He lifted his hands to it. He could feel her inhaling slowly as he worked the first button free of its buttonhole and moved his hands down to the next and the next. It took him a long time, but finally her dress was open to below the waist. He took the corners of the neck and moved them back.

She was wearing a shift. Even so he could

see that he had not been mistaken. He wondered again for a moment if he was going to faint. Or vomit. He moved her dress down her arms and hooked two fingers beneath the straps of her shift just in front of her shoulders. He lifted them as gently as he could and drew her shift down to her hips.

"How many?" he asked through lips that seemed too stiff to obey his will. He was looking at raw, inflamed welts crisscrossing all that was exposed of her back.

It took her a while to answer. "Fifteen," she said.

Fifteen. Iestyn Jones had been given ten. Alex remembered watching and counting the ten and thinking them endless. He remembered the state the boy had been in afterward.

"Why?" His voice had become a whisper.

"I don't know," she said.

"Why, Siân?"

"They believe I was your informer," she said. "They believe I told you about the meeting."

"Bloody hell!" he said.

He could remember Owen Parry demanding to know who his informer had been and his own refusal to give the man's name — he did not even know the man's name. He could remember Parry telling him that he would find out.

Bloody, bloody hell!

"Come," he said, and he crossed to the bed and drew back the covers. "Come and lie down."

She was holding her dress and shift to her breasts at the front. Her mask had come off, he saw, looking at her. Her eyes were pain-drugged.

"Come, Siân," he said. "I am afraid to touch you. I may hurt more than help."

But he did take her hands when she came close to him and unclenched her fingers from the fabric of her dress so that it could fall to the floor. Her shift lodged about her hips. He was in no mood to be aroused by her near nakedness, or she to be embarrassed by it.

"Lie down," he said.

He hovered over her helplessly while she got herself onto the bed facedown. She lay there eventually, clutching the pillow to her face, breathing loudly and raggedly. He knew that she was fighting pain.

He forced himself to look long and hard at the welts the whips had made on her back. All were red and swollen. Some had bled.

"How has this mess been treated?" he

asked. "What did your grandmother do for you?"

"She bathed it with water," she said.

"It needs ointments," he said. "And you need something for pain. Whose idea was it that you come to work today?"

"Mine," she said. "They might have misinterpreted my staying away."

He did not question her meaning but told her he would be back and left the room. He should send Miss Haines to her, but this was something he must do himself. Good God, she had been whipped because of him. She had been whipped! Fifteen times. By Scotch Cattle. Up on the mountain, spread-eagled and confined on the ground. Siân. His Siân. The feeling of cold dizziness in his head was becoming almost familiar.

He returned to the guest bedroom less than ten minutes later with a basin of tepid water and a soft flannel cloth, ointment that both Miss Haines and the cook swore was a miracle cure for minor bumps or major cuts, and a double dose of laudanum.

She was lying in the same position as before except that she had turned her head to the side, the better to breathe. She watched him come into the room and cross to the bed. Pain almost pulsed from her pale face and her dark, shadowed eyes.

"This first," he said, indicating the laudanum. "You will have to raise your head to drink it, and that will be painful, but it will dull the pain after a few minutes and help you sleep. When was the last time you slept?"

"I don't know," she said. "What is it?"

"Laudanum," he said.

"I have never taken it." She eyed it suspiciously.

"You will now," he said firmly.

Her eyes were closed and she was breathing raggedly through her mouth by the time she had raised herself, drunk it down, and lowered herself to the bed again.

"You are unlike any other woman I have ever known," he said, dipping the flannel into the water, squeezing it out, and feeling his knees turn weak as he eyed her back and knew that the time had come to touch it and cause her more pain. "Have you cried at all?"

"No," she said.

"Did you scream?"

"No."

She flinched when he touched the cloth to her back, and then lay still. He cleansed the welts and cooled them with the cloth and then spread the ointment liberally over her back, moving his fingers over her as lightly as he could. Even after the cooling water, her back felt as if it were on fire.

"Siân," he said, "I could have prevented this. Why did you not tell me? Why did you extract that promise from me?"

"What better way would there have been to suggest that I really was guilty than appealing to you for help?" she asked.

"What was their warning four nights ago?" he asked.

"That I leave my job," she said. "That I not come back here."

"And yet," he said, "you came."

"Yes."

"Knowing that you were going to get the whips last night."

"Yes."

"Did your grandfather and your uncle do nothing?" he asked.

"They were tied to chairs before I was taken away," she said. "And cursing fit to be driven from chapel."

"Did Parry do nothing?" he asked.

There was a pause. "No," she said.

"How did you get down from the mountain?" He was moving a sheet gingerly up her body.

"Grandad and Uncle Emrys came for me," she said. "And Huw and Iestyn."

"Not Parry?"

Again the pause. "No," she said.

He went down on his haunches beside the bed and looked into her face. Her eyes were closed. The laudanum should be taking effect soon, he thought. She would be able to sleep and forget her pain for a time — while he went out hunting. His mouth tightened into a grim line.

"Siân," he said.

She opened her eyes and looked into his. She was still in pain, he could see.

"Did you know any of them?" he asked. "Did you recognize any of them?"

"No," she said hastily. "They were wearing hoods. They were whispering."

He watched her silently as she closed her eyes. Her eyelashes grew wet as he watched.

"They are usually men from other valleys," she said. "I would not have recognized them even if they had not worn the hoods and even if they had spoken in their normal voices."

He remained silent, watching one tear trickle diagonally down her cheek to be absorbed in the pillow. The tear from the other eye pooled against her nose.

"Siân?" he said after a while. "Who were they?"

She sobbed then, a wrenching sob that seemed to have been dragged out from deep

476

inside her. She lifted one shaking hand to cover her face and sobbed as if her heart would break. Alex stayed where he was, watching her. He could not draw her into his arms. He did set one hand lightly against the side of her head.

"Who were they?" he repeated.

He knew the answer. He sensed it. But he had to hear it from her own lips.

"I wouldn't have known," she managed to jerk out between helpless sobs. "He was whispering like the others. He pleaded for ten lashes instead of twenty and they changed it to fifteen. He stopped them after a few strokes to put a cloth between my teeth so that I would not bite my lips raw. I didn't think I noticed or heard him. But he forgot to whisper when he was pushing the cloth into my mouth." She could say no more for a while.

He watched her, feeling the cold knot of fury ball inside his stomach.

"Who was he, Siân?" he asked.

"O-w-e-n," she wailed, misery and despair stark in her voice. "He was Owen."

He stroked the side of her head as she wept. His hand was warm and gentle. His heart was as cold as steel.

"It's over now," he murmured to her while the crying eased and he could tell from the lesser tension in her body that the pain was receding. "You defied them and you faced them with more courage and dignity than I have ever known in a woman — or in most men for that matter. When you stand on your own feet, Siân Jones, you stand quite firmly and quite alone on them, don't you? Some would call you a fool. I would wager that many have in the last few days. I honor you. I deeply honor you."

She smiled fleetingly. "That was strong medicine?" she asked. "I feel fuzzy all over."

"It was strong medicine," he said. "Are you comfortable?"

"I can never sleep on my stomach," she said.

"You would prefer your back?" he asked. "Let me help you, then."

It would be safer to help her, now — her eyes looked heavily drugged, but no longer with pain. He helped ease her over onto her back and covered her nakedness with the sheet and with two blankets. She was very nearly asleep.

"I should go home," she said, her words slow and slurred.

He looked down at her, watching her eyelids droop over her eyes. He touched the backs of his fingers to her cheek and then leaned over her and set his mouth lightly to hers.

"You are home, Siân," he whispered.

He did not believe she heard him. Her eyes were closed and remained closed. Her breathing was quiet and even.

She opened her eyes once to see Miss Haines standing beside her bed.

"I have brought you a drink," the house-keeper said. "Would you like it? May I help you sit up?"

But Siân shook her head and closed her eyes again. She was floating on cotton wool. She was cotton wool. She could not remember why, but she had a feeling that this was a state to be clung to for as long as possible. She vaguely wondered what Miss Haines was doing leaning inside her cupboard bed.

"I have sent a message to Mr. Hywel Rhys," Miss Haines said, "to inform him and Mrs. Rhys that you will be staying here at least for tonight."

Yes, that was good. Gran would not worry now. Siân sank gratefully back into fuzz. *I honor you. I deeply honor you.* She wrapped herself about with his voice and the soft gentleness of his words. They had been more soothing than the ointments. They had made the whipping worthwhile. No, not that, perhaps. But they had made its aftermath bearable.

Alexander. She opened her eyes and looked about the room for him. But he had gone away. There was no one else in the room.

You are home, Siân. She could hear his voice saying the words, though she could not remember where or when he had spoken them. *You are home.*

She sank back into sleep.

She woke up later to find someone else beside her bed. He was standing there gazing silently down at her. She had seen that look on his face only once before.

"Siân," he said softly as she closed her eyes again, "Siân, my little one."

She wanted him to go away. She did not want him in her dreams. Not with that look on his face. Not with those words on his lips. It could only be a cruel, mocking dream, the sort she could remember from childhood. Never reality. Only a dream.

"My little one," he said, "what have they done to you? Why didn't you come to me? Why have you never come to me?"

Because it was a dream, she said what she had always longed to say to him and never been invited to say. "Dada," she said, her eyes closed.

She had heard him cry once before. It was also when she had seen him look like that before. When her mother had died and he had come to the house. He had never cried over her, Siân. Or laughed with her. Or shown any emotion over her. She had never existed for him. But this was a dream. Anything could happen in a dream. In the dream he was crying over her.

"Things are going to change," she heard Sir John Fowler say before she sank back into sleep. "By God things are going to change. They are not going to hurt you again, my little one."

Where was Alexander? She opened her eyes to look about for him, but he was not there. There was no one there. She was in a strange room, she saw. She did not recognize it. She did not know quite why she was there. Alexander had brought her there. There was a twinge of discomfort when she tried to move. But she did not need to move. She was comfortable and warm and deliciously sleepy.

She sank back into sleep.

The atmosphere at the ironworks and in the coal mines and in the houses of the town was always somewhat subdued the morning after Scotch Cattle had dealt out punishment. Everyone knew about it and everyone knew who the victim or victims had been, yet no one wanted to discuss it. There was always a dual feeling of almost shamed sympathy for the victim on the one hand and approval of what the enforcers had done to safeguard the will of the majority on the other.

The atmosphere was more marked than usual this morning. No one could remember a time when a woman had run afoul of Scotch Cattle. But Siân Jones had. It was almost beyond belief that she had defied their warnings when she could so easily have complied with their one demand. But she had defied them.

Everyone knew by the morning that she had been dragged up the mountain last night and given the whips. Everyone even knew how many — fifteen lashes. Those who had been willing to discuss the matter in the days previous to it had bet on ten. Perhaps even five. She was a woman.

But she had been given fifteen lashes — with damp whips. She had been spread on the wet ground and her back bared for the whips, just as if she had been a man. Emrys Rhys had carried her home across his own back. Hywel Rhys had used enough curse words to be expelled from chapel for at least two eternities if anyone had cared to take the matter up with the Reverend Llewellyn and the deacons.

Owen Parry had not been able to control her obstinacy, the shocked whisper went around. There were those who had predicted that he would give her backside a good tanning before the Scotch Cattle could get at her, and thus save her from herself. But he had not been able to stop her. And he had not gone to her after the Cattle had howled the end of the whipping and their departure. Only her kin and Gwyn Jones's kin had gone up the mountain to bring her home.

Owen Parry was at work today among the puddlers, his face hard and set so that no one spoke to him unless he had to or stepped into his path.

Another amazing fact was that Siân Jones had gone to work this morning — a few hours after being dealt fifteen lashes with wet Scotch Cattle whips. One could not help but be rather awed at her spirit.

And one could not but be rather uneasily aware that such defiance and such courage did not seem quite to denote an informer. There were very few who had ever wholeheartedly believed that it was she who had informed against them. Why would she have done so when her own man would be the one most in danger from discovery? She must have known that Parry was to chair the meeting. And if she had been the informer, why had she apparently done nothing after the warning to enlist the help of the Marquess of Craille? Why had she done nothing to avoid the whips?

Men and women went about their work that morning subdued and a little fearful and a little puzzled.

The ironworkers were the first to hear it — the distinct, authoritative voice of the Marquess of Craille. It was not particularly loud, but it was a voice of his they had not heard before — a voice trained from birth to be heard and obeyed without question.

Work was finished for the day, he announced. He would see them in one hour's time on the mountain, in their usual meeting place. Every last man of them. The women were to return to their homes.

The men looked at one another, stunned. And yet, as they laid down their tools and left their work areas, there was not one of them who even thought of disobeying.

The miners received the same message less than half an hour later as the marquess's voice rang along first one coal seam and then another until every man, boy, and woman had heard the summons at least twice.

There was not a man who dared absent himself from the summons to the mountain. And not a man who would have done so even if he dared. The Scotch Cattle had gone too far this time. They had whipped a woman — the teacher Craille had employed to teach his daughter. Every man wondered in some fascination and not a little dread what the Marquess of Craille planned to do about it.

21

He stood on the rise at one end of the hollow, where the speakers at the two meetings he had observed had stood. He waited, still and silent, for the last stragglers to come up from Cwmbran, though most of the men had been there ahead of him. They were uneasily quiet and were eyeing him warily.

He was driven by a cold fury. He had not thought of what he would say. He did not think of it now. The words would come when he began. He knew at least what he was going to do. But first he would speak. He tapped his riding whip slowly against his boot.

The men seemed to sense the moment when he was ready to begin though he did not raise his arms or make any other signal. All fidgeting and whispering stopped. All faces gazed up at him. It was a self-conscious silence, a faintly hostile one, perhaps. He did not care.

"I am tired of being at war with you," he said, looking around at the upturned faces. "I am tired of being considered the enemy merely because I am an English aristocrat and the owner of the land on which you live and the industry at which you work. I am sorry that anyone who gives me information about your lives must be considered a base informer and punished with whips."

There was a barely audible murmuring. Some men shifted their weight from one foot to the other. A few gazes slipped from his own.

"No woman has ever given me such information," he said slowly and distinctly.

He waited while discomfort among the men grew visibly.

"The woman who was whipped last night was innocent of the charge against her," he said. "She is my daughter's teacher, not my spy."

There was more shuffling, louder murmuring.

"More of that later," he said, and the hush was suddenly loud. "I disapprove of the planned march on Newport. I disapprove because it will accomplish nothing but will put you all in considerable danger of injury and arrest. Government authorities are expecting such a move and are preparing for it. I disapprove of your going but will do nothing to stop you provided no one is coerced by Scotch Cattle whips to join those of you who decide to go and provided that there is no other violence concerning it here in Cwmbran. The decision is yours. You are all free men."

He waited through the swell of sound that followed his words. It was unclear to him if it was merely surprise or if it was suspicion that set them all to talking at once.

"But in the meantime," he said, "there is much to do here at home. I have owned Cwmbran and been your employer for two years. I have been deeply shamed in the past few months to discover how irresponsible I have been during those years, assuming all was well here when I should have come to find out for myself. There is enough to do here to occupy us all for a decade or more — new housing, waterworks and sewers, schools for the children, to name but a few of the more obvious. It has angered me and — yes — hurt me that you have not met me halfway on this, that you have ignored my requests to meet with your representatives so that we might get started."

There was a roar of protest, most of it directed at him. So many men were speaking to him that he heard none of them. For the first time he held up a hand for silence.

"Do I understand," he asked, "that you knew nothing of my requests?"

The men's reaction convinced him that he had guessed correctly.

"Perhaps," he said, "your leader saw fit to make a decision without consulting you. Perhaps Owen Parry decided not to accord you the democratic rights you have been demanding in the Charter. Perhaps he assumed that you would be unwilling to trust and to work with the enemy."

"We should have been given the choice," someone cried out with a growl, and there was a loud murmuring of assent.

"What Parry decided is good enough for me," someone else shouted, and won for himself his own chorus of approval.

Alex held up one hand. "If I must make improvements alone," he said, "I will do so. Both the right and the responsibility are mine. I would prefer to make decisions with you rather than for you, but I consider it your democratic right not to participate in democracy. I will ask the Reverend Llewellyn if a meeting may be held in the chapel schoolroom one day next week — on your ground rather than on mine. I will ask him to chair that meeting. I will attend it. I invite all of you to attend too — and to bring your women with you."

"Oh, *Duw,*" someone said, "that is all we would need."

There was a gust of laughter in which Alex briefly joined.

"Your women live in your houses all day and care for your children while you are at work," he said when there was silence again. "You can be certain that they will have very strong ideas, and sensible ones too, about what is needed to make life healthier and more comfortable in Cwmbran. Perhaps we should learn to listen to them and give their ideas the respect they deserve."

It was an idea with which the men were uncomfortable, he could see. But he had no wish to labor the point or any others he had made. They were there. He had spoken them in the hearing of almost every man from the valley. It was up to them now. Their lives would improve whether they wished it or not. But he could not change their attitudes or their perception of himself. It was up to them.

He waited until there was full silence, and then he waited a little longer until the silence became tense and expectant.

"Where is Owen Parry?" he asked.

"Here I am." A voice rang out firm and clear from near the back of the crowd of

490

men packed into the hollow.

Alex took his time locating the man in the crowd and then looked directly at him.

"Owen Parry," he said, dropping his whip to the ground and removing his coat with deliberate slowness, "I once told you that if the Scotch Cattle returned to Cwmbran to terrorize and hurt any of my people, I would hunt them down and give them as good as they gave."

"You did," Owen said, challenge and defiance in his voice.

Alex unbuttoned his waistcoat and pulled it off, dropping it to the ground to join his whip and his coat. "They came back," he said, "and put terror into a woman too courageous either to give in to their demands or to seek help from someone who might have given it. She suffered that terror for three days."

The silence was louder than Scotch Cattle howls.

"Last night she was dragged up the mountain by men too cowardly to show their faces or speak above a whisper and confined to the ground and whipped," Alex said. "Fifteen times. This morning she came to work and said nothing by way of complaint." His cravat was on the ground with his other clothes. He pulled his shirt free of his breeches and began to unbutton it. All the while he spoke he had not taken his eyes off Owen Parry.

"Even if she were guilty of the offense for which she was punished," Alex said. "Even if, I would be her champion. She is a woman. You were one of those Scotch Cattle, Owen Parry."

"Yes," Owen said as the great swell of sound succeeding the accusation died down.

"The bloody bastard!" one voice roared. Alex recognized it as Hywel Rhys's, though he did not take his eyes off Owen Parry. "Let me get at him. I will tear him limb from limb and go to hell for it too. It will be a pleasure to spend eternity in hellfire with the devil, knowing that Parry is there with me."

But the men about him subdued him and silence fell again. Parry was looking directly back at him, Alex saw, his head lifted proudly.

"Strip down, Parry," Alex said. "Perhaps the men you lead and I employ will be good enough to clear a space in the middle of this hollow. I will fight you man to man. If I defeat you, I will punish you as you and your thugs punished Siân Jones last night. Fifteen lashes with my whip."

Owen Parry laughed. Alex could understand why, having seen the man stripped to the waist at the works. But then perhaps Parry had not had a good look at him, and certainly he could not know that Alex had been trained in one of the prestigious boxing saloons of London. And perhaps he did not understand what murderous rage love could find in a man's heart and in his muscles.

An empty square appeared in the middle of the hollow as if by magic, and two paths, one leading down from the rise on which Alex stood and the other from the spot on which Owen Parry stood.

Alex pulled off his boots and his stockings and took the path to the square. "You may choose your seconds, Parry," he said. "There are doubtless any number of men who will stand in your corner. I will stand alone — as I have done since coming to Cwmbran."

"No, you won't," a light, youthful voice said from close by. "I'll be in your corner, sir. For Siân."

For the first time Alex removed his eyes from Owen. He looked in some surprise at Iestyn Jones, who had stepped into the square and moved now to one corner of it.

"And I."

"Me too."

The voices spoke simultaneously, and

Huw Jones and Emrys Rhys joined Iestyn in the corner.

"Thank you," Alex said, and turned his attention back to Owen Parry, who was stripping to the waist in the opposite corner of the square.

"I hope you don't knock the bastard senseless," Emrys Rhys said. "I want that pleasure for myself."

It was a lengthy fight. Owen Parry's sheer strength was pitted against Alex's strength and skill and they gave punch for punch for long minutes, neither pausing to circle the other looking for an opening, neither backing up from the other, neither staying down when he was put down. For both it was more than a mere fistfight. It was a battle of the classes and of ideas. It was a battle of hatred on one side, determination on the other.

Alex was not at all sure he could win. He had not been sure from the start. And yet, win or lose, it was a fight he had to fight. But as they fought on, surrounded by hundreds of curiously quiet men, their landed punches and their grunts audible to all, he knew ultimately that he had the advantage. He fought to avenge what had been done to Siân. He detached his mind from his opponent and the pain that was being inflicted on his own body and focused his thought on the remembered sight of the red thread above Siân's dress that morning and the raw welts across her back when he had bared it. He thought of her face, pale and controlled, her eyes dark-shadowed.

And he thought of her finally losing her control and weeping, not because of the pain but because she had had to admit at last to both him and herself that Owen Parry had been one of the Scotch Cattle who had dragged her from her home.

He focused on Parry again, his mind coldly furious, his own pain and near-exhaustion forgotten, the skills he had learned from a master suddenly remembered. He waited for an opening, for a momentary dropping of guard — not difficult at this stage of the fight, when they were both on the verge of collapse. And then with one powerful right and all his remaining strength, he hit Owen full in the face and felled him.

They had both been down before. Both had got up each time, shrugging off aid from their corners. But this time Parry lay where he was, facedown on the thin heather, breathing heavily. He had not lost consciousness, but the strength and the will to get up and fight on had gone from him.

The men of Cwmbran watched in awe and near-silence. It was many years since any man had dared face Owen Parry's fists and even more years since any man had put him down. Those who had considered the aristocratic owner of Cwmbran an effete weakling — especially after the hasty way he had given in to the threat of a strike — looked uneasily at the evidence to the contrary stretched out on the ground in the empty square they surrounded.

Alex strode back to the rise from which he had addressed them earlier and slid his whip out from beneath the mound of his clothes. Men fell away from either side of him as he walked back again. He stood over the prostrate form of Owen Parry, feet apart, whip clenched in his right hand, gazing down at him. Owen watched him. He had made no move to get up and had waved away his seconds with weary annoyance. He had made no move to roll over onto his back or otherwise protect himself from the promised punishment.

"The whips were wet last night," he said, defiance in his voice. "They were wielded full force."

Alex gazed down at him for a long time. Parry would not move, he knew. He would lie there and take his punishment. But Siân had been given no choice. She had been spread-eagled on the ground, wrists and ankles tied to stakes. Wet whips. Wielded full force.

"Coward!" Owen Parry hissed up at him suddenly. "Are you afraid to draw a little blood, Craille? Or afraid that your arm is not strong enough to do so?"

Alex felt sick suddenly. Hatred upon hatred. Violence upon violence. An eye for an eye. He dropped his whip onto Owen Parry's back and turned away.

"I'll leave you to your conscience, Parry," he said, "and I will hope sincerely that it will pain you far worse and for far longer than the lash of a whip." He walked away toward his clothes.

"Right, you, Owen," Emrys Rhys growled from behind him. "This is for Siân, you bloody cowardly bastard."

There was the whistle of a whip, a thud as it connected with flesh, a grunt.

Alex did not look back. He dressed himself with slow deliberateness, ignoring the stiffness of his muscles and the soreness of his flesh.

The men were no longer silent as he walked down the mountain a few minutes later, minus his whip. He could hear a swell of sound from behind him. He wondered

497

who would ultimately win the battle that had been fought that day — Owen Parry or himself.

He wondered if Siân still slept.

She had woken up at last and knew where she was and why she was there. She must have slept for a long time, she thought. She had had no idea that the effects of a drug could be so powerful. She shrugged her shoulders tentatively one at a time. Her back was sore again — the drug was wearing off, then — but not so painful that it enclosed her world in a nightmarish vise, as it had done that morning when she had come to work and sat with Verity.

She edged her legs over the side of the bed and sat up slowly and gingerly. The door on the opposite side of the room must lead to a dressing room, she guessed. She needed one badly. Her legs felt rather as if they were made of cotton wool but they conveyed her where she wanted to go and brought her back to the bed again five minutes later. She sank down onto it gratefully. It was a powerful drug, he had said. Powerful, indeed. She closed her eyes. Her back was tingling, but lying still eased the pain. She supposed that she must learn to live with it for several weeks. It had been a severe whipping. Perhaps the men wielding the whips had tried to make up for the fact that they were to give only fifteen lashes instead of the planned twenty.

She had intended, when she got up, to go home. Gran would be worried. But she would be unable to get home. She was still so very tired. There was a voice in her memory — Miss Haines's voice? — telling her that a message had been sent to Gran and Grandad that she would be staying at the castle at least for tonight.

She sighed with sleepy contentment. She would not have to make the effort. She could stay where she was. And sleep.

Someone had called her his little one. There had been a tenderness in his voice that she had yearned and yearned for all her life. He had cried over her. Dada, she had called him. Not Father or Papa, but Dada. There had always been an aching emptiness in her because there had never been any man to call Dada. An emptiness made worse by the fact that there was a man who might have been called that but never had. The man who had fathered her.

Dada, she had called him. In her dream. It must have been a dream. She ached to believe that it had been reality. But it had been a drug-induced dream.

"Siân?"

She had not heard the door open and close. She must have dozed off again. She opened her eyes and smiled.

"Alexander."

"How is the back?" he asked.

"Bearable," she said. "I am still drugged."

"Good," he said. "You needed its help."

"Yes." Her eyes roamed over his face. She swallowed. "You have been fighting?"

He nodded.

"Because of me?" she whispered. "Owen?"

He nodded again.

She closed her eyes. "Does he look as bad as you?" she asked.

"Worse," he said. He spoke very quietly. "All the men of Cwmbran now know that you were wrongly accused and convicted, Siân, that the whips were given to an innocent woman. All watched you being avenged."

"No one has beaten Owen in a fight for as far back as I can remember," she said.

"I had powerful motivation," he said.

She opened her eyes and gazed up at him. "You made it public, Alexander?" she said. "Everyone heard and saw?"

"Everyone," he said. "Every man of Cwmbran."

She closed her eyes once more. She did

500

not have to have it explained further. She could picture it just as if she had been there. He would have taken them up the mountain to the meeting place. It would be fitting for it to happen there. He had used his authority to draw all the men up there and then he had told them the truth and administered punishment. But no — something better than that.

"It was a fair fight?" she asked without opening her eyes.

"A fair fight," he said. "I avenged you with my fists. He made me look like this with his."

It was primitive and bloodthirsty and unchristian to be pleased. But she was pleased.

"Thank you," she whispered, and opened her eyes again.

He gazed down at her and took a step closer to the bed in order to touch the backs of his fingers to her cheek. She set her hand over his and turned her face toward it so that she could lay her lips against his palm. He did not move his hand.

"Thank you," she said again, and she looked up into his blue eyes and smiled.

"You are still drugged?" he asked.

She nodded.

"There is no pain?"

She shook her head.

"Too drugged to know what is happening?" he asked.

No, not too drugged for that. She understood him immediately. And answered him without hesitation by looking into his eyes and shaking her head again.

He did not move for a moment but gazed searchingly into her eyes. Then he withdrew his hand from hers and crossed the room to the door. She heard the key turn in the lock. When he came back to the bed, he began to undress, his eyes on hers.

He was bruised, she saw. Bruised and beautiful. She had not seen him up on the mountain that first time. She had only felt him. Now her eyes devoured all his muscled, well-proportioned beauty. And she wanted him with a languorous, half-drugged desire. She wanted to be joined with him, one with him. She wanted to be healed by him. She wanted to heal him.

"Siân." He drew back the bedclothes when he was naked and eased her shift and other garments gently down her body and off over her feet. "My beautiful Siân."

"Beautiful Alexander." She smiled and reached up her arms for him.

He did not come on top of her. He set one knee between hers and eased her legs wide with both of his so that he could kneel between her thighs.

"Don't move," he said. "I'll do everything that needs to be done. Lie still."

And yet he said it not so that he might thrust into her and take his own pleasure as quickly as possible, she discovered over the next half hour or so. He gave her pleasure, slow pleasure that her body could absorb without the frenzied need to writhe and lift to him.

His hands caressed her breasts, tightening them with sweet sensation, bringing her nipples to aching peaks. His head, bent over her, reached down for them. His mouth suckled them and eased them while his tongue lightly caressed the sore nipples and sent throbbing need down through her womb to settle between her thighs.

She spread her arms wide across the bed and gripped its sides. It struck her for a moment that she was spread-eagled as she had been last night, but the other way up and voluntarily this time. There were no bonds at her wrists and ankles to hold her in position. And today her body was being caressed, loved instead of whipped.

"Take away the memories and the ugliness," she whispered to him.

He lifted his head from her breast and

looked down at her, along one of her arms, and down to one spread leg. And she could see in his eyes that he understood.

He nodded and smiled down at her. "Yes," he said. "No ugliness today, Siân. And no force and no violence. Only love."

Her eyes yearned up into his. Love? Yes, it was love. He had called her his love up on the mountain and she had believed him. She believed the word he used now. It was an impossibility, what was between them. But it was real and beautiful nevertheless and in the here and now it was exquisitely right.

"Yes," she said. "Love me, Alexander."

And so he loved her, first with his hand, so that she almost swooned with the rapture of it. She did not understand how he knew to arouse desire and rapture without the frenzy that might have caused her pain, but she accepted his knowledge and his expertise with gratitude and love. Sweet glory flowed against his hand and had her moaning and then smiling up into his eyes. He was smiling back.

"Don't move," he said. "I will try not to jar you. If there is any pain, stop me immediately. There is to be no pain for you today."

His hand slid beneath her but lifted her only slightly. He did not come down on top of her but continued to kneel between her thighs. Her eyes dropped from his and watched as he slid his length deeply and firmly into her. She drew in on him and throbbed about him.

"Ah," she said.

It was wonderfully pleasurable, she found, to be able to watch herself being loved, to watch thrust and withdrawal as well as to feel. He did it slowly and gently without sacrificing either depth or intensity. Her grip on the sides of the bed tightened as she watched and as her muscles pulled him farther inward and relaxed for his withdrawals.

His eyes looked as drugged as hers felt when he spoke and she looked up into his face again.

"Shall I come alone?" he asked her. "Will it hurt you? Shall I wait for you?"

"Wait for me." She smiled at him once more. "I am coming. I want to be with you. It won't hurt. Wait for me."

And so he stroked her with gentle patience while she closed her eyes and focused on the inner ache that would blossom about him and take her into the world that they could occupy together and simultaneously. One body, one soul. One impossibility made gloriously possible for one single moment in eternity.

"Yes," he was saying. "Yes. Now, my love. Now. Yes, Siân. Now."

And they entered that moment together.

"Cariad," she heard him say as they went in.

22

She had asked to see him. And so he was waiting, very formally, in his study for her to come downstairs. His first instinct had been to go up to her, to take the stairs two or even three at a time in his eagerness. But he would not do that. There was probably talk enough belowstairs about the fact that he had personally tended to her wounded back yesterday morning. Perhaps it had even been noted that he had spent longer than an hour in her room later in the afternoon. Doubtless it was already known in the house that he had fought for her honor up on the mountain.

And so he waited for her to come down. She had fallen asleep after they had made love, so deeply asleep that he had realized how much under the influence of the laudanum she still was. He had felt guilty, lying beside her, her hand clasped in his. Perhaps after all he had taken advantage of her at a time when she could not make a rational decision. He had eased himself off the bed and left the room, not to return.

But he could not believe that she had not fully understood what was happening and had not fully acquiesced in it. He had never made love like that before. He had never before joined himself to a woman and felt unity. One body, one life, one soul. It sounded silly put into words. But it had happened. It could have happened only if it really had been so. He could not have felt that alone. She must have felt it too.

The door opened and he turned to watch her come inside his study. She was her usual neat and lovely self — and very straight-backed. Someone closed the door behind her. He hurried across the room to her, but something stopped him from holding out his hands to her. Her self-containment, perhaps.

"How is your back?" he asked.

"Sore," she said. "Miss Haines rubbed more ointment on it a short while ago. It will heal. I knew yesterday that your right eye was going to be black this morning."

"I think it makes me look rather like a pirate," he said. "Don't all women fall for a pirate?"

She smiled fleetingly. "Alexander," she

said, "I am going home."

"I would prefer that you stayed here until you are quite better," he said, "but I know how close you are to your grandparents. Go, then, Siân. Take a few days off — until you can move freely and without pain. I will persuade Verity that holidays are meant to be relished." He grinned at her.

She was looking not quite into his eyes, he noticed, and he felt the first twinge of alarm. "I meant that I am going home to stay," she said quietly. "I will not be coming back."

"I did take advantage of you, then," he said. "I am sorry, Siân. I thought you were free enough of the drug's effects to know exactly what you were agreeing to."

"I did." She looked up into his eyes. "It was wonderful, Alexander. It was the most wonderful experience of my life. Thank you."

He stared blankly at her. "But you are leaving my house," he said, "and my employment."

"It happened beneath your own roof," she said, "a few rooms from your daughter's room."

"It was not sordid," he said quickly, hurt.

"No, it was not," she agreed. "It should have been, but it was not. What happened

509

between us on the mountain should have been sordid but was not. They were saved from ugliness by being moments of spontaneous — tenderness. But they cannot be repeated, Alexander. Now we know times like that can happen, it would be sordid to allow them. I cannot be your mistress and I will not be your casual love, either. I thought perhaps I could. But I can't."

"Siân." He possessed himself of her hands and kissed the palms, one at a time. "You are not my casual love. There is nothing casual about my feelings for you."

"It doesn't matter," she said. "The result is the same. This town and these people are important to me, Alexander. I have fought to belong to them, to be accepted by them. I suppose I will never be truly one of them. My background and upbringing set me somewhat apart. But I value their respect. I need to be able to look them all in the eye."

"And you cannot?" he said harshly. "Because you love the common enemy and have slept with him?"

"I still can," she said, "because I am not ashamed of what we have done. But I would be ashamed if I deliberately invited more by continuing to come here."

He hated himself for sneering, but he sneered. "So the people of Cwmbran mean more to you than I do," he said.

She looked at him calmly for a long time. He could not believe that her answer was not instant. He had expected dismayed denial.

"Yes," she said so quietly that he hardly heard the word.

They stared at each other. The one word had erected a brick wall between them, or perhaps a wide ocean, or miles and miles of sky and space.

It was an impossibility, then. A foolishness. A stupidity. An idiocy. In his life before Cwmbran he had never thought to try to bridge the gap. He had taken his responsibilities seriously and had always treated his subordinates well. But he had always accepted that the gap was there. It was the way of the world. Here in Cwmbran the gap was wider than he had ever known it because here he was separated from his people by suspicion and perhaps even hatred and he was guilty of neglect. And yet it was here that he had conceived the notion of closing the gap?

Simply because he had fallen in love with her?

"Then you had better go," he said, clasping his hands behind him, "before I debauch you beyond redemption."

"Don't be angry," she said. "Please, Alexander, try to understand."

"I understand," he said, "that I have been foolish to fall in love with this place and these people. And with you. I stand alone. So be it. Perhaps you and your people would be more comfortable if I went away and if life continued as before. I am not going to go away and life here is not going to be as it has been in the past years. I will act alone if I must. Good-bye, Siân."

"Alexander," she said softly.

"Go," he said. "I'll have your week's pay sent to your grandfather's house. You are no longer in my employ."

He thought she would never go away. She stood and gazed at him wide-eyed.

"I've hurt you," she said at last. "I'm sorry. I'm so sorry."

And then she whisked herself around, wincing noticeably at the sudden movement, and let herself out of the room before he could reach beyond her to open the door for her. He stayed where he was, resisting the urge to go after her.

He swore silently and at some length as he stared at the door.

Her grandmother fussed over her, feeding her at frequent intervals through the day as

512

if she needed fattening up. Emrys had taken all her things up to his room and brought all his things down. His room upstairs was to be permanently hers. Her grandfather was inordinately pleased that at last she was at home and he could support her, as a man should support his women. There was no question now — it was tacitly understood — of her marrying next week.

It was good to be home. It felt almost as if she had been gone a month instead of just one night.

No one mentioned Owen. Or the Marquess of Craille. She had to wait for visitors to do either.

Mari hugged her and brought her some freshly baked Welsh cakes — and told her that during the fight up on the mountain Iestyn and Huw and Emrys had acted as seconds to the marquess. Iestyn came later on his way over the mountain to call on his girl. He kissed Siân's cheek and told her again that he was proud of her — and told her that he thought the Marquess of Craille a decent sort for not dismissing Owen from his job.

"I don't think he likes to use his power in any negative way, Siân," he said. "He is handy with his fists, mind — we never thought to see the man who could put

513

Owen down in a fair fight. But he was content to leave it at that. No dismissal. And he did not use his whip after all."

"His whip?" Siân looked at him sharply.

"No," he said. "He was going to. But you could see that he was unable to hit a man when he was down. He would not take an eye for an eye. Which I was glad to see because that idea came very early in the Good Book, Siân, before people realized that God is not really like that at all."

It was Huw who told her later that Emrys had used the whip — fifteen times across Owen's back. And that Owen had made no attempt to avoid the lashes, though no one was holding him down.

"I almost admired the bastard," Huw said, and then had to apologize because Hywel was there and heard him. He went on to tell Siân about the meeting the marquess had called at the chapel. The townspeople were divided between those who were willing to give him a chance and those who still sided with Owen and were suspicious of any good thing the marquess seemed to be offering them.

Siân had shut her mind to Owen. She did not want to think of him. She did not want to hear about him. Or see him. She felt hurt and bruised and raw all over. She wanted to heal. There were two men she wanted to blot from her memory, from her very being. She wanted to be given time.

But when a knock came on the door one evening and no one followed it up by lifting the latch, Emrys opened the door and then immediately stepped into the doorway to block it.

"Get away from here," he said, "where you are not wanted and where you might be given two black eyes as a welcome."

"I want to speak to Siân," Owen said quite steadily.

"Oh, do you?" Emrys said, his voice menacing. "And where is your whip, man? Everyone knows that our Siân can be controlled only with a whip. And not always even then. It is a pity you could not whip her spirit as well as her back."

"Get away from my door, Owen Parry," Hywel Rhys said from his chair. "And don't come back."

"There is wicked of you, Owen, to come here, knocking on the door as if nothing had happened," Gwynneth said. "Unchristian it is of me, but I must ask you to leave. Siân has nothing to say to you."

Siân had set her head back against her chair and closed her eyes. She could hear him again telling her in a voice he had forgotten to disguise to open her mouth so that he could stuff the rag between her teeth.

"Siân," Owen said from behind the protective bulk of Emrys in the doorway, "will you come for a little walk with me? There are things that must be said."

She wondered suddenly what it must have cost him to come here like this, knowing very well what reception he was facing. And he was right. There were things to be said. It was the eve of what was to have been their wedding day.

"Which eye would you like me to blacken first?" Emrys asked. "It is all the same to me, Owen Parry."

Siân got to her feet. "It's all right, Uncle Emrys," she said. "I will go for a walk with him."

"Over my bloody dead body," Emrys said.

Siân noticed irrelevantly that her grandfather did not reprimand her uncle. "Sit down, *fach,*" he said to her instead.

"I'll go, Grandad," she said. "Owen will not hurt me. And there are things we need to say to each other."

"Crazy woman," Emrys said, standing aside. "You should be put on a leash, Siân Jones, and kept on it. Go on, then. But you set one finger on her, Owen Parry, just one finger . . ." He did not complete the threat.

"Have her back within the hour, mind," Gwynneth said.

Siân lifted her warm cloak from behind the door and drew it about her. It was autumn and chilly and damp, the sort of evening best spent indoors before a crackling fire. She did not look at Owen as she stepped past him out the door. They walked along the street, a few feet of space between them. Neither spoke until they turned and took the familiar route up into the lower hills.

"Siân," he said at last, "I am not proud of what I had to do. Neither am I ashamed. I want you to know both those things."

She said nothing for a while. What could she say? She had expected either abject apologies or angry self-justification. He had given her neither.

"I was innocent," she said quietly. "You knew I was innocent."

"But others did not," he said. "There was a very powerful rumor circulating. If I had defended you too vigorously, if I had forbidden the punishment, it would have been thought that I was putting my woman before the common good. I could not do that, Siân. I am the leader. I have to be seen to be impartial."

Somehow she was reminded of the answer

she had given Alexander when he had asked her if she loved her people more than she loved him.

"You were given warning enough," Owen said, his tone more defensive. "It was madness to ignore it, Siân. You deserved what you got."

"Your life is full of violence, Owen, isn't it?" she said sadly. "It is the only solution to a problem that you seem able to see. I am glad I saw that fully before it was too late."

"Sometimes," he said, "violence is the only answer. When there is nothing else, one has to have the courage to take any means to achieve what should be. These are not times when quiet acceptance can achieve anything."

"Perhaps it can," she said. "Are you going to the meeting at chapel tomorrow night? Huw told me about it. There is a chance, perhaps, for something to be achieved peacefully and amicably."

"He is clever, I grant him that," Owen said. "He thinks to quieten us with trivialities and make us forget the greater injustices we have suffered for centuries."

Siân sighed. "I am going back home, Owen," she said. "There is nothing to say after all."

"Siân." He stopped on the hillside and

faced her. "Siân, you don't know how it hurt me, seeing you helpless on the ground like that, watching what happened to you."

"On the other hand," she said, "you do know how it hurt me, Owen. You learned how much the next day. Why did you take it so quietly?"

She was surprised and somewhat alarmed to see tears spring to his eyes.

"I would have lain there for twice as many lashes," he said, "if they could have taken away the memory of yours, Siân. I felt I had deserved them, though I was not ashamed of what I had done. And I am not ashamed."

She bit her upper lip.

"I betrayed my love for you," he said. "For that I will never forgive myself. But sometimes something has to be put before love. I would ask you to forgive my betrayal, but it somehow does not seem appropriate. I would do it again, you see, if it seemed necessary. You took it bravely, *fach.* I was proud of you — if I have a right to be proud."

Even now — oh, even now, she thought, looking up at him, she wished she loved him. Owen! And she was no better than he. No better at all.

It had to be said. "I betrayed you too, Owen," she said.

His eyes widened. "It was you who told him after all, then?" he asked.

She shook her head. "In a personal way," she said. "I betrayed you in a personal way."

She saw comprehension dawn in his eyes before he nodded and turned away. "Well, I never did that at least, Siân," he said, beginning to walk back toward the town, his hands shoved into his pockets. "I loved you. Past tense and present tense. I won't ask for details. I have no right to know now and don't want to know. Perhaps we can forgive each other and learn to live together in the same town without hatred."

"Yes," she said.

He stopped outside the gate into the back garden. "I won't come any farther," he said. "I have no stomach for a brawl with Emrys."

"Owen," she said, "you are not going to go ahead with plans for the march, are you? You are not secretly making weapons?"

He laughed rather bleakly. "You don't think I am going to answer those questions, do you, Siân?" he asked. "When you are his woman?"

"I suppose," she said, "that like you, I have no right to know now and do not really want to know. Be careful, Owen. I don't want to see you hurt. I cared for you. I care for you."

He ran one knuckle along her jawline to her chin. "Good-bye, *cariad*," he said. He hesitated before leaning forward and kissing her softly on the forehead.

"Good-bye, Owen."

She stood at the gate for a few minutes watching him walk away toward his own house. He did not look back. She swallowed against a lump in her throat. And then she continued to gaze along the empty street as if she was looking along the avenue of her own future. Sometimes it was hard not to give in to self-pity. Sometimes it seemed as if there was nothing and no one left to live for.

Siân was rolling out dough on the table when someone knocked on the door the following afternoon. She let her grandmother answer the summons. But she straightened up quickly, startled, when she heard the voice.

Her grandmother looked back at her, tight-lipped. "It is for you, Siân," she said. Although it was a chilly day outside, she left the door open and did not invite Sir John Fowler inside.

"Siân?" he said. He looked uncomfortable and embarrassed.

She had thought many times about the

strange dream she had had at Glanrhyd Castle. Perhaps she had known all the time that it had not really been a dream. She knew it now, and her cheeks grew hot at the memories. She pushed at a stray lock of hair with the back of one wrist.

"May I speak with you?" he asked.

Her grandmother was poking furiously at the fire, which did not need poking, Siân could see.

Siân looked down at her floury hands and at the half-rolled dough on the table. "I'll wash my hands and get my cloak," she said.

Her grandmother looked speakingly up at her, but Siân ignored the look. He had come, she thought. He had come. It seemed she had waited all her life for him to come to her. But she hated him. She despised him. She wanted nothing to do with him. She had never been able to think of him as her father. She could not do so now. Her heart beat painfully as she washed her hands in silence, took the pins from her hair and shook it loose, and took her cloak from behind the door. Sir John had nodded at her words and closed the door. He was waiting outside.

"Gran," Siân said.

"I will finish rolling the dough," Gwynneth said without looking at her. "Go, you."

Sir John Fowler had ruined Gran's daughter, Siân thought, and caused her to be driven from chapel and from Cwmbran. It was no wonder that Gran had no love for him. As Siân herself did not. She hesitated, but there was nothing to be said. She left the house without another word.

"Shall we walk?" he suggested. "Along the river?" He did not offer his arm or smile. Of course he did neither. He was as cold and as impersonal as he had ever been.

"How is your back?" he asked as they walked.

"Still quite sore," she said. "Iestyn still has the marks on his back. I suppose I will too for a long time. Perhaps always."

"You have no job?" he asked. "Craille told me that you resigned as his daughter's governess."

"Yes," she said. "It seemed the right thing to do."

"Siân," he said as they were walking past the ugliest section of the river, next to the coal mine, "you must let me support you. I'll buy you a house somewhere and give you an allowance. Or I'll find you employment somewhere if you would prefer. If you want a good husband, I'll see what I can do. Whatever you wish. I'll do whatever you wish."

"I don't want anything from you," she said quietly, "thank you." And yet her heart cried out to her that she lied.

He did not pursue the matter. He was quiet for a while. "Why did you not come to me for help?" he asked. "I have heard that they gave you the customary three days' warning, Siân. You must know Scotch Cattle well enough to realize that they are not to be defied. Why did you not come to me?"

She looked at him in some amazement. "You are the last person I would have thought of turning to," she said quite truthfully.

His mouth and his jawline tightened. "I don't know where you came from, Siân," he said. "Apart from the fact that you look like your mother, I can see nothing of her in you. You are cold to the very heart and always have been. Even as a very young child."

"Well, then," she said, shivering inside her cloak, "I must resemble my other parent, I suppose."

They had passed the mine and were in pleasant countryside if they did not look back. Siân was reminded of the Sunday afternoon walk she had taken there with Alexander and Verity weeks before.

"You resented me," he said, "because I

was not married to your mother."

"I did not even realize for many years," she said, "that there was something odd about that. I think I always hoped that you would look at me as you looked at her. I think that as a child I used to watch for you for hours and days on end. And then when you came you had eyes only for her. You used to disappear upstairs with her and I had to amuse myself downstairs. In time, I suppose, I stopped watching for you."

"You used to hide from me," he said, "and glower at me. You used to throw down the toys I brought you and deliberately play with some old thing your mother had made for you. You were cold."

"They were bribes," she said, "to keep me quiet while you spent your hour or so with Mam."

"They were gifts, Siân," he said. "You were my little girl."

She sighed. "Why did you come now?" she asked. "And why did you come to Glanrhyd Castle? I didn't dream it, did I?"

"Craille sent to tell me what had happened," he said.

"Did he?" She turned her head sharply to look at him. "And you came."

"I came," he said, "as I did not come when your husband died, Siân, or when my grandson was stillborn. I stayed away from you then because you had rejected me and put me from your life. But I saw you that day at the castle when my wife and daughter were with me. It had been so long. This time I could not stay away."

Siân closed her eyes briefly and drew in a breath of chilly air. "What did you call me?" she asked. "What was dream and what was reality?"

"Your mother used to use the Welsh word," he said. "I could never bring myself to use it or even the English equivalent out loud. You hated me. But in my heart you were always my little one, Siân."

She felt absurdly close to tears. "Then why did you never say so?" she asked. She was surprised to hear her voice shaky and accusing. "Did you not understand that when a child is cold and sullen, she is crying out for love?"

"I didn't know much about children, Siân," he said. "I was afraid of you. I used to dream of holding you on my lap, your head against my shoulder while I told you stories. But you would have nothing to do with me."

"Oh," she said, "Mam always used to say we were two peas in a pod, you and I. I used to think the idea was absurd."

"Do you remember what you called me at the castle?" he asked her softly.

"Yes," she said. "Absurd coming from a twenty-five-year-old woman, wasn't it?"

"You made me cry," he said.

"Sir John Fowler crying," she said. "It seems a contradiction in terms. Except that I remember you cried when Mam died. Alexand— The marquess had given me a double dose of laudanum. I was very heavily drugged. I called you Dada, didn't I?"

"Yes, my little one," he said.

"Oh, don't." She looked sharply away from him. "You cannot know how much I need love and tenderness at the moment. I get them from Gran and Grandad and Emrys and from Gwyn's family too. But I am weak at present. I crave more. I crave —"

"A father's love?" he said. "You have it, Siân."

"Oh." She stopped walking and spread her hands over her face. "Did you know why I was whipped? Did you know that Owen was one of the Scotch Cattle who took me away? Did you know that Alex —, that Alexander fought him up on the mountain in front of all the men of Cwmbran over it? Did you know that I love Alexander and left my employment at the castle because I cannot be his mistress as Mam was yours? Did you

527

know that my heart is breaking? Did you know how much I needed you?"

She could not remember his ever holding her in his arms. The touch of him was unfamiliar and the smell of him. She had never before really noticed that they were almost the same height. She fit comfortably against him. Her head fit comfortably on his shoulder. On Sir John Fowler's shoulder. She closed her eyes very tightly.

"Dada," she whispered.

"Siân." He rocked her. "My little one."

He held her hand when they walked on. A broad, square hand. An older man's hand. A father's hand.

"Tell me what I may do for you, then," he said. "A cottage somewhere quiet in the country, Siân? Where I can visit you sometimes and be the father I have always failed at being? Or a job? Or a husband?"

She did not want to leave Cwmbran. Cwmbran had always been her dream of home. It had haunted her during her school years in England. It had been the obvious place of refuge after her mother's death even though she had never lived there and did not know her grandparents. But the dream had turned sour. Owen lived in Cwmbran. People who had suspected her of being an informer and perhaps still did lived in

Cwmbran. And Alexander lived there and had said that he would continue to do so.

"A teaching job?" she said. "I like teaching. I think I do well at it. Somewhere away from this valley. But not outside Wales. My spirit would die if I had to leave my country. Perhaps down Cardiff way? Or even Swansea? Can you find me something?"

He squeezed her hand. "I'll find you something," he said. "You'll be happy, Siân. I'll see to it that you are happy, my little one."

She laughed suddenly with genuine amusement. "I am almost as tall as you," she said.

He laughed — she could not remember his laughing before. "But I see you with a father's eye," he said. "If you were a foot taller than me, Siân, you would still be my little one."

They walked on quietly. She felt rather as if someone had applied cooling cloths and ointments to her raw and battered emotions, Siân thought, looking across at the man who had fathered her and now held her hand.

Alexander had sent for him. He had known that she would need him. And he had come, her father.

He had come.

23

He was going to have to do something about Verity. She had become sullen and bad-tempered. She was not willing to do any of her usual indoor activities. Nor was she willing to go outside. Even when he suggested walks, she would not go with him. "No" had become her favorite word — spoken sharply and petulantly more often than not. When he had suggested sending to London for another governess, she had had a screaming tantrum. When he had offered to send her to her grandmother for a few weeks, she had locked herself in her bedroom and refused for longer than eight hours to come out.

There was so much else to occupy his time and his energies. The meeting at the chapel was more poorly attended than he had hoped, though both men and women came. He knew the reason. A meeting had been called on the mountain for the same night. Barnes had found out about it and told him. But Alex had told them they were free to meet and make their own decisions. He made no attempt either to stop or to spy on the meeting.

It was a Chartist meeting. They had not given up, then. They must still be planning their march. He had just hoped that it would be peaceable, that there would be no weapons involved. But he did not know for sure. Weapons had been seized in other places, he read in his letters from London, and there were many caves in the hills that would be suitable for both making and storing weapons.

One fact at least relieved him. All the men of Cwmbran did not attend the Chartist meeting, and yet the following nights were blessedly free of Scotch Cattle howls. Perhaps at least he had been able to persuade the men that each one should be left to make up his own mind. Unanimity was not always necessary for the success of an enterprise.

In the meantime he was busy having the records of both the works and the mine for ten years back gone over carefully to identify those men and women who had been forced permanently from work by injuries sustained on the job or by the coughing sickness that seemed to attack miners more than other workers. Those people were to be put on pensions for life. Pensions were to be given to widows of men who had died on the job, unless or until the widow remarried.

There was so much to do. If it were not for Verity, Alex thought, he would be able to bury himself in work and perhaps forget his personal unhappiness. But there was Verity, and when all was said and done, she was the most important person in his world. If he must hire a manager — someone different from Barnes — and take her back to England, then so be it. Perhaps it would be better for him to go back there, to treat Cwmbran only as a business enterprise — to keep control of it, but from a distance.

"You don't want to take a walk in the hills?" he asked Verity early one evening. "With Papa?"

"No," she said, reaching for her doll but setting it down again almost immediately. "It is cold outside."

"We can wrap up warm," he said, "and see who has the brightest cherry nose when we come home."

"No," she said. "I don't want to go."

Pouting and sullenness always made him impatient. He resisted the urge to stalk from the room and leave her to her misery. But they were out of character with Verity. He sat down on one of the nursery chairs and looked at her. Feeling his eyes on her, she snatched up her doll again and began to rock it without even watching it.

"Sweetheart," he said, "what is it?"

He knew very well what. For more than a week he had been persuading himself that with the resilience of childhood she would forget and return to her more normal sunny nature. But *he* could not forget. The ache inside him was still raw — it was pain more than ache.

"Nothing," Verity said crossly. "I just don't want to go for a silly walk."

"A book, then?" he asked. "Will you read to me? Or shall I read to you?"

The poor doll was tossed down onto the floor. "I don't want to do anything," Verity said, and stared at him with hostile, unhappy eyes.

He looked back. The name had to be spoken. He did not want to say it. He did not want to think it, though for more than a week he had thought nothing else. "You are missing Mrs. Jones?" he asked.

"No!" Her eyes blazed for a moment. "I hate her. I don't ever want to see her again. She was not a good teacher."

He inhaled slowly. "Why do you hate

her?" he asked.

"Because she doesn't like me," Verity said. "She went away without saying a word to me. But I don't care. I hate her anyway."

He reached out a hand to her. "Come here," he said.

She looked sullenly at his hand for a minute and then came to climb onto his lap. She set her face against his waistcoat and began to cry noisily. "Am I a bad girl?" she managed to jerk out. "I tried not to be a bad girl, Dada. She shouldn't hate me. I tried to be good. I hate her."

He held her in the warm cocoon of his arms and kissed the top of her head. "I didn't tell you what happened to Mrs. Jones," he said. "I thought you would be upset. I told you only that she was not feeling well that day she went to bed in one of the guest rooms. I think I had better tell you."

"She didn't feel well because she didn't like me," Verity said.

"'No." He kissed her head again. "Some wicked men had whipped her the night before and made her back all swollen and raw. Do you remember the wild animals you heard out in the hills one night?"

He told her about the Scotch Cattle and about what they had done to Siân and why.

"She went home," he said at last, "because the people of this town would always have been suspicious of her if she had kept coming here, and she loves the people of Cwmbran."

Verity was silent for a while. "Doesn't she love us, Papa?" she asked.

He closed his eyes and saw Siân naked below him on the bed, her body joined to his, her eyes soft and luminous with love. He felt as if a knife tip were needling at his heart.

"Yes," he said, "she loves us. But she belongs with them."

"And we don't, do we?" Verity said sadly.

That feeling of intense yearning with which he was becoming familiar was so strong on him for a moment that it was almost like despair.

"Yes, we do," he said, "but in a different way. We live here in Glanrhyd Castle and are very wealthy. Papa owns all this land and pays the wages of the people who work here. I am responsible for seeing to it that their lives are comfortable. We are English."

"But I speak some Welsh," she said. "Mrs. Jones said that soon I would be able to speak it fluently."

He laughed softly. "My little Welsh Verity," he said. "but we will always be a little apart, sweetheart. It is part of the price we pay for the privileges of our life. But we can always work for the respect and loyalty and even affection of our people."

She seemed comforted and fetched him some of her books a short while later. She read him one and he read her three. When he tucked her into bed, she seemed quite her old self.

Yet much later in the night Alex was woken by his valet, who had been sent by Verity's nurse. Verity was crying inconsolably and the woman was beside herself, not knowing what to do. Alex dismissed her when he reached his daughter's bedroom, and scooped the child up and sat with her as he had on a previous occasion, a blanket wrapped warmly about her.

"What is this all about?" he asked, kissing her. "A pain?"

"I want Mrs. J-o-n-e-s," she wailed.

God. A thousand devils. Damnation. So did he.

"Mrs. Jones will be sleeping," he said.

Her wailings increased in volume.

"I tell you what," he said. "You stop crying and Papa will put you back to bed and tuck you in, and tomorrow I will take you to visit Mrs. Jones. How does that sound?"

She sniffed and hiccuped. "Will she see

me?" she asked.

"If she is at home, I am quite sure she will," he said.

"Will she come back here?" She looked up at him suddenly with reddened eyes and glistening cheeks.

"No," he said, kissing her eyes one at a time. "But I think she will agree to let you visit occasionally. I'm sure she will, in fact."

It was not quite the answer she had hoped for, but he could see that she was very tired. She settled her head against his shoulder and sighed. Though he could not see her face, he could tell five minutes later that she was asleep again. He held her close. He could not think of a warmer, more comforting feeling than to hold one's sleeping child in one's arms. To feel oneself so trusted. So loved. He set his head against the chair back and closed his eyes.

He had not seen her in more than a week. She had not come to the meeting in the chapel. He had not expected her to do so and had been disappointed when she had not. He had not once set eyes on her.

Siân!

He should not have let her go. He should have persuaded her to stay until her back was properly healed. He should have refused to allow her to leave her job. He should have pressed ahead with the impossibility, with the idea that had terrified him at the time and still terrified him now.

But no — he had been right to let her go. He could not possibly make her his wife. She was an ironworker's granddaughter, a coal miner's widow. She was illegitimate. It was unthinkable. He would never be able to take her back to England with him. She would not fit into his world. It was not that he would be ashamed of her, but it would be impossible for her. And here in Wales the lines seemed to be even more firmly drawn. He could not pull her over into the loneliness of his world.

But he needed her. His need for her was almost a tangible thing. He wondered if her need for him was as powerful. He wondered if she lay awake at nights longing for him, reliving those three occasions when they had come together.

Well, tomorrow he would take Verity to her and ask if his daughter could spend an hour with her. He would go back for her after the hour was over. For two brief spells he would be able to feast his eyes and his senses on Siân Jones. For two brief spells he would be able to torture himself.

Alex fell asleep, his daughter curled up warmly on his lap.

■ ■ ■ ■

Siân was on her knees on the floor, singing while she rubbed blacking into the grate. It was a hard and a dirty job, but she liked to be able to sit back on her heels every so often and admire the gleaming surface of what she had already done. She looked ruefully down at her blackened hands and smiled. Not so long ago blackened hands and face and hair and body had been the norm of her days. And yet now she was wrinkling her nose at a small area of dirt. She sang on and polished on.

It was not that she was feeling happy. She wondered if it would be possible ever to feel happy again. But life was reasserting itself, and life, when all was said and done, was worth living. She knew that from the ups and downs of past experience. And she had had more than her fair share of downs, it seemed.

Sir John Fowler — her father — was going to find her a teaching job. It would not be easy to find a good one since most of the teachers in Wales were men, but she trusted him to find her something suitable. He had sent her a note the day after her visit and a silver locket that had been her mother's.

She wore it about her neck now despite the dirtiness of her job. Soon she would be moving away to a new job — there was a great emptiness in the pit of her stomach at the very thought. But there was also a welling of optimism. She would be able to start a new life.

She needed to get away and start afresh. It was painful now to live in Cwmbran. She dreaded coming face-to-face with Alexander, yet it was bound to happen sooner or later if she stayed. And she did not want to live in the same town as Owen. She could never quite forgive him for what he had done to her or herself for what she had done to him. And yet there was a leftover affection for him that pained her. She had come so close to loving him. She had come so close to living the life she had always dreamed of living.

She would miss her family. And Iestyn. He had called on her the evening before and gone walking with her. She had not even known about the Chartist meeting up in the hills. She did not even know if Emrys or her grandfather had been to it — it was not so easy to know now that she slept upstairs. It seemed that everyone was being very careful to withhold from her any information that she might leak to someone who did not know, she thought rather bitterly. Iestyn had not attended it — he had gone to the meeting in the chapel instead. She did not ask him about it.

"Is the demonstration still planned, then?" she had asked him.

"Yes," he had said. "It will be soon too, I think, Siân. I have heard that there are piles of iron-tipped pikes up in the caves and some guns."

"Oh, Iestyn." She had looked at him sharply. His face was rather pale. "There will be trouble."

"I am afraid of it," he had said, "though everyone insists that it will be peaceful, that the weapons are just for defense."

She had caught at his arm. "You will not go, Iestyn? Oh, please don't go," she pleaded.

He patted her hand. "No, I will not go," he had said. "I believe in the Charter, Siân. I signed it. But I cannot agree to using force. Better to put up with years more of oppression than to risk revolution. And here in Cwmbran we have it good. We have a good master. Dada is to have a pension. Did you know?"

She shook her head and he told her about the new pensions. She would be eligible for one, she realized with a jolt. But she was going away. Anyway, she did not want to hear anything about Alexander. Not even about his kindness. Perhaps especially not about his kindness.

"Iestyn," she had said, returning to the former topic, "they will not try to make you go on the march? The Scotch Cattle will not come after you?" She shuddered violently at the mere thought of Scotch Cattle.

"I don't know," he had said. "There has been no mention of them yet. Only some private attempts at persuasion at work. But I will not go. I will sign any petition that is made up, but I will not take part in anything that might turn violent."

They had left it at that. But Siân was hopeful. Perhaps the violence of the last few months — the two separate visits of Scotch Cattle, the fight up on the mountain — had taught their own lesson. Perhaps all the people of her town were yearning for the atmosphere of the *eisteddfod* day to be the more dominant mood again. Perhaps they were all beginning to realize that force and suspicion and hatred could only drive them permanently apart and destroy them.

Perhaps the march would never happen after all. And perhaps, if it did, it would involve only those men who chose to participate. Perhaps her people could finally agree to disagree. It would be a giant step forward.

She sat back on her heels to admire a section of work she had completed and brushed back a lock of hair from her face with the back of her hand. She noticed ruefully after she had done so that the back of her hand was dirty too.

And then there was a knock on the door. Siân waited a moment for the door to open to admit Mari or one of the neighbors — her grandmother had gone down to the shop. But whoever was there was waiting outside. She got to her feet, wiped her hands ineffectually on her apron, and opened the door.

And felt rather as if a giant fist had shot through it and punched her full on the stomach.

Her cheeks and forehead were smudged black. Her hair was caught back in a rather untidy knot, but several errant locks had fallen down over her shoulders. Her dress was old and faded, her apron dirty. Her hands were black. She looked quite incredibly lovely.

"Good afternoon, Mrs. Jones," he said. "Verity wanted to come and visit you."

Verity was hiding half behind him. Siân's eyes dropped to her. She did not return his greeting.

"It looks as if we have chosen a bad time," he said. "You are busy."

But she seemed to have recovered from the shock of seeing him. "Hello, Verity," she said. She smiled, and something turned over inside him. "I have missed you."

Verity, he saw, looking down, was regarding Siân warily from one eye as she hid behind him.

"I thought perhaps," he said, "she could stay with you for an hour if you are not too busy. I will come back for her." He looked directly at her. "She has been crying for you."

She bit her lip and looked down. "Verity," she said, "I did not leave because of you. I left because of — other things."

"Because you love us but belong here," Verity said.

Siân flushed and then smiled. "Yes," she said. "Something like that. I am awfully dirty. I have been cleaning the grate. But of course you can stay — for an hour or longer. Just give me a moment to wash my hands. Oh, and my face too. Is it dirty?" The flush returned.

She was ignoring him, Alex realized, acting rather as if he were not there. He greedily drank in the sight of her.

Verity giggled.

Siân whisked around to pour water into a bowl.

"I'll leave her, then?" Alex said. "And return in an hour?"

She nodded in his general direction and plunged her hands into the bowl.

"I want to climb the hill to the top," Verity said, all her usual animation suddenly returned.

"We will do so," Siân said. "It is nice and sunny today and not nearly as cold as it has been. We will go all the way to the top. Don't you like the look of my shiny black grate? You can almost see your face in it."

Alex, standing in the doorway, turned for one last wistful glance back. She was drying her face with a towel.

"You must come too, Papa," Verity said. "I want you to come up the hill too."

He found his eyes locked on Siân's. The towel had stilled over her mouth. She lowered it slowly.

"You might as well," she said. "It is hardly worth going home for an hour just to have to come all the way back again."

He hesitated, but more because he felt he ought, he realized, than because he was seriously considering refusing. How could he refuse? A whole hour with her? Perhaps longer? He had missed her so very much. He felt as if he had not seen her for a year.

"Very well, then," he said, addressing himself to Verity. "You are sure it has to be the very top?"

She giggled again. It felt so good to see her looking like a happy child once more.

They climbed the hill, the sun almost warm on their backs, the breeze cooling their faces and blowing back their hair. Verity had placed herself between the two of them, holding to a hand of each, skipping along when the gradient was not too steep, prattling about everything she could think of that had happened since Siân had left, practicing her Welsh, singing some of the songs Siân had taught her. Siân joined in, and Alex hummed along until Verity decided to teach him the words and Siân corrected her pronunciation. There was an absurd moment near the top of the mountain when all three of them were singing the same tune with varying degrees of recognizable Welsh words.

"Whee!" Verity cried when they were at the top and she could look down at the valleys on both sides, her arms stretched out to the sides. "We are at the top of the world."

"Only to find that there is no stairway to heaven," Alex said. "Thank goodness for that. No more climbing."

Verity laughed and twirled around and around. She raced off along the top, arms out, screeching with exuberance. Alex and Siân watched her go, both smiling at her, and then turned and looked at each other. Their smiles faded.

He acted from pure instinct. He leaned down and set his mouth, open, over hers for a brief moment.

"How is the back?" he asked.

"Much better," she said. "I can move freely now, at least."

"I couldn't deny her, Siân," he said. "She needed to see you."

"I needed to see her too," she said softly. "I love her."

Siân as Verity's mother. And as the mother of his other children. Siân as his wife and his companion and lover. The impossibility became yearningly real suddenly.

"Siân." He reached out a hand and touched her cheek.

"Sir John Fowler — my father — is going to help me find a teaching job somewhere else in Wales," she said quickly. "I am going to be moving away."

She might as well have plunged a knife into him.

"It is what you want?" he asked.

She nodded. "I like teaching," she said. "I think I would enjoy teaching in a school. There would be challenge in teaching more than one child. And I need to get away. I need to start over again."

"Do you?" he said. "It would not work here, Siân?"

She shook her head. "No," she said, "it would not work here."

He took his hand away from her cheek. Verity, he could see, was absorbed with something she had found on the ground some distance away.

"Your father," he said. He raised his eyebrows. "Your *father,* Siân?"

She nodded. "He came to see me at Glanrhyd Castle after you had sent word to him," she said. "And he came to Grandad's house a few days ago." She smiled fleetingly. "Yes, my father."

"Well," he said, "I am glad."

She pulled on a silver chain he had noticed about her neck and drew a locket out from inside her dress. "He sent me this," she said. "It was my mother's. He took it after she died."

He took the locket from her fingers and opened it. A miniature — a flattering portrait — of a younger Sir John Fowler looked up at him from one side and one of Siân from the other — except that it could not be Siân.

"Your mother?" he asked.

She nodded. "I look like her."

"I can understand," he said, closing the locket and tucking it back into the neckline of her dress, "why he fell in love with her." He looked into her eyes.

"I can accept now that it was love," she said. "I used to tell myself that it was merely lust. But I think I was a product of a love affair."

He smiled at her and then sobered. There was something that had been worrying him. "Siân," he asked, "is there any chance that you are with child?"

She blushed and bit her lower lip. "No," she said. "None at all."

It was hard to understand the stab of disappointment he felt since the last thing he wanted to have done was to have impregnated her and forced her under his protection.

"Siân." He took one of her hands in both of his. He could not let her go. He would not. "Is it really what you want for yourself? This teaching job?"

"Yes." She looked back into his eyes. She seemed very calm, very sure of herself. "I know now that I can never belong fully in a place like Cwmbran. I mean, I can never become like everyone else merely by trying or by taking the same sort of job as they have or by marrying one of them. I have to accept the fact that I am somewhat different. I have to find out where I do belong and I have to learn to be happy with who I am and what I am. I know that I belong in Wales. And I am almost sure that I belong here as a teacher. But I need to be in a different place, where I can establish my real identity from the start."

"Perhaps," he said, "you belong with me, Siân."

She shook her head. "No," she said, "of that at least I am sure. I could never be happy with you, Alexander. I could never be me if I stayed with you. My identity would be submerged in yours as it would have in Owen's had I married him. Selfish and unchristian as it may sound, I have to be me. My father is going to help me find myself. It is fitting, I believe. I am excited by the prospect of the future."

He felt as if a leaden weight had settled in the pit of his stomach. Verity was sailing back toward them, her arms extended again.

"Siân," he said quickly, desperate to say it before it was too late, "you know that I love you. I'll not burden you with the fact and

I'll do no more to persuade you into a way of life that would only bring you unhappiness. But I believe I have said the words before only when we have been making love. I want you to know that they are true even when we are not. I love you."

She stared mutely back at him.

"I will never marry again," he said. "There will never be anyone else. If ever you need me, I am here. I love you."

He watched her swallow and open her mouth to speak.

And then Verity was on them, happy and prattling.

She took a hand of each again and raced them down the hill, shrieking with delight when they sometimes moved so fast that she lost her footing and was rushed downward, suspended by her arms. Somehow, before they reached the valley, they were all laughing again.

24

The Crowthers had recently opened a school on their estate in Carmarthenshire. Lady Crowther and her daughter were teaching there at present with some help from the village rector and the nonconformist minister. But Lord Crowther was eager to hire a regular teacher. He had been thinking of a schoolmaster, but he was prepared, as a favor to his old friend, Sir John Fowler, to give Mrs. Siân Jones a try. He understood, though it had never been stated baldly, that Mrs. Jones was Fowler's byblow.

Sir John told Siân about the offer during another afternoon stroll by the river. It was a good offer, he said. The job came with a small cottage on the estate and a newly equipped schoolhouse and a generous salary. She could start after Christmas, in a little over two months' time.

"I should take it, then," she said, feeling

breathless. "It is too good a chance to miss, isn't it?" And yet she was terrified, feeling like a bird being thrust out of the nest. More terrified than she had been after her mother's death.

He took her hand. "Only if you want, Siân," he said. "If it is too far away, then I will keep looking for something closer. Or if you want you can come and live close to me again. The cottage is still empty."

No, definitely not that. She could not go back there. She would rather stay where she was.

"Will you say yes to Lord Crowther for me?" she asked. "And thank you." She smiled at him a little self-consciously. "Thank you, Dada."

He squeezed her hand.

Gran was upset. Grandad was in a rage. Emrys shook his head and refused to get involved. But Siân began to plan ahead, began to detach herself from the life she had so desperately wanted to be hers. She quietly and doggedly ignored the memory of Alexander's voice on top of the mountain saying, "Perhaps you belong with me, Siân." If he had only known at that moment how vulnerable she was, how desperate to be persuaded, she would indeed be his now, housed no doubt in a cottage as her mother had been, receiving his calls two or three times a week and his visits to her bed.

She was glad he had not known.

Yet a treacherous part of her desperately wished that he would come to realize it and would come to her to persuade her to stay before it came time for her to leave.

She did not see him again. Although Verity came several times to spend an hour with her, she was brought and fetched each time by a groom — the one who had come that very first time to summon Siân to the castle.

She tried to detach herself from what was going on around her. And something was definitely going on. Emrys was out of the house far more than usual, down at the Three Lions, he always said, though he was rarely drunk when he arrived home. There were meetings there, Siân knew, and meetings up on the mountain. There was a tension and an air of expectancy in the town.

Normally she would have known all about it. Owen would have told her, and Grandad and Emrys would have talked about it at home. And normally she would have been painfully interested in finding out what was going on. Normally her curiosity would have overwhelmed her and sent her up the mountain to find out at firsthand what was being planned.

But this time, though she knew that something important was happening, probably the approach of the planned march on Newport, she deliberately kept herself detached. She did not want to know. She did not want to be caught up in the passions of her people. They were no longer her people.

But some of them were, of course. There was still her family and Gwyn's. Still Iestyn, whom she sometimes felt she loved more than anyone else in the world. She walked home from chapel with him the last Sunday in October, when the trees about them were a riot of autumn color.

"Iestyn," she said, "it is going to be soon, isn't it?"

She did not have to explain to what she referred. The whole town pulsed with the knowledge that she had been trying to ignore.

"Any day now," he said. "John Frost is to send word. Three giant columns of men there are to be, Siân, from all parts of the valleys, one led by Frost himself and the others by Zephaniah Williams and William Jones. There is great pressure being put on us to join the Association. Many men are giving in and doing so. Owen Parry is insistent that the government will sit up and take notice only if all of us march and close down all the ironworks and mines in the valleys."

She did not want to know, Siân thought. And yet every night for weeks her sleep had been tense and broken by the expectation of hearing Scotch Cattle in the hills. But expectation had never yet become reality.

And of course she was constantly worried about Iestyn, who had been whipped once, and who was determined now to hold out against persuasion and refuse to march.

Oh, it was impossible to remain totally detached.

And it was impossible too to try to remain ignorant as the week worn on. Tension mounted. According to Iestyn, who had become Siân's only confidant, more and more pressure was being put on those men who had not yet joined the Association. They were being called traitors. If they only joined in, Owen had told them, five thousand men would march on Newport, and workers in other parts of the British Isles would rise with them. The government would have no choice but to grant their demands. The Charter would be law within a month. And all would be accomplished peaceably. There was to be no violence.

Iestyn and a few other men held out stubbornly.

By Saturday there could be no mistaking the fact that the date had been set, though Siân knew no details. The streets were unnaturally quiet. Men who should have been at work were not there. Siân dared not ask a grim-faced Emrys why he was at home. The unnatural silence had crept even inside the walls of her grandfather's house.

And then on Sunday after chapel and Sunday School, during lashing and miserable rain, they were gone. Her grandfather and Emrys were not at home when Siân returned for tea, and when she asked about them, her grandmother turned without a word and hurried upstairs to shut herself behind her bedroom door. Siân felt sick. She understood instantly where they had gone.

In the pouring rain. They were going to trudge all the way to Newport in the pouring rain — perhaps to violence and disaster. She felt dizzy with panic. And yet she forced herself to pour boiling water from the kettle into the teapot and to sit down at the table.

It was not her concern. It no longer mattered to her what happened in Cwmbran. She would no longer allow it to matter. She pushed thoughts of Emrys and her grandfather and Huw from her mind.

Angharad was breathless and sobbing —
and wet through — when she arrived at
Josiah Barnes's lodge cottage on Sunday
afternoon. She knocked urgently on the
door twice before it opened.

"They have gone, Mr. Barnes," she gasped
out as she stumbled into the cottage. "Even
though it is Sunday and even though it is
raining. I didn't know the exact time yesterday or even this morning. Honest, I didn't.
Even when my dada went out I wasn't sure.
But I stopped Ifor Richards and he told me.
I came as soon as I knew. Don't be angry
with me. I only just found out."

But Barnes, though he had not known,
was not angry, as she expected him to be.
He was even in a good mood — as far as
his mood could be good when everything
he had worked for in the past dozen years
was disintegrating before his eyes. At least
now the full disaster was upon them. He
would see how Craille would react to all
that would follow today's business. Within
the week, if Barnes knew his man, the
marquess would be on his way back to
England, defeated and humiliated. Barnes
would be in charge again. It would not be
easy putting things back together, but he

had always enjoyed a challenge.

No, he was not fuming. He had no intention of going out and getting soaking wet himself just in order to go after the men or in order to go up to the house to warn Craille. Let him find out for himself.

"So they are on their way to Newport," he said, rubbing his hands together.

"They were going up the mountain first," Angharad said, "to organize and to wait for the men from Penybont to come down the valley. Perhaps you can stop them yet, Mr. Barnes. There is frightened they will be when they see you. But at least they will be safe."

Barnes laughed. "I have better ways to spend my Sunday afternoons," he said. "Upstairs with you, woman, and get undressed." And with her father on his way to Newport, he would be able to have her as many times as he wanted before sending her home again.

Angharad looked at him a little uncertainly, but she went scurrying upstairs willing enough when he helped her on her way with a pat on the backside.

It was fortunate, he thought less than ten minutes later, that he never wasted time in going about his business with a woman. He had finished and was already relaxing when someone else knocked on his door. But he was warm and comfortable and sleepy. He grunted in protest.

Whoever was there was knocking as urgently as Angharad had earlier. Barnes grunted again at the third knock, pulled on his trousers, and went downstairs, buttoning them as he went. There had better be a good reason, he thought, as yet a fourth knock sounded at the door.

It was Gwilym Jenkins, the man who had spread the rumor about Siân for Barnes. He was breathless and wet and frightened.

"They are on their way," he said. "They are gathering up on the mountain."

"I have been disturbed from my Sunday rest for this?" Barnes asked, frowning. "I knew that half an hour ago. Let the fools go. With any luck they will be mown down by soldiers' guns and learn a lesson that this valley will remember for generations to come."

"I have to hide," Gwilym said, desperation in his eyes and his voice. "They are after everyone and making everyone go. I saw them drag Iestyn Jones up the mountain. I have to hide until they are well gone. Will you let me stay here, Mr. Barnes?"

Barnes moved to block the doorway more firmly. "Not here," he said. "They have probably all gone by now anyway. If you are scared, Jenkins, beg a place in the stables for an hour or two." He jerked his head up the driveway and viewed the worker with some contempt.

But as Gwilym turned away, looking as if fear was still clawing at his back, Barnes held up a hand. "Wait a minute," he said. "Iestyn Jones, did you say?"

"I saw it with my own eyes," Gwilym said. "I don't want it to be me, Mr. Barnes. There is no knowing what will happen in New-port."

Barnes beckoned impatiently and moved away from the door, where he was getting wet himself. "Come inside," he said. He stood frowning down into the fire for a few moments, while Gwilym hurried gratefully into the kitchen, shutting the door firmly behind him. He breathed an audible sigh of relief.

Josiah Barnes was not normally a vindic-tive man. He had worked hard at Cwmbran for many years and had made prosperous industries of the ironworks and mine there. He was a hard man and ruled with an iron fist — as one had to in order to prosper, he believed. But he was not usually a spiteful man.

Times had changed, of course. For many

years there had been only the occasional reminder that he was not in fact on an equal footing with the other owners — one of those reminders had come when Sir John Fowler's bastard had refused to marry him. But now suddenly the truth had been revealed to him in the cruelest of ways. Not only was the real owner in residence at Glanrhyd Castle, and not only was he trying to take charge of the works, but also he was wresting all power from Barnes and making changes that would be disastrous for profits and discipline. Perhaps the last straw — a small one, but the one that had broken the camel's back, so to speak — was Craille's hiring of the bastard to teach his daughter and releasing her from where he, Barnes, had put her — in the mine.

Yes, frustration and anger had made him vicious. And spiteful. And a taste of success had made him greedy for more. The knowledge that Siân Jones had been dragged up the mountain and had her back bared and whipped could still make his mouth water. And the fact that Parry had been humiliated in front of all the men of Cwmbran when he was leveled by the fists of Craille added to Barnes's pleasure — and the fact that there had been no further mention of a wedding between Siân and Parry.

Yes, he was greedy for more. Viciously greedy. Iestyn Jones. Her brother-in-law. She was fond of the boy. Word had come to Barnes that she had gone up the mountain after him the night he was whipped.

"You will go back into town," he said, turning decisively and looking at Gwilym Jenkins, who was wiping ineffectually at a wet face with a wetter cap.

Gwilym's hand paused, mid-wipe. "Oh, no, Mr. Barnes," he said. "Not yet. I dare not go back there yet."

"Nevertheless you will," Barnes said, "for twice what I paid you last time. All you have to do is get to Hywel Rhys's house and pass along a message. Mrs. Rhys will no doubt let you hide there until all is safe."

Gwilym, saucer-eyed, was shaking his head.

"You have to tell Siân Jones that her brother-in-law has been taken," Barnes said. "Embellish the story in any way you see fit. His hands were tied. Maybe there was a loop about his neck too. Maybe they were cuffing him and threatening him with whips. And a gun. They were telling him they would hold a gun to his head all the way to Newport and would use it too if he tried to hold back or escape."

Gwilym was turning his cap about and

about in his hands. "I would be caught for sure," he said.

"But the money would more than buy the rest of the furniture you need," Josiah Barnes said. "She will follow him and doubtless try to rescue him herself. The bitch will finally get what she deserves. They will not dare let her go, believing her to be Craille's informer. They will be afraid that she will run straight to him."

"Good God, man," Gwilym said, his conscience pricked, "she is a woman."

Barnes smiled. "Did I say twice as much as before?" he said. "Make it three times as much. One third now. Another third when the message is given. And the other if she goes up the mountain and does not come back again."

Gwilym swallowed. "I'll do it," he said. "But it doesn't seem right somehow."

Barnes stood in the middle of the kitchen after he had sent Jenkins on his way. He smiled at nothing in particular. The bitch! At the very least she would suffer from Jenkins's tale. But he did not believe she would sit passively at home once she had heard about her precious Iestyn.

He remembered suddenly that Angharad was in bed upstairs. And a good thing too. Contemplating the sort of fate that might be awaiting Siân Jones had made him uncomfortably hard. It was good to know that there was a woman close by on whom to relieve his discomfort. He unbuttoned his trousers as he climbed the stairs and stripped them off when he reached the top. Angharad was fast asleep.

"Wake up, sleepyhead," he said, chuckling, "and get those legs spread. I have something for you."

Angharad did as she was told then and twice more within the next couple of hours. And part of her could not help but rejoice at what was happening. There was nothing more cozy and intimate than Sunday afternoon lovings — nothing more calculated to make a man realize that he needed a woman permanently in his home.

But another part of her was troubled and had been even before the interruption. She had come running to Josiah Barnes only partly because she had thought he would be angry if she did not. Partly too she had wanted him to stop the march even if it meant trouble for some. She was afraid of what would happen in Newport. She was afraid some of the men would die.

She was afraid Emrys Rhys would die.

But then there was the interruption.

Curious as to the identity and message of the visitor when Josiah Barnes did not come back to bed after a few minutes, she had crept out onto the landing and down a few stairs, avoiding the one that she knew to be squeaky. And so she had heard all that had been said after Gwilym Jenkins came inside the cottage.

And it troubled her. Her own message might have caused some trouble, but this was deliberate and malicious trouble being brought on someone innocent. Siân was her friend. She had always admired Siân's dignity and ladylike demeanor — and the fact that Siân was never uppity. It shocked Angharad to hear Josiah call Siân a bitch and plot to have her hurt. It shocked her even more to realize that it was Josiah who had had those rumors about Siân put about so that Siân had been whipped by Scotch Cattle.

"I think," Angharad said when she felt that a suitable time had elapsed after his fourth use of her body, "that I had better be going, Mr. Barnes."

He was half asleep. He grunted. "As you wish," he muttered.

Angharad looked at him wistfully. She knew suddenly that she had been fooling herself all these months. And that even if she had not, even if there was still a flicker of hope, she was about to snuff it out herself.

She got out of bed and dressed herself in clothes that were still not quite dry. By the time she was finished, Josiah Barnes was snoring in the bed. She gazed at him for a long time and sighed. One tear trickled unheeded down each cheek. She turned away and hurried downstairs, stepping over the squeaky stair. She drew on her cloak, pulled up the hood, and stepped outside. The rain had not eased at all.

She hesitated for only a moment before turning in the direction of the castle and hurrying head down up the driveway. She had never been to the castle. She did not know where to go. But like Siân before her, she ascended the steep steps to the front door, and knocked hastily before she could give herself time to think again.

The servant who answered her knock looked at her as if she was a worm and blocked the doorway quite dauntingly. He would have sent her away, but having got up her courage to come this far, Angharad was not to be denied. She told the man that it was a matter of life and death and on his own head be it if he stopped her from talking to the marquess.

She almost died of fright when she was told to wait in a room grander than anything she had ever seen in her life. She almost died again when the Marquess of Craille stepped into the room a few minutes later, looking far more awesomely grand than he had ever looked in the few glimpses Angharad had had of him in the past.

"Yes?" he said. "You have an important message for me?"

He looked directly at her and his voice was kind. Paradoxically Angharad was even more unnerved. She tried to speak but no sound came out.

"You are soaked," he said kindly. "Were you afraid to step closer to the fire? Please do so now."

Angharad had not even noticed the fire or the fact that she was wet.

"They have gone," she blurted out. "He is tricking her to go after them and she will be caught. I don't know what will happen to her then."

He looked at her keenly. "They have gone," he said. "Who have gone where?"

Was he stupid? Did he not realize that time was of the essence? "He sent him almost two hours ago," she said breathlessly, her words tripping over themselves in her haste to get them out. "She would have gone right away. But they all went long before that."

He came toward her suddenly and Angharad took a hasty step backward. But he merely smiled and took her by the arm and led her toward the fire. He seated her in a very grand chair to one side of it. She was scared of dripping all over it and ruining it.

"I am sorry," he said, "I do not know your name."

She stared at him a moment until she noticed his raised eyebrows. "Oh," she said. "Angharad. Angharad Lewis, sir. I mean your lord, my lordship. Oh." She closed her eyes, mortified.

"Angharad," he said, "there is nothing to be frightened about here. What are you trying to tell me? Take your time. There is no point in haste when I am too stupid to understand." He smiled. "Start at the beginning."

"The men are gone," she said. "To Newport. They went up the mountain ages ago. They were going to wait for the men to come from Penybont, but they have probably gone by now. Oh, it will be too late. He sent the message to her two hours ago. Goodness knows what will have happened to her."

He had crossed the room while she spoke.

He was back now and was handing her a glass with an inch or so of dark liquid in the bottom of it.

"Drink it," he said. "It will warm you."

"I am chapel," she said. "I can't . . ."

"Think of it as medicine," he said, "to stop you from catching a chill. So they have gone, have they? I am sorry about it, but I told them I would not stop them. It was their own decision, Angharad. Who is the 'she' you have been mentioning?"

Angharad was coughing and grimacing over her first ever taste of alcohol. "Siân Jones," she said, her voice an agony.

He was down on his haunches in front of her suddenly, his expression taut, his eyes fully focused on her.

"What about Siân Jones?" he snapped out. "Tell me clearly, Angharad."

She swallowed. "They forced all the men to go," she said. "They forced Iestyn Jones to go."

She watched his jaw harden and was frightened again. She thought irrelevantly that this man would be too masterful for her. She would be too afraid of him to enjoy anything with him. Even though he had been kind to her.

"And Siân saw and went after him?" he said, frowning.

It was only afterward that Angharad realized that she should have gone along with his assumption. She did not think of it at the time.

"No," she said. "Gwilym Jenkins saw it and came to tell Mr. Barnes." She flushed at the realization of what her choice of verb had revealed, but he did not seem to notice. "He was running away so that they would not take him too. But he told Mr. Barnes about Iestyn Jones, and Mr. Barnes paid him a lot of money to go back and tell Siân. He was to make it sound even worse than it was so that she would go after him and get caught. He called her a b-b-" — she swallowed again — "he called her a bitch. But she is not. She is my friend."

He stood up in front of her. Angharad risked only one glance up at him. She was terrified by what she saw. He looked as if he was ready to tear her limb from limb.

"And this was two hours ago?" he asked, his voice tight.

"Yes," she said. "I was busy. I was too busy to come until now. I am sorry. I could not get away. He . . . We . . . I — I could not get away."

"I understand," he said. And she had no doubt at all that he did. She hung her head in shame. "Thank you, Angharad. You are very brave. And a true friend to Siân. I will have you taken down to the kitchen so that you can dry yourself and have some tea before going home. Did he know you were coming here? Are you afraid for your safety?"

"No," she said. "He was s-sleeping."

"This was hard for you to do," he said, reaching out a hand toward her. "Thank you for doing it. He will never know how I found out."

She realized that she was to put her hand in his. She did so and looked up at him. His face was still blazing, but she realized that it was not with her he was angry.

"What are you going to do?" she whispered as he helped her to her feet.

"I am going to bring her safely home," he said. "I must hurry, Angharad. Stay here and warm yourself. I'll send someone to take you downstairs."

Angharad's teeth chattered as she waited after he had hurried from the room. He would kill her if he ever found out. Mr. Barnes would kill her. And she would deserve it. She had betrayed all her own people just as Gwilym Jenkins had. She was no better. She bit her upper lip as she absorbed the thought. She had betrayed them. All because she wanted a rich hus-

band and a good home and luxuries. Siân
Jones was not a bitch. Siân was her friend.
She did not deserve to get into trouble.

It was she, Angharad, who deserved that.
Siân had been whipped for what Angharad
had done.

25

Siân's determination to remain uninvolved shattered like a crystal glass on a stone floor.

"Oh, *Duw, Duw,*" her grandmother said when Gwilym Jenkins called with the news about Iestyn. "There is wicked the men have become and all over an old Charter. Well, just don't let them be expecting me to visit them in the old jail when they are caught and thrown in it, that is all. I wash my hands of them all — Hywel, Emrys, the lot of them." She threw her apron over her head and burst into tears.

Siân, white-faced, was on her feet. "Could they not let him alone?" she said. "One boy is going to make all the difference to their cause that he must be dragged away with his hands bound and a n-noose about his neck and a gun thrust into his back? So they will hang him or shoot him if he makes any more protest? And Iestyn will not keep his mouth shut just because he is afraid. Oh,

Iestyn, my pet." She covered her face with shaking hands for a few moments.

"There is no telling what they will do," Gwilym said. "They are in an ugly mood. Is it all right with you, Mrs. Rhys, if I stay here for a bit? If I go home, they will drag me off too. And I have the wife and little ones to think of."

"Of course you must stay," Gwynneth said, "and have a cup of tea." But she looked up sharply suddenly. "Where are you going, Siân?"

Siân was pulling a dry cloak about her and lifting the hood to cover her head. "I am going down to Mam and Mari's to find out the truth of it," she said. "Perhaps they let him come home after all. Perhaps Huw spoke up for him."

"But only to Mari's, mind," her grandmother said, getting to her feet and grabbing for Siân's arm. "You are not to go in pursuit of them, Siân. Promise me, *fach*. You can do no good by going after them."

Siân drew free and opened the door. "I must find out what has happened," she said, and ran out into the rain before her grandmother could extract any promises from her.

Iestyn, she thought as she hurried toward his home. Surely they would have allowed him to return home. Why drag an unwilling man with them all the way to Newport? And in such terrible weather. The rain beat down on her, and the wetness of it and the chill of early November seemed to seep into her very bones. They were mad. All of them were mad — Emrys, Huw, Grandad, Owen. All of them.

Her mother-in-law and Mari were in the kitchen with the children. They were eating tea, both women with pale, set faces.

"Where is Iestyn?" Siân asked without preamble.

His mother sucked in her breath. "They took him," she said. "Four of them came for him, Siân, and took him away with them. Everyone has to march, they said. There are to be no exceptions."

So the miracle had not happened. He had not come back home. She had not expected it, Siân realized.

"Not Iestyn," she said, almost in a whisper. "Oh, dear God, not Iestyn. There is going to be trouble on that march."

"Do you go, then, Siân," her mother-in-law said bitterly, "and bring him back. Fight off a few hundred men carrying sticks and guns and bring my boy home. They will whip you to death this time and there is no man left down here who will be able to go up to carry you home."

Mari wept. "There is wicked it was of Huw to go," she said. "He will leave the little ones orphans."

Siân turned without a word and ran back out into the rain. She did not fully realize where she was going until she found herself scrambling and slithering upward over wet grass above the houses. They were gathering on the hill, Gwilym had said. Probably in the usual place. She did not even allow herself to wonder what she would do if and when she came up to them.

But before she reached the usual meeting place, she looked downward and could see that she was too late. Even through the driving rain she could see the long, dark column moving down the valley, well past the mine. The men had begun their march, and from the look of the length of the column it would appear that there were hundreds of them. More than the men of Cwmbran. The men must have come down from Penybont too and they were marching onward together until the one dense column, picking up more and more as it went along, met up with the other two and prepared to enter Newport.

It was suddenly and sickeningly real. And yet it was not a totally secret thing. Although the exact date appeared to have been kept a closely guarded secret, everyone knew that this was going to happen. Goodness only knew what was awaiting the men in Newport. Perhaps a whole army of soldiers and guns and cannon.

Siân pressed a hand to her mouth and closed her eyes. Iestyn. Her dear boy. With a noose about his neck and a gun thrust against his back — being forced onward to provide fodder for government guns. For one moment she felt that her knees would buckle under her.

And for another moment she hesitated, a strong part of herself urging her to run back across the hill toward Glanrhyd Castle and Alexander. He would help her. He would go after them and force them to release Iestyn.

But perhaps he did not know about the march. Perhaps if he did, despite everything, he would try to end it, call out some forces against it. Perhaps if she went to him now she really would be an informer. Grandad and Emrys were in that march. And Huw. And Owen.

Her hesitation did not last long. Within a few moments she was running across the hill, slipping and sliding on the wet and slippery heather. But it was not toward the castle she ran, but away from it. She ran in pursuit of the marching column of men, moving downward as well as across. She wished she had put boots on. But there was no time now to return for them. If she did not go immediately, and run while they marched, she would never catch up to them and she would never free Iestyn.

It seemed as if hours had passed before she was finally above the stragglers of the column. By that time she felt soaked to the very bone, and her lungs hurt from the exertion of half-running across an uneven and slippery hillside. There was almost nowhere to hide. Although there were trees farther down the valley, here there were few. She could only hope that the rain would keep the men's eyes directed downward.

Her own eyes searched frantically for Iestyn. And unwillingly they saw something else. Many of the men were carrying wooden pikes. Even from some distance above it was obvious to Siân that those pikes had been tipped with iron. Someone had been very busy preparing weapons — probably in hill caves with iron stolen from the works. The sight made her feel physically sick.

And eventually, as she moved farther forward, she began to see the guns. Not just a few of them, but many, carried by the men on the outside of the columns. Oh, God. Oh, dear God.

There was something incongruous and rather horrible about the fact that the men were singing as they marched — in full and glorious harmony. They were singing Welsh hymns.

"God. Oh, dear God." Siân found herself sobbing out the inarticulate prayer.

She saw Iestyn eventually, marching between two particularly large and burly miners. There was no noose about his neck, thank goodness. That was what she noticed first. Neither was there a gun pointed against his back. But his hands were bound, one wrist attached to a wrist of the man on either side of him. Being Iestyn, he looked neither angry nor sullen. But neither was he singing. He was marching quietly along.

She knew she had been spotted at the same moment as she decided that she was going to go down there. Arms were pointing up at her and one or two voices calling. There was one whistle. She turned sharply downward and ran and slithered down into the mass of marching men. She pushed through them, ignoring reaching hands and amused and lewd remarks, until she was beside Iestyn's jailers.

"Let him go," she said. "You have no right."

"Duw," one of the men said. "Siân Jones. We might have guessed. There is no other woman who would dare. Be off home with you before Owen or someone else in authority sees you."

"Siân," Iestyn said, surprise and some alarm in his face. "Go home, *fach.* I am all right. After all I suppose I should go where my brother and my friends are going. Go home. Tell Mam that I am all right."

"But your hands are tied," she said. She looked indignantly at the two miners who flanked him. "Untie him. Let him go."

"And feel the fists of Owen Parry?" the other one said. "No, thank you, Siân Jones. Guard him, Owen said. Everyone must march. So guard him we will. Don't worry. We are not breaking his ribs or smashing his teeth."

Siân half ran to keep up with their strides. She did not believe it would be possible to feel wetter or more miserable. And yet the men had hours of marching to do before reaching Newport and then the demonstration to participate in and then — if by some miracle everything went according to their plans — hours and hours more of marching home.

"Then I am coming too," she said firmly.

There were some hearty cheers and a few ribald comments from the men who were within earshot, and some gentle persuasions from Iestyn to go home, but Siân walked stubbornly on. If they would not release Iestyn, then she would go with him to protect him.

But word of her presence in the column somehow reached farther down the line. A short while later a grim-faced Owen appeared beside her.

"I might have known it," he said. "The only surprise would have been if you had not come, Siân. I should have the march stopped and have you publicly beaten."

"Don't be silly," she said, not even looking at him.

"I will give you my word not to try to escape even if you release me," Iestyn said. "But leave Siân alone, Owen. Let her go home."

"So that she can tell her bloody lover that we are on the march and that we have prisoners with us?" Owen said.

"Lover?" Iestyn's voice was shaking. "Watch your mouth, Owen Parry."

"It is all right, Iestyn," Siân said quietly. "You need not fear that I will inform against you, Owen. I am going with you to New-port."

"Bloody right you are," he said through his teeth. "And don't think you are going to slip away into the hills once we get into trees, either. You and you." He pointed at two men Siân did not even know, two men presumably from Penybont. "Find two lengths of rope and confine her wrists as with the men who had to be persuaded to come with us. And don't let her go, or you will have me to answer to."

"Owen," Siân said coldly, "how ridiculous you make yourself. I told you I am coming. I have no intention of escaping."

But he did not stay to listen. He length-ened his stride in order to return to his place at the head of the column, and one of the Penybont men, grinning, clamped a hand on her arm while the other went in search of rope. Five minutes later she was walking between the two of them, her wrists firmly bound.

And so she marched for what seemed like days more than hours though the gloom of daylight gave way only gradually to the greater gloom of dusk and then the full dark of night. They stopped twice to eat at small public houses that were far too small to en-able them all to get out of the wet even for a few minutes or to provide them all with adequate supplies of food and drink.

Sometimes they sang to keep up their spirits. But mostly it was just the sheer press of numbers and an individual stubbornness of will that kept them all trudging onward down the valley until very late — Siân found it unbelievable that morning had not dawned hours ago — a halt was called and even those toward the back of the column could see that they had come to a place where hundreds — perhaps thousands — more men were waiting for them.

They were at Cefn, just north of Newport, the men around Siân were beginning to say. John Frost was there and had been for hours, but he was in a roaring temper because they were late and the other two columns had made no appearance at all.

They waited around in the cold and the wet and the dark for what seemed hours longer. It had seemed while they marched that there could be no greater discomfort or misery, and yet the wait was far worse. They did not know why they waited or for how long they were to stand around. They did not know where they were to go from here or for what purpose.

Some of the men, sullen and almost mutinous, began to wonder if there was any plan or organization at all. Or any leader capable of making some decision.

And then finally there was the suggestion of morning on the horizon and the darkness began to lift. And finally too they were on the move again. Through the means of imperfect communication, they gathered that John Frost was not going to wait any longer for the other columns to arrive. Already his planned march on the town was hours later than scheduled. They were to circle around the town and enter it from the southwest. They were to march to the Westgate Inn, the largest building in Newport, and the focal point of its existence.

Word was somehow passed down the line that prisoners were to be untied.

"I suppose they feel that you will not desert now, *fach,*" one of Siân's jailers said as she rubbed at her wrists. "It will be safer to stay with the column. You stay next to me and I will shield you from harm."

"Thank you." Siân smiled at him. He had done his best through the night to keep her cheerful. He had even released her once and persuaded his companion to do likewise so that she could go into the trees to put herself comfortable, and had stood guard to make sure that no one interrupted her and embarrassed her.

■ ■ ■ ■

Something went drastically wrong. No one afterward could ever explain exactly what it was. Perhaps the best explanation was that it was an explosive situation and that it was almost inevitable that a spark be ignited. Who ignited it was not the important question. Someone did as someone inevitably was fated to do.

The large column that descended on the Westgate Inn was armed, the front and side lines with guns. Inside the inn the mayor waited with special constables and soldiers, all armed, all ready to face trouble. Some of the demonstrators entered the inn and shots were fired. No one ever knew who shot first.

But the demonstrators got the worst of it. Several of them were fired on at point-blank range inside the inn and yet could not retreat quickly because of the press of more men behind them. As some demonstrators, hearing the sound of shots from outside, broke windows in their attempt to get inside to help their comrades, the soldiers began to direct their fire outside the inn as well as inside.

Shortly after the demonstrators had begun to arrive at the inn, and long before all of them had done so, word began to spread that the crowd was being fired upon and the order was given to retreat. It did not take long for panic to spread.

The demonstration broke up as hundreds of men fled along every available street or hid in any available building. It did not help matters that one of the missing columns, arrived at last, was trying to enter the town from the north, the route along which most of the fleers were escaping.

Siân was not outside the hotel when the shooting began, but she was close enough to hear the sound of shots. It felt rather as if the bottom was falling out of her stomach, she thought even before others reacted and confirmed her suspicion that it was indeed guns she heard.

She looked around, panicked, for Iestyn, but there was no sign of him. She had not seen her grandfather or Emrys or Huw all night, but she knew they must be up ahead. And up ahead were the guns.

And then the crowd ahead of her was pressing back and breaking into a run and panic became a blind and a clawing thing that threatened madness and death. Siân's staunch companion from Penybont took a firm hold on her arm and drew her close against him, but she shook him off and found herself pushing against the tide of humanity. She was reacting with as little thought as they. Pure instinct, pure panic, drove her forward into danger.

Iestyn. Emrys, Grandad, Huw. She had to find them. She had to know they were safe.

By the time she had fought her way into the square before the inn, it was no longer dense with humanity but was filled instead with fleeing men and dotted with some who lay still on the ground. Siân looked about her with panic and terror. Where were they? Were they on the ground? Were they dead? She ran out into the open.

But before she had taken more than two steps, an iron-hard arm came around her waist and lifted her right off her feet.

"All the devils in hell!" a voice bellowed in her ear. "Are you mad?"

"Iestyn." She was sobbing. "I have to find Iestyn."

"Get out of here," Owen said. "They are shooting. Aah!"

She crashed painfully down onto cobbles, her forehead thudding against them, almost robbing her of consciousness for a few moments. Owen's weight came down heavily on top of her. But she was still sobbing.

"I have to find Iestyn," she said. "Please,

Owen, I have to find him."

It was only gradually that she became aware that something was wrong. Foolish to think of something being wrong under the circumstances, but she had the unmistakable feeling that something was. He should be shaking her, yelling at her, threatening her.

"Owen?"

He grunted.

Somehow, despite his great weight, she turned herself over under him. His head flopped against her shoulder.

"Owen?" she whispered again.

There was a curious silence all about them. Everyone must have fled.

"Cariad." His voice was very faint.

She got her arms about him. But the wetness she felt with one hand was not the expected wetness of rain. It was warm and thick to the touch.

"You have been hurt?" she asked foolishly. She listened to her voice as if it belonged to someone else. She felt almost as if she was above her own body, looking down. A spectator.

There was no answer. She knew with absolute certainty that there would be no answer. Ever.

Cariad, he had said.

589

His last word.

Cariad.

She held Owen's lifeless body in her arms and closed her eyes.

Time was a meaningless commodity. She did not know how much of it passed before she opened her eyes. Someone was leaning over her and then coming down on his knees beside her.

"He is dead," she told the Marquess of Craille in a voice that matched the announcement. "He died saving my life."

He had managed things badly, Alex admitted to himself as the night wore on. Unbelievably badly. It came to feel almost as if he were in one of those dreams in which a person is trying to run and cannot seem to propel himself forward or trying to accomplish something but unable even to start.

His first instinct when he left Angharad was to rush to Siân's home to find out if indeed she had gone up the mountain in pursuit of her brother-in-law. It was an instinct he followed. He took the time only to grab a cloak and hat and went into town at a run. It would take as long to have a horse saddled and ride there, he thought, as to go there on foot.

But of course she was gone. Her grandmother looked at him with wide and frightened eyes and tried to pretend that nothing was amiss at all. He grasped her upper arms and looked intently into her face.

"I know they have gone," he said. "You must tell me if Siân has gone too, ma'am. I shall go and bring her home for you."

She nodded. "Mari sent one of the children to tell me she went after Iestyn," she said.

There was a man sitting silently beside the fire. He was neither Siân's grandfather nor her uncle, Alex saw when he looked fully at him. He frowned at a sudden suspicion.

"You are the man who brought the news about Iestyn Jones?" he asked.

The man shrank back against the chair. His eyes shifted from Alex to Mrs. Rhys.

"I shall want a word with you when I return," Alex said curtly, and left the house.

He half ran up the mountain in the hope that the men would still be gathered there — and that Siân would be doing nothing more dangerous than spying on them as she had done on two previous occasions. Even apart from Siân, he was lividly angry. He would do nothing to interfere with their freedom to march, he had told the men, provided they did nothing to coerce anyone into joining them. They had defied him.

He had accomplished nothing at all in his months at Cwmbran.

The meeting place was empty. And though he shaded his eyes and squinted off into the distance, so was the valley below. The men must be well on their way. Perhaps Angharad had been wrong about the time. She had spent the afternoon in bed with Barnes. Probably more time had passed than she had realized. Though over two hours was long enough.

Despite the coldness and wetness that had already seeped beneath his clothing, Alex was aware of an extra coldness about his heart. Siân had not returned home. He had seen no sign of her on the mountain. That could mean only one thing.

She had been caught and taken along on the march.

And he had wasted precious time running after her on foot. There was at least a mile and a half of rough hillside between him and his stables. Instinct would have sent him off and running again — running in pursuit of his marching men — and Siân. But belatedly he decided to use thought and common sense. It would take time to go back for a horse. But in the long run he would be faster. It would take the men many hours to march to Newport. He would overtake them long before they arrived there.

Quite what he would do, one man against hundreds, when he came up to them, he did not know. He would think of that when the time came.

And so he went back for a horse — because it was the sensible thing to do and he should have done it to start with. And while it was being saddled, he went into the house to change into dry clothes and to kiss Verity and tell her he would be away on business until tomorrow.

And then he galloped away along the valley, in pursuit of a column of men who could march at only a fraction of his pace.

Except that his horse threw a shoe after less than an hour because he was pushing it too hard over rough terrain, taking risks that he had no business taking. And because he would not abandon the horse in the middle of nowhere, he had to lead it slowly to the nearest smithy — a walk at snail's pace of well over an hour.

Good sense in the end had served him no better than impetuosity. He had to walk the rest of the way and was severely hampered during the night by the oppressive darkness and his unfamiliarity with the landscape. For long stretches, when trees blocked out even the suggestion of light from the sky, he had to walk with his arms stretched out ahead of him, like a blind man.

He ground his teeth impotently, worried sick about Siân. And about his men. But mainly and constantly about Siân.

And so he arrived at Newport too late. Just too late as was the nature of nightmares. Men by the hundreds were fleeing in undisciplined panic, wildness and fear in their eyes. He caught one of them by the arm and forced him to a halt, though the man took a swing at him. He was no one Alex recognized.

"What has happened?" he demanded to know.

"Thousands of soldiers," the man gasped out. "All shooting at us. Hunting us down."

"Where?" Alex snapped out the question. "Where were they shooting from?"

"There," the man said, waving back vaguely into the town with his free arm.

Alex let him go. He drew a few steadying breaths. It would be the easiest thing in the world to panic himself. Where was she? Where to God was she? How was he to find her in the midst of this madness?

It was somehow easy to find his way to the focal point of the whole trouble — a cobbled square with a large building to one side of it, seemingly an inn. It was strangely empty of panicked men, like the eye of a storm. But it was swarming with armed constables and uniformed soldiers. They were turning over dead bodies with their boots and pointing bayonets at those few who were groaning or even screaming from their wounds.

Alex felt cold at heart again. They were all men, one quick glance around at the dead and wounded revealed to him. But the welling of relief the realization brought lasted for only a moment. God in heaven. His worst fears had been realized. There had been a bloody battle here, or more likely a bloody massacre. There were perhaps twenty dead lying on the ground. Were any of them his men?

His mind was almost paralyzed with anxiety over Siân's whereabouts, but he forced himself to walk about the square, looking down at the dead and the wounded. He breathed a fresh sigh of relief each time he looked into a stranger's face.

And then he saw two bodies tangled together, the one sprawled over the other. And his heart lurched again as he noticed that the lower body wore skirts. She was a woman.

He was not sure how his legs carried him across the short distance. But they did. And he stood looking down, his heart turned to stone.

She was wet and disheveled and as pale as parchment. Her forehead was smeared with blood. Sprawled across her, his head cradled on her shoulder, her arms about him, was Owen Parry, a huge bloodstain on the back of his coat.

Alex gazed down at them, unable to move or to think or to feel.

And then she opened her eyes.

He dropped to his knees beside her, hardly daring to hope that this was more than her last gasp of life.

"He is dead," she said to him, her voice flat but quite firm. "He died saving my life."

She was, he realized — and he was glad that he was on his knees so that they could not buckle under him — very much alive.

"Siân," he said to her. "Siân, my love."

26

Siân lay lethargically on the ground, holding Owen. His weight was squashing the breath from her. Her head was sore. She was cold and wet. But now suddenly there was only one thought in her mind, one focus of her being. He had come. All would be well now. He had come.

"Alexander." She tried to smile at him.

And then there were others there, scarlet-coated soldiers, one of them pointing a gun down at her, while two of them grabbed Alex by the arms and dragged him to his feet.

"The game is over," one soldier said roughly. "You can dry off and cool your heels in jail for a while, the pair of you. That one is dead by the look of him."

But while the soldier whose gun was pointed at Siân gave Owen's body a great shove with his boot so that he rolled off her, Alex was transformed before her eyes. He shrugged off the hold of his captors with apparent ease and looked at them with cold hauteur. Despite the fact that he was soaked through and liberally splattered with mud, there was obviously no mistaking the fact that his clothes were costly and fashionable. And even if one discounted the clothes, there was something about him, Siân thought, some indefinable air, that would have convinced the soldiers that he was not of the common rabble. They stared at him without trying to take hold of him again.

"I am the Marquess of Craille," he said, looking down at Siân with steely eyes and thin lips, "owner of the land and works at Cwmbran. And come in pursuit of my truant workers." There was something coldly malicious about his tone.

"Begging your pardon, my lord," one of the soldiers said, clearly embarrassed. "We did not look closely enough."

Siân sat up slowly. The one gun was still pointed at her. Her mouth felt dry despite all the wetness about her.

"We will take the woman and see to the body," the soldier said. "The mayor would doubtless be pleased to receive you inside the inn, my lord. You probably need a good stiff drink."

Alex laughed unpleasantly. "She comes

with me," he said. "I came all this way at considerable discomfort to myself, Lieutenant, as you can see, to round up as many of them as I can and take them home. I cannot allow you to have all the joy of dealing with them. I really cannot. The pleasure of seeing them suitably punished will more than make up for a sleepless night and one ruined suit of clothes. On your feet, Siân Jones."

Siân stared at him in disbelief. He was every inch the cold, sneering, cruel aristocrat. Alexander had totally disappeared; the Marquess of Craille had taken his place.

"I can see your point, my lord," the lieutenant said. "But it is a long way back to Cwmbran, I believe. Would you not prefer to have me jail her here and you can come back for the trial?"

Alex sneered. "I shall enjoy every mile of the journey," he said, so deliberately undressing her with his eyes that the other soldiers snickered. His voice became low and menacing. "Perhaps you did not hear me, woman. Perhaps you need some help." And he bent over her and jerked her to her feet with one hand clasped about her upper arm. With the other hand he whacked her painfully on the bottom.

The lieutenant chuckled. "Well, we have a

manhunt to conduct, my lord," he said. "The inn is already full of prisoners. I doubt the jails hereabouts will all hold the number we will catch today. This will be the last we hear of the Charter at any rate." He touched his shako and beckoned his soldiers away.

"Let me go." Siân's voice was shaking. She felt dizzy. She would not look up into his face. "Let me go."

But his grip on her arm tightened more painfully. "Siân," he said with quiet urgency, "you must be my abject prisoner. Or if you choose to fight me, you must expect that I will strike you. You are in terrible danger."

She looked up at him, understanding suddenly.

"It was the idea that I will rape you every mile of the journey home and then punish you at the end of it that appealed to them and made them agree to let me have custody of you," he said. "Come, we must get out of this town as quickly as we can. This is going to develop into a witch hunt." He pulled firmly on her arm.

"No!" she said sharply. "No. Please." When he stopped, she looked down. Owen was on his back. His face looked peaceful though his eyes were open.

"He is dead, Siân," Alex said gently. But

when she pulled again on her arm, he let her go.

She went down on her knees beside Owen's body and smoothed the wet hair back from his forehead. With shaking, shrinking hands she closed his eyes. "Owen," she whispered. "Owen." She bent over him and kissed his lips. They were cold, though whether from the wintry chill or from death she did not know. She got back to her feet.

"Come," Alex said, one arm about her shoulders.

"We cannot just leave him." She looked at him in an agony.

"Yes, we must," he said, and he was again the Marquess of Craille, though neither cold nor cruel. "I will have him brought home for burial, Siân. But now we must leave him."

"I can't leave," she said. "I don't know what has happened to Iestyn. Or Emrys or Grandad. Or Huw. I can't leave without them. I have to find them."

He swore softly. "I suppose you have heard of needles and haystacks," he said. "After this morning's rout it will be every man for himself, Siân. We will have to hope that everyone returns safely home within the next few days."

"Alexander." He was quite right, of course. But she could not yet think either rationally or sensibly. She wanted miracles worked. She wanted him to work them. "Please?"

He closed his eyes for a moment and then opened them to watch as five dispirited men were marched briskly under armed escort toward the inn. He recognized none of the men.

"Come, then," he said. "I should pay my respects to the mayor while I am here, I suppose." But he did not immediately move. He fumbled beneath his cloak and came out with his cravat, wet and limp and bedraggled. He took Siân's right wrist and bound the cravat tightly about it while she watched in incomprehension, before securing the ends to the belt at his waist.

"I was brought here with both wrists confined," she said dully.

"For goodness' sake," he said, "act the part of sullen prisoner, will you, Siân? If you appear defiant or abusive, I will have to give you the back of my hand across the face."

"I'll be sullen," she said. "Do you think they have taken Iestyn?" Please God they had not taken him. Not Iestyn. What was going to happen to the prisoners? A firing squad? Hanging? Transportation? A long incarceration? Please God they had not taken Iestyn.

"We will hope not," Alex said, moving toward the Westgate Inn with arrogant, purposeful strides, so that Siân had to run to keep up with him.

It was late afternoon by the time they left Newport to begin the long walk home. Despite the fact that at first his relief at finding Siân alive and relatively uninjured had given him only the one purpose of getting her away from all danger as fast as he possibly could, Alex found after a while that his need to ensure the safety of his people kept him in the town. Siân looked about her fearfully and eagerly for her relatives. He looked for any of his people.

There was no particular danger, he realized early. There was no more shooting. It had all ended before he even arrived at the Westgate. And fortunately his appearance was so different from that of the workers, and his voice and accent, that no one questioned his claim to be who and what he was — and no one questioned his right to take his own prisoners. Of course, there had not been many women among the demonstrators.

The mayor and everyone else in authority he spoke to in the course of the day appeared amused more than anything else to see Siân with her wrist confined to his belt and to see her abject demeanor — slumped shoulders, downcast eyes. And to imagine the rapes that he hinted she would have to endure between Newport and Cwmbran. Men seemed generally to consider a rape a suitable and amusing punishment for female wrongdoing, Alex thought with inner anger.

There were more dead bodies inside the inn. None of them looked familiar, and Siân, pale and listless, shook her head when he looked down at her inquiringly. He was not sure that he knew every man of Cwmbran by sight. There were many prisoners. By some miracle none of them were from Cwmbran either.

They wandered the streets endlessly after finally leaving the inn — Siân had been forced to stand by Alex's side while he sat eating a cold dinner with the mayor and drinking a bottle of wine. He had not dared suggest that a chair be brought for her and he risked offering her only a few mouthfuls of food from his plate, sneering at her each time he did so and forcing her to say thank you before giving each to her. The mayor thought it great sport.

Alex wondered what the mayor would say if he knew that Siân was Alex's love — and that Alex was not a magistrate.

The streets were almost totally deserted except for small bands of soldiers and constables and occasionally some prisoners, rooted out from their hiding places within the town. Even the lawful citizens would not risk being seen out on the streets that day and perhaps being mistaken for demonstrators.

"I think all the men of Cwmbran must have made their escape, Siân," Alex said finally, relieved in one way but anxious in another. It seemed too good to be true. And dammit, he thought, they did not deserve their good fortune. They had been warned. "We are not going to find any of them in the streets and we can hardly knock on every door and ask if by any chance there is a man from Cwmbran hiding in a cupboard."

Her shoulders were slumped. It was not all act, he thought, looking into her face.

"He will be safe, Siân," he said, resisting the urge to set an arm about her shoulders. "He is probably halfway home to Cwmbran by now."

"They forced him to come too," she said, "though he had been brave enough to say no and to stand for his principles. Owen could never understand such convictions. He believed that all people should think the same way — his way." She shuddered suddenly. "Owen is dead."

"He knew the risks, Siân," he said. "He believed in his cause so strongly that he was willing to die for it. I felt no love for the man, but I have to admit to a grudging respect for him."

She did not reply. She hung her head.

"Did you love him?" He was almost whispering.

"Yes," she said, and his heart plummeted to somewhere around the level of his boots. "There are many kinds of love. I did not love him quite as a woman loves a man. And I did not like his approach to life. I did not like his intolerance or the way he condoned violence and was even willing to use it himself. I hated him for what he did to Iestyn yesterday — was it only yesterday? But in some inexplicable way and despite all I loved him. Yes, I did. Even though he was among the Scotch Cattle who took me up the mountain. I loved him. Does it make sense?"

"Yes," Alex said, relieved. Yes, it made sense. "Siân, we must leave. Perhaps we will find him on the way home. Probably we will find him at home, anxious for your safety."

"Yes," she said. "Yes, we must leave. I pray God that Owen is the only Cwmbran casualty of all this madness."

"Amen," he said. "Let's go, then. Once we are clear of the town I will be able to release your wrist."

"So much madness," she said, following him as he made his way to the outskirts of the town. "And so much violence. And it is not at an end. I will not ask you what will happen to all these prisoners. I don't think I want to know. Not now." She shivered. "And all in the name of freedom, Alexander. Is there any such thing?"

"In the heart and mind," he said. "In the individual life if one is fortunate and perhaps in the individual family and community. Perhaps the secret is to look inward and then to look outward just at what is within the radius of one's personal influence. Even that is not possible for all people, of course. But for us it is, Siân. For Cwmbran it is."

"Because you are our owner," she said. "Ah, that word *owner.* It says volumes."

"Small ways," he said. "A little at a time. We live according to a certain social and political system, Siân. None of us can change the world in one sweep. We can only do our small part, starting with who we are and what we are. Don't blame me because I am in a position of power. It is what I do with that power that counts, surely."

She laughed suddenly though there was not much amusement in the sound. "This does not seem quite the time or place to be having this discussion," she said. "You have used your power to keep me free today. By keeping me tethered to your belt and by treating me with contempt when we have been in company, you have ensured my freedom. A strange paradox. I must thank you."

"At the same time as you resent the fact that I have that power," he said. "We are outside the town, Siân. I think I may untie your wrist." He stopped to do so and smiled at her. "I should be angry with you for doing anything as foolhardy as rushing after your brother-in-law when it must have been obvious to you that you were not going to persuade Parry to let him go. But as usual I honor you instead." He chafed the wrist he had just freed and briefly lifted it to set his mouth against the inside of it.

But there was no safety in the countryside for anyone who had no good reason for being there. Soldiers and constables were out in force, all of them armed, hunting down fugitives. Some poor devils were being marched back into town, Alex saw, almost unconsciously putting on his aristocratic air and drawing Siân close against his side.

"Anyone with any sense," he said, "would have taken to his heels early this morning and been miles along on his way home by now."

"Perhaps some lingered to look for friends or brothers," she said.

"Like someone I know." He took her hand. "Siân, you are so cold that there is not a shred of warmth in you. And we are both still wet though the rain has stopped at last. We are going to stop at the first inn we come to and have a bath and a meal and a good sleep. I don't suppose there are many men who have dared to stop at any today. I would not expect any difficulty in finding an empty room."

He wanted to make love to her, he thought. He wanted to warm her with his own body and with a shared passion. He wanted to take away the drawn, unhappy look from her face even if only for a brief hour. They were both wet and cold and exhausted. But more than anything else in the world at this precise moment he wanted to make love to her.

"I can't," she said. "I must find Iestyn."

"From what I have seen of that young man," he said, "he has enough courage and enough stubbornness to make me wonder that he does not share blood with you. And he is no child. He will look after himself."

"I sometimes forget," she said, "that he is no longer twelve years old as he was when I married Gwyn."

"We will be stopping at the next inn," he said, "even if I have to use force. I want you in dry clothes before we go much farther."

"It sounds like heaven," she admitted. "But it seems so unfair when there must be so many hundreds of men on the run and just as wet and cold and miserable as we are."

"Again," he said, trying not to feel guilty, "it is the way of the world, Siân."

It seemed that they must have walked halfway back to Cwmbran before they came across an inn, and even then it was so small and squat that it looked little different from a farmhouse. In reality, Alex realized, they had probably walked only a mile or two. Exhaustion was beginning to take its toll.

There was a real farmhouse not far from the inn, and a large stone barn beside it. Alex, steering Siân toward the inn, felt his heart sink as two redcoats and a few other armed men in civilian clothes appeared at the door of the barn prodding a group of men out ahead of them. All of the men had their hands raised above their heads, except one who had only one arm raised. Poor devils, Alex thought, and tried to rush Siân inside before she saw.

But he jerked to a halt suddenly. "The devil!" he muttered.

"What?" Siân said, and she turned her head to look across the meadow to the barn. She said nothing for a few moments, but he felt her tense though she was not touching him. "Oh, dear God in heaven. Oh, dear God."

They were all men from Cwmbran. They included all the relatives she had searched for all day in Newport.

Alex clenched his teeth. "This is going to be tricky," he said. "Stay here, Siân. Go inside and find a fire to warm yourself by."

He did not look to see if she obeyed him. He strode off in the direction of the barn, putting on arrogance and hauteur and coldness as he went. He swore fluently as soon as he was within earshot of the men. He saw recognition in the eyes of his men, though all of them wore admirably passive expressions.

"So here you are, you lily-livered, good-for-nothing sons of bitches!" Alex said, cold fury tightening his jaw and his lips and flashing from his eyes. "Hiding where it is safe and warm and dry. Thank you, Sergeant." He nodded curtly at the senior of the two redcoats. "Had you not flushed them out they might have cowered here for a week until all danger had passed. It seems I did not put enough fear or enough backbone into them during their training." He let his eyes sweep the line of his men with contempt and loathing. Iestyn Jones had a broken arm, he noticed. It was resting awkwardly against his stomach. It must be unbearably painful without the other arm to support it.

The sergeant coughed. "Would you identify yourself, please, sir?" he asked.

Alex regarded him coldly and raised his eyebrows haughtily. "Craille," he said. "The Marquess of Craille. Owner at Cwmbran. And losing money every hour that my workers are away on this scandalous escapade. I brought a supposedly trained group of constables to help me round them up and herd them home again. But it seems they heard a few shots in Newport, saw the rioters flee in panic, and decided to make themselves scarce."

He clasped his hands behind his back and stepped in front of the first prisoner in line.

"Jones," he barked out at Huw Jones, "where is your gun?"

With some relief Alex saw dawning comprehension in the man's eyes. "I don't know — sir," he said.

"And yours, Rhys?" Alex moved to the next man in the line.

"I lost it, sir," Emrys Rhys said. There was full comprehension in his eyes.

"And yours?" he asked the next man, whose name he did not know.

"The soldiers took it, sir."

"We confiscated three guns, my lord," the sergeant said. "We had no idea these men were constables. We took them for fugitives. Your pardon, my lord."

"Three guns," Alex said, contempt in his voice. "Three guns for the seven of you. Perhaps I should let you take them away to jail after all, Sergeant. It appears they are useless to me."

The sergeant coughed. "I would not want to interfere between you and your employees, my lord," he said, clearly uncomfortable. "Provided you can vouch for them all, my men and I will be taking our leave."

"It is as well," Alex said, smiling arctically. "By the time I have disciplined them at home, they will doubtless wish I had not shown up when I did."

The sergeant coughed again. "And the woman, my lord?" he asked.

Alex turned, unsurprised, to find Siân standing close behind him. Damned woman. He kept the smile. "She is my —" he said, pausing suggestively. "She is mine."

The sergeant coughed once more. "Quite, my lord," he said. "Begging your pardon for the interference, my lord," And he and his men marched briskly back to the road.

"You may lower your arms," Alex said conversationally. "As you see, I have no gun. Only the three that the soldiers so obligingly left on the grass at my feet."

"Iestyn!" Siân flew toward him. "What has happened? Oh, your poor arm. It is broken?"

The boy smiled weakly at her, but she covered her face with her hands before he could say anything. "Oh, you are all safe," she said. "We have been searching for you all day. I imagined all the worst fates."

There was a chorus of voices. "We have been searching for you, *fach*," Hywel Rhys said over them all. "Why do you think we are still this close to Newport at the end of the day? We have been worried sick about you."

"Iestyn's arm was broken with a pike when he tried to swim against the tide of fleeing men, looking for you," Huw said. "But he was too stubborn and stupid to go on home and let the rest of us look. He is as pale as a ghost but just as stubbornly refuses to faint."

Alex watched them all in silence. As usual when he was around, they were speaking English out of deference to him, though he was quite convinced they had forgotten his presence. Until Emrys Rhys looked at him and cleared his throat. They all fell into an uneasy and self-conscious silence.

"I don't know why you did it, sir," Emrys said gruffly. "But thank you."

Alex nodded as the others followed suit. "There will be a price to pay," he said quietly.

They all eyed him warily, including Siân.

"I will be calling another meeting after we return home," Alex said. "I will expect you all to be there with your wives and your parents and your sisters and adult children and anyone else over whom you have any influence. Life at Cwmbran is going to become more livable and we are all going to have a hand in making it so."

"I will be there, sir," Iestyn said faintly. "And I will bring my mam and dada."

"And I will do likewise, sir," Emrys said.

There was a general mumbling from the

other men, which Alex took to be assent.

"We have to have that arm attended to, boy," Alex said to Iestyn. "At the inn, where all of you can dry off and have a good meal and a beer or two inside you — if chapel men drink beer, that is."

There was a gust of laughter, which sounded strange to all their ears.

"We daren't go there," Hywel Rhys said, nodding rather wistfully in the direction of the inn.

"My special constables can go anywhere I wish them to go," Alex said. "And that arm needs to be set."

Siân hovered close to Iestyn as they all walked toward the inn and insisted on staying with him while, in the absence of a doctor, Alex himself set the arm as best he could and bound it into makeshift splints. She smoothed the boy's hair back from his face and murmured endearments to him in Welsh as if he were still a child instead of a remarkably brave young man. The inexpert setting of the arm must hurt like a thousand devils, Alex thought, but the boy did not flinch even once and even looked at Siân with a half smile as she talked.

Alex had reserved a room upstairs. He sent Siân up to get out of her wet clothes and have a hot bath while the men steamed before the fire downstairs and waited to be served with the meal Alex had ordered.

But Siân turned when she had one foot on the bottom stair. "Owen is dead," she said quietly, though the hush that followed her words was assurance enough that everyone had heard. "He was shot in the back outside the Westgate Inn while trying to hurry me to safety. He died in my arms."

She turned back and continued on her way up before anyone seemed able to think of anything to say.

After they had eaten and drunk and even dozed a little by the fire and dried off, the men insisted on continuing on their way home. They seemed to feel guilty about being so comfortable.

"The women will worry," Hywel Rhys said. "Especially when some of the other men start arriving back and we are still missing. It would be a sin and a self-indulgence to worry our women unnecessarily. We walked through last night. We will walk through tonight as well. At least tonight it is not raining."

"Siân is staying here," Alex said firmly. "She is exhausted and needs a good night's rest."

The triumvirate of Hywel and Emrys Rhys and Huw Jones all looked hard at him, but none of them said anything. Hywel nodded and got to his feet.

"Bring her safely home tomorrow," was all he said.

Even Iestyn Jones insisted on going. "The walk and the fresh air will do me good after all that food," he said, laughing.

Fortunately Alex thought of something before they left. He acquired paper, pen, and ink from the landlord and wrote a note naming each of the men and vouching for the fact that they were all special constables in the employ of the Marquess of Craille from Cwmbran.

He watched them on their way from the doorway of the inn. It was dark already. Such was the nature of November evenings. Then he climbed the stairs to the room he had reserved, tapped on the door, and opened it.

She was sitting beside the fire, wrapped in a blanket. Her hair, spread over her shoulders, was almost dry. The bath was half hidden behind a screen. The tray on which her meal had been brought to her was standing empty beside her.

She turned her head and smiled at him as he stepped inside the room and closed the door quietly behind him.

27

It was good-bye, she thought. She had hoped — part of her had hoped — to avoid him for the next two months, until she could take up her new teaching post. She had hoped to slip away without fuss to start a new life. She was looking forward to her new life.

But after all there was to be a good-bye. A quite decisive one. And after all she could not be sorry. How could she be sorry? He had come for her. Despite the fact that she had been foolish to go herself, and despite the discomfort of the rain and the danger, he had come for her.

He had saved her from captivity, from some unknown and dreadful fate. And he had done the like for her relatives, though he had had no reason to do so when they had defied him and ignored his warnings by coming — with the exception of Iestyn. He had set Iestyn's broken arm when everyone else had been too squeamish to touch it, and he had ordered them all a meal. And he intended to go back to Cwmbran and organize another meeting.

It was a great, great gift he had given her.

Yes, it was fitting there be this good-bye. After it, she was going to ask her father if her leaving could be hastened forward. Perhaps she could go to her new school to observe for a month before she started drawing a salary. She would want to leave soon after this good-bye.

She had bathed and eaten and was cozily warm before the fire. The landlady had taken her clothes away, promising to have them all washed, dried, and ironed by the morning.

Perhaps he would not stay, Siân thought fleetingly. Or if he did, perhaps he would stay in a different room, especially if her relatives and friends stayed too. But it was only a fleeting thought. She knew with a near certainty that he would come and that they would have a whole night in which to say good-bye.

A whole night. In a clean and quiet room and in a wide bed that looked cozy, though she had not lain on it.

There was no sense of wrongness about the occasion. No sense that it would be sordid or that she would be sinning. She loved him. She was leaving him because of the total impossibility of any sort of relationship in which they could meet each other as equals. But there was a good-bye to be said, and they had been presented with this unexpected gift of a night together.

She had no doubt that the problem of her grandfather and Emrys and Huw being at the inn would be solved.

And so she turned her head and smiled at Alex when he tapped on the door and came inside. It had begun, their precious night together, and she would not look beyond it. She would live it intensely so that she would look back on the memory of it for the rest of her life.

"They foolishly decided to walk through the night again," he said. "Even Iestyn."

"Yes, they would," she said. "They would not want to worry Gran and Mam and Mari for longer than necessary. Alexander, thank you." She reached out one bare arm toward him.

He came forward to take her hand and raise it to his lips. "You look cozy and sleepy," he said.

She smiled.

"What are you wearing?" he asked.

"A blanket," she said.

"The mayor and various soldiers we have spoken to in the course of the day would be delighted to witness this scene," he said. "Except that you seem far too aquiescent, Siân."

"I am acquiescent," she said.

She heard him draw breath slowly. "I don't suppose that bathwater is still warm," he said.

"I doubt it." She hated the thought of a long delay while he ordered more heated and carried up.

"I'll use it anyway," he said, pulling off his coat and tossing it aside. "Just to feel clean will be worth a little chilliness."

She climbed into the bed while he was behind the screen bathing. She left the blanket on the chair beside the fire. There was something seductively domestic about the scene, she thought as she drew the bedclothes up about her. She lay in bed waiting for her man and listening to the sounds of water being splashed over his back and head. There was no awkwardness between them, no embarrassment, no question of what would happen when he had dried himself off. He would come to bed.

She ached at the impossibility of it all, at the knowledge that it was for this night only. But she suppressed the thought quite ruthlessly. There was this night.

She had never before slept naked. There was something arousing about feeling sheets against her bare legs and breasts. She was tired, she thought, remembering that there had been no sleep at all the night before and constant exertion. She felt as if she could sleep for a week. But love first. Oh, yes, love first, and then sleep.

He was naked when he came out from behind the screen. He did not even have a towel about his waist. "I thought you might be asleep," he said.

She shook her head. "Not yet."

He leaned over her, one hand on either side of her head. "What were you waiting for?" he asked. He was smiling and looking wonderfully handsome, his blond hair damp from the toweling he had given it, his eyes very blue.

"For you," she said.

"To sing you lullabies?" He grinned.

"You forget that you are wearing nothing," she said. "I have been able to see that you know what I have been waiting for and that you want the same thing."

"For shame." He rubbed his nose lightly across hers. "You peeked. Have you no modesty?"

Her heart turned over rather painfully at

this new teasing, affectionate Alexander. As if they belonged together. As if they were familiar and comfortable with each other. Ah, would it be a memory that she would ever be able to look back upon without pain?

"None whatsoever," she said. "Guess what I am wearing."

He frowned in thought. "A blanket?" he asked.

"If you look over your shoulder," she said, "you will see that I left it on the chair."

"You are never naked, Siân," he said, his eyes laughing while he affected shock.

"I am afraid so," she said.

"Well," he said, "this could be dangerous. I have no sword, drawn or otherwise, to set between us on the bed."

"Oh, dear," she said.

"There is only one solution, as I see it," he said, "short of my sleeping on the floor, which I absolutely refuse to do."

"What?" she asked.

"There is going to have to be sexual intercourse between us," he said.

Her cheeks flamed foolishly at having it spoken so openly between them. "I could sleep on the floor," she said, reaching up with both arms and linking them about his neck, "but I know you are too much the gentleman to allow it. Sexual intercourse it will have to be, then, I suppose."

They smiled at each other for a while longer, their eyes wandering hungrily over each other's face before he lowered his own and touched her lips with his tongue, tracing first the upper one and then the lower, creating raw need deep in her breasts and her womb. But he did not kiss her.

"Siân," he said, raising his head a few inches to look into her eyes. "Siân, my love. It will be more than sexual intercourse. You know that."

"Yes," she said. Yes, she knew it though she was not sure it was something that should be admitted aloud between them. But why not? Why not one glorious night with no barriers at all between them? One night — and one night only — to make dreams come true. "Yes, it will be far more than that, Alexander. *Cariad.*"

"It will be nothing," he said, grinning, "if we don't do something about all these blankets between us."

"If we had thought," she said as he stood up and pulled back the bedclothes, first to look at her appreciatively, and then to climb in beside her, "we might have used them instead of a drawn sword."

"Our trouble," he said, sliding one arm beneath her neck and turning her over onto her side so that her body came against his along its full length, "is that we do not think."

Siân was having trouble with her breathing. "Praise be for thoughtlessness," she said.

"A fervent amen to that." But his voice had lost its light, teasing tone. "Siân." It was warm and husky against her ear. "You are more beautiful than I can put into words. I will worship you with my hands and my mouth and my body, but I will still not be able to show you how beautiful you are."

She whimpered as he began to suit action to words. He was all warm, hard, wonderful masculinity. Adam to her Eve. Antony to her Cleopatra. Romeo to her Juliet. Alexander. She wanted to draw him into herself, to lose herself in him. Forever and ever and ever.

"In all eternity I could not love you enough to adequately worship your beauty," he whispered into her mouth as his hand, down in the secret part of herself, found a most secret part and brought her to the precipice of need. "Come to me, Siân. Give it all to me. Give me your trust."

She came, giving him all that she most valued in her life — her independence, her personhood, herself, her soul. She shuddered against him, utterly helpless, utterly vulnerable, utterly pleasured.

But he continued to worship her, to give everything, to demand everything in return. Several times he used his skill to make her shatter about him and against him and held her while she savored the pleasure and the wonder of it. But always his hands and his lips and his tongue went back to work until pleasure seemed not a single moment or experience, but a garden of endless delight.

And finally she knew that it was a reciprocal thing, that there must be more pleasure for a man — for her man — than merely the releasing of his seed. She caressed him with her hands and her lips and tongue and teeth. She touched that part of him that she would have thought herself incapable of touching, holding it in her two hands, closing them about it, feeling its hardness and length, touching its tip with her thumb and pulsing lightly there until it grew slightly sticky and he groaned.

She wanted it inside her. All the way deep inside, pumping into her so that pleasure could be finally a shared thing, united in the deepest core of her femininity. She wanted his seed. She wanted to feel it spring. She wanted it to take root. She wanted to be fruitful for him. And for herself. For them.

"Please, please," she was moaning against his mouth.

Although there had been release over and over again and pleasures untold, she knew that she was still this side of the ultimate pleasure. The ultimate pleasure would not be for her alone. Or for him alone. The ultimate pleasure would be their final union. One body. One heart. One soul.

His body was on hers, pressing it downward into the mattress. His legs pushed hers wide until she twined them about his and tilted herself for penetration. But he had far more control than she. He lifted his head and smiled down at her.

"I think," he said, "it is time for that sexual intercourse we talked about, Siân."

She had not thought it possible to be any more aroused than she already was, but his words proved her wrong. There was a gush of aching longing at the entrance to her body where he was pressing against her. He continued to smile at her as he came in, hard and long and deep, sliding into the slick heat of her need.

"Most beautiful of all," he said. "Hot, Siân, and wet. Ah, yes, and tight. Those are wonderful muscles. Is it all mine, my love?

Just mine?"

"Just yours," she said. "Only and ever yours, Alexander. And this — is it all mine?"

"Yours," he said, "and yours only, Siân, from the moment I first set eyes on you. It is for your pleasure and for yours alone. Like this? Does this give pleasure?" He withdrew slowly to her entrance and thrust swiftly and firmly back inside.

She exhaled through her mouth as her inner muscles clenched about him again and drew him deeper. "Yes," she said. "But not mine alone, Alexander. It must be together. Please, it must be together."

"Together, then," he said, and he watched her face as he began a slow rhythm, adjusting it to the rhythm of her own body until they moved together. His eyes grew heavy with passion. His face glistened with perspiration.

"Ah," Siân said from deep in her throat, watching his eyes. It was sweet, exquisite agony, this deep spearing of his body into hers.

"Not much longer," he said. "Are you ready to come with me, my love?"

"Yes." Her voice was almost a sob. "Please. Oh, please."

His weight was on her again, one arm tight about her shoulders, the other about her hips as she clung to him with arms and legs and closed her eyes so that all her focus could be on the point deep inside her where they worked with a frenzied expenditure of energy to unite.

And suddenly there it was, that indescribable moment of surprise as peace was recognized for what it was, and the long, mindless, boneless free fall into its heart began. Together.

For long moments they were twined tautly together before they both — together — gradually relaxed and became again two people who had loved. Lover and beloved. No longer one person, though he was still deeply embedded in her body.

Siân held him, though his weight was heavy on her, knowing that he slept. She had one frightening glimpse ahead to the great cold wall of impossibility, but she closed her eyes and breathed in deeply, drawing in the scent of soap and sweat from his shoulder — into her nostrils and into her mind. It was still only evening. There was still the night.

Their good-byes were not all said yet. There was time.

She was deeply asleep. Her head was on his shoulder, her face turned in against his neck so that he could feel her breath warm against it. He could feel her breasts against his chest, her arm about his waist, her abdomen and her thighs against his. When he had woken earlier, feeling guilty that he had allowed himself to use her soft body as a mattress, and had disengaged himself from her and moved off her, they had turned instinctively in to each other, touching at every part, as if only so could they sleep with the assurance that what had happened between them had been real.

They had become one. For one incredible moment — or one incredible eternity — he had been unaware of his own identity and had forgotten hers. For one moment he had been them and she had been them and they had been one. Not the plural them, but some singular form that was neither he nor she nor it. They had been one.

And so they had clung to each other wordlessly as they had both sunk into a sleep of exhaustion.

He had felt as if he could sleep the clock around without stirring even once. But he had come to the surface of sleep again. How could he not when he was holding such an armful? He smiled and rubbed his cheek against the top of her head.

He felt utterly happy. He tested the

thought in his mind. Happiness was elusive and transitory, he knew from past experience. But it was definitely true — he felt it now. He held it now in his arms. He would do so forever. He tightened his hold on her so that she muttered sleepily against his neck. He was not naive enough to imagine that he could feel with her this level of intense happiness for the rest of a lifetime, but he did know something equally satisfying or even more so.

She was his happiness. All the happiness he would know in his life — whatever portion was allotted him — would center about her. Siân.

He had been so close to letting her go. Even now if he allowed his mind to start thinking with cold rationality he was not sure that there was a truly workable way of keeping her. But he would not allow such thoughts. Not now. Not yet.

He set a hand beneath her chin, lifted her face, and kissed her mouth with soft, feathering kisses.

"Mm," she said sleepily, and her lips pouted softly against his own.

He was being very unfair. She must be exhausted after all she had been through in the last couple of days. And after the vigorous lovemaking they had shared before falling asleep.

He turned her onto her back, moving with her, spread her legs with his own, and pushed inside her. She was warm and wet and relaxed. He held still in her, savoring the feel of woman about his masculinity. The feel of Siân.

"Mm," she said again, and he could feel her slide her feet up the bed so that he could nestle more comfortably inside her.

He could tell that she was still not fully awake. He found the knowledge arousing. He enjoyed her participation. He could equally enjoy her passivity, provided it was the passivity of acquiescence. He would not question that now with Siân.

"Relax," he murmured into her ear. "Lie still and let me love you."

He loved her over many minutes with slow, firm strokes, only very gradually increasing in pace. He knew that a woman did not become easily aroused from intercourse alone, unlike men, for whom it was everything. And so he gave her time, and himself too. Time to enjoy the heat and softness of the inside of her body about his erect manhood, time to enjoy the treacherous male delight in possession and mastery, his woman's body spread and mounted beneath his own. But a possession and a mastery to be used for her delight.

He felt her muscles gradually clench involuntarily as he continued to pump rhythmically into her, and her breathing quicken and her inner heat intensify. He took her hands in his, lifted them above her head, crossing them at the wrists, and laced his fingers with hers. She gripped his hands tightly as he changed rhythm, coaxing her to come with him again to climax. She sighed and relaxed beneath him as his seed sprang.

"Mm," she said when he was at her side again, his arm beneath her head. "I just had a wonderful dream."

"Did you?" He kissed her. "Tell me about it."

"You made love to me," she said.

"Say no more." He rubbed his nose against hers. "I had the same dream. I'm sorry I woke you up, Siân. Blame it on this shocking habit you have of sleeping naked."

"And the fact that you did not bring a sword with you," she said. "Alexander? You meant what you said to Grandad and the others? You are going to go ahead with the improvements at Cwmbran? You are not going to punish them by going back to England?"

"I suppose I might have at that," he said.

"But how could I punish myself?"

"You love Wales, don't you?" she said, some wonder in her voice.

"I don't know much of Wales," he said. "I love Cwmbran. And its people. And one of its citizens in particular."

She set the tips of her fingers over his lips. "Hush," she said. "If you mean me, I am not going to be one of its citizens for much longer. I am going to have my father send me away before Christmas. As soon as possible. I am eager to start my new life. No." Her fingers pressed harder as he started to speak. "Not tonight, Alexander. Let us give each other tonight — just as if tomorrow does not exist."

He was going to say anyway what he had been about to say. But he stopped himself. There were all sorts of things to consider — her lifelong happiness, his obligations to his line and his title, his relatives, Verity. It was not something to be blurted out during a night of passion. He had thought of it before and rejected it. Perhaps he would do so again once the night of passion was over.

He kissed her lingeringly.

"Iestyn," he said. "He is not happy as a miner, Siân?"

"You would never wring a word of complaint from him," she said, "or find him working one whit less hard than any other man. But when he was a younger boy, before reality intruded and set up a wall behind which he has barricaded himself, he used to tell me his dreams. Books and school and preaching and a chapel of his own and people to minister to."

"Was it just a boy's dream, do you think?" he asked. "One not based at all on reality? Could it have been reality if he had had the chance?"

"I used to think perhaps not," she said. "I used to think that perhaps he was too sweet and gentle to control a congregation and to guide the moral and spiritual life of a community. But recently I have been forced to admit that there is a streak of iron in Iestyn. Nothing to spoil the sweetness and gentleness, but enough to make me realize that there is no weakness in him. None at all. In his own way I think he is stronger than someone like — well, Owen."

"He smiled and listened to your nonsense while I was putting him through the agonies of hell setting his arm," he said. "I think he was trying to make you feel better, Siân."

"Yes," she said. "I noticed. *Was* it nonsense? I did not know what I was saying."

"Utter nonsense," he said. "The sort of thing I used to drool at Verity before her

636

first birthday. I could tell from the tone of your voice, though you spoke Welsh. If I take him from the mine and make him my secretary for a while so that both he and I can explore some future options for him at our leisure, would I incite a riot in Cwmbran? I never know with your people, Siân. They are quite unpredictable."

Even in the darkness he could see the wideness of her eyes as she jerked her head back and looked up at him. "You would do that?" she said. "For Iestyn? Oh, Alexander."

"That does not answer my question," he said.

"It does not matter how anyone else reacts," she said. "It does not matter how I am reacting. Ask him, Alexander. Oh, please, ask him. Oh, I love you."

He smiled slowly. "Do you, Siân?"

She stared at him for a long time and then nodded.

"And I love you," he said. "You must be quite, quite exhausted."

She lay quietly looking at him.

"We must sleep," he said.

"Yes."

"Of course," he said, "it does seem rather a waste to make no use of a time when we are both awake, doesn't it?"

"I hate waste," she said.

"How shall we use the time?" He grinned at her.

"Kiss me," she said. "Perhaps one of us will have thought of something by the time you have finished."

He kissed her.

He had never joked with a woman before. Not, anyway, as a prelude to sex. It added a quite delightful dimension to the experience, he was finding. They were both mad. They were both desperate for sleep.

"We are mad," he said, lifting his head.

"What do mad people do not to waste time in the middle of the night when they should be sleeping?" she asked.

"A tough one," he said. "I am mad and cannot be expected to know the answer. Perhaps this, though." He slid one arm beneath her and lifted her over to lie on top of him. "Shall I show you what I mean?"

"Yes, please," she said.

Another half hour passed before they settled for sleep once more, having agreed that perhaps that was what mad people did and if so, then sane people had a great deal to learn from them.

28

Angharad was to receive a pension as the widow of a man who had died in the mine. It was as well, she thought, alone in her father's house. She was left with only one house to clean and she was afraid to go to the Reverend Llewellyn's house. She was afraid he would know. If he did, he would give her a dreadful lecture. Perhaps worse. Perhaps he would have her publicly driven from chapel.

It did not seem to matter. Nothing much seemed to matter anymore.

Owen Parry was dead.

Emrys Rhys had returned safely.

It did not matter. It did not concern her.

She had gone to Josiah Barnes's house on Monday morning, her regular day there. He had been at home, the works being closed down with all the men gone.

And he knew. The Marquess of Craille had gone to Hywel Rhys's house when Gwilym Jenkins was there, and Gwilym had gone back to Mr. Barnes's and he had put two and two together.

He knew.

At first Angharad had felt only the shame and humiliation of being treated like a child when she was twenty-eight years old. Although even when she was a child her father had never put her over his knee. Mr. Barnes did, and lifted her skirt so that only a thin shift was between her flesh and his hand.

But humiliation had given place to pain and finally to an agony that enclosed her world and had her sobbing hysterically. She would have sworn afterward that he beat her for all of five minutes. And he had a very hard hand.

Somehow, because she was not ashamed of what she had done but because she knew that in other ways she had deserved the beating and more, she managed to control her sobs and lift her chin when he set her back on her feet. She managed to look him in the eye.

It was a mistake.

He slapped both sides of her face several times, and when that did not seem to satisfy him, he used his fists.

"Go on," he said finally, when Angharad was not even quite sure she was on her feet, "get out of here before I kill you. You are not worth swinging for. Welsh scum!"

Angharad went home and stayed there.

Siân wrote a note to her father the morning after her return from Newport — and after an uninterrupted twelve hours of sleep. But he arrived in person on her grandfather's doorstep almost before the ink had dried on the letter. He caught her up in a bear hug as soon as she answered the door, despite the fact that they were in full view of her grandmother.

He took off his hat and inclined his head to Gwynneth, but she gave him only a curt "Good morning" before passing him and leaving the house. She was going to help a neighbor who had just given birth.

Siân smiled apologetically at her father. She wrapped her arms about his neck and rested her cheek against his shoulder as he hugged her again. The novelty of having a father could still make her turn weak inside even if Gran was of the firm opinion that he had done enough wrong in the past that he did not deserve to be forgiven now. She relaxed against him as if he could remove all the burdens of the world from her shoulders.

"You are back and safe," he said when he

finally loosened his hold on her. He gave her a smacking kiss on the lips. "Craille sent word last night as he did when you first disappeared. I thought I would go out of my mind, Siân. As if there was not enough weighing on it with all my men closing down the works and taking themselves off to Newport. Ten of them have not returned. I know for certain that six of those have been arrested. There is no word on the other four. And then you going off in pursuit — it was the last straw."

"I am sorry," she said stiffly, pulling away from him. "You need not have worried about me. I am not your responsibility."

He clucked his tongue. "That is my cue to say that is just fine with me," he said. "No, we are not going to fall into that trap again. I was out of my mind because I love you, my little one."

She came closer again and patted the lapels of his heavy winter coat with both hands. "I know, Dada," she said. She smiled at him. "It is a good thing we are father and daughter and not husband and wife. We would be forever at each other's throats."

"You took no harm?" he asked. "Craille brought you home?"

"I am all right." She patted his lapels again and turned to the fire to make a pot of tea.

"Take your coat off and stay a while. Dada, can I go before Christmas? Can you arrange it? I want to go soon. Or sooner."

He took off his coat and tossed it over the back of a chair before coming to warm his hands at the fire and sit down. "He will offer only what I offered your mother?" he asked.

She set down the heavy kettle and arranged the cozy over the teapot. "He said nothing yesterday," he said. "He offered nothing. But you know I could not accept. I believe Mam was happy. I could not be. Can you arrange something?"

"I'll write," he said. "They will probably be quite delighted that you are eager enough to want to go early — especially if I pay your salary until the end of the year. Close your mouth again, Siân. You must not argue. I am your father."

"Yes," she said. "Thank you. How soon do you think it will be before they reply?"

"Come to the cottage while we wait, Siân," he said. "Let me take you there today. Pack your things and come with me now. You can be comfortable there until I have a reply. And I will be able to call on you every day. We have much to catch up on, my little one, and soon you will be gone."

It was tempting. Siân poured the tea in

silence. To be back in the familiar setting of her childhood. To take one step forward into her future. To take that decisive step away from him. Why had Alexander not offered yesterday even what she could not possibly accept? They had walked in near silence for hours, hand in hand. And then he had collected his horse and they had ridden the rest of the way home — it was the first time she had been on horseback. They had exchanged hardly a word. Not that words had seemed necessary. Sometimes words did not. And then he had delivered her to Grandad's and left her there amid the flurry of welcomes without a private word or look.

She had said no before, of course. He knew the impossibility as well as she. He knew as well as she that their night together had been good-bye. But, oh, she had wanted to fight the impossibility. She had wanted him to fight it. She had expected him to ask again. She had been steeling herself to say no again and had not been at all sure that she would be able to.

But he had accepted good-bye for what it was.

As she must.

He had been stronger than she.

She should pack her things as soon as their tea was drunk. She should go without giving herself a chance for second thoughts.

"Siân?" her father said.

"Give me a week," she said. "There are people I must say good-bye to, loose ends I must tie up. If you have not heard within a week, will you come anyway, Dada, and take me to the cottage?"

He nodded and picked up his cup. "You are doing the right thing," he said, "although I know your heart is sore. You are a strong woman, Siân, and will make a new life for yourself. You would not be happy with the life he could offer. He could probably give you little ones and you would certainly never want for anything, but it would hurt you when both you and your children were rejected by the chapel and your people. And it would hurt you when he marries again and has children on his wife. Your mother was deeply hurt when she knew Tess was on the way."

"Yes," Siân said.

"Siân" — he set his cup down in its saucer on the table — "forgive me. I was married already when I met Marged the year the *eisteddfod* was in Penybont. She was the most beautiful thing I had ever seen and so I took her, wronging both her and my wife. And you. And yet, to be honest with you, I am not sure I would have married her even

645

if I had been free. It is not done, you know, and I was never a man with the courage to break new ground. But I always loved her — and you."

"Morality is not a simple thing," she said, "though it should be. It sounds simple enough when one listens to sermons and reads good books. But it is not. Love and morality are not always in agreement, and sometimes love is stronger. Perhaps it should not be, but it is. How can I not forgive you? I have loved Alexander. And besides I would not be here if you had not given in to your love for Mam, would I?" She smiled.

He left soon after, having hugged her tightly again and assured her once more that she was doing the right thing. He would be back next week, he told her, unless he had a favorable reply to his letter before then.

She was not a strong person, Siân thought, sitting down beside the fire again and gazing into its dancing flames. If she were strong, she would have taken the opportunity of the cottage and gone with her father now, today. It was what she had longed for since waking up from her lengthy sleep and discovering that there was only intense pain to wake up to. It was why she had written to him. She had been desperate to get away, to put the memories behind her and the terrible danger of seeing Alexander again and bringing on more pain.

But when it had come to the point, she had not had the courage to go. She had made an excuse to stay for one more week.

It was absurd to feel that one could not go on living when there was no physical illness. She knew it was absurd. Her head told her so. She knew that the pain would recede and that life would reassert itself. She knew that at the age of twenty-five she might still hope that life had a great deal of richness and happiness in store. But it was the heart that was ruling today.

And her heart was breaking. Her heart felt as if it could not go on beating.

Although a day and a night and part of another day had passed since their goodbye, she still felt that distinctive soreness that was not really soreness inside where he had loved her four separate times. And her breasts were still tender to the touch. She set a hand flat over her abdomen. And she still yearned to discover that she had been fruitful for him. She wanted his child to be in her womb.

Oh, yes, it was definitely the heart that was ruling today.

And yet not a word to suggest that perhaps

good-bye had not been quite good-bye after all. Just the almost silent journey home — two people yearning to be one as they had been one through the night, both sleeping and waking, but now very decisively two. Two separate entities. Two different worlds.

And then the terrible anticlimax of his slipping away while Gran was sobbing over her.

Emptiness was a terrifying thing, Siân thought. It sounded harmless — emptiness, nothingness. But emptiness was not a nothingness. It was a something. It was a heavy, all-encompassing, smothering load of despair.

She felt quite, quite empty.

There was much to do. There were his men to get back to work and a meeting to arrange — at the chapel again. There were arrangements to be made to bring home the body of Owen Parry. There was Iestyn Jones to talk to — the boy stood in his study, looking him steadily in the eye, and accepted the job Alex offered, promising to give it every effort of which he was capable though he had no experience of such work. The fact that his right arm was in a sling would not hinder him from beginning immediately, he explained — he was left-handed.

If the boy showed dedication and aptitude and character — all of which Alex fully expected — then next autumn Alex would send him to university or whatever type of college trained nonconformist ministers. The Reverend Llewellyn would be able to supply the necessary information.

And there were other, less pleasant matters to handle. It was not necessary to keep the mind dead, Alex found, just to keep it crowded with other matters. It would be best if he continued to do so for another two months. Then she would be gone to her new teaching post in Carmarthenshire. It would be best to let her go without another word. It would be unfair to offer what she might in a moment of weakness accept and make her unhappy for the rest of her life. She would not be happy having a function only in his bed. Neither would he.

Siân was a woman for his life, not just for his bed.

And yet he shied away from the implications of the thought. It would not be right either for her or for himself. He could not make it right just by wishing it were. But by God, he wished it. If he did not keep his mind and his days occupied with other thoughts and actions, he would go mad with the wishing.

And he might end up letting his heart rule his head. No good could come of that. Could it? But he would not let doubts intrude.

There were those less pleasant matters. He summoned Gwilym Jenkins to the castle. He suspected that just the fact of having to come there would put the fear of God into the man. He had Jenkins shown into his study and deliberately kept him waiting there a full ten minutes.

But he did not dismiss the man from his job or impose any punishment other than the visit itself and a severe tongue-lashing. Jenkins was the one who had put about the rumors that had resulted in Siân's whipping, and he was the one who had sent her off in pursuit of the marchers to Newport and into a danger that might well have proved a great deal worse for her than had been the case.

But Alex did not dismiss him. The man had himself been whipped and had had all his furniture destroyed before his very eyes. And he had a wife and five children to support.

Alex sent him back to work with only one penance to perform. Gwilym Jenkins was to attend the meeting in the chapel, and he was to bring his wife with him if any of the children were old enough to look after the others.

And then there was Josiah Barnes to be dealt with. The man had worked hard for twelve years and made the Cwmbran mine and works efficient and profitable. If he had run the industry harshly, then so had every other owner in the surrounding valleys. And yet the man had done some dastardly things. He had allowed chagrin over the fact that Siân had refused to marry him seven years ago to fester in him and turn into vicious spite. And that spite had hurt her reputation and caused her anguish and terror and severe physical harm. In the Newport march it might have cost her her liberty or even her life — Alex frequently found himself waking up from sleep in a cold sweat, remembering how close she had been to Parry when the latter had been killed. The bullet might just as easily have taken her life.

Barnes just might have been a murderer.

And so Barnes was dismissed from his job. Alex forced himself to treat the matter in a dispassionate, professional manner, though his hands itched to deal out punishment as they had dealt it out to Owen Parry after the whipping. Barnes was summoned to the office, given a chance to defend himself, and

651

dismissed when he could not do so. He was dismissed without a reference. Alex had agonized over that point, imagining what sort of a future he was dooming his former agent to. But he could not in all conscience vouch for the man's character and integrity to another prospective employer.

He gave Josiah Barnes three days to leave his cottage and Cwmbran.

"If I see you here after that time, I will physically remove you myself," he said coldly, face-to-face with a furious, defiant Barnes. "If I ever hear of your being within a one-mile radius of Mrs. Jones, I will kill you. I will not ask if you understand. You are dismissed."

"You will be bankrupt before spring," Josiah Barnes said. "All your workers will be starving and rioting. I will greet the news with all delight."

Alex looked steadily and coldly at him until he turned and stalked from the room.

And there was another call to be made. Alex did not want to summon Angharad Lewis to the castle. He did not want to frighten her. He found out where her father lived and paid a call on her there.

She answered the door herself, half hiding in the shadow behind it. Alex looked, appalled, at bruised cheeks, a blackened eye, swollen closed, and a swollen lip. She disappeared completely behind the door when she saw him.

"Ah, Angharad," he said, stepping inside and closing the door quietly. "Barnes?"

"He found out," she said. "He guessed. But I don't care. Siân Jones came back alive."

"Oh, my dear," he said, "I am so sorry." He closed his eyes briefly and remembered telling Gwilym Jenkins that he would be speaking with him on his return from Newport. Jenkins would have reported to Barnes, and Barnes would have drawn the obvious conclusion. And yet he, Alex, had promised her that no one would ever know who had told him. "Are there hidden bruises too?"

"It doesn't matter," she said. But she blurted as he took her hands in his, "He took me over his knee. Just like a naughty child. It still hurts to sit down. I am glad he never married me. I would have seen him more clearly from the start if he was not rich and powerful, I suppose. There is wicked I was to want to move up in the world. I deserved what I got. That is what my dada says. I will be run out of chapel if the Reverend Llewellyn finds out."

Alex squeezed her hands. "You have a

good heart, Angharad," he said. "You put yourself in danger and gave up your hopes for the sake of your friend. No one can show any greater love than that — I am sure you know the Bible as well as I do, if not better."

She hung her head and looked suddenly self-conscious with her hands in his. He released them.

"You work for the minister," he said. "And you worked for Barnes. And Parry too, I believe?"

She swallowed and nodded.

"I would like to offer you employment at the castle if you are interested," he said. "Miss Haines has been complaining of too few maids now that my daughter and I are in residence." Miss Haines had complained of no such thing. "Would you like to call on her and discuss the matter — perhaps next week when your face should be back to rights?"

Angharad regarded him from one wide eye. "Oh," she said. "Yes, please. I'll be getting a pension, but I do like to work."

He smiled. "I shall tell Miss Haines to expect you one day next week, then," he said, his hand on the door latch. "And thank you again, Angharad, for your courage and your goodness. I shall consider myself in your debt for a long time to come."

"Thank you, my lordship," she said, looking flustered, as he let himself out.

Perhaps it was as well, he thought as he strode along the street, that he had visited her after his dismissal of Barnes. He was tempted even now to call at the lodge cottage on his way home and beat the stuffing out of the man. But he would not do it. Violence only seemed to breed more violence. And when all was said and done, the loss of his job and all his prospects was probably the worst possible punishment for Josiah Barnes.

Yes, it was the best possible course he could take, he decided during the first few days after his return from Newport, to keep himself busy, to keep his mind active, to fill his leisure hours with amusing his daughter. He would not think about Siân until after Christmas. Until after she had gone.

Perhaps then it would be safe to think about her. And safe to remember.

But not now. Not yet.

If possible, the chapel was more crowded than it was for Sunday services on the morning of Owen Parry's funeral. There were a few who had always openly opposed him and more who had been intimidated by his physical strength and his power. There were those who had been shocked by the revelation that he was a member of the Scotch Cattle and that he had actually participated in the raid that had carried off his fiancée for whipping. There were those — mostly women — who blamed him for the fiasco of the demonstration on Newport, though by some miracle he had been the only casualty of that march from Cwmbran.

But there was scarcely a person in Cwmbran who did not respect him and who did not feel that his loss somehow diminished them all. Besides, he had been one of their own, and despite everything — despite the heightened feelings of the past months and the fears and the violence — their sense of community was central to their very lives.

Owen Parry had no remaining family. But in a sense every man, woman, and child in Cwmbran was his family. They turned out in force to mourn him and to raise the roof off the chapel with their singing so that he could not miss hearing them even from his place in heaven. They came to lay him to rest and to sing again in the cemetery across the river, under the wide sky, in case after all the chapel roof had prevented their songs of praise from reaching him in heaven.

The male voice choir lined up in their

usual order, a deliberate and conspicuous space between two of the baritones to show that someone was missing, that the choir was the poorer for his absence. They sang *"Hiraeth"* for one who no longer had to feel the nameless longings that only prisoners of the flesh felt. They sang *"Hiraeth"* for one who had progressed past longing into the great fulfillment of the hereafter.

Siân sat in her grandfather's pew at the front of the church and later stood close to the open grave, too numb to weep. He had wanted to marry her — she might now be experiencing widowhood again. He had wanted her to go up the mountain with him. He had threatened her with violence if she ever crossed his will after marriage. He had threatened violence to save her from a whipping. And then he had participated in that night of terror and violence — and had persuaded those with him to reduce her sentence from twenty to fifteen lashes. He had stopped the whipping when he had seen her biting her lips to shreds and stuffed a rag between her teeth for her to bite on. He had had her bound when he found her among the men on the march to Newport. He had cursed and yelled at her when he found her on the square before the Westgate Inn.

And then he had died for her.

She had held him in her arms as he died. He had called her *cariad*.

Owen. It was impossible to believe that the cold, silent coffin held Owen. All that power and energy and determination and passion and tenderness.

Owen.

Her eyes were drawn unwillingly to the gap in the lines of the male voice choir when they were out in the cemetery. And back to the coffin being lowered into the earth. As Mam had been lowered. And Gwyn. And Dafydd.

Owen. Ah, Owen.

Emrys's arm came about her shoulders and held her like a vise. And finally she felt the tears course down her cheeks and drip off her chin. She would not brush them away, or look away from the fact of his death, or hide her face against Emrys's shoulder.

Love had many faces. Owen had worn one of them. She did not try to hide from the pain of her grief for him or try to analyze the love she had felt for him. She had loved him and she grieved for his death.

He had been a part of her life. A part of her life was gone with him.

The Marquess of Craille was standing

close by when she finally turned away from the grave. She had known he was at the chapel though she had not once turned her head to see. She had known he was at the cemetery. He took the few steps that separated them now.

"I loved him," she said, looking up into his eyes.

He did not smile though there was a smile in him. She felt it. "I know," he said gently. And he took both her cold hands in his, squeezed them almost painfully, and raised one of them to his lips. "I am sorry for your grief, Siân."

Emrys still had an arm about her shoulders. She did not know or care who else saw or heard.

I loved him. I love you. The many faces of love.

The many faces of pain.

29

Emrys knew that Josiah Barnes was leaving. Everyone knew that. Emrys even knew the full reason, though rumor had to suffice for most people. He knew that Barnes was to leave the day of the funeral. But it was not until he was at the funeral that he found out what had happened to Angharad Lewis.

He took Siân home and left her in the care of his mother before changing out of his Sunday clothes and paying a call at the lodge house in Glanrhyd Park. He prayed as he strode through the town and past the ironworks that Barnes had not already left.

He had not.

Angharad's father had gone to the Three Lions with a crowd of other men after the funeral. She was at home alone when Emrys knocked on the door. She only half opened it and peeped fearfully around it.

"Oh," she said, leaving the door ajar and hurrying away from it into the room, "it is you. Dada is at the pub."

"Angharad," he said, stepping inside the house and shutting the door behind him, "Craille has sent him away. But even if he had not, Barnes would not be bothering you again."

She turned her head and looked over her shoulder. He was holding up his hands, palms in. His knuckles were red and raw. Her eyes filled with tears.

"Sit down at the table," she said, "and I will bathe your hands for you."

He did as she told him and sat in silence while she filled a bowl, half with cold water and half with water from the kettle on the fire. She selected a soft cloth from a drawer and then came to stand beside him at the table. She bathed his hands with trembling care.

"Shall I find bandages?" she asked when she had finished. She had not once looked up into his face.

"Don't be daft," he said.

She stepped back. "Go, then, Emrys Rhys," she said. "And thank you."

"Angharad," he said softly, "I have applied for Owen Parry's job and his house. Maybe I won't get either. But Craille is talking about building more houses in the spring."

"Look at me," Angharad said, though she

did not look at him. "I deserved every one of these bruises and the ones you cannot see. I am a whore and an informer."

"We all do stupid things sometimes," he said. "You are still Angharad to me, *fach.*"

She hung her head, but he could see the glisten of tears in her eyes.

"I went back to chapel today for Owen's funeral," he said. "It wasn't so bad. I would like to go back again — for a wedding."

Angharad sobbed and set the back of one hand against her mouth.

"But I may not get the job," he said. "I may not get a house of my own until next summer. Perhaps not even then."

"I would live with your mam and your dada and ten other people as well," she said, "if you were in the house too, Emrys Rhys."

"Would you?" he said. "Will you come with me for that wedding, then, Angharad?"

"Yes," she said. "If you can forgive me."

He stood up and reached out a hand toward her. "Come and be kissed then, is it?" he said. "I'll see if I can kiss you without hurting the poor lip."

"I don't mind if you hurt it," she said, hurrying into his arms. "I don't mind. Emrys. Ah, Emrys, I'm sorry. I'm so sorry."

"Sh," he said, "and let me kiss you. And then we will forget all about the past. After this kiss, *fach.* "

He kissed her and gave them a long time in which to forget.

Sir John Fowler had written to Siân three times during the week, but he had not yet heard from the Crowthers in Carmarthenshire. It was to be the cottage, then, until they did hear. Perhaps until after Christmas. He was coming for her tomorrow. Her bag was packed — she really had very few possessions — and most of the farewells had been said. Just Grandad and Emrys in the morning and Gran whenever her father arrived.

Farewells were so difficult to say. Even Huw, when it had come his turn, had hugged her as if he was trying to break every bone in her body. And the Reverend Llewellyn had tried to crush every bone in her hand.

Angharad was happy. Despite the severe beating she had suffered at the hands of Josiah Barnes, she was happy. She had been offered a maid's job at Glanrhyd Castle, but she had found a better job than that. She was going to marry Emrys before Christmas. And Iestyn had a job at the castle too, as Alexander's secretary. He was happier than Siân had ever seen him. And it was

663

not just the happiness that the sweetness of his nature imposed on him, but the happiness of dreams beginning to come true. It shone out of him.

And all because of Alexander.

She could not think of Alexander.

His meeting had taken place the night before. The Sunday School hall had been so full that the meeting had been moved to the chapel itself. Everyone had wanted to talk, Emrys had reported. And things were to happen — a school within a month, waterworks in the spring as soon as the cold weather was at an end, a minimum wage at the works and mine, a public library. The list went on and on.

Almost all the things she had told him she would do if she had unlimited supplies of time and money, Siân thought. As if he were offering her one more gift.

But she would not think of Alexander. Not yet. Not when she was still in danger of rushing off to him for one last good-bye.

She had not seen him since Owen's funeral.

There was one more good-bye, though. And she would do it now in the afternoon, before the early winter dusk came down. She had to say good-bye to Cwmbran.

She took the route she had taken so often

with Owen, up onto the lower hills, reliving their evenings together. She stood still and looked down at the town, ignoring the November wind, which whipped at her cloak and made wild tangles of her loose hair.

Glanrhyd Castle half hidden among the trees of the park. The works below it with smoke curling from the tall chimneys and a general look of grayness about buildings and yards. The houses in terraces rising above one another as the streets ascended from the valley floor. The coal tips and colliery wheel farther down the valley with greenness beyond. The river, looking clean from up here and soon to be clean indeed. The chapel. The footbridge across the river and the cemetery beyond.

And the people. Her family, Gwyn's family, the neighbors, her choir partners, Glenys Richards, who played the harp for her, Angharad, her friends from the mine, the Reverend Llewellyn, Verity, Alexander.

Siân turned sharply suddenly and began to climb higher, away from the pain. But she took it with her. It was not easy to say good-bye even when it was to something as inanimate as a valley and hills and a town. Oh, it was not easy to say good-bye.

She had never felt that she fully belonged.

Because she had not grown up there, because she was half English and illegitimate, because her upbringing and education made her different from the other townspeople, she had always felt that she was not fully a part of Cwmbran. She had tried in so many ways to belong, to fit in. She had taken a job, even when that had meant working in the mine. She had married Gwyn, a fellow miner. She had joined the chapel and the choir. She had taught in the Sunday School. She had agreed to marry Owen. But she had always felt that she had somehow failed. She had never felt that she belonged.

She had been wrong. She realized that now it was time to leave, now that she was saying good-bye. She belonged.

She was climbing up toward the meeting place. But she paused in one hollow and crossed to a rock face. She laid one hand flat against it. He had set her back against it while he questioned her about the Chartist meeting. She had become suddenly frightened that he intended to rape her. She had threatened to scream. And he had kissed her. A blond, handsome English stranger.

She continued on her way up to the meeting place and stood on the spot where she had twice hidden to observe a meeting. It was quiet and deserted now. And the town below was quiet and peaceful.

Her town. Her valley. Her people.

Belonging did not always mean being the same as everyone else. Belonging meant accepting and being accepted, loving and being loved. She remembered being hugged and kissed outside the *eisteddfod* pavilion by almost everyone from Cwmbran. She remembered being lifted to the shoulders of some of the men and carried in triumph. Not just her personal triumph, but theirs. Cwmbran's.

She was different. She would always be different. But people had come to accept her and even love her for what she was. She could see that now that it no longer mattered. This was good-bye. She felt a sharp stabbing of grief as she looked down at her valley. Her mother's valley. Her people's valley. Hers.

She turned and toiled on upward, not looking back, not even knowing where she was going until she arrived there.

One final good-bye. She stood looking down at the spot on which Alexander had first made love to her. It was a chilly day, though she was sheltered from the wind when she sat down. The ground was dry — there had been no rain since the day of the march to Newport.

She sat hugging her knees and gazing downward. The end. Tomorrow would be a new beginning. She did not know what was ahead. She could not know. But today it did not matter. Today was an end. Good-bye to Cwmbran. Good-bye to her people. Good-bye to Alexander.

Alexander. Alexander.

She set her forehead against her knees and closed her eyes. And allowed herself to remember and to touch despair again.

She sat thus for a long time.

The meeting had gone well. It had exceeded his most optimistic expectations, in fact, in both numbers and enthusiasm. The Reverend Llewellyn had begun it with a long prayer, beginning in English and switching to Welsh as the emotion grew. Ideas Alex had suggested were accepted with eagerness, but he had not had to suggest many. Soon the people had taken charge of the meeting, pleasing him with the good sense and practicality of their insights. Iestyn had recorded it all with meticulous thoroughness despite the fact that he had only one workable arm.

Committees had been formed to investigate some ideas and to make definite plans and proposals — the location and size and design of a schoolhouse, for example. But no one — including Alex — had been willing to fall into the trap of losing momentum and enthusiasm by waiting for committee reports. Much could be done without delay. The chapel and the Sunday School hall would serve as a school for the time being. A teacher was to be hired as soon as possible. Perhaps the school could be in operation by the new year.

Siân's name had been suggested.

Alex had felt a wave of approval from his people, an acceptance that he had felt only on brief occasions before, like the day of the *eisteddfod*. He felt respect from his people, almost affection. In his prayer, before he had switched to Welsh, the Reverend Llewellyn had given thanks for an owner who cared enough for his workmen to follow after them to Newport and diligently to protect their lives and freedom there so that there had been only one casualty. The Lord would forgive him for the untruths he had felt compelled to tell in order to do so. There had been a chorus of fervent amens while Alex, with bowed head, had smiled.

It had all been very wonderful. And yet now, the day after, he could not shake off a feeling of depression that was threatening to spoil it all. A general flatness of mood just at the time when he should be feeling most elated. Verity was gone for the day. Lady Fowler and Tess had invited her to spend it with them and had sent a carriage late in the morning.

He felt lonely without Verity.

He felt lonely.

After a solitary luncheon he wandered about his study, watching Iestyn writing some letters and knowing that his idleness and his restlessness were making the boy self-conscious. He went out onto the hills so that he would be a burden to no one but himself.

The wind was invigorating. It was a chilly day, but more because of the wind than anything else. There was none of the icy dampness in the air that was so characteristic of this part of the world.

He wandered across the lower hills, pausing frequently to look down into the valley. It was all so familiar now. He could picture individual streets, and his eyes could alight on some individual houses and know who lived in them. The works were familiar and the mine. The chapel was familiar — focal point of the spiritual and social life of Cwmbran. Focal point of their wonderful music. Soon to be a temporary school.

And the hills were familiar. They were a

mere extension of the town below. He had wandered them frequently. He had first met Siân in the hills. He glanced up to the spot, close by, and strolled up to it. Just here. He set his palms against the rock and leaned toward it, his eyes closed. She had been frightened and courageous and defiant. He had kissed her.

He pushed himself away from the rock.

The hills were meeting place, playground, recreation area, courting place, and more. He remembered the whole town trekking over the mountain to the next valley for the *eisteddfod,* taking Glenys Richards's harp with them. He remembered the wonderful, heart-warming absurdity of the *gymanfa ganu* on top of the mountain.

It had been one of the happiest days of his life.

He strolled on to the meeting place and looked down into the valley again. Perhaps after all he should leave, he thought. Perhaps he should go back to the life and the land that were familiar to him and appoint a competent and sensitive manager to look after developments here. Perhaps that would be best.

Perhaps she would stay and teach in Cwmbran if he left. She should stay. This was where she belonged. Yet she was leaving tomorrow. Someone had mentioned that last night when she had been suggested as a teacher.

She was leaving tomorrow. His depression was suddenly converted to a deep stabbing of despair.

He was the one who should be leaving, not her. She was the one who belonged here. He did not. He belonged in England. He had roots there — memories and relatives and friends and an estate. It was his world. He should go back there.

Yes, he was the one who should leave. He should have someone talk to Siân today, before it was too late, and persuade her to stay and take on the challenge of the new school. He would leave with Verity. They would go tomorrow. Anything that could not be packed in time could be sent on later.

He was gazing sightlessly downward. His valley. His. It all belonged to him. His eyes focused again. But it was all a matter of wealth and property and inheritance. It belonged to him, but he did not belong to it.

He stood very still as the now familiar feeling washed over him again, leaving him shaken and bereft. *Hiraeth.* The deep — the bone deep — longing for something beyond himself. The longing to be a part of the beauty and the struggle and the passion and the soul of this little part of Wales. The yearning for — he shook his head. There was no real word for it.

He had stepped into the unknown in coming here. And he had continued to step forward, unwilling to accept facts and conditions that he had been told were essential to the prosperity of Cwmbran. He was breaking new ground now with all the plans he and his people were about to put into effect.

Walking always forward into the excitement of the unknown. It was something he had never done before. He had always accepted his life for what it was and enjoyed what it had to offer while taking his responsibilities seriously. He had never thought of himself as a rebel or a radical or a stirrer of troubled waters.

Was he to go back now and leave all the excitement behind? So that Siân could stay?

Was she not his final step into the unknown? The woman he could not think of marrying because it was simply not done in his world to marry so beneath himself socially? The woman who could not be happy with him because he would be removing her from her world but would be unable to take her into his?

The world was changing. And even if it were not, could not one man change? One man and one woman? He had no doubt that she was as miserable as he over the fact that they could not be together. Were the conventions, the rules, so much more important than they were?

He did belong to Cwmbran, Alex thought, turning at last and beginning to plod upward. He had lived there for several months and he had loved it from the start. He loved its people. One did not have to live in a place from birth to belong there. One did not have to be the same as the other inhabitants to belong. One merely had to love — and be loved.

It was his place. He had come home when he had come to Cwmbran, driven by the need for some solitude and peace after a broken engagement. Yes, it was not an utterly fanciful thought. He had come home.

His head was down, watching the ground beneath his feet. But he glanced up eventually, realizing with a start where it was he was going.

And he stopped.

She was there before him.

She was sitting on the level piece of ground where they had loved, her knees drawn up, her forehead resting against them.

He stood quietly watching her for a while. Siân. His love. His world. His home. And then he continued on his way up.

She heard him when he was quite close and looked up sharply. She was almost not surprised. And she was not as upset as she might have expected to be to find that good-bye was to be said all over again. She could never feel distress or despair when he was with her, though she knew she would feel them even more intensely when he left. She could only feel rightness and peace with Alexander.

He sat down beside her, his shoulder not quite touching hers, saying nothing. She looked back down into the valley.

"I am saying good-bye to it all," she said. "My father is coming for me tomorrow."

"It was mentioned at the meeting," he said.

"I heard it went well." She smiled though she did not look at him. "I am glad, Alexander. I am glad you have been accepted here and that life is going to improve. I will always think of it as your gift to me, though I hope you would have done it anyway."

"There seemed to be common agreement that you would make the best teacher for the new school," he said.

Oh. She closed her eyes briefly. "No," she said.

"You would," he said. "You are a good teacher, and you are loved here. You belong here."

"No." No, she did not want this turmoil. There was no decision to make. But oh, the sweet seductive thought.

"Because I will be here?" he asked.

"Yes." He knew the full truth. She had never tried to hide it. She would not pretend now, then. "Yes, because of that, Alexander. But I am happy that you will be here. There are many good schoolmasters who will be only too happy to take the teaching job."

"It does not seem right," he said, "that you not be here to see it all, Siân, when you were the one to dream it. Do you remember the afternoon when you told me your dreams — what you would do in Cwmbran if you could?"

"Yes," she said. She remembered and cherished every moment she had ever spent with him. She would always remember.

"I want you to stay." His arm came loosely about her shoulders. His hand clasped her upper arm.

"No." She knew what it would mean to stay. She knew the limits of her strength. No, she had to go. Tomorrow. She should have gone last week.

"Siân," he said, "I don't know that I have the will to do it without you. I don't want to contemplate life without you. I don't think I can live it alone."

She had counted on his honor. Even though a part of her had hoped and even expected during their return from Newport that he would renew his offer, a firmer part of herself had trusted him to behave with honor. She had trusted him to let her go, her own personhood intact.

"Don't," she said, sagging sideways against him despite herself and burrowing her head against his shoulder. "I could not do it, Alexander. I would give myself and you temporary happiness and ultimate misery. And I would become a pariah. Don't ask me. I know now that I will not give in to the temptation, but I don't want to remember you as a tempter. I want to remember you as a man of honor and integrity. I want to remember you as a man worthy of my love."

"Siân —" he said, his mouth an inch from her own.

"Make love to me," she said, closing her eyes, bringing her arm up about his neck. "Let there be one final good-bye. But let me go, then. Let me be able to remember that you set me free." She was crying.

He turned her in to him, crushing her with his arms. "Not as my mistress," he said. "I am not asking you to stay as my mistress, Siân. I am begging you to stay as my wife."

She felt as if all the air had been knocked from her lungs. "No," she said. "No." The dream was too painfully sweet to contemplate.

"I love you," he said. "You know I love you, Siân. And I know you love me."

She buried her head against his shoulder, her mouth open in her agony. "Alexander," she said. "Alexander, we can't. It is an impossibility. Please. I have accepted that. I must go tomorrow. Let me go. Please let me go."

He cradled her in his arms, rocked her against him. He said nothing for a while. She knew he was waiting for the tension to go out of the moment. But she knew too that he was not going to let her go. She knew he was not going to accept the impossibility as she had. *I am begging you to stay as my wife.* Had he really spoken those words? *My wife.* Alexander's wife. His friend and companion. His lover. Mother of his children. His wife.

She relaxed against him.

"We are both widowed," he murmured

against her ear. "We have both recently been freed of engagements. We love each other. We are lovers. Tell me why we should not take the logical step of marrying, Siân."

For a few moments she could think of no reason. There seemed only to be every reason why they should marry. But there were reasons — several of them, each an insurmountable barrier.

"You are the Marquess of Craille," she said. "I am a nobody, and an illegitimate nobody at that. There are those who would say that you had looked too low even for a mistress if you took me."

"And I would remind those impertinent persons that my life and your life are none of their business," he said.

"Alexander." She drew a deep breath. "It is not as simple as that. You know it is not."

"No, it is not." He set a hand beneath her chin suddenly and lifted her face. He kissed her warmly and deeply. "It is not a simple matter at all. It would not be easy for you to feel at ease in the sort of life I am accustomed to and expected to live in England. And I know it is very possible that you would not be readily accepted there. I know that here it might be difficult for you suddenly to be lady of the manor. I know that in time our children may find themselves having to fight against well-bred contempt at their birth. I know that you are the one who would do most of the suffering and that I would suffer knowing that you did and that I had caused it. But, Siân, think of the alternative. Are you really willing to live with the alternative?"

A month or two in the cottage in which she had lived with her mother. And then strangers and a strange place and a new teaching job. A new life. And no Alexander.

"You would be ashamed of me," she said.

"Never!" His answer was quite vehement. He still held her chin. He was gazing into her eyes. "That at least will never be one of our difficulties, Siân. You must know that it won't be. Marry me. Our lives are controlled so much by rules and social conventions. I have been asking myself during my walk on the hills why it is we are usually so willing to put the rules before people. Siân, are we willing to part today, never to see each other again, when the only obstacle between us is a rule? And not even quite that — a social expectation. A lifetime without each other because we were born into different social strata. No other reason. There is nothing else, is there?"

She could think of no answer. If she could look at anything except his blue eyes perhaps she would be able to think clearly. But his hand was firm beneath her chin. Short of closing her eyes, there was nowhere else to look.

"Alexander," she whispered. And then she thought of something. "Verity?"

"Now you are grasping at straws." He smiled unexpectedly. "The prospect of having you as a mother will have her running up hills and down hills for three days at a stretch, transported by delight."

She laughed despite herself.

"Is there any chance you are with child?" he asked.

She shrugged and felt herself flush. "I suppose so," she said. "There is a chance, though it was only one night."

"And four separate assaults on your fertility," he said. He was actually grinning. "If we only knew for sure, Siân, there would be an end to the matter without further discussion. I insist that all my children be legitimate, you see." His smile softened. "I want children with you, my love. I want to give you a son to console you for your Dafydd, though not to take his place. He will always be your first-born, as Verity will always be mine. But I want sons and daughters with you. I want a life with you. That is not an unrealistic ambition, is it?"

Her womb was throbbing with need — for him and for his child. She shook her head.

He looked deeply into her eyes. "No, it is not unrealistic?" he asked. "Or no, you will have none of me."

"Alexander," she whispered.

He drew her head to his shoulder again, wrapped his arms tightly about her, and waited. She knew that he had come to the end of his arguments. She knew that he could use one more method of persuasion that would surely work. He could make love to her. But she knew that he would not do so. Not until her answer was given.

He had given her her freedom after all. Freedom to decide for herself. It was the reason too why he had brought her head to his shoulder. He would not use even his eyes to make her decide in a way that she might regret. It was her choice now.

She relaxed against him, breathing in the distinctive smell of him. "We would live most of our lives in England?" she asked.

"Hardly any, I think," he said. "Even before I got to know Cwmbran, Siân, I felt a strange feeling of homecoming here. I felt it again this afternoon when I was deciding to take Verity back to England so that you could stay here. I would not be going home,

I realized. I would be leaving home."

"You were prepared to go away so that I could stay?" she asked.

"And still would," he said. "If one of us must leave, Siân, it should be me. You have more right to be here than I do. And more to lose by leaving."

She thought about it. "No," she said, "we have an equal amount to lose, Alexander. Each other."

His arms tightened a little.

"I loved Gwyn," she said. "He was a decent, caring, hardworking man. And I loved Owen. If you had not come, my love for him would have been enough to have seen us through a lifetime. It would have been enough to have helped me over the difficulties there would have been — there was much over which we did not see eye to eye. But you did come. And I have discovered with you what I believe few people are privileged to know in a lifetime. It is the sort of love immortalized in great literature. In poetry. I am not exaggerating, am I?"

"No," he said.

"It is a love worth fighting for," she said.

His arms tightened still further.

"I want to fight for it," she said. "It won't be easy. Not for either of us. And not for our children. But if you think there is a chance for us, Alexander, I want to take it. I think our love is a precious gift. I don't want to throw it away. I won't throw it away."

He kissed her cheek, the only part of her face exposed to him. "I'll call on your father tomorrow and ask for you," he said.

She chuckled against his shoulder and then sobered again. She lifted her head and looked into his eyes. "Will you, Alexander?" she asked. "It will mean so much to him. And to me."

"And then I will call on your grandparents," he said, "and ask them. A more thorny matter, I believe. If I get past those hurdles, I will take you to Glanrhyd and we can ask Verity together."

She smiled slowly at him. "Alexander," she said, "are you sure? Are you quite, quite sure?"

"Yes," he said. "Are you?"

She nodded. "Yes, I am sure."

He kissed her then and they clung together, breathless with the realization of how close they had come after all to cowardice, to giving in to the fear of facing down the unknown and stepping firmly into an impossibility.

"It is dusk already," he said. "Darkness has fallen while we have been sitting here."

She was aware of her surroundings for the

first time in many minutes. "It comes early at this time of year," she said.

"It is chilly up here," he said. But his words were more question than statement.

"But not too chilly." She lay back against the ground, drawing him down with her. "It is not too cold, my love." She smiled into his eyes, so blue, so intense with his love, so close to her own. "My love."

He smiled back as his hands began to love her, before his mouth followed suit. *"Cariad,"* he whispered. "You are going to teach me Welsh, Siân. My vocabulary is severely limited. But I learned the best word first." He rubbed his nose against hers. *"Cariad."*

But then for a long time he did not need words at all.

HISTORICAL NOTE

The failure of the demonstration at Newport in November 1839 spelled the effective end of Chartism in the British Isles, though it limped on for several more years.

Of the many men who were arrested after the demonstration very few were actually put on trial. Of those who were, most were jailed for a year. Some were transported.

The three leaders — John Frost, Zephaniah Williams, and William Jones — were all sentenced to death. However, at the last moment they were reprieved and sentenced to transportation for life instead. Only John Frost ever came back home.

I have taken two deliberate liberties with history.

Some women did attend the Chartist meetings and take out membership in the Chartist Association. For the sake of my plot I have made it seem as if women were forbidden to have anything to do with the movement.

The mayor of Newport was wounded in the shooting at the Westgate Inn. I have been kinder to him. In my story he is still hale and hearty enough to entertain my hero after all the shooting has stopped.

ABOUT THE AUTHOR

Mary Balogh grew up in Wales and now lives with her husband, Robert, in Saskatchewan, Canada. She has written more than one hundred historical novels and novellas, more than thirty of which have been *New York Times* bestsellers. They include the Slightly sestet (the Bedwyn saga), the Simply quartet, the Huxtable quintet, and the ongoing seven-part Survivors' Club series.